A JUNIOR-HI[GH]

Romance of the Airman

BY

PAULINE A. HUMPHREYS

HEAD OF THE DEPARTMENT OF EDUCATION, CENTRAL MISSOURI

STATE TEACHERS COLLEGE, WARRENSBURG

AND

GERTRUDE HOSEY

ASSOCIATE PROFESSOR OF EDUCATION, CENTRAL MISSOURI

STATE TEACHERS COLLEGE, WARRENSBURG

GINN AND COMPANY

COPYRIGHT, 1931, BY PAULINE A. HUMPHREYS AND GERTRUDE HOSEY

ALL RIGHTS RESERVED

PRINTED IN THE UNITED STATES OF AMERICA

431.2

GINN AND COMPANY

BOSTON · NEW YORK · CHICAGO · LONDON
ATLANTA · DALLAS · COLUMBUS · SAN FRANCISCO

Orville Wright witnesses the Presentation of the Harmon Trophy to Colonel Charles A. Lindbergh

Delegates from forty-four nations to the First Civil Aëronautics Conference held in America met in Washington, D.C., on December 12, 1928, to celebrate the twenty-fifth anniversary of the first successful flight. Orville Wright was the guest of honor at this conference, and Colonel Charles A. Lindbergh received the Harmon Trophy

Preface

THE work of attempting to locate material which should be interwoven into the traditional subject matter of the school was inspired by a program of the Department of Superintendence of the National Education Association held in Boston in 1928. An entire evening was given over to authoritative speakers who discussed aspects of aviation that affect our public schools. In opening this meeting Superintendent Joseph M. Gwinn, of San Francisco, then president of the organization, said that education, which must ever respond to the changes that come, *must give attention to aviation*, and that this program was proposed as a beginning in aëronautic education. W. F. Durand, of Stanford University, one of the principal speakers on this program, called to the attention of the five thousand superintendents of schools who were present the opportunities that teachers have for enlisting the interest of the youth in this timely subject. Speaking of the features of the subject that lend themselves to the field of general education, Dr. Durand said : "There is the history of the development of aëronautics, a marvelously inspiring page of the general domain of historic development. We may go back to mythology, and from there down we may find a wonderfully interesting story of the development from those early days down to the present time. Those are things which might in some way be interwoven — worked into the general program of the school — without undue dislocation or disturbance." This last suggestion was taken as a guide in the organization of the materials of this book.

The direct result of this program was the preparation of a handbook for teachers which suggested phases of the subject of aëronautics, drawn from literature, history, and

vi *Romance of the Airman*

biography, that might be used in the classroom. Three thousand copies of this handbook were printed as a bulletin of the Central Missouri State Teachers College and distributed to the teachers in the area which this college serves.

The enthusiastic reception of this handbook was most gratifying, and the numerous requests for materials to put into the hands of pupils led the authors of the bulletin to undertake the compilation of available materials for a textbook on the subject of aviation. A careful and exhaustive study has been made of the classics, current literature, biography, autobiography, and history in order to select representative materials treating all phases of aëronautics from the legendary period to the present time. Care has been exercised in the selection of materials from authentic sources. Those episodes in the development of aviation that will become history have been chosen with discrimination. Special effort has been made to secure selections that correlate with the classics usually prescribed for courses in junior-high-school English.

PAULINE A. HUMPHREYS
GERTRUDE HOSEY

Acknowledgments

Grateful acknowledgment is made to the following holders of copyright who have given permission to include material: *Aëronautics* for "Le Bourget," by Paul E. Lamarche, Jr., and for "Plant Protection by Airplane," by S. R. Winters; *Air Travel News* for "Hunting Whales by Airship," by Roman J. Miller, reprinted from the June, 1929, issue, by special permission of the publisher; the *Annals of the American Academy of Political and Social Science* for "The First Official Recognition of Aviation," by Adrian Van Muffling, reprinted from the May, 1927, issue of the *Annals*, Vol. CXXXI, No. 220, pp. 1–6; the *American Aviator: Airplanes and Airports* for "Peace on Earth," by Abbuh Randlaw, and for "The Wright Brothers, the First Successful Flyers," by D. Thompson White; the *Atlantic Monthly* for "A Record-breaking Balloon Voyage," by Henry H. Clayton; *Baltimore Sun* for "Floyd Bennett laid to Rest as the Elements Rage," by W. A. S. Douglas; The Century Co. for "The First Flyers," by Florence B. Davis, from the *St. Nicholas Magazine*, copyright, January, 1927, by The Century Co., and for "My First Balloon Ascent," from "My Airships," by A. Santos-Dumont, copyright, 1904, by The Century Co.; Thomas Y. Crowell Company for "Byrd's Flight to the North Pole," from "Heroes of the Air," by C. C. Fraser; *Des Moines Register* for "Homage to the Lilienthal Brothers by a Frenchman"; Dodd, Mead & Company, Inc., for "Nungesser and Coli fly to Death in the *White Bird*" and "The *Dixmude*," from "The Boys' Book of Airmen," by Irving Crump, copyright, 1927, by Dodd, Mead & Company, Inc.; Doubleday, Doran and Company, Inc., for "The Perils of Flying the Night Air Mail," by Howard Mingos, and for "Flying the Mail," by Donald Wilhelm, both reprinted from *World's Work*; Ginn and Company for "The Enchanted Horse," from "Arabian Nights' Entertainments," told by M. A. L. Lane; *Harlow's Weekly* for "The Westbound Mail," by Phil Braniff; Houghton Mifflin Company for "Pegasus, the Winged Horse," by Nathaniel Hawthorne, and "Darius Green and his Flying Machine," by John T. Trowbridge, used by permission of, and by arrangement with, Houghton Mifflin Company; Hut-

viii *Romance of the Airman*

chinson and Company, Ltd., for "The *Southern Cross* visits the Fiji Islands," from "The Flight of the *Southern Cross*," by C. E. Kingsford-Smith and C. T. P. Ulm; Horace Liveright for "From Foot to Flying Machine," from "Man the Miracle Maker," by Hendrik Van Loon, published by Horace Liveright, Inc., New York, copyright; *The Independent* for "The Experiments of a Flying Man," by Wilbur Wright; *Living Age* for "Bisecting the Arctic," by F. Ramm, for "Lady Heath flies across Africa," by Lady Mary Heath, and for "A Peruvian Aviator of the Eighteenth Century," by F. P. Farrar; London *Saturday Review* for "Lady Heath flies across Africa," by Lady Mary Heath; Robert M. McBride & Co. for "The *Southern Cross* visits the Fiji Islands," from "The Flight of the *Southern Cross*," by C. E. Kingsford-Smith and C. T. P. Ulm; *Magazine of Business* for "Aviation's Varied Uses in Business," by P. G. Johnson, reprinted by their special permission; Thomas Nelson & Sons for "Lindbergh, America's Ambassador of Good Will," from "Conquering the Air," by A. Williams; *North American Review* for "Columbus of the Air," by Augustus Post; Parke, Austin and Lipscomb for "A Balloon Flight across Africa," from "Five Weeks in a Balloon," by Jules Verne; *Popular Science Monthly* for "Alaska's Flying Gold Hunters," by James M. Nelson, and for "Da Vinci Did it First," by Edwin W. Teale; G. P. Putnam's Sons for "Our Flight in the *Friendship*," from "20 Hrs. 40 Min.," by Amelia Earhart; *San Francisco Examiner* for "*Gjoa* — To Amundsen," by John J. Jury; *Scientific American* for "Life-saving Airplanes," by S. R. Winters; Seeley, Service and Company, Ltd., for "Andrée's Polar Expedition," "The Montgolfier Brothers," "Otto Lilienthal," and "The Story of the Zeppelin," from "Marvels of Aviation," by C. C. Turner; *Toledo Blade* for "The Lost Fliers," by Isabelle Elling; *Youth's Companion* for "Preparation for the Antarctic Expedition," by Richard E. Byrd; John H. Finley for "American Youth honors Lindbergh"; George Godoy for "Ave, Lindbergh!" from *El Universal*; C. E. Kingsford-Smith and C. T. P. Ulm for "The *Southern Cross* visits the Fiji Islands," from "The Flight of the *Southern Cross*"; and Archibald Williams for "Lindbergh, America's Ambassador of Good Will," from "Conquering the Air."

Contents

	PAGE
INTRODUCTION	xiii

I. *The Airman Dreams*

Some Ancient Stories of Man's Attempts to Fly		3
Dædalus and Icarus	*Ovid*	11
Pegasus, the Winged Horse	*Nathaniel Hawthorne*	16
The Enchanted Horse	*The Arabian Nights' Entertainments*	43
The Magic Carpet	*Washington Irving*	50
The Unparalleled Adventure of One Hans Pfaall	*Edgar Allan Poe*	56
A Balloon Flight across Africa	*Jules Verne*	71
The Flying Warrior of Uganda	*Henry M. Stanley*	83
Darius Green and his Flying Machine	*J. T. Trowbridge*	86
Argosies of the Air	*Alfred, Lord Tennyson*	97

II. *The Airman Experiments*

Early Scientific Experimenters		101
"Da Vinci Did it First"	*Edwin W. Teale*	114
Otto Lilienthal, Inspirer of the Wright Brothers	*C. C. Turner*	124
The First Official Recognition of Aviation	*Adrian Van Muffling*	131
A Peruvian Aviator of the Eighteenth Century	*F. P. Farrar*	136
Benjamin Franklin as a Patron of Aviation		147
Alexander Bell's Contribution to Aviation		155

III. *The Airman Invents*

From Foot to Flying Machine	*Hendrik Van Loon*	165
The Montgolfier Brothers, Inventors of the Balloon	*C. C. Turner*	170
The First Flyers	*Florence Boyce Davis*	181

Romance of the Airman

The Wright Brothers, the First Successful Flyers
D. Thompson White 185
The Experiments of a Flying Man *Wilbur Wright* 197
The Story of Zeppelin's Early Projects *C. C. Turner* 208

IV. The Airman becomes a Pathfinder

My First Balloon Ascent *Alberto Santos-Dumont* 217
A Record-breaking Balloon Voyage *Henry Helm Clayton* 225
Andrée's Polar Expedition *Charles C. Turner* 250
Bleriot crosses the English Channel 257
The Amundsen-Ellsworth Polar Flight
Roald Amundsen and *Lincoln Ellsworth* 262
Byrd's Flight to the North Pole *Chelsea Fraser* 275
Bisecting the Arctic *F. Ramm* 289
Crossing the Atlantic 299
Nungesser and Coli fly to Death in the *White Bird*
Irving Crump 307
An Airman drops in on a German Farm
Clarence D. Chamberlin 319
Our Flight in the *Friendship* *Amelia Earhart* 326
The *Southern Cross* visits the Fiji Islands
Kingsford-Smith and *Ulm* 338
Lady Heath flies across Africa *Lady Mary Heath* 345
Preparation for the Antarctic Expedition
Commander Richard E. Byrd 352
Le Bourget *Paul E. Lamarche, Jr.* 373
The First Dirigible to circumnavigate the Globe 381

V. The Airman soars to Fame

Columbus of the Air *Augustus Post* 391
Wings of Lead *Nathalia Crane* 408
American Youth honors Lindbergh *John H. Finley* 414
Floyd Bennett, Martyr of the Air 422
Floyd Bennett laid to Rest as the Elements Rage
W. A. S. Douglas 426

Contents

xi

		PAGE
Gjoa — To Amundsen	*John J. Jury*	431
The *Dixmude*, Mystery of the Air	*Irving Crump*	433
The Lost Fliers, Nungesser and Coli	*Isabelle Elling*	441
Some Historic Aircraft		442
Homage to the Lilienthal Brothers by a Frenchman		
Editorial in the *Des Moines Register*		454

VI. The Airman Serves

Lindbergh, America's Ambassador of Good Will		
	Archibald Williams	459
Ave, Lindbergh!	*George Godoy*	465
The Perils of Flying the Night Air Mail	*Howard Mingos*	468
Flying the Mail	*Donald Wilhelm*	482
Peace on Earth	*Dr. Abbuh Randlaw*	490
Lindbergh makes a Parachute Jump	*Charles A. Lindbergh*	492
The Westbound Mail	*Phil Braniff*	497
Plant Protection by Airplane	*S. R. Winters*	500
Hunting Whales by Airship	*Roman J. Miller*	508
Life-saving Airplanes	*S. R. Winters*	516
Alaska's Flying Gold Hunters	*James M. Nelson*	525
Aviation's Varied Uses in Business	*P. G. Johnson*	532

CHRONOLOGY OF AVIATION	539
GLOSSARY	541
CLASSIFIED LIST OF RELATED TOPICS	549
BOOKS LISTED IN "OTHER READINGS"	557
A LIST OF BOOKS, PERIODICALS, AND BULLETINS ON AVIATION	561
INDEX	563

Introduction

To the Teacher

Aim. The purpose of this reader is to extend the experiences of the junior-high-school pupil and broaden his sympathies by utilizing his native interest in and enthusiasm for adventure, exploration, heroic daring, and noble self-sacrifice in such a way that he may take his place in society more happily and more efficiently.

Material. The lack of any concrete and definite material on aviation for classroom use has prompted the authors to prepare this reader. An attempt has been made to select material that is authentic, of literary value, and simple enough for those whose interests are keenest in this, man's latest romantic field of adventure.

Outstanding achievements of men of many nations have been selected in order to generate a respect and an admiration for people of other lands. As a further means of developing world-mindedness, emphasis has been placed upon the aviator in peaceful pursuits rather than in pursuits of war.

Magazine material has been drawn upon liberally for two reasons: first, the major part of the present-day reading of adults is found in magazines and newspapers; secondly, acquaintance with authentic material found in our best magazines will develop an abiding interest in and a preference for the better class of magazines.

The selection of writings from Hawthorne, Poe, Tennyson, Irving, and other writers of equal rank is evidence that the book contains material of literary merit. Byrd, Amundsen, Chamberlin, Lindbergh, Earhart, and other skillful aviators have made generous contributions con-

xiii

xiv   *Romance of the Airman*

cerning their experiences. Others, specialists in their particular field of air service, have contributed to the wealth of material collected, the reading of which will enable pupils to develop sympathetic contacts with a wide variety of human endeavor.

Organization. The several periods of the development of aviation, chronologically speaking, have been followed in sequence in the organization of the material.

For centuries man "stood upon the edge of space and yearned while sparrows from the hedge took flight and taunted us." This, the "dream period" of aviation, is a record of man's flight of mind. The selections from the classics contribute material highly imaginative and delightfully pleasing to the youth who is often living in a dream world.

The next period, that of experimentation by man, from Leonardo da Vinci to the Wright brothers, is designed to impress on the student that every great accomplishment of man is the result of years of painstaking study, and that that which seems to the uninterested observer to be failure may, in reality, be a definite step toward success.

The period of invention brings the reader down to our own age — the age of conquest of the air after centuries of seemingly fruitless work. The persistent efforts of the Montgolfiers and Wrights, in spite of discouragement and failure and in the face of an indifferent if not a scornful public, should serve to inspire youth to patient endeavor.

The spirit of adventure dominant in all young people is adequately provided for in the section "The Airman becomes a Pathfinder." Here we have the picture of youth who dares the elements, explores the unknown, and even challenges death.

The section entitled "The Airman Soars to Fame" provides material for the hero worship which youth so

Introduction xv

freely indulges in during the high-school period. Men and the craft that they control so skillfully inspire young readers to serve others and to forget self in the effort to accomplish goals set by themselves — "to dare and do the impossible."

Human history offers no examples of more noble self-sacrifice or greater loyalty to a cause than those told in the section "The Airman Serves." These daring spirits who have been pioneers in the practical use of aircraft present qualities of character most desirable for emulation.

HELPS IN TEACHING

The glossary. According to the report of the United States Department of Commerce, five hundred and sixty-five new words have been added to the language since aviation has developed to its present proportions. Reliable authorities state that two hundred or three hundred of these must of necessity become a part of the average man's vocabulary if he is to read the newspapers and magazines intelligently. Of these new words those not found in any word list before 1926 have been placed in the glossary.

Three classes of words have been listed at the close of the lessons:

1. Those peculiar to the special selection in which they are found. They appear under the caption "To aid in understanding this selection."
2. Those that junior-high-school students should add to their vocabulary, indicated as words "To add to your vocabulary."
3. Technical words, — aëronautical terms which are defined in the glossary.

The informal tests. These give the student a means of checking his comprehension of the subject matter and also xvi *Romance of the Airman*

offer suggestions to the busy teacher for preparing her own tests for checking the class.

Exercises and topics related to other subjects. These give suggestions for the correlation of this reading with the other subjects and for unifying the student's whole program. These exercises and the informal tests are not intended to supplant questions for study or class discussion which any good teacher will include in her lesson plan, but rather to provide additional material and suggestions for the busy teacher. Since the superior student is so frequently neglected in the regular classroom, especial effort has been made to prepare exercises that will stimulate him to do additional reading and thinking. These exercises should not be assigned to the class as a whole, but the teacher, in assigning these topics for class reports, should give careful attention to the individual student's abilities and interests. They give opportunity to provide for such individual differences in ability and interests as are found in the usual classroom. The information required in them may be found in the student's texts for his other subjects or in the encyclopedias or reference books found in all junior high schools.

Other readings. Reading that is done in school should develop the student's ability to make wise choices when he is left to his own resources. The cross references to other selections in this book, included under the head of "Other Readings," give the student practice in pursuing the general subject which interests him and in organizing several selections into a single theme. In the list of readings from other sources the authors have sought not only to stimulate the student to further reading on aviation but also to direct his interest in this subject toward reading in history, geography, literature, science, and other fields.

Introduction   xvii

To the Student

In the preparation of your lesson always read the explanatory note before you read the selection. When you come to the words that are starred in the text, turn at once to the exercises at the end of the selection, where you will find these explained under the heading "To aid in understanding this selection." When you have finished your reading, check yourself with the informal test at the close, and score by the key that your teacher provides for you.

Some students will need to study other words than those given in the list called "To aid in understanding the selection." If you find such words, consult the dictionary and encyclopedia. Remember that the material in this book, for the most part, is taken from books, magazines, and newspapers of the present time. Your ability to read these understandingly is one of the things necessary to make you a good citizen.

The dictionary should, if necessary, be consulted for the meaning and pronunciation of the list of words marked "To add to your vocabulary." For some students many of the words suggested will already be a part of their speaking vocabulary. One good way to add to your speaking vocabulary is to select from the list words that you do not use in your informal everyday speech and make a conscious effort to use them in the class discussion. When you have deliberately used a word a few times, you may feel pretty sure that it has become a part of your vocabulary and will come to your aid, unsought, when needed.

The topics related to your other subjects give you many opportunities to enrich your understanding of these subjects and to appreciate the place they have in the world of affairs today. The themes give you opportunity to im-

xviii   *Romance of the Airman*

prove your command of oral and written English. One type of subject that you will find valuable for giving you the ability to express yourself clearly is that which asks you to inform yourself about a person, place, or process and then explain this topic to the class. The degree of understanding thereby gained by the other members of your class is a test of your ability to express yourself clearly.

The references to other readings in this book will enable you to make comparisons between topics or gain additional information about certain things.

The references to readings from other sources give you suggestions for reading on those subjects you desire to pursue for further information.

You will find it both interesting and instructive to keep a notebook with a "Who's Who" section and to make maps of the various regions studied. Clippings, pictures, and maps added to this will make it valuable as a reference book in years to come.

ROMANCE OF THE AIRMAN

I. The Airman Dreams

Oh that I had wings like a dove; for then would I fly away, and be at rest

Psalms lv, 6

Some Ancient Stories of Man's Attempts to Fly

> *Explanatory Note.* The selections in this first section, "The Airman Dreams," are taken from literature dealing with imaginative flights through the air. Remember while you are reading these that they are merely the creation of an author's fancy. Also bear in mind that the remainder of the book recounts actual happenings. You can match every imaginary story in this first section with a real one from the later sections—one that has happened in your own age. Truly, *truth is stranger than fiction.*

THE present generation sees man's realization of an aspiration that extends back to earliest times. Many prehistoric myths and legends give accounts of man's flight through the air, of his rapid but safe passage over perilous ocean and mountains. Man's imagination created gods and supernatural creatures endowed with qualities and powers that he himself desired to possess, and so among the prehistoric tales of most peoples are found gods or legendary heroes that have the power of aërial navigation.

In many of these legendary stories man dons a cap, winged sandals, or other magic garments that give him the power of traveling through the air with safety and ease. In Greek mythology Mercury, the messenger of the gods, flew through the air by means of a winged hat and winged sandals. Perseus is the hero of another Greek myth in which the power of flight was obtained from sandals. He was sent to conquer the Medusa, a terrible monster who caused all living beings who gazed upon her to turn into stone. Perseus was equipped with winged sandals that gave him the power of flight through the air, a helmet that rendered him invisible, and a bright shield to reflect the image of the monster. Thus armed, he swooped down on

Romance of the Airman

her while she slept and severed her head from her body. With the head as his trophy he winged his way over mountains and sea until he reached the country of the Ethiopians. There he saw the beautiful maiden Andromeda chained to a rock as the prisoner of a sea monster. The hero undertook to slay the maiden's captor on condition that her parents give her to him as his bride. Again he swooped down from the sky on his enemy, and again he achieved a victory over a hideous monster. When his right to the maiden was contested by her former suitor, who appeared at the wedding feast with his forces to claim the maiden, Perseus turned the head of the Medusa on them and changed them all to stone.

Similar legends of man's power to fly have come down to us from other nations. Among the many legends from ancient China is one of magic shoes that enabled the wearer, surrounded by a smoky mist, to rise into the clouds. An old Swedish story, "The Beautiful Palace East of the Sun and North of the Earth," tells of a youth who had boots with which he could take steps a hundred miles in length, and a cloak that made him invisible. In an Icelandic tale, magic shoes made of the skin from the soles of the feet carried the wearer through the air. Descriptions of thousand-league boots that could transport the wearer swiftly through the air are found in the folk tales of several European countries.

Another set of legends gives man the power of flight by means of some kind of mechanical contrivance fastened to his body. The most widely told of all these is the Greek myth of Dædalus. He, with his son, Icarus, had been imprisoned on the island of Crete. He was released, but could not get away, as the ships had all been taken by the angry King Minos. Dædalus therefore devised wings for himself and his son which were fastened to their bodies with wax.

Perseus Swoops down to Slay the Sea Monster and Free Andromeda

Romance of the Airman

They were thus able to leave Crete. Icarus disobeyed his father's warning and flew too near the sun. The heat melted the wax, and poor Icarus dropped into the sea.

A similar story is found in the Teutonic myth of Wieland the Smith. The king of Jutland kept him a prisoner by making him lame. This clever prisoner made himself a cloak of feathers and flew to his home. A legendary king of Britain, Bladud, who was the father of King Lear,* is reputed to have made wings of feathers, with which he attempted to fly through the air. He, like Icarus, met his death when he tried out his wings.

In Chinese history there is an emperor by the name of Shun, who lived more than two thousand years before the birth of Christ. A story goes that as a youth he learned the art of flying from the two beautiful daughters of the Emperor Yao, and afterwards married them and received from his father-in-law a share in the government. After Yao's death Shun became the emperor and ruled long and well. Once, when he was imprisoned in a burning building, he put on the working clothes of a bird and flew out; another time, when he was imprisoned in a deep well, he clothed himself as a dragon and winged his way to safety.

A third form of legendary flight is with magic carriages or steeds. In Grecian mythology Phaëthon, the son of the sun-god, desired to drive his father's chariot across the sky. His father reluctantly consented to his son's insistent plea, but warned the lad of the danger of losing his way. In spite of his father's precautions the headstrong youth got off the usual track and drove so near the earth that the inhabitants were scorched black and a great area of the earth was dried into a desert. In order to save the earth from complete ruin, Jupiter was forced to strike this reckless driver with a thunderbolt that hurled him headlong into a river.

The Airman Dreams 7

Among the Chinese there are several stories of flying chariots. A famous poem, "Fallen into Sorrow," written by a disappointed statesman who lived about three hundred years before Christ, tells of an aërial chariot. The poet pictures himself kneeling at the grave of Emperor Shun, from which he is carried aloft by a chariot drawn by four dragons. He views the four corners of the earth from his chariot and then descends again.

About the time this poem was written, Chinese history records that Ki-Kung-Shi made a flying chariot that could travel a great distance with a fair wind. The emperor had the chariot destroyed because he did not want his people to know of it.

Among the legends of India is one of the jeweled car owned by a king of Benares who rode about in the air at great speed. Another Indian story tells of an airship in the shape of a huge bird, painted so that it could not be distinguished from a real one. This bird was equipped with springs by which it could be made to ascend, to descend, and to change its velocity. The stories of the movements of this bird sound much like those of movements of modern aircraft.

Among Persian stories is one of a foolish king who essayed to fly by means of a throne drawn by four eagles. Each eagle had a piece of flesh fastened before him which enticed him to fly forward; but the scheme failed, and the poor king fell in disgrace before his people.

A similar story is told of Alexander the Great. He was supposed to have navigated the air in a vehicle drawn by hungry birds that had a horse liver attached in front of them. He carried with him magicians that understood the language of the birds.

A Mohammedan legend tells of King Solomon's magic carpet of green silk. When he desired to travel, he placed

Romance of the Airman

his throne and all his forces upon it and told the wind where he wished to go. The carpet with all its contents soared into the air and alighted at the place named.

The best-known legend of a flying horse is that of Pegasus. In Greek mythology Pegasus is the winged steed fashioned by Neptune from the drops of blood which dropped from the head of the Medusa as Perseus flew across the ocean with his hideous burden. Bellerophon captured this wild steed with the aid of the golden bridle given him by Minerva, and rode him through many thrilling adventures. Pegasus was finally translated to the sky and became the constellation that now bears his name.

Several Persian legends tell of mechanical horses that were constructed and used by young heroes to carry beautiful princesses from imprisonment. These horses had a mechanism by which their movements might be directed and their speed changed. The Persians had the idea, at least, of a man-controlled flying machine.

Some ancient men, however, went further and made contrivances that are said to have actually traveled in the air. About 500 B.C. a Chinese by the name of Lu Pau made a magpie from wood and bamboo that is reputed to have flown aloft for three days. A Latin writer by the name of Aulus Gellius related the story of a wooden dove that had the power of flight. It was constructed by Archytas, a Greek philosopher who lived in Italy about 428–347 B.C., and, so Gellius reported, was balanced by weights and put in motion by inclosed air. A story of the fifteenth century tells of Johann Müller of Nuremberg, who is said to have made a mechanical eagle that could fly. This eagle was sent out from the gates to meet Emperor Charles V on his approach to the city. When man began to make these mechanical devices that could fly, he was no longer a dreamer but an experimenter.

The Airman Dreams

9

Words and Phrases

To aid in understanding this selection

King Lear: the story of this legendary king of Britain is told by Shakespeare in his play by that name.

To add to your vocabulary

aërial	myth
prehistoric	velocity
legendary	

Informal Test (Matching)

In the notes to the student you are told the purpose of the informal tests. This one is called a matching test. All matching tests in this book should be done as follows: On your test paper, number as many lines as you have items in the first list (in this test you number ten lines). Look at the first word, or group of words, in the numbered list, and then find in the second list the item that is associated with that word, or group of words, in the story. Write it after 1 on your paper. For example, in this test, No. 1 in the first list is *Bladud*. The item in the second list that goes with *Bladud* is *father of King Lear*. Write after 1 on your paper *father of King Lear*. Do all others like this.

You will find more items in the second list than you will use. Think carefully and be sure to choose the right ones.

1. **Bladud**	owner of a magic carpet
2. **Mercury**	had the power of turning everything to stone
3. **Perseus**	winged steed
4. **Medusa**	son of the sun-god
5. **Phaëthon**	made wings fastened with wax
6. **Andromeda**	messenger of the gods
7. **Dædalus**	Latin writer
8. **King Solomon**	possessor of a reflecting shield
9. **Pegasus**	receiver of the golden bridle
10. **Bellerophon**	father of King Lear
	a maiden chained to a rock
	mechanical eagle

10 *Romance of the Airman*

When you have finished your test, mark each item that you missed. Your score is the number right. Compute your percentage of accuracy by dividing the number you have right by the total number, which in this test is 10.

Exercises and Topics related to your Other Subjects

1. Bring to the class pictures of works of art showing Mercury, Perseus, Andromeda, Dædalus, Phaëthon, Pegasus, Neptune, and Medusa. Consult mythologies and reference books as well as books on art for these.

2. Consult historical references and give a short talk on "The Life of Alexander the Great"; "The Life of Charles the Fifth."

3. The story of the wooden dove of Archytas is written in the Latin language. Students of the history of aviation have gone back to this old book, "Attic Nights," to get authentic information about this early flying machine. Use similar illustrations and give a short talk on "The Necessity for some Latin Students in Each Generation." Ask a Latin teacher to give you some suggestions on this topic.

Other Readings

In this book

"The Enchanted Horse," page 43.
"The Magic Carpet," page 50.
"Dædalus and Icarus," page 11.
"Pegasus, The Winged Horse," page 16.

Dædalus and Icarus

OVID

Explanatory Note. This poem is a translation from the great Latin work "Metamorphoses." This was written by Ovid, a Roman poet born in 43 B. C. Selections from "Metamorphoses" are often studied by Latin classes in high school and college.

This translation is from Samuel Croxall, an English clergyman and writer of the eighteenth century.

IN TEDIOUS exile now too long detain'd,
Dædalus * languish'd for his native land:
The sea foreclos'd his flight; yet thus he said;
"Though earth and water in subjection laid,
O cruel Minos, thy dominion be,
We'll go through air; for sure the air is free."
Then to new arts his cunning thought applies,
And to improve the work of nature tries.
A row of quills in gradual order plac'd,
Rise by degrees in length from first to last;
As on a cliff th' ascending thicket grows,
Or different reeds the rural pipe compose.
Along the middle runs a twine of flax,
The bottom stems are join'd by pliant wax.
Thus, well compact, a hollow bending brings
The fine composure into real wings.
His boy, young Icarus, that near him stood,
Unthinking of his fate, with smiles pursu'd
The floating feathers, which the moving air
Bore loosely from the ground, and wafted here and there;
Or with the wax impertinently play'd,
And with his childish tricks the great design delay'd.
The final master-stroke at last impos'd,
And now the neat machine completely clos'd;
Fitting his pinions on, a flight he tries,

Dædalus teaches his Son to use the Wings

And hung self-balanc'd in the beaten skies.
Then thus instructs his child: "My boy, take care
To wing your course along the middle air;
If low, the surges wet your flagging plumes;
If high, the Sun the melting wax consumes:
Steer between both: nor to the northern skies,
Nor south Orion,* turn your giddy eyes:
But follow me: let me before you lay
Rules for the flight, and mark the pathless way."
Then teaching, with a fond concern, his son,
He took the untry'd wings, and fix'd them on;
But fix'd with trembling hands, and as he speaks,
The tears roll gently down his aged cheeks:
Then kiss'd, and in his arms embrac'd him fast,
But knew not this embrace must be the last.

The Airman Dreams

13

And mounting upward, as he wings his flight,
Back on his charge he turns his aching sight;
As parent birds, when first their callow care
Leave the high nest to tempt the liquid air.
Then cheers him on, and oft, with fatal art,
Reminds the stripling to perform his part.
These, as the angler at the silent brook,
Or mountain shepherd leaning on his crook,
Or gaping plowman, from the vale descries,
They stare, and view them with religious eyes,
And straight conclude them gods; since none, but they,
Through their own azure skies could find a way.
Now Delos,* Paros,* on the left are seen,
And Samos,* favor'd by Jove's haughty queen;*
Upon the right, the isle Lebynthos * nam'd,
And fair Calymne* for its honey fam'd.
When now the boy, whose childish thoughts aspire
To loftier aims, and make him ramble higher,
Grown wild, and wanton, more embolden'd flies
Far from his guide, and soars among the skies,
The soft'ning wax, that felt a nearer sun,
Dissolv'd apace, and soon began to run.
The youth in vain his melting pinions shakes;
His feathers gone, no longer air he takes.
"Oh! father, father," as he strove to cry,
Down to the sea he tumbled from on high,
And found his fate; yet still subsists by fame,
Among those waters that retain his name.
The father, now no more a father, cries,
"Ho, Icarus! where are you?" as he flies;
"Where shall I seek my boy?" he cried again,
And saw his feathers scatter'd on the main.
Then curs'd his art; and funeral rites conferr'd,
Naming the country from the youth interr'd.

14 *Romance of the Airman*

Words and Phrases

To aid in understanding this selection

Dædalus: the word means "cunning worker."

Orion: a star in the southern sky.

Delos, Paros, Samos, Lebynthos, Calymne: islands in the Ægean Sea.

Jove's haughty queen: the island of Samos was one of the principal seats of worship of Juno, the wife of Jupiter, or Jove.

To add to your vocabulary

callow	pinions
wanton	quill

Informal Test (Completion)

All completion tests in this book should be done as follows: On your test paper, number as many lines as there are numbers in the test (in this test you will number seven lines). After each number on your paper write the words necessary to complete the sentence of the corresponding number in the test. For example, after 1 you write *his native land*.

1. Dædalus longed for _ _ _ _ _ _.

2. The materials used by Dædalus in making the wings were _ _ _ _ _ _, _ _ _ _ _ _, and _ _ _ _ _ _.

3. While the father worked, his son _ _ _ _ _ _ or _ _ _ _ _ _.

4. After Dædalus finished the wings, the first thing he did was _ _ _ _ _ _.

5. He told Icarus not to fly too low because _ _ _ _ _ _.

6. He told Icarus not to fly too high because _ _ _ _ _ _.

7. The people below believed the flyers in the sky were _ _ _ _ _ _.

Exercises and Topics related to your Other Subjects

On a map of ancient Greece locate the places named in this poem. Bring to the class for oral reading the passage or passages you like best in the poem.

The Airman Dreams 15

Subjects for oral themes

A Modern Icarus. [A boy who does not heed his father's warning and has a downfall.]

The Flight viewed from Below. [Compare with similar incidents of modern times.]

The Myth of Orion.

Other Readings

In this book

"Some Ancient Stories of Man's Attempts to Fly," page 3.

Pegasus, the Winged Horse

NATHANIEL HAWTHORNE

> *Explanatory Note.* According to the classic Greek myth, Pegasus was a beautiful winged horse that sprang from the body of Medusa, the Gorgon whom Perseus slew. The story given here was written by Nathaniel Hawthorne for the entertainment of his own children, Una, Julian, and Rose. His interpretation of the ancient myth is so highly imaginative and delightful that for many years it has given pleasure to other readers.

Pegasus and the Fountain of Pirene

ONCE, in the old, old times — for all the strange things which I tell you about happened long before anybody can remember — a fountain gushed out of a hillside, in the marvelous land of Greece. And, for aught I know, after so many thousand years, it is still gushing out of the very selfsame spot. At any rate, there was the pleasant fountain, welling freshly forth and sparkling adown the hillside, in the golden sunset, when a handsome young man named Bellerophon* drew near its margin. In his hand he held a bridle, studded with brilliant gems and adorned with a golden bit. Seeing an old man, and another of middle age, and a little boy, near the fountain, and likewise a maiden, who was dipping up some of the water in a pitcher, he paused, and begged that he might refresh himself with a draft.

"This is very delicious water," he said to the maiden as he rinsed and filled her pitcher, after drinking out of it. "Will you be kind enough to tell me whether the fountain has any name?"

"Yes; it is called the Fountain of Pirene," * answered the maiden; and then she added: "My grandmother has told me that this clear fountain was once a beautiful

Pegasus carries Bellerophon into the Clouds

From a painting by Vesper L. George, Boston

18   Romance of the Airman

woman; and when her son was killed by the arrows of the huntress Diana, she melted all away into tears. And so the water, which you find so cool and sweet, is the sorrow of that poor mother's heart!"

"I should not have dreamed," observed the young stranger, "that so clear a wellspring, with its gush and gurgle, and its cheery dance out of the shade into the sunlight, had so much as one teardrop in its bosom! And this, then, is Pirene? I thank you, pretty maiden, for telling me its name. I have come from a far-away country to find this very spot."

A middle-aged country fellow — he had driven his cow to drink out of the spring — stared hard at young Bellerophon, and at the handsome bridle which he carried.

"The watercourses must be getting low, friend, in your part of the world," remarked he, "if you come so far only to find the Fountain of Pirene. But, pray, have you lost a horse? I see you carry the bridle in your hand; and a very pretty one it is with that double row of bright stones upon it. If the horse was as fine as the bridle, you are much to be pitied for losing him."

"I have lost no horse," said Bellerophon, with a smile. "But I happen to be seeking a very famous one, which, as wise people have informed me, must be found hereabouts, if anywhere. Do you know whether the winged horse Pegasus still haunts the Fountain of Pirene, as he used to do in your forefathers' days?"

But then the country fellow laughed.

Some of you have probably heard that this Pegasus was a snow-white steed, with beautiful silvery wings, who spent most of his time on the summit of Mount Helicon.* He was as wild and as swift and as buoyant in his flight through the air as any eagle that ever soared into the clouds. There was nothing else like him in the world. He

The Airman Dreams 19

had no mate, he never had been backed or bridled by a master; and, for many a long year, he led a solitary and happy life.

Oh, how fine a thing it is to be a winged horse! Sleeping at night, as he did, on a lofty mountain-top, and passing the greater part of the day in the air, Pegasus seemed hardly to be a creature of the earth. Whenever he was seen, up very high above people's heads, with the sunshine on his silvery wings, you would have thought that he belonged to the sky, and that, skimming a little too low, he had got astray among our mists and vapors, and was seeking his way back again. It was very pretty to behold him plunge into the fleecy bosom of a bright cloud, and be lost in it, for a moment or two, and then break forth from the other side. Or, in a sullen rainstorm, when there was a gray pavement of clouds over the whole sky, it would sometimes happen that the winged horse descended right through it, and the glad light of the upper region would gleam after him. In another instant, it is true, both Pegasus and the pleasant light would be gone away together. But anyone that was fortunate enough to see this wondrous spectacle felt cheerful the whole day afterwards, and as much longer as the storm lasted.

In the summer-time, and in the beautifullest of weather, Pegasus often alighted on the solid earth, and, closing his silvery wings, would gallop over hill and dale for pastime, as fleetly as the wind. Oftener than in any other place, he had been seen near the Fountain of Pirene, drinking the delicious water or rolling himself upon the soft grass of the margin. Sometimes, too, — but Pegasus was very dainty in his food, — he would crop a few of the clover blossoms that happened to be sweetest.

To the Fountain of Pirene, therefore, people's great-grandfathers had been in the habit of going — as long

20 *Romance of the Airman*

as they were youthful, and retained their faith in winged horses — in hopes of getting a glimpse at the beautiful Pegasus. But of late years he had been very seldom seen. Indeed, there were many of the country folks, dwelling within half an hour's walk of the fountain, who had never beheld Pegasus, and did not believe that there was any such creature in existence. The country fellow to whom Bellerophon was speaking chanced to be one of those incredulous persons.

And that was the reason why he laughed.

"Pegasus, indeed!" cried he, turning up his nose as high as such a flat nose could be turned up — "Pegasus, indeed! A winged horse, truly! Why, friend, are you in your senses? Of what use would wings be to a horse? Could he drag the plow so well, think you? To be sure, then, how would a man like to see his horse flying out of the stable windows? — yes, or whisking him up above the clouds, when he only wanted to ride to mill? No, no! I don't believe in Pegasus. There never was such a ridiculous kind of horse-fowl made!"

"I have some reason to think otherwise," said Bellerophon, quietly.

And then he turned to an old, gray man, who was leaning on a staff, and listening very attentively, with his head stretched forward, and one hand at his ear, because, for the last twenty years, he had been getting rather deaf.

"And what say you, venerable sir?" inquired he. "In your younger days, I should imagine, you must frequently have seen the winged steed!"

"Ah, young stranger, my memory is very poor!" said the aged man. "When I was a lad, if I remember rightly, I used to believe there was such a horse, and so did everybody else. But, nowadays, I hardly know what to think, and very seldom think about the winged horse at all. If

The Airman Dreams 21

I ever saw the creature, it was a long, long while ago;
and, to tell you the truth, I doubt whether I ever did
see him. One day, to be sure, when I was quite a youth,
I remember seeing some hoof-tramps round about the
brink of the fountain. Pegasus might have made those
hoof-marks; and so might some other horse."

"And have you never seen him, my fair maiden?"
asked Bellerophon of the girl, who stood with the pitcher
on her head while this talk went on. "You certainly
could see Pegasus, if anybody can, for your eyes are very
bright."

"Once I thought I saw him," replied the maiden, with
a smile and a blush. "It was either Pegasus, or a large
white bird, a very great way up in the air. And one other
time, as I was coming to the fountain with my pitcher, I
heard a neigh. Oh, such a brisk and melodious neigh as
that was! My very heart leaped with delight at the sound.
But it startled me, nevertheless; so that I ran home without filling my pitcher."

"That was truly a pity!" said Bellerophon.

And he turned to the child, whom I mentioned at the
beginning of the story, and who was gazing at him, as
children gaze at strangers, with his rosy mouth wide open.

"Well, my little fellow," cried Bellerophon, playfully
pulling one of his curls, "I suppose you have often seen
the winged horse."

"That I have," answered the child, very readily. "I
saw him yesterday, and many times before."

"You are a fine little man!" said Bellerophon, drawing
the child closer to him. "Come, tell me all about it."

"Why," replied the child, "I often come here to sail
little boats in the fountain, and to gather pretty pebbles
out of its basin. And sometimes, when I look down into
the water, I see the image of the winged horse, in the pic-

ture of the sky that is there. I wish he would come down, and take me on his back, and let me ride him up to the moon! But if I so much as stir to look at him, he flies far away out of sight."

And Bellerophon put his faith in the child, who had seen the image of Pegasus in the water, and in the maiden, who had heard him neigh so melodiously, rather than in the middle-aged clown, who believed only in cart horses, or in the old man, who had forgotten the beautiful things of his youth.

Therefore he haunted about the Fountain of Pirene for a great many days afterwards. He kept continually on the watch, looking upward at the sky, or else down into the water, hoping forever that he should see either the reflected image of the winged horse, or the marvelous reality. He held the bridle, with its bright gems and golden bit, always ready in his hand. The rustic people, who dwelt in the neighborhood, and drove their cattle to the fountain to drink, would often laugh at poor Bellerophon, and sometimes take him pretty severely to task. They told him that an able-bodied young man, like himself, ought to have better business than to be wasting his time in such an idle pursuit. They offered to sell him a horse, if he wanted one; and when Bellerophon declined the purchase, they tried to drive a bargain with him for his fine bridle.

Even the country boys thought him so very foolish that they used to have a great deal of sport about him, and were rude enough not to care a fig, although Bellerophon saw and heard it. One little urchin, for example, would play Pegasus, and cut the oddest imaginable capers, by way of flying; while one of his schoolfellows would scamper after him, holding forth a twist of bulrushes, which was intended to represent Bellerophon's ornamental bridle.

The Airman Dreams 23

But the gentle child, who had seen the picture of Pegasus in the water, comforted the young stranger. The dear little fellow, in his play-hours, often sat down beside him, and, without speaking a word, would look down into the fountain and up toward the sky, with so innocent a faith that Bellerophon could not help feeling encouraged.

Why Bellerophon Sought Pegasus

Now you will, perhaps, wish to be told why it was that Bellerophon had undertaken to catch the winged horse. And we shall find no better opportunity to speak about this matter than while he is waiting for Pegasus to appear.

If I were to relate the whole of Bellerophon's previous adventures, they might easily grow into a very long story. It will be quite enough to say, that, in a certain country of Asia, a terrible monster, called a Chimera,* had made its appearance, and was doing more mischief than could be talked about between now and sunset. According to the best accounts which I have been able to obtain, this Chimera was nearly, if not quite, the ugliest and most poisonous creature, and the strangest and unaccountablest, and the hardest to fight with, and the most difficult to run away from, that ever came out of the earth's inside. It had a tail like a boa constrictor; its body was like I do not care what; and it had three separate heads, one of which was a lion's, the second a goat's, and the third an abominable great snake's. And a hot blast of fire came flaming out of each of its three mouths! Being an earthly monster, I doubt whether it had any wings; but, wings or no, it ran like a goat and a lion and wriggled along like a serpent, and thus contrived to make about as much speed as all the three together.

Oh, the mischief, and mischief, and mischief that this

24 *Romance of the Airman*

naughty creature did! With its flaming breath, it could set a forest on fire, or burn up a field of grain, or, for that matter, a village, with all its fences and houses. It laid waste the whole country round about, and used to eat up people and animals alive, and cook them afterwards in the burning oven of its stomach. Mercy on us, little children, I hope neither you nor I will ever happen to meet a Chimera!

While the hateful beast — if a beast we can anywise call it — was doing all these horrible things, it so chanced that Bellerophon came to that part of the world, on a visit to the king. The king's name was Iobates,* and Lycia * was the country which he ruled over. Bellerophon was one of the bravest youths in the world, and desired nothing so much as to do some valiant and beneficent deed, such as would make all mankind admire and love him. In those days the only way for a young man to distinguish himself was by fighting battles, either with the enemies of his country, or with wicked giants, or with troublesome dragons, or with wild beasts when he could find nothing more dangerous to encounter. King Iobates, perceiving the courage of his youthful visitor, proposed to him to go and fight the Chimera, which everybody else was afraid of, and which, unless it should be soon killed, was likely to convert Lycia into a desert. Bellerophon would either slay this dreaded Chimera, or perish in the attempt.

But, in the first place, as the monster was so prodigiously swift, he bethought himself that he should never win the victory by fighting on foot. The wisest thing he could do, therefore, was to get the very best and fleetest horse that could anywhere be found. And what other horse, in all the world, was half so fleet as the marvelous horse Pegasus, who had wings as well as legs, and was even more active in the air than on the earth? To be sure, a great many

The Airman Dreams

people denied that there was any such horse with wings, and said that the stories about him were all poetry and nonsense. But, wonderful as it appeared, Bellerophon believed that Pegasus was a real steed, and hoped that he himself might be fortunate enough to find him; and, once fairly mounted on his back, he would be able to fight the Chimera at better advantage.

The Capture of Pegasus

And this was the purpose with which he had traveled from Lycia to Greece, and had brought the beautifully ornamented bridle in his hand. It was an enchanted bridle. If he could only succeed in putting the golden bit into the mouth of Pegasus, the winged horse would be submissive, and would own Bellerophon for his master, and fly whithersoever he might choose to turn the rein.

But, indeed, it was a weary and anxious time, while Bellerophon waited for Pegasus, in hopes that he would come and drink at the Fountain of Pirene. He was afraid lest King Iobates should imagine that he had fled from the Chimera. It pained him, too, to think how much mischief the monster was doing, while he himself, instead of fighting it, was compelled to sit idly poring over the bright waters of Pirene, as they gushed out of the sparkling sand. And as Pegasus came thither so seldom in these latter years, and scarcely alighted there more than once in a lifetime, Bellerophon feared that he might grow an old man, and have no strength left in his arms or courage in his heart, before the winged horse would appear. Oh, how heavily passes the time while an adventurous youth is yearning to do his part in life, and to gather in the harvest of his renown! How hard a lesson it is to wait! Our life is brief, and how much of it is spent in teaching us only this!

26   Romance of the Airman

Well was it for Bellerophon that the gentle child had grown so fond of him, and was never weary of keeping him company. Every morning the child gave him a new hope to put in his bosom, instead of yesterday's withered one.

"Dear Bellerophon," he would cry, looking up hopefully into his face, "I think we shall see Pegasus today!"

And, at length, if it had not been for the little boy's unwavering faith, Bellerophon would have given up all hope, and would have gone back to Lycia, and have done his best to slay the Chimera without the help of the winged horse. And in that case poor Bellerophon would at least have been terribly scorched by the creature's breath, and would most probably have been killed and devoured. Nobody should ever try to fight an earthborn Chimera, unless he can first get upon the back of an aërial steed.

One morning the child spoke to Bellerophon even more hopefully than usual.

"Dear Bellerophon," cried he, "I know not why it is, but I feel as if we should certainly see Pegasus today!"

And all that day he would not stir a step from Bellerophon's side; so they ate a crust of bread together, and drank some of the water of the fountain. In the afternoon there they sat, and Bellerophon had thrown his arm around the child, who likewise had put one of his little hands into Bellerophon's. The latter was lost in his own thoughts, and was fixing his eyes vacantly on the trunks of the trees that overshadowed the fountain, and on the grapevines that clambered up among their branches. But the child was gazing down into the water; he was grieved, for Bellerophon's sake, that the hope of another day should be deceived, like so many before it; and two or three quiet teardrops fell from his eyes, and mingled with what were said to be the many tears of Pirene, when she wept for her slain children.

The Airman Dreams   27

But when he least thought of it, Bellerophon felt the pressure of the child's little hand, and heard a soft, almost breathless, whisper.

"See there, dear Bellerophon! There is an image in the water!"

The young man looked down into the dimpling mirror of the fountain, and saw what he took to be the reflection of a bird flying at a great height in the air, with a gleam of sunshine on its snowy or silvery wings.

"What a splendid bird it must be!" said he. "And how very large it looks, though it must really be flying higher than the clouds!"

"It makes me tremble!" whispered the child. "I am afraid to look up into the air! It is very beautiful, and yet I dare only look at its image in the water. Dear Bellerophon, do you not see that it is no bird? It is the winged horse, Pegasus!"

Bellerophon's heart began to throb! He gazed keenly upward, but could not see the winged creature, whether bird or horse; because, just then, it had plunged into the fleecy depths of a summer cloud. It was but a moment, however, before the object reappeared, sinking lightly down out of the cloud, although still at a vast distance from the earth. Bellerophon caught the child in his arms, and shrank back with him, so that they were both hidden among the thick shrubbery which grew all around the fountain. Not that he was afraid of any harm, but he dreaded lest, if Pegasus caught a glimpse of them, he would fly far away, and alight in some inaccessible mountain-top. For it was really the winged horse. After they had expected him so long, he was coming to quench his thirst with the water of Pirene.

Nearer and nearer came the aërial wonder, flying in great circles, as you may have seen a dove when about

28   *Romance of the Airman*

to alight. Downward came Pegasus, in those wide, sweeping circles, which grew narrower, and narrower still, as he gradually approached the earth. The nigher the view of him, the more beautiful he was, and the more marvelous the sweep of his silvery wings. At last, with so light a pressure as hardly to bend the grass about the fountain, or imprint a hoof-tramp in the sand of its margin, he alighted, and, stooping his wild head, began to drink. He drew in the water, with long and pleasant sighs, and tranquil pauses of enjoyment; and then another draft, and another, and another. For nowhere in the world or up among the clouds did Pegasus love any water as he loved this of Pirene. And when his thirst was slaked, he cropped a few of the honey-blossoms of the clover, delicately tasting them, but not caring to make a hearty meal, because the herbage, just beneath the clouds, on the lofty sides of Mount Helicon, suited his palate better than this ordinary grass.

After thus drinking to his heart's content, and in his dainty fashion condescending to take a little food, the winged horse began to caper to and fro, and dance as it were, out of mere idleness and sport. There never was a more playful creature made than this very Pegasus. So there he frisked in a way that it delights me to think about, fluttering his great wings as lightly as ever did a linnet, and running little races, half on earth and half in air, and which I know not whether to call a flight or a gallop. When a creature is perfectly able to fly, he sometimes chooses to run, just for the pastime of the thing; and so did Pegasus, although it cost him some little trouble to keep his hoofs so near the ground. Bellerophon, meanwhile, holding the child's hand, peeped forth from the shrubbery, and thought that never was any sight so beautiful as this, nor ever a horse's eyes so wild and spirited as those of

The Airman Dreams

Pegasus. It seemed a sin to think of bridling him and riding on his back.

Once or twice Pegasus stopped and snuffed the air, pricking up his ears, tossing his head, and turning it on all sides, as if he partly suspected some mischief or other. Seeing nothing, however, and hearing no sound, he soon began his antics again.

At length — not that he was weary, but only idle and luxurious — Pegasus folded his wings, and lay down on the soft green turf. But, being too full of aërial life to remain quiet for many moments together, he soon rolled over on his back, with his four slender legs in the air. It was beautiful to see him, this one solitary creature, whose mate had never been created, but who needed no companion, and, living a great many hundred years, was as happy as the centuries were long. The more he did such things as mortal horses are accustomed to do, the less earthly and the more wonderful he seemed. Bellerophon and the child almost held their breath, partly from a delightful awe, but still more because they dreaded lest the slightest stir or murmur should send him up, with the speed of an arrow-flight, into the farthest blue of the sky.

Finally, when he had had enough of rolling over and over, Pegasus turned himself about, and, indolently, like any other horse, put out his forelegs, in order to rise from the ground; and Bellerophon, who had guessed that he would do so, darted suddenly from the thicket, and leaped astride of his back.

Yes, there he sat, on the back of the winged horse!

But what a bound did Pegasus make, when, for the first time, he felt the weight of a mortal man upon his loins! A bound, indeed! Before he had time to draw a breath, Bellerophon found himself five hundred feet aloft, and still shooting upward, while the winged horse snorted

30 *Romance of the Airman*

and trembled with terror and anger. Upward he went, up, up, up, until he plunged into the cold misty bosom of a cloud, at which, only a little while before, Bellerophon had been gazing, and fancying it a very pleasant spot. Then again, out of the heart of the cloud, Pegasus shot down like a thunderbolt, as if he meant to dash both himself and his rider headlong against a rock. Then he went through about a thousand of the wildest caprioles that had ever been performed either by a bird or a horse.

I cannot tell you half that he did. He skimmed straight forward, and sideways, and backward. He reared himself erect, with his forelegs on a wreath of mist, and his hind legs on nothing at all. He flung out his heels behind, and put down his head between his legs, with his wings pointing upward. At about two miles' height above the earth, he turned a somersault, so that Bellerophon's heels were where his head should have been, and he seemed to look down into the sky, instead of up. He twisted his head about, and, looking Bellerophon in the face, with fire flashing from his eyes, made a terrible attempt to bite him. He fluttered his pinions so wildly that one of the silver feathers was shaken out and, floating earthward, was picked up by the child, who kept it as long as he lived, in memory of Pegasus and Bellerophon.

But the latter — who, as you may judge, was as good a horseman as ever galloped — had been watching his opportunity, and at last clapped the golden bit of the enchanted bridle between the winged steed's jaws. No sooner was this done than Pegasus became as manageable as if he had taken food, all his life, out of Bellerophon's hand. To speak what I really feel, it was almost a sadness to see so wild a creature grow suddenly so tame. And Pegasus seemed to feel it so, likewise. He looked round to Bellerophon, with the tears in his beautiful eyes, instead

The Airman Dreams 31

of the fire that so recently flashed from them. But when Bellerophon patted his head and spoke a few kind and soothing words, another look came into the eyes of Pegasus; for he was glad, after so many lonely centuries, to have found a companion and a master.

Thus it always is with winged horses, and with all such wild and solitary creatures. If you can catch and overcome them, it is the surest way to win their love.

Bellerophon and Pegasus become Friends

While Pegasus had been doing his utmost to shake Bellerophon off his back, he had flown a very long distance; and they had come within sight of a lofty mountain by the time the bit was in his mouth. Bellerophon had seen this mountain before, and knew it to be Helicon, on the summit of which was the winged horse's abode. Thither, after looking gently into his rider's face, as if to ask leave, Pegasus now flew, and, alighting, waited patiently until Bellerophon should please to dismount. The young man, accordingly, leaped from his steed's back, but still held him fast by the bridle. Meeting his eyes, however, he was so affected by the gentleness of his aspect and the thought of the free life which Pegasus had heretofore lived that he could not bear to keep him a prisoner, if he really desired his liberty.

Obeying this generous impulse he slipped the enchanted bridle off the head of Pegasus, and took the bit from his mouth.

"Leave me, Pegasus!" said he. "Either leave me, or love me."

In an instant the winged horse shot almost out of sight, soaring straight upward from the summit of Mount Helicon. Being long after sunset, it was now twilight on the

32 *Romance of the Airman*

mountain-top, and dusky evening over all the country round about. But Pegasus flew so high that he overtook the departed day, and was bathed in the upper radiance of the sun. Ascending higher and higher, he looked like a bright speck, and, at last, could no longer be seen in the hollow waste of the sky. And Bellerophon was afraid that he should never behold him more. But while he was lamenting his own folly, the bright speck reappeared, and drew nearer and nearer, until it descended lower than the sunshine; and, behold, Pegasus had come back! After this trial there was no more fear of the winged horse's making his escape. He and Bellerophon were friends, and put loving faith in one another.

That night they lay down and slept together, with Bellerophon's arm about the neck of Pegasus, not as a caution, but for kindness. And they awoke at peep of day, and bade one another good morning, each in his own language.

In this manner Bellerophon and the wondrous steed spent several days, and grew better acquainted and fonder of each other all the time. They went on long aërial journeys, and sometimes ascended so high that the earth looked hardly bigger than — the moon. They visited distant countries, and amazed the inhabitants, who thought that the beautiful young man, on the back of the winged horse, must have come down out of the sky. A thousand miles a day was no more than an easy space for the fleet Pegasus to pass over. Bellerophon was delighted with this kind of life, and would have liked nothing better than to live always in the same way, aloft in the clear atmosphere; for it was always sunny weather up there, however cheerless and rainy it might be in the lower region. But he could not forget the horrible Chimera, which he had promised King Iobates to slay. So, at last,

The Airman Dreams

33

when he had become well accustomed to feats of horsemanship in the air, and could manage Pegasus with the least motion of his hand, and had taught him to obey his voice, he determined to attempt the performance of this perilous adventure.

At daybreak, therefore, as soon as he unclosed his eyes, he gently pinched the winged horse's ear, in order to arouse him. Pegasus immediately started from the ground, and pranced about a quarter of a mile aloft, and made a grand sweep around the mountain-top, by way of showing that he was wide awake, and ready for any kind of excursion. During the whole of this little flight, he uttered a loud, brisk, and melodious neigh, and finally came down at Bellerophon's side, as lightly as ever you saw a sparrow hop upon a twig.

"Well done, dear Pegasus! well done, my sky-skimmer!" cried Bellerophon, fondly stroking the horse's neck. "And now, my fleet and beautiful friend, we must break our fast. Today we are to fight the terrible Chimera."

The Fight with the Chimera

As soon as they had eaten their morning meal and drunk some sparkling water from a spring called Hippocrene, Pegasus held out his head, of his own accord, so that his master might put on the bridle. Then, with a great many playful leaps and airy caperings, he showed his impatience to be gone; while Bellerophon was girding on his sword, and hanging his shield about his neck, and preparing himself for battle. When everything was ready, the rider mounted, and, as was his custom, when going a long distance, ascended five miles perpendicularly, so as better to see whither he was directing his course. He then turned the head of Pegasus toward the east, and set out for Lycia.

34 *Romance of the Airman*

In their flight they overtook an eagle, and came so nigh him, before he could get out of their way, that Bellerophon might easily have caught him by the leg. Hastening onward at this rate, it was still early in the forenoon when they beheld the lofty mountains of Lycia, with their deep valleys. If Bellerophon had been told truly, it was in one of those valleys that the Chimera had taken up its abode.

Being now so near their journey's end, the winged horse gradually descended with his rider; and they took advantage of some clouds that were floating over the mountain-tops, in order to conceal themselves. Hovering on the upper surface of a cloud, and peeping over its edge, Bellerophon had a pretty distinct view of the mountainous part of Lycia, and could look into all its shadowy vales at once. At first there appeared to be nothing remarkable. It was a wild, savage, and rocky tract of high hills. In the more level part of the country there were ruins of houses that had been burnt, and, here and there, the carcasses of dead cattle, strewn about the pastures where they had been feeding.

"The Chimera must have done this mischief," thought Bellerophon. "But where can the monster be?"

As I have already said, there was nothing remarkable to be detected, at first sight, in any of the valleys and dells that lay among the heights of the mountain. Nothing at all; unless, indeed, it were three spires of black smoke, which issued from what seemed to be the mouth of a cavern, and clambered sullenly into the atmosphere. Before reaching the mountain-top, these three black smoke-wreaths mingled themselves into one. The cavern was almost directly beneath the winged horse and his rider, at the distance of about a thousand feet. The smoke, as it crept heavily upward, had an ugly, sulphurous, stifling scent, which caused Pegasus to snort and Bellero-

The Airman Dreams 35

phon to sneeze. So disagreeable was it to the marvelous steed, who was accustomed to breathe only the purest air, that he waved his wings, and shot half a mile out of the range of this offensive vapor.

But on looking behind him Bellerophon saw something that induced him first to draw the bridle, and then to turn Pegasus about. He made a sign, which the winged horse understood, and sank slowly through the air, until his hoofs were scarcely more than a man's height above the rocky bottom of the valley. In front, as far off as you could throw a stone, was the cavern's mouth, with the three smoke-wreaths oozing out of it. And what else did Bellerophon behold there?

There seemed to be a heap of strange and terrible creatures curled up within the cavern. Their bodies lay so close together that Bellerophon could not distinguish them apart; but, judging by their heads, one of these creatures was a huge snake, the second a fierce lion, and the third an ugly goat. The lion and the goat were asleep; the snake was broad awake, and kept staring around him with fiery eyes. But — and this was the most wonderful part of the matter — the three spires of smoke issued from the nostrils of these three heads! So strange was the spectacle that, though Bellerophon had been all along expecting it, the truth did not immediately occur to him, that here was the terrible three-headed Chimera. He had found out the Chimera's cavern. The snake, the lion, and the goat, as he supposed them to be, were not three separate creatures, but one monster!

The wicked, hateful thing! Slumbering as two thirds of it were, it still held, in its abominable claws, the remnant of an unfortunate lamb, which its three mouths had been gnawing, before two of them fell asleep!

All at once Bellerophon started as from a dream, and

36   *Romance of the Airman*

knew it to be the Chimera. Pegasus seemed to know it,
at the same instant, and sent forth a neigh that sounded
like the call of a trumpet to battle. At this sound the
three heads reared themselves erect, and belched out great
flashes of flame. Before Bellerophon had time to consider
what to do next, the monster flung itself out of the cavern
and sprang straight toward him, with its immense claws
extended and its snaky tail twisting itself behind. If Pegasus had not been as nimble as a bird, both he and his
rider would have been overthrown by the Chimera's headlong rush, and thus the battle have been ended before it
was well begun. But the winged horse was not to be caught
so. In the twinkling of an eye he was up aloft, halfway
to the clouds, snorting with anger. He shuddered, too,
not with affright, but with utter disgust at the loath-
someness of this poisonous thing with three heads.

The Chimera, on the other hand, raised itself up so as
to stand absolutely on the tip-end of its tail, with its talons
pawing fiercely in the air, and its three heads spluttering
fire at Pegasus and his rider. My stars, how it roared, and
hissed, and bellowed! Bellerophon, meanwhile, was fitting
his shield on his arm, and drawing his sword.

"Now, my beloved Pegasus," whispered he in the winged
horse's ear, "thou must help me to slay this monster; or
else thou shalt fly back to thy mountain-peak without
thy friend Bellerophon. For either the Chimera dies, or
its three mouths shall gnaw this head of mine, which has
slumbered upon thy neck!"

Pegasus whinnied, and, turning back his head, rubbed
his nose tenderly against his rider's cheek. It was his way
of telling him that, though he had wings and was an
immortal horse, yet he would perish, if it were possible
for immortality to perish, rather than leave Bellerophon
behind.

The Airman Dreams
37

"I thank you, Pegasus," answered Bellerophon. "Now, then, let us make a dash at the monster!"

Uttering these words, he shook the bridle; and Pegasus darted down aslant, as swift as the flight of an arrow, right toward the Chimera's threefold head, which, all this time, was poking itself as high as it could into the air. As he came within arm's length, Bellerophon made a cut at the monster, but was carried onward by his steed, before he could see whether the blow had been successful. Pegasus continued his course, but soon wheeled round, at about the same distance from the Chimera as before. Bellerophon then perceived that he had cut the goat's head of the monster almost off, so that it dangled downward by the skin, and seemed quite dead.

But, to make amends, the snake's head and the lion's head had taken all the fierceness of the dead one into themselves, and spit flame, and hissed, and roared, with a vast deal more fury than before.

"Never mind, my brave Pegasus!" cried Bellerophon. "With another stroke like that, we will stop either its hissing or its roaring."

And again he shook the bridle. Dashing aslantwise, as before, the winged horse made another arrow flight toward the Chimera, and Bellerophon aimed another downright stroke at one of the two remaining heads, as he shot by. But this time neither he nor Pegasus escaped so well as at first. With one of its claws the Chimera had given the young man a deep scratch in his shoulder, and had slightly damaged the left wing of the flying steed with the other. On his part, Bellerophon had mortally wounded the lion's head of the monster, insomuch that it now hung downward, with its fire almost extinguished, and sending out gasps of thick black smoke. The snake's head, however, which was the only one now left, was twice as fierce

38 *Romance of the Airman*

as ever before. It belched forth shoots of fire five hundred yards long, and emitted hisses so loud, so harsh, and so ear-piercing that King Iobates heard them, fifty miles off, and trembled till the throne shook under him.

"Welladay!" thought the poor king; "the Chimera is certainly coming to devour me!"

Meanwhile Pegasus had again paused in the air, and neighed angrily, while sparkles of pure crystal flame darted out of his eyes. How unlike the lurid fire of the Chimera! The aërial steed's spirit was all aroused, and so was that of Bellerophon.

"Dost thou bleed, my immortal horse?" cried the young man, caring less for his own hurt than for the anguish of this glorious creature, that ought never to have tasted pain. "The Chimera shall pay for this mischief with his last head!"

Then he shook the bridle, shouted loudly, and guided Pegasus, not aslantwise as before, but straight at the monster's hideous front. So rapid was the onset, that it seemed but a dazzle and a flash before Bellerophon was at close grips with his enemy.

The Chimera, by this time, after losing its second head, had got into a red-hot passion of pain and rampant rage. It so flounced about, half on earth and partly in the air, that it was impossible to say which element it rested upon. It opened its snake-jaws to such an abominable width, that Pegasus might almost, I was going to say, have flown right down its throat, wings outspread, rider and all! At their approach it shot out a tremendous blast of its fiery breath, and enveloped Bellerophon and his steed in a perfect atmosphere of flame, singeing the wings of Pegasus, scorching off one whole side of the young man's golden ringlets, and making them both far hotter than was comfortable, from head to foot.

The Airman Dreams 39

But this was nothing to what followed.

When the airy rush of the winged horse had brought him within the distance of a hundred yards, the Chimera gave a spring, and flung its huge, awkward, and utterly detestable carcass right upon poor Pegasus, clung round him with might and main, and tied up its snaky tail into a knot! Up flew the aërial steed, higher, higher, higher, above the mountain-peaks, above the clouds, and almost out of sight of the solid earth. But still the earthborn monster kept its hold, and was borne upward, along with the creature of light and air. Bellerophon, meanwhile, turning about, found himself face to face with the ugly grimness of the Chimera's visage, and could only avoid being scorched to death, or bitten in twain, by holding up his shield. Over the upper edge of the shield, he looked sternly into the savage eyes of the monster.

But the Chimera was so mad and wild with pain that it did not guard itself so well as might else have been the case. Perhaps, after all, the best way to fight a Chimera is by getting as close to it as you can. In its efforts to stick its horrible iron claws into its enemy, the creature left its own breast quite exposed; and perceiving this, Bellerophon thrust his sword up to the hilt into its cruel heart. Immediately the snaky tail untied its knot. The monster let go its hold of Pegasus, and fell from that vast height; while the fire within its bosom burned fiercer than ever. Thus it fell out of the sky, all aflame, and — it being nightfall before it reached the earth — was mistaken for a shooting star. But, at early sunrise, some cottagers were going to their day's labor, and saw, to their astonishment, that several acres of ground were strewn with black ashes. In the middle of a field, there was a heap of whitened bones, higher than a haystack. Nothing else was ever seen of the dreadful Chimera!

The Return to the Fountain of Pirene

And when Bellerophon had won the victory, he bent forward and kissed Pegasus, while tears stood in his eyes.

"Back now, my beloved steed!" said he. "Back to the Fountain of Pirene!"

Pegasus skimmed through the air, quicker than ever he did before, and reached the fountain in a very short time. And there he found the old man leaning on his staff, and the country fellow watering his cow, and the pretty maiden filling her pitcher.

"I remember now," quoth the old man, "I saw this winged horse once before, when I was quite a lad. But he was ten times handsomer in those days."

"I own a cart horse worth three of him!" cried the country fellow. "If this pony were mine, the first thing I should do would be to clip his wings!"

But the poor maiden said nothing, for she had always the luck to be afraid at the wrong time. So she ran away, and let her pitcher tumble down, and broke it.

"Where is the gentle child," asked Bellerophon, "who used to keep me company, and never lost his faith, and never was weary of gazing into the fountain?"

"Here am I, dear Bellerophon!" said the child, softly.

For the little boy had spent day after day, on the margin of Pirene, waiting for his friend to come back; but when he perceived Bellerophon descending through the clouds, mounted on the winged horse, he had shrunk back into the shrubbery. He was a delicate and tender child, and dreaded lest the old man and the country fellow should see the tears gushing from his eyes.

"Thou hast won the victory," said he joyfully, running to the knee of Bellerophon, who still sat on the back of Pegasus. "I knew thou wouldst."

The Airman Dreams 41

"Yes, dear child!" replied Bellerophon, alighting from the winged horse. "But if thy faith had not helped me, I should never have waited for Pegasus, never have gone up above the clouds, and never have conquered the terrible Chimera. Thou, my beloved little friend, hast done it all. And now let us give Pegasus his liberty."

So he slipped off the enchanted bridle from the head of the marvelous steed.

"Be free, forevermore, my Pegasus!" cried he, with a shade of sadness in his tone. "Be as free as thou art fleet!"

But Pegasus rested his head on Bellerophon's shoulder, and would not be persuaded to take flight.

"Well, then," said Bellerophon, caressing the airy horse, "thou shalt be with me, as long as thou wilt; and we will go together, forthwith, and tell King Iobates that the Chimera is destroyed."

Then Bellerophon embraced the gentle child, and promised to come to him again. and departed. But, in after years, that child took higher flights upon the aërial steed than ever did Bellerophon, and achieved more honorable deeds than his friend's victory over the Chimera. For, gentle and tender as he was, he grew to be a mighty poet!

Words and Phrases

To aid in understanding this selection

Bellerophon: son of the king of Corinth.

Pirene: a fountain in Corinth said to have started from the ground under the kick of Pegasus.

Helicon: a mountain.

Chimera: a monster that breathed fire and made great havoc throughout the land.

Iobates: king of Lycia.

Lycia: the country in which the Chimera was found.

42 *Romance of the Airman*

Informal Test (Completion) [1]

1. When Bellerophon approached the fountain he saw four persons; namely, _____ _____, _____ _____, _____ _____, and a _____.

2. The fountain was called _____.

3. The color of the winged horse was _____, and it had _____ wings.

4. The Chimera lived in a _____.

5. The Chimera threatened to convert Lycia into a _____.

6. Bellerophon and Pegasus returned to _____ _____ after the monster was killed.

7. The child that helped Bellerophon to capture Pegasus became a great _____.

Exercises and Topics related to your Other Subjects

1. On your map locate Greece and Asia Minor.

2. List all the descriptive words that are applicable to each of the following characters: Bellerophon; the child; the maiden.

3. List the words and phrases that describe the country.

Other Readings

In this book

"The Enchanted Horse," page 43.

From other sources

For the myths that form the basis for this story, read Gayley's "Classic Myths," published by Ginn and Company.

Read from Hawthorne's "Wonder Book" the story of "The Gorgon's Head."

[1] For directions, see completion test on page 14.

The Enchanted Horse[1]

> *Explanatory Note.* "The Arabian Nights' Entertainments," or "The Thousand and One Nights," is a collection of stories of romance and adventure. The author is unknown; but the stories, which are supposed to have come from India to Persia and from Persia to Arabia, have been translated into many modern languages. These stories are valued not only for their charm and wonder but also for the pictures they give of the customs and manners of the Old East.

THERE was in ancient times, in the country of the Persians, a mighty king who had one son and three beautiful daughters. It was the custom in that country to observe every year two festivals — that of the New Year and that of the autumnal equinox. At these times the king would open his palaces, reward the worthy, pardon the offenders, and receive the congratulations of his people.

On a certain day during one of these festivals three sages appeared before him: one had a peacock of gold, the second a trumpet of brass, and the third a horse made of ebony and ivory.

The king said to the sages, "What are these things, and what is their use?"

The owner of the peacock said, "Whenever an hour of the night or the day passes, this bird will flap its wings and utter a cry."

The owner of the trumpet said, "If my trumpet is placed at the gate of the city, it will act as defender of it; for when an enemy attempts to enter, it will send forth a warning sound."

The owner of the horse said, "O my lord, the use of this horse is that if any man mount it, it will carry him wherever he desires to go."

[1] From "The Arabian Nights' Entertainments."

44 *Romance of the Airman*

Upon this the king said, "I will make trial of all these things."

Then he made trial of the peacock and found that it was as its owner had said. And he made trial of the trumpet and found it as its owner had said. He then said to these two sages, "Ask of me what favor you will." And they replied, "Give each of us one of thy daughters in marriage." Whereupon the king gave them two of his daughters.

Then the third sage came forward and said, "O king, bestow upon me a like favor."

"When I shall have made trial of the horse," said the king.

Upon this the king's son came forward and said, "O my father, let me mount the horse and make trial of it, lest we disgrace our house by permitting my only remaining sister to marry a mere juggler." And the king said, "Try it, my son, as thou desirest."

The king's son accordingly mounted the horse and urged it forward, but it would not move.

"O sage," said he, "what is this? Does this seem to thee a rapid pace?"

"Turn the peg," said the owner of the horse, pointing out a wooden pin which was on its neck. And when the prince had turned it, the horse moved and rose with him toward the sky.

Then was the king's son greatly alarmed and bitterly did he repent his desire to make trial of the horse. He examined the steed carefully to find, if possible, another peg which might control its rapid flight, but none was to be seen. At last he discovered two screws, one upon each shoulder of the horse. When he turned one of these he shot upward with increasing swiftness so that he could scarcely keep his seat. Instantly he grasped the other screw and found, to his delight, that as he turned it his upward flight was stopped and he began to descend. He

The Airman Dreams

45

ceased not to descend for a whole day, for in his ascent the earth had become distant from him. And as he descended he found that he could guide his horse whithersoever he desired.

Now as he came nearer the earth he discovered countries and cities which he had never before seen, and among them was a beautiful city in the midst of a green valley.

"Here will I spend the night," said the prince, "and in the morning I will return to my father and tell him of my strange adventure."

Accordingly he began to search for a safe shelter and soon saw in the center of the city a palace rising high into the air and guarded by strong walls.

"This place is attractive," said he to himself, and dismounted upon the palace roof. Here he waited until he was sure that the inmates were asleep, and then, being both hungry and thirsty, he went down a flight of steps into the building to look for something to eat.

After roaming about in the dark for a long time he found himself in a dimly lighted room, where some slave girls were sleeping. Beyond, on a couch, lay a beautiful princess, who started up in terror at his approach. She, was, however, soon soothed by his courtesy and kindness.

"Perhaps," said she to him, "thou art he who demanded me yesterday in marriage of my father, and who was re-jected because he was disagreeable in appearance. Surely my father is mistaken, for thou art none other than a handsome person."

But the slave-girls said: "This is not the man, O our mistress. Verily this youth is of high rank, and the other was not fit to be his servant."

At this moment came the king, who had been aroused by a frightened slave, and who rushed upon the young man as if he would kill him.

"How is it," he cried out in anger, "that thou art come into my palace without permission? Have I not refused all who would take my daughter from me in marriage, and shall I suffer thee to escape with her by stealth?"

But the prince said: "Verily I wonder at thee. Dost thou ask for thy daughter a husband of nobler birth than I am? Hast thou seen anyone whom thou canst truly say is a better man?"

"No, young man," answered the king, craftily; "but I would have thee ask me for the princess publicly."

"Thou has said well," said the prince; "but when thy servants and thy slaves and thy soldiers are assembled and when they fall upon me and kill me, thou wilt be disgraced in the eyes of all honest men. If, however, thou wilt permit me to meet them in fair combat, the result will save thine honor; for should I overcome and subdue them all, then am I proved to be such a man as the king would choose for a son-in-law."

The king was astonished beyond measure at the young man's speech and said to him, "The number of my horsemen is forty thousand, besides the slaves belonging to me and their followers, who are equal in number."

"When the day dawns," said the prince, "send them forth to meet me and say to them, 'This person has asked for the hand of my daughter in marriage on condition that he overcomes and subdues you all and that you cannot prevail against him.'"

"So be it," said the king.

He then called his vizier * and commanded him to collect all the troops and to mount them upon their horses. Then said the young man: "O king, thou dost not treat me fairly. How shall I go forth on foot to overcome thy people who are mounted on horses? Send me, then, the horse on which I came."

The Airman Dreams

47

"Where is thy horse?" the king asked him.

"It is on the roof of thy palace," answered the prince.

"Nay, how can that be?" cried the king. But he sent one of his chief officers, saying, "Bring down what thou shalt find upon the roof of the palace."

So the officer went up to the roof and found there the horse made of ebony and ivory. And when the other officers saw it they laughed and said, "The young man is a madman." But they lifted the horse and carried it down the stairs and placed it before the king. And the people gazed at it and were amazed at its beauty and the richness of its bridle and saddle.

Then said the young man, "O king, I am going to mount my horse and charge upon thine army."

"Do as thou wilt," said the king, "and pity them not, for they will not pity thee."

So the prince seated himself firmly upon his horse and turned the peg. As the king saw the young man ascend into the sky he cried out to his troops, "Take him before he escapes!" But the vizier said: "O king, can we catch the flying bird? This is a great enchanter. Rejoice, therefore, that thou hast escaped from his hand."

Then the king returned to his daughter and told her what had happened, and she mourned greatly for the young man, saying, "I will not eat or drink till he is brought back to me." Such was her case.

The prince, meantime, was pursuing his journey and came before long within sight of his native city. Turning the other peg, he swiftly descended and found himself in his own home. Great was the rejoicing at his return; but after a little time the young man was overcome with longing to see again his beloved princess, so, mounting the enchanted horse, he flew back to her father's palace.

There he went about searching for her from room to

48 *Romance of the Airman*

room until at last he found her ill in bed in a remote part of the palace, surrounded by her slaves and nurses. And she said to him, "How couldst thou leave me?"

"O princess," said he, "wilt thou listen to my words and comply with my wishes?"

And she said, "I will not oppose thee in anything."

"Then," said he, "come with me to my country and my kingdom."

"I obey most willingly," she answered him.

Having taken her by the hand, he led her up to the roof of the palace and mounted his horse; then, placing her behind him, he turned the peg and soared with her into the sky, while, below, her father and mother cried out to her to return.

"Fairest lady," said the king's son, tenderly, "dost thou wish me to restore thee to thy father and mother?"

"O my master," she answered, "I am content to go with thee."

Then the king's son rejoiced exceedingly, and the horse began to move with great swiftness, and they ceased not to journey until they arrived at their destination.

Words and Phrases

To aid in understanding this selection

vizier: a high executive officer in various Mohammedan countries.

To add to your vocabulary

sage	craftily
juggler	destination

The Airman Dreams   49

Informal Test (Completion) [1]

1. The gifts of the three sages were (1) _____, (2) _____, (3) _____.

2. The trial flight of the horse was made by _____.

3. The rate of flight was controlled by means of _____.

4. The princess thought the rider of the horse was _____.

5. The king's horsemen numbered _____.

6. The enchanted horse was made of _____.

7. When the rider of the horse left, the princess vowed _____ _____.

8. When he soared away with the princess, he was watched by _____.

Exercises and Topics related to your Other Subjects

Subjects for themes

Comparison of the Imaginary Landing with a Real Landing of some Modern Aviator.

Comparison of the Imaginary Take-off with a Real Take-off.

Find pictures of ancient Persian buildings showing the high walls and flat roofs. Give a class talk on these houses.

Other Readings

In this book

"The Magic Carpet," page 50.

From other sources

" The Arabian Nights' Entertainments," by Martha A. L. Lane.

[1] For directions, see page 14.

The Magic Carpet

WASHINGTON IRVING

Explanatory Note. This selection is taken from the "Legend of Prince Ahmed Al Kamel," one of the collection of stories told by Washington Irving in "The Alhambra." Its hero is a young Moorish prince, Ahmed Al Kamel, who fell in love with the picture of the beautiful daughter of the Christian king of Toledo. He wooed her by letters and verses carried by a friendly dove. Hearing that a combat was to be held by the rivals for her hand, Prince Ahmed presented himself at the lists, clad in magic armor and mounted on a magic horse. Because he was a Moslem he was denied the right to contend for a Christian princess. When the rival princes sneered at him, however, he defied them; and so great was the magic power of his horse that, once in the fray, he defeated all his rivals and even unhorsed the king himself. This, of course, so aroused the king's anger that all chance of winning the princess by ordinary means was now lost to Ahmed. Hearing that the princess was ill from grief and that her father had offered his richest jewel to the one who would restore her, Ahmed appealed to his friend the owl for advice. The wise old owl told him of a magic box possessed by the king and advised him to secure possession of it by strategy.

THE next day the prince laid aside his rich attire and arrayed himself in the simple garb of an Arab of the desert. He dyed his complexion to a tawny hue, and no one could have recognized in him the splendid warrior who had caused such admiration and dismay at the tournament. With staff in hand and scrip * by his side, and a small pastoral reed, he repaired to Toledo and, presenting himself at the gate of the royal palace, announced himself as a candidate for the reward offered for the cure of the princess. The guards would have driven him away with blows: "What can a vagrant Arab like thyself pretend to do," said they, "in a case where the most learned of the land have failed?" The king, however, overheard the tumult, and ordered the Arab to be brought into his presence.

The Airman Dreams

51

"Most potent king," said Ahmed, "you behold before you a Bedouin * Arab, the greater part of whose life has been passed in the solitudes of the desert. Those solitudes, it is well known, are the haunts of demons and evil spirits, who beset us poor shepherds in our lonely watchings, enter into and possess our flocks and herds, and sometimes render even the patient camel furious. Against these, our counter charm is music; and we have legendary airs handed down from generation to generation, that we chant and pipe to cast forth these evil spirits. I am of a gifted line, and possess this power in its fullest force. If it be any evil influence of the kind that holds a spell over thy daughter, I pledge my head to free her from its sway."

The king, who was a man of understanding, and knew the wonderful secrets possessed by the Arabs, was inspired with hope by the confident language of the prince. He conducted him immediately to the lofty tower secured by several doors, in the summit of which was the chamber of the princess. The windows opened upon a terrace with balustrades, commanding a view over Toledo and all the surrounding country. The windows were darkened, for the princess lay within, a prey to devouring grief that refused all alleviation.

The prince seated himself on the terrace, and performed several wild Arabian airs on his pastoral pipe. The princess continued insensible, and the doctors, who were present, shook their heads, and smiled with incredulity and contempt. At length the prince laid aside the reed, and, to a simple melody, he chanted the verses of the letter which had declared his passion.

The princess recognized the strain. A fluttering joy stole to her heart; she raised her head and listened; tears rushed to her eyes and streamed down her cheeks; her bosom rose and fell with a tumult of emotions. She

52 Romance of the Airman

would have asked for the minstrel to be brought into her presence, but maiden coyness held her silent. The king read her wishes, and at his command Ahmed was conducted into her chamber. The lovers were discreet; they but exchanged glances, yet those glances spoke volumes. Never was the triumph of music more complete. The rose had returned to the soft cheek of the princess, the freshness to her lip, and the dewy light to her languishing eye.

All the physicians present stared at each other with astonishment. The king regarded the Arab minstrel with admiration, mixed with awe. "Wonderful youth," exclaimed he, "thou shalt henceforth be the first physician of my court, and no other prescription will I take but thy melody. For the present, receive thy reward, the most precious jewel in my treasury."

"O king," replied Ahmed, "I care not for silver, or gold, or precious stones. One relic hast thou in thy treasury, handed down from the Moslems,* who once owned Toledo. A box of sandalwood containing a silken carpet. Give me that box, and I am content."

All present were surprised at the moderation of the Arab; and still more, when the box of sandalwood was brought and the carpet drawn forth. It was of fine green silk, covered with Hebrew and Chaldaic characters. The court physicians looked at each other, shrugged their shoulders, and smiled at the simplicity of this new practitioner, who could be content with so paltry a fee.

"This carpet," said the prince, "once covered the throne of Solomon the Wise; it is worthy of being placed beneath the feet of beauty."

So saying, he spread it on the terrace beneath an ottoman that had been brought forth for the princess; then seating himself at her feet,—

The Carpet rose in the Air, bearing off the Prince and Princess

The Airman Dreams 53

"Who," said he, "shall counteract what is written in the book of fate? Behold the prediction of the astrologers verified. Know, O king, that your daughter and I have long loved each other in secret. Behold in me the pilgrim of love."

These words were scarcely from his lips, when the carpet rose in the air, bearing off the prince and princess. The king and the physicians gazed after it with open mouths and straining eyes, until it became a little speck on the white bosom of a cloud, and then disappeared in the blue vault of heaven.

The king in a rage summoned his treasurer. "How is this," said he, "that thou hast suffered an infidel to get possession of such a talisman*?"

"Alas! sir, we knew not its nature, nor could we decipher the inscription of the box. If it be indeed the carpet of the throne of the wise Solomon, it is possessed of magic power, and can transport its owner from place to place through the air."

The king assembled a mighty army, and set off for Granada* in pursuit of the fugitives. His march was long and toilsome. Encamping in the Vega, he sent a herald to demand restitution of his daughter. The king himself came forth with all his court to meet him. In the king he beheld the Arab minstrel, for Ahmed had succeeded to the throne on the death of his father, and the beautiful Aldegonda was his Sultana.*

The Christian king was easily pacified. Instead of bloody battles, there was a succession of feasts and rejoicings; after which, the king returned well pleased to Toledo, and the youthful couple continued to reign, as happily as wisely, in the Alhambra.

54 *Romance of the Airman*

Words and Phrases

To aid in understanding this selection

scrip: an old word for a bag or sack.
Bedouin: a name for an Arab of the desert in Asia or Africa.
Moslems: Mohammedans.
talisman: an object decorated with drawings or writing which gives it magic power.
Granada: an ancient kingdom, now a part of southern Spain.
Sultana: queen.

To add to your vocabulary

vagrant	astrologers
alleviation	restitution

Informal Test (True-False)

All True-False tests in this book should be done the same way. On your test paper, number as many lines as there are sentences in the test (in this test you number eleven lines). Then read the first sentence. If this tells something as it is told in the story, write the word *True*, or a capital *T*, after the 1 on your paper; if the statement is not as told in the story, write the word *False*, or a capital *F*. Do all the others in the same way. For example, *The prince arrayed himself in rich attire* is not true; write *False*, or *F*, after the 1 on your paper. *The king ordered the Arab brought to his presence* is true; write *True*, or *T*, after the 2 on your paper.

1. The prince arrayed himself in rich attire.

2. The king ordered the Arab brought to his presence.

3. Ahmed said he had spent his life in great cities.

4. In the desert music was used as a charm against evil spirits.

5. The king had never heard of the wonderful secrets of the Arabs.

6. The princess recognized Ahmed when she heard his first note.

7. When she recognized him she pronounced his name at once.

The Airman Dreams 55

8. The king said he would never use any other cure but the Arab's music.

9. All were surprised at the smallness of the gift for which the Arab asked.

10. The king knew the carpet had magic power.

11. When the king went after his daughter, he found she had become queen of the land.

Exercises and Topics related to your Other Subjects

Tell an interesting event which happened to the ancient kingdom of Granada the year that Columbus discovered America.

Subjects for oral themes

A short biography of Washington Irving.
How Irving happened to write " The Alhambra."

Other Readings

In this book

"The Enchanted Horse," page 43.

From other sources

Read the complete legend of Prince Ahmed Al Kamel in " The Alhambra," by Washington Irving.

The Unparalleled Adventure of One Hans Pfaall

EDGAR ALLAN POE

Explanatory Note. Edgar Allan Poe (1809–1849) was an American poet and short-story writer. No American writer has surpassed Poe in creating fascinating stories of mystery and romance, and according to John Macy, in his "Story of the World's Literature," no other American has had such a powerful influence upon the literature of Europe.

It is especially interesting to trace the influence of this story and of a similar one, "The Balloon Hoax," on subsequent fiction. Jules Verne, a French novelist whose works have been widely translated and read, created a number of stories that very clearly show that they originated from these tales of Poe's. In "From the Earth to the Moon," a tale of a trip to the moon in a kind of elongated cannon ball which was hurled into space by a tremendous blast of powder, Verne gives credit to Poe's "Hans Pfaall" as the source of his idea. "Five Weeks in a Balloon," and "Around the World in a Flying Machine," are other stories in which Verne shows the influence of these two tales from Poe. Many present-day writers of stories for boys are of the same type. In his story "With the Night Mail" Rudyard Kipling follows Verne's style of detailed description purporting to give scientific exactness. Notice how much of this kind of description there is in "Hans Pfaall."

Another interesting point to note is that Poe mentions a pair of pigeons and a cat as passengers in the balloon; Verne says that some chickens and a dog were carried along; and Kipling makes the rescue of a kitten from the wrecked airship one of the dramatic incidents.

The story of "Hans Pfaall" opens about noon one hot summer day in the great square of the city of Rotterdam. A large crowd of people had gathered, and all were gazing excitedly toward the sky. Suddenly there burst from their lips a shout that resounded loudly throughout the entire city.

THE origin of this hubbub soon became sufficiently evident. From behind the huge bulk of one of those sharply defined masses of cloud already mentioned, was seen slowly to emerge into an open area of blue space, a queer, heterogeneous, but apparently solid substance, so oddly shaped,

The Airman Dreams 57

so whimsically put together as not to be in any manner comprehended, and never to be sufficiently admired, by the host of sturdy burghers * who stood open-mouthed below. What could it be? In the name of all the devils in Rotterdam, what could it possibly portend? No one knew; no one could imagine; no one — not even the burgomaster * Mynheer Superbus Von Underduk — had the slightest clue by which to unravel the mystery; so, as nothing more reasonable could be done, everyone to a man replaced his pipe carefully in the corner of his mouth, and maintaining an eye steadily upon the phenomenon, puffed, paused, waddled about, and grunted significantly — then waddled back, grunted, paused, and finally — puffed again.

In the meantime, however, lower and still lower toward the goodly city, came the object of so much curiosity and the cause of so much smoke. In a very few minutes it arrived near enough to be accurately discerned. It appeared to be — yes! it *was* undoubtedly a species of balloon; but surely no *such* balloon had ever been seen in Rotterdam before. For who, let me ask, ever heard of a balloon manufactured entirely of dirty newspapers? No man in Holland certainly; yet here, under the very noses of the people, or rather at some distance *above* their noses, was the identical thing in question, and composed, I have it on the best authority, of the precise material which no one had ever before known to be used for a similar purpose. It was an egregious insult to the good sense of the burghers of Rotterdam. As to the shape of the phenomenon, it was even still more reprehensible. Being little or nothing better than a huge fool's-cap turned upside down. And this similitude was regarded as by no means lessened, when, upon nearer inspection, the crowd saw a large tassel depending from its apex, and, around the upper rim or

58 *Romance of the Airman*

base of the cone, a circle of little instruments, resembling sheep bells, which kept up a continual tinkling to the tune of "Betty Martin." But still worse.—Suspended by blue ribbons to the end of this fantastic machine, there hung, by way of car, an enormous drab beaver hat, with a brim superlatively broad, and a hemispherical crown with a black band and a silver buckle. It is, however, somewhat remarkable that many citizens of Rotterdam swore to having seen the same hat repeatedly before; and indeed the whole assembly seemed to regard it with eyes of familiarity; while the vrow Grettel Pfaall, upon sight of it, uttered an exclamation of joyful surprise, and declared it to be the identical hat of her good man himself. Now this was a circumstance the more to be observed, as Pfaall, with three companions, had actually disappeared from Rotterdam, about five years before, in a very sudden and unaccountable manner, and up to the date of this narrative all attempts at obtaining intelligence concerning them had failed. To be sure, some bones which were thought to be human, mixed up with a quantity of odd-looking rubbish, had been lately discovered in a retired situation to the east of the city; and some people went so far as to imagine that in this spot a foul murder had been committed, and that the sufferers were in all probability Hans Pfaall and his associates.—But to return.

The balloon (for such no doubt it was) had now descended to within a hundred feet of the earth, allowing the crowd below a sufficiently distinct view of the person of its occupant. This was in truth a very singular somebody. He could not have been more than two feet in height; but this altitude, little as it was, would have been sufficient to destroy his equilibrium, and tilt him over the edge of his tiny car, but for the intervention of a circular rim reaching as high as the breast, and rigged on to the

The Airman Dreams 59

cords of the balloon. The body of the little man was more than proportionally broad, giving to his entire figure a rotundity highly absurd. His feet, of course, could not be seen at all. His hands were enormously large. His hair was gray, and collected into a queue behind. His nose was prodigiously long, crooked, and inflammatory; his eyes full, brilliant, and acute; his chin and cheeks, although wrinkled with age, were broad, puffy, and double; but of ears of any kind there was not a semblance to be discovered upon any portion of his head. This odd little gentleman was dressed in a loose surtout of sky-blue satin, with tight breeches to match, fastened with silver buckles at the knees. His vest was of some bright yellow material; a white taffety cap was set jauntily on one side of his head; and, to complete his equipment, a blood-red silk handkerchief enveloped his throat and fell down, in a dainty manner, upon his bosom, in a fantastic bowknot of super-eminent dimensions.

Having descended, as I said before, to about one hundred feet from the surface of the earth, the little old gentleman was suddenly seized with a fit of trepidation, and appeared disinclined to make any nearer approach to *terra firma*. Throwing out, therefore, a quantity of sand from a canvas bag, which he lifted with great difficulty, he became stationary in an instant. He then proceeded in a hurried and agitated manner to extract from a side pocket in his surtout a large morocco pocketbook. This he poised suspiciously in his hand; then eyed it with an air of extreme surprise, and was evidently astonished at its weight. He at length opened it, and, drawing therefrom a huge letter sealed with red sealing wax and tied carefully with red tape, let it fall precisely at the feet of the burgomaster Superbus Von Underduk. His Excellency stooped to take it up. But the aëronaut, still greatly dis-

60 *Romance of the Airman*

composed, and having apparently no further business to detain him in Rotterdam, began at this moment to make busy preparations for departure; and, it being necessary to discharge a portion of ballast to enable him to reascend, the half-dozen bags which he threw out, one after another, without taking the trouble to empty their contents, tumbled, every one of them, most unfortunately, upon the back of the burgomaster, and rolled him over and over no less than half a dozen times, in the face of every individual in Rotterdam. It is not to be supposed, however, that the great Underduk suffered this impertinence on the part of the little old man to pass off with impunity. It is said, on the contrary, that during each of his half-dozen circumvolutions, he emitted no less than half a dozen distinct and furious whiffs from his pipe, to which he held fast the whole time with all his might, and to which he intends holding fast (God willing) until the day of his decease.

In the meantime the balloon arose like a lark, and, soaring far away from the city, at length drifted quietly behind a cloud similar to that from which it had so oddly emerged, and was thus lost forever to the wondering eyes of the good citizens of Rotterdam. All attention was now directed to the letter, the descent of which, and the consequences attending thereupon, had proved so fatally subversive of both person and personal dignity to his Excellency, Von Underduk. That functionary, however, had not failed, during his circumgyratory movements, to bestow a thought upon the important object of securing the epistle, which was seen, upon inspection, to have fallen into the most proper hands, being actually addressed to himself and Professor Rubadub, in their official capacities of President and Vice President of the Rotterdam College of Astronomy. It was accordingly opened

The Airman Dreams 61

by those dignitaries upon the spot, and found to contain the following extraordinary, and indeed very serious, communication:

To their Excellencies Von Underduk and Rubadub, President and Vice President of the States' College of Astronomers, in the city of Rotterdam.

Your Excellencies may perhaps be able to remember an humble artisan, by name Hans Pfaall, and by occupation a mender of bellows, who, with three others, disappeared from Rotterdam, about five years ago, in a manner which must have been considered unaccountable. If, however, it so please your Excellencies, I, the writer of this communication, am the identical Hans Pfaall himself.

[He then tells how his business dwindled away and he fell more and more deeply into debt. Finally one day a book which he came across suggested to him "the execution of a certain design with which either the devil or my better genius had inspired me."]

I contrived, by the aid of my wife, and with the greatest secrecy and caution, to dispose of what property I had remaining, and to borrow, in small sums, under various pretenses, and without giving any attention (I am ashamed to say) to my future means of repayment, no inconsiderable quantity of ready money. With the means thus accruing I proceeded to procure at intervals cambric, muslin, very fine, in pieces of twelve yards each; twine; a lot of the varnish of caoutchouc *; a large and deep basket of wickerwork, made to order; and several other articles necessary in the construction and equipment of a balloon of extraordinary dimensions. This I directed my wife to make up as soon as possible, and gave her all requisite information as to the particular method of proceeding. In the meantime I worked up the twine into

62 Romance of the Airman

network of sufficient dimensions; rigged it with a hoop and the necessary cords; and made purchase of numerous instruments and materials for experiment in the upper regions of the upper atmosphere. I then took opportunities of conveying by night, to a retired situation east of Rotterdam, five iron-bound casks, to contain about fifty gallons each, and one of a larger size; six tin tubes, three inches in diameter, properly shaped, and ten feet in length; a quantity of a particular metallic substance, or semimetal which I shall not name, and a dozen demijohns* of a very common acid. The gas to be formed from these latter materials is a gas never yet generated by any other person than myself — or at least never applied to any similar purpose.

[The writer here enters into a lengthy description of this gas and of the way it was to be generated.]

Everything being now ready, I exacted from my wife an oath of secrecy in relation to all my actions from the day of my first visit to the bookseller's stall; and promising, on my part, to return as soon as circumstances would permit, I gave her what little money I had left, and bade her farewell. Indeed I had no fear on her account. She was what people call a notable woman, and could manage matters in the world without my assistance. I believe, to tell the truth, she always looked upon me as an idle body — a mere make-weight — good for nothing but building castles in the air — and was rather glad to get rid of me. It was a dark night when I bade her good-by, and taking with me, as *aides-de-camp*, the three creditors who had given me so much trouble, we carried the balloon, with the car and accouterments, by a roundabout way, to the station where the other articles were deposited. We there found them all unmolested, and I proceeded immediately to business.

The Airman Dreams   63

It was the first of April. The night, as I said before, was dark; there was not a star to be seen; and a drizzling rain, falling at intervals, rendered us very uncomfortable. But my chief anxiety was concerning the balloon, which, in spite of the varnish with which it was defended, began to grow rather heavy with the moisture; the powder also was liable to damage. I therefore kept my three duns* working with great diligence, pounding down ice around the central cask, and stirring the acid in the others. They did not cease, however, importuning me with questions as to what I intended to do with all this apparatus, and expressed much dissatisfaction at the terrible labor I made them undergo. They could not perceive (so they said) what good was likely to result from their getting wet to the skin, merely to take a part in such horrible incantations. I began to get uneasy, and worked away with all my might; for I verily believe the idiots supposed that I had entered into a compact with the devil, and that, in short, what I was now doing was nothing better than it should be. I was, therefore, in great fear of their leaving me altogether. I contrived, however, to pacify them by promises of payment of all scores in full, as soon as I could bring the present business to a termination. To these speeches they gave of course their own interpretation; fancying, no doubt, that at all events I should come into possession of vast quantities of ready money; and provided I paid them all I owed, and a trifle more, in consideration of their services, I dare say they cared very little what became of either my soul or my carcass.

In about four hours and a half I found the balloon sufficiently inflated. I attached the car, therefore, and put all my implements in it — a telescope; a barometer, with some important modifications; a thermometer; an electrometer; a compass; a magnetic needle; a seconds

Romance of the Airman

watch; a bell; a speaking trumpet, etc., etc., etc., — also a globe of glass, exhausted of air, and carefully closed with a stopper — not forgetting the condensing apparatus, some unslacked lime, a stick of sealing wax, a copious supply of water, and a large quantity of provisions, such as pemmican, in which much nutriment is contained in comparatively little bulk. I also secured in the car a pair of pigeons and a cat.

It was now nearly daybreak, and I thought it high time to take my departure. Dropping a lighted cigar on the ground, as if by accident, I took the opportunity, in stooping to pick it up, of igniting privately the piece of slow match, the end of which protruded a little beyond the lower rim of one of the smaller casks. This maneuver was totally unperceived on the part of the three duns; and, jumping into the car, I immediately cut the single cord which held me to the earth, and was pleased to find that I shot upwards with inconceivable rapidity, carrying with all ease one hundred and seventy-five pounds of leaden ballast, and able to have carried up as many more. As I left the earth, the barometer stood at thirty inches, and the centigrade thermometer at nineteen degrees.

Scarcely, however, had I attained the height of fifty yards, when, roaring and rumbling up after me in the most tumultuous and terrible manner, came so dense a hurricane of fire, and gravel, and burning wood, and blazing metal, and mangled limbs, that my very heart sank within me, and I fell down in the bottom of the car, trembling with terror. Indeed, I now perceived that I had entirely overdone the business, and that the main consequences of the shock were yet to be experienced. Accordingly, in less than a second, I felt all the blood in my body rushing to my temples, and, immediately thereupon, a concussion, which I shall never forget, burst

The Airman Dreams   65

abruptly through the night, and seemed to rip the very firmament asunder. When I afterwards had time for reflection, I did not fail to attribute the extreme violence of the explosion, as regarded myself, to its proper cause — my situation directly above it, and in the line of its greatest power. But at the time, I thought only of preserving my life. The balloon at first collapsed, then furiously expanded, then whirled round and round with sickening velocity, and finally, reeling and staggering like a drunken man, hurled me over the rim of the car, and left me dangling, at a terrific height, with my head downward, and my face outward, by a piece of slender cord about three feet in length, which hung accidentally through a crevice near the bottom of the wickerwork, and in which, as I fell, my left foot became most providentially entangled. It is impossible — utterly impossible — to form any adequate idea of the horror of my situation. I gasped convulsively for breath — a shudder resembling a fit of the ague agitated every nerve and muscle in my frame — I felt my eyes starting from their sockets — a horrible nausea overwhelmed me — and at length I lost all consciousness in a swoon. . . . But this weakness was, luckily for me, of no very long duration. In good time came to my rescue the spirit of despair, and, with frantic cries and struggles, I jerked my way bodily upwards, till, at length, clutching with a vice-like grip the long-desired rim, I writhed my person over it, and fell headlong and shuddering within the car.

It was not until some time afterward that I recovered myself sufficiently to attend to the ordinary cares of the balloon. I then, however, examined it with attention, and found it, to my great relief, uninjured. My implements were all safe, and, fortunately, I had lost neither ballast nor provisions. Indeed, I had so well secured them in their

66 *Romance of the Airman*

places, that such an accident was entirely out of the question. Looking at my watch, I found it six o'clock. I was still rapidly ascending, and the barometer gave a present altitude of three and three-quarters miles. Immediately beneath me in the ocean, lay a small black object, slightly oblong in shape, seemingly about the size of a domino, and in every respect bearing a great resemblance to one of those toys. Bringing my telescope to bear upon it, I plainly discerned it to be a British ninety-four gun ship, close-hauled, and pitching heavily in the sea with her head to the W. S. W.* Besides this ship, I saw nothing but the ocean and the sky, and the sun, which had long arisen.

It is now high time that I should explain to your Excellencies the object of my voyage. Your Excellencies will bear in mind that distressed circumstances in Rotterdam had at length driven me to the resolution of committing suicide. It was not, however, that to life itself I had any positive disgust, but that I was harassed beyond endurance by the adventitious miseries attending my situation. In this state of mind, wishing to live, yet wearied with life, the treatise at the stall of the bookseller, backed by the opportune discovery of my cousin of Nantz, opened a resource to my imagination. I then finally made up my mind. I determined to depart, yet live — to leave the world, yet continue to exist — in short, to drop enigmas, I resolved, let what would ensue, to force a passage, if I could, to the moon.

[After setting forth his reasons for believing such a trip possible, Pfaall gives a long and fantastic description of a flight which covered eighteen days.]

I was now close upon the planet, and coming down with the most terrible impetuosity. I lost not a moment, accordingly, in throwing overboard first my ballast, then

The Airman Dreams

67

my water kegs, then my condensing apparatus and gum-elastic chambers, and finally every article within the car. But it was all to no purpose. I still fell with horrible rapidity, and was now not more than half a mile from the surface. As a last resource, therefore, having got rid of my coat, hat, and boots, I cut loose from the balloon *the car itself*, which was of no inconsiderable weight, and thus, clinging with both hands to the network, I had barely time to observe that the whole country, as far as the eye could reach, was thickly interspersed with diminutive habitations, ere I tumbled headlong into the very heart of a fantastical-looking city, and into the middle of a vast crowd of ugly little people, who none of them uttered a single syllable or gave themselves the least trouble to render me assistance, but stood, like a parcel of idiots, grinning in a ludicrous manner, and eyeing me and my balloon askant, with their arms set akimbo. I turned from them in contempt, and, gazing upwards at the earth so lately left, and left perhaps forever, beheld it like a huge, dull, copper shield, about two degrees in diameter, fixed immovably in the heavens overhead, and tipped on one of its edges with a crescent border of the most brilliant gold. No traces of land or water could be discovered, and the whole was clouded with variable spots, and belted with tropical and equatorial zones.

Thus, may it please your Excellencies, after a series of great anxieties, unheard-of dangers, and unparalleled escapes, I had, at length, on the nineteenth day of my departure from Rotterdam, arrived in safety at the conclusion of a voyage undoubtedly the most extraordinary, and the most momentous, ever accomplished, undertaken, or conceived by any denizen of earth. But my adventures yet remain to be related. And indeed your Excellencies . may well imagine that, after a residence of five years

68 *Romance of the Airman*

upon a planet not only deeply interesting in its own peculiar character, but rendered doubly so by its intimate connection, in capacity of satellite, with the world inhabited by man, I may have intelligence for the private ear of the States' College of Astronomers of far more importance than the details, however wonderful, of the mere *voyage* which so happily concluded. This is, in fact, the case. I have much — very much which it would give me the greatest pleasure to communicate. . . . But, to be brief, I must have my reward. I am pining for a return to my family and to my home: and as the price of any further communications on my part — in consideration of the light which I have it in my power to throw upon many very important branches of physical and metaphysical science — I must solicit, through the influence of your honorable body, a pardon for the crime of which I have been guilty in the death of the creditors upon my departure from Rotterdam. This, then, is the object of the present paper. Its bearer, an inhabitant of the moon, whom I have prevailed upon, and properly instructed, to be my messenger to the earth, will await your Excellencies' pleasure, and return to me with the pardon in question, if it can, in any manner, be obtained.

I have the honor to be, etc., your Excellencies' very humble servant,

HANS PFAALL

Upon finishing the perusal of this very extraordinary document, Professor Rubadub, it is said, dropped his pipe upon the ground in the extremity of his surprise, and Mynheer Superbus Von Underduk, having taken off his spectacles, wiped them, and deposited them in his pocket, so far forgot both himself and his dignity, as to turn round three times upon his heel in the quintessence of astonish-

The Airman Dreams 69

ment and admiration. There was no doubt about the matter — the pardon should be obtained. So at least swore, with a round oath, Professor Rubadub, and so finally thought the illustrious Von Underduk, as he took the arm of his brother in science, and without saying a word, began to make the best of his way home to deliberate upon the measures to be adopted. Having reached the door, however, of the burgomaster's dwelling, the professor ventured to suggest that as the messenger had thought proper to disappear — no doubt frightened to death by the savage appearance of the burghers of Rotterdam — the pardon would be of little use, as no one but a man of the moon would undertake a voyage to so vast a distance. To the truth of this observation the burgomaster assented, and the matter was therefore at an end.

Words and Phrases

To aid in understanding this selection

burghers: citizens.
burgomaster: in Holland the officer that corresponds to mayor in this country.
caoutchouc: the gummy coagulated juice of tropical plants; india rubber.
demijohn: a large glass bottle with a small neck, usually cased in wickerwork.
dun: one who duns; an insistent creditor.
W. S. W.: west-southwest.

To add to your vocabulary

heterogeneous	reprehensible	trepidation
whimsically	equilibrium	pemmican
portend	rotundity	ballast
egregious	surtout	subversive

Technical terms

car   aëronaut

70 *Romance of the Airman*

Informal Test (Completion) [1]

1. The scene of this story is in _____.
2. The balloon from the moon was made of _____.
3. The shape of this balloon was that of _____.
4. The basket of this balloon was _____.
5. The person in this balloon was about _____ feet high.
6. He had no _____.
7. Hans Pfaall flew to the moon because he wished to escape from _____.
8. He was helped in his scheme by _____.
9. Among his provisions he took a large supply of _____.
10. From the moon the earth looked like _____.
11. His voyage to the moon occupied _____ days.
12. He had been there _____ years.

Exercises and Topics related to your Other Subjects

1. Write a short biography of Edgar Allan Poe.

2. Read Washington Irving's description of the Dutch of New York in his "Knickerbocker's History" and compare it with Poe's description of the Dutch of Rotterdam.

3. Read Kipling's "With the Night Mail," and bring to class selections that show the influence of Poe's "scientific fiction."

Other Readings

In this book

"A Balloon Flight across Africa," page 71.

From other sources

"With the Night Mail," by Rudyard Kipling.
"The Balloon Hoax," by Edgar Allan Poe.
"From the Earth to the Moon," by Jules Verne.

[1] For directions, see page 14.

A Balloon Flight across Africa

JULES VERNE

> *Explanatory Note.* Jules Verne's story "Five Weeks in a Balloon," from which "A Balloon Flight across Africa" is taken, was his first masterpiece. It was published in 1862, and almost overnight he became famous. It is a strange mixture of fact and fancy.
>
> The voyage of the balloon was a most extravagant flight of fancy, but Verne's descriptions of Africa are said to represent with painstaking accuracy the reports of the explorers and to be truly valuable as a piece of geographical work. He refers several times to the African explorers Burton and Speke, whose explorations in this section had just been published in the "Journal of the Discovery of the Source of the Nile," by Captain John Hanning Speke. Probably this book was the source from which Verne gathered the geography for his story; probably also Dr. Burton, who was a scholar versed in the Arabian language, suggested to Verne the character of Dr. Ferguson.
>
> The balloon used by Dr. Ferguson was elongated in shape and consisted of a smaller balloon within a larger one. It had been made in England and brought in the English ship *Resolute* to the starting point on the coast of Africa. The car had ample room for the three passengers, a good supply of provisions, and all necessary instruments and tools.

AT NINE o'clock the three traveling companions took their places in the car. The doctor lighted his blowpipe, and heated it so as to produce a high temperature. The balloon, which had hitherto remained *in equilibrio*, began to sway. The sailors were obliged to slacken the ropes they held. The car ascended twenty feet.

"My friends," cried the doctor, coming forward and waving his hat, "let us give our aërial vessel a name which carries happiness everywhere; let us call it the *Victoria*!"

A ringing cheer was the reply. "God save the Queen! Hurrah for Old England!"

At this moment the ascending force reached a tremendous pitch. Ferguson, Kennedy, and Joe waved a last adieu to their friends.

72   *Romance of the Airman*

"Let go, all!" cried the doctor. And the *Victoria* rose rapidly, while the four carronades* of the *Resolute* thundered out a salute as she glided upwards on her perilous journey.

The air was clear, the wind was moderate, the *Victoria* mounted almost perpendicularly to a height of fifteen hundred feet, which was indicated by a depression of nearly two inches in the barometrical column.

At this elevation a more decided current carried the balloon toward the southwest. What a magnificent panorama unfolded itself beneath the eyes of the travelers! The island of Zanzibar was in sight from end to end, and stood out in its rich coloring as upon a huge board; the field presented an appearance of patchwork, and the large clumps of trees indicated the woods and coppices.

The inhabitants appeared like insects. The cheers and cries died away in the air by degrees, and the reports of the ship's guns vibrated only in the lower concavity of the balloon. "How splendid all that is!" cried Joe, breaking the silence for the first time.

No reply was vouchsafed. The doctor was occupied in observing the barometrical changes and taking note of the various details of the ascent. Kennedy stared at it and could not take it all in.

The sun added to the heat of the blowpipe and increased the expansion of the gas. The *Victoria* reached a height of twenty-five hundred feet. The *Resolute* now appeared like a small bark, and the African coast loomed in the west like an enormous line of foam.

"Why don't you speak?" said Joe.

"We are making observations," replied the doctor, as he turned his glass toward the continent.

"Well, I feel as if I must speak," said Joe.

"Fire away, Joe; talk as much as you like."

Joe therefore gave way to a tremendous string of excla-

The Airman Dreams 73

mations. The "oh's" and the "ah's" followed one another in astonishing succession.

While they were crossing the sea, the doctor thought it better to maintain this elevation, as he could observe a greater extent of coast; the thermometer and the barometer, suspended in the interior of the half-opened tent, were almost incessantly consulted; a second barometer, placed outside, was for use during the night.

After two hours the *Victoria*, impelled at a rate of a little over eight miles, neared the coast. The doctor determined to approach the earth; he moderated the flame of the blowpipe, and soon the balloon descended to within three hundred feet of the ground.

He perceived that he was just over Mrima, the name bestowed on this portion of the coast of Eastern Africa. Thick lines of mango bushes lined the shore; their roots, lacerated by the Indian Ocean, were left plainly visible by the ebb-tide. The sand hills, which formerly constituted the coast line, rose above the horizon, and Mount Nguru showed its head in the northwest.

The *Victoria* passed close to a village, which, from the map, the doctor pronounced to be Kaole. All the population assembled to utter yells of anger and fear as the travelers passed. Arrows were vainly directed against the air monster, which floated majestically above the reach of their futile fury. (Two days later the *Victoria* passed over the town of Kazeh, situated about three hundred and fifty miles from the coast.)

"We left Zanzibar at nine o'clock in the morning," said Doctor Ferguson, consulting his notes, "and after two days' traveling we have accomplished, including our deviations, nearly five hundred geographical miles. Captain Burton and Captain Speke took four months and a half to accomplish the same distance."

74 *Romance of the Airman*

Kazeh, an important place in Central Africa, is scarcely a town, properly called; there is not a town in the interior, and Kazeh is only a collection of six immense camps. Within these are collected the houses and huts of slaves with small courts and gardens, carefully cultivated with onions, yams, melons, pumpkins, and mushrooms of a perfect flavor there grown to perfection.

Unyamwezy is a veritable Land of the Moon, the fertile and beautiful park of Africa, in the center of the Unyanembé, a delightful country, where some Omini families, who are Arabs of the purest blood, live in idleness. These people have for a long time trafficked in the interior of Africa and in Arabia; they deal in gum, ivory, striped cloth, slaves; their caravans penetrate these equatorial regions in all directions; they there seek upon the coast objects of pleasure and luxury for the rich merchants, and they, surrounded by wives and slaves, live in this beautiful country and enjoy an existence the least agitated and the most horizontal possible, always stretched at full length, laughing, smoking, or sleeping.

Around the camps are numerous native huts, large spaces for the market fields of cannabis and datura, of lovely trees and most refreshing shade. Such is Kazeh.

There is also the general rendezvous for the caravans — those from the south with slaves and ivory, and from the west, which bring cotton and glassware to the tribes around the Great Lakes. Also in the market there is a continual movement, a regular hubbub, in which the cries of the half-breed porters mingle with the sound of drums and cornets, the whinnying of mules, the braying of donkeys, the songs of women, the crying of children, and the blows of the rattan of the jemadar,* who beats time in this pastoral symphony.

There are some wares exposed to sale without any kind

The Airman Dreams

of order, even in a charming disorder. Showy stuffs, colored beads, ivory rhinoceros' teeth, sharks' teeth, honey, tobacco, and cotton. There they carry on the most strange bargains, each object having just so much value as it excites desire.

Suddenly this hubbub and movement ceased, the noise immediately subsided. The *Victoria* had appeared in the sky, sailing• along majestically and descending slowly without losing its vertical position. Men, women, children, slaves, merchants, Arabs, and negroes all disappeared and glided away into the "tembes" and beneath the huts.

"My dear Samuel," said Kennedy, "if we continue to produce such an effect as this we shall have some difficulty to establish commercial relations with these people."

"There is, nevertheless, one very simple mercantile transaction to be carried out," said Joe; "that is, to quietly descend and carry away the most valuable merchandise without troubling the merchants. We should then get rich."

"You see," said the doctor, "that the natives have only been terrified for the moment. They will not delay to return, impelled either by superstition or curiosity."

"You think so?"

"We shall soon see, but it will be prudent to keep at a safe distance. The *Victoria* is neither an ironclad nor armored. There is no shelter from a bullet nor from an arrow."

"Do you then intend to enter into conference with these Africans, my dear Samuel?"

"Perhaps so; why not? There ought to be in Kazeh Arab merchants who are not ignorant men. I remember that Burton and Speke were much pleased with the hospitality of this town. So we can try our luck."

76 *Romance of the Airman*

The *Victoria* gradually approached the earth, and made fast one of the grapnels to the top of a tree near the market place.

The entire population now turned out; heads were cautiously advanced. Many "waganga," easily recognizable by their badges of shellfish, advanced boldly. They were the sorcerers of the place. They carried at the waist small gourds rubbed over with grease, and many objects for the practice of their magic and all of a dirtiness quite professional. By degrees the crowd advanced to the sorcerers, the women and children surrounding them; the drummers rivaled each other in din; hands were clasped and held up toward the sky.

"That is their manner of praying," said Doctor Ferguson. "If I am not in error, we shall be called upon to undertake an important part."

"Very well, sir," said Joe, "play it."

"Even you, my brave Joe, may perhaps become a god."

"Well, sir, that won't worry me much, and the incense will be rather agreeable than otherwise."

At this moment one of the sorcerers made a gesture, and the clamor sank into profound silence. He addressed some words to the travelers, but in a tongue unknown to them.

Doctor Ferguson, not understanding what was said, replied at hazard in a few words of Arabic, and was immediately answered in that language.

The orator then delivered a flowing speech, very flowery and distinct. The doctor had no difficulty in perceiving that the *Victoria* was actually taken for the moon in person, and that this amiable goddess had deigned to approach the town with her three sons, an honor which would never be forgotten in that country beloved by the sun.

The doctor replied, with great dignity, that the moon

The Airman Dreams

made every thousand years a departmental tour, feeling the necessity of showing herself to her worshipers. He then prayed them to take advantage of her divine presence by making known their wants and vows.

The sorcerer replied that the sultan, the "mwani," who had been ill for many years, had asked the assistance of heaven, and that he now begged the sons of the moon to come to him.

The doctor imparted the invitation to his companions.

"And will you go to that Negro king?" said the Scotchman.

"Certainly. These people appear to me to be well disposed; the day is calm; there is scarcely a breath of wind. We have nothing to fear for the *Victoria.*"

"But what will you do?"

"Be quiet, my dear Dick; with a little medicine I will manage to get out of it."

Then addressing the crowd he said: "The moon, taking pity upon the sovereign who is so dear to the people of Unyamwezy, has confided his recovery to our hands. Let him prepare to receive us."

The cries, shouts, and gesticulations were redoubled, and the entire vast ant hill of black heads were in motion.

"Now, my friends," said Doctor Ferguson, "it will be necessary to be ready for anything; we may be obliged to retreat at any moment. Dick shall remain in the car and, by means of the blowpipe, keep up a sufficient ascensional power. The grapnel is firmly fixed; so there is no danger on that score. I will get down. Joe will also get down, but will remain at the foot of the ladder."

"What! are you going alone to the blackamoor's house?" asked Kennedy.

"Why, Mr. Samuel, don't you want me to go with you?" said Joe.

78 Romance of the Airman

"No, I shall go alone; these people imagine that the moon has come to pay them a visit. I am protected by their superstition; so have no fear. Stay at your posts as I have arranged."

"Since you wish it," said the Scot, "it shall be so."

"Mind you attend to the expansion of the gas."

"All right."

The cries of the natives again increased. They were demanding very energetically indeed the intervention of heaven.

"Do you hear?" cried Joe. "I think they are a little too dictatorial to their beautiful moon and her sons."

The doctor, carrying his medicine chest, came down from the balloon, preceded by Joe. The latter was as grave and dignified as was in his nature to be. He sat down at the foot of the ladder and crossed his legs, Arabfashion. A portion of the crowd surrounded him at a respectful distance.

Meantime Doctor Ferguson, preceded by the musicians, and groups of religious dancers, advanced slowly toward the royal "tembe," situated some distance from the town. It was now about three o'clock, and the sun was shining brilliantly. It could scarcely do otherwise under the circumstances!

The doctor advanced with dignity; the Waganga surrounded him, and kept back the crowd. Ferguson was soon joined by the son of the sultan, a well-made young fellow, who, following the custom of the country, was the sole inheritor of the parent's goods and possessions. He prostrated himself before the son of the moon, who raised him with a gracious gesture.

Three quarters of an hour afterwards, through shady paths in the midst of a luxuriant vegetation, the enthusiastic procession arrived at the palace of the sultan. It was

The Airman Dreams 79

a square house, called Iiténya, situated upon the slope of a hill. A species of veranda, made by a straw roof, covered the exterior, and was supported by wooden posts, with some pretension to carving displayed upon them. Long streaks of reddish clay ornamented the walls in an attempt to depict men and snakes, the latter being naturally more successful than the former. The roof of this habitation did not rest directly upon the walls; and so the air could circulate freely, though there were no windows and scarcely a door.

Doctor Ferguson was received with great honor by the guards and favorites, who were men of a handsome race, the Wanyamwezi — a pure type of the population of Central Africa, strong and healthy, well-made, and erect in their bearing. Their hair, divided into a quantity of curls, fell down upon their shoulders; and by means of incisions colored blue or black they tattooed their cheeks from the temples to the mouth. Their ears, very much distended, were ornamented with disks of wood and gum copal.* They were clothed with emeu,* brilliantly colored. The soldiers were well armed with bows and arrows barbed and poisoned, with cutlasses, with the "sima," a long saw-toothed sword, and with hatchets.

The doctor entered the palace. There, in spite of the sultan's illness, the hubbub, already great, was redoubled. The doctor noticed on the lintel of the door that rabbits' tails and zebras' manes were suspended as talismans. He was received by a troop of His Majesty's wives to the harmonious accompaniment of cymbals and drums, which were played by hammering them as hard as possible with the fists.

The greater number of women appeared very pretty, and laughingly smoked tobacco and "thang" in large black pipes. They seemed well formed, so far as the long

80 Romance of the Airman

and graceful robe permitted their figures to be seen, and wore a kind of kilt of calabash fibers fastened round their waists.

Six of them, though destined to be sacrificed, were by no means the least gay of the assembly. At the death of the sultan they were to be buried alive with him, so as to keep him company in his otherwise somewhat distressing solitude.

Doctor Ferguson, having taken all this in at a glance, advanced toward the monarch's couch. There he saw a man of about forty, perfectly brutalized by dissipation of all kinds, and for whom he could do nothing. His malady, which had lasted some years, was nothing but constant intoxication. This royal drunkard had by degrees lost consciousness, and all the ammonia in the world could not cure him.

The favorites and the women, bending their knees, bowed themselves down during this solemn visit. By means of a few drops of a strong cordial, the doctor for a moment animated the stupefied body. The sultan moved; and for a corpse which had given no sign of existence for hours, to move at all was hailed with acclamation in honor of the doctor.

He, however, had had enough of it, and, pushing his worshipers aside, he left the palace and started in the direction of the balloon.

[Meanwhile Joe, at the foot of the ladder, had been receiving the homage of his subjects like the true son of a goddess. After bringing him gifts of many kinds, the natives danced before him. Not to be outdone, he joined them in a dance of his own and soon had the whole crowd imitating his every movement. In the midst of this excitement he saw the doctor hurrying toward him surrounded by a wildly excited group of natives.]

The sorcerers and priests appeared to be the most excited. They surrounded and pressed upon the doctor with

The Airman Dreams 81

threatening gestures. What a strange alteration! What had happened? Had the sultan unfortunately died under the celestial doctor's hands?

Kennedy, from his position, perceived the danger without comprehending the cause. The balloon, pulling strongly, was stretching the rope that held it as if impatient to rise into the air.

The doctor came to the foot of the ladder. A superstitious fear still kept back the crowd and prevented their using violence; he rapidly ascended, and Joe followed.

"There is not an instant to lose," said his master. "Never mind detaching the grapnel. We must cut the cord. Follow me."

"What is it?" said Joe, ascending.

"What has happened?" cried Kennedy, carbine in hand.

"Look there!" replied the doctor, pointing toward the horizon.

"Well?" asked the Scot.

"Well! it's the *moon*!"

In fact, the moon, red and glorious as a globe of fire upon an azure background, was then rising — she and the *Victoria* together.

Either, therefore, there were two moons, or the strangers were nothing but impostors and false gods. Such were the natural thoughts of the crowd. Hence the change.

Words and Phrases

To aid in understanding this selection

carronade: a short, light cannon formerly used.

jemadar: a native officer; usually the leader of a caravan.

copal: a hard gum from various tropical trees, used in making varnish.

emeu: the emu, a bird similar to an ostrich.

82   *Romance of the Airman*

To add to your vocabulary

grapnel	sorcerers	lintel
coppice	dictatorial	

Informal Test (Completion) [1]

1. The balloon was named _____.

2. As the balloon rose the doctor was busy _____.

3. The country in which they landed was called "the land of the _____."

4. Dr. Ferguson found that he could speak to the natives in the _____ language.

5. He told them that the moon made a tour every _____ years.

6. They implored his help for _____.

7. The house was ornamented with pictures of _____ and _____.

8. Six of the women were doomed _____.

9. Dr. Ferguson's life was endangered when _____.

Exercises and Topics related to your Other Subjects

1. Write a short biography of Jules Verne.

2. Explain how the blowpipe was used to control the balloon.

3. Consult your geography and reference books and prepare a short talk on the region around Lake Victoria Nyanza.

Other Readings

In this book

"The *Southern Cross* visits the Fiji Islands," page 338.

"The Unparalleled Adventure of One Hans Pfaall," page 56.

From other sources

"Five Weeks in a Balloon," by Jules Verne.

"Tom Sawyer Abroad," by Mark Twain.

[1] For directions, see page 14.

The Flying Warrior of Uganda[1]

HENRY M. STANLEY

> *Explanatory Note.* In 1870 James Gordon Bennett, of the *New York Herald*, financed an expedition into Africa to search for David Livingstone, the missionary. The leader of the expedition was Henry M. Stanley, a newspaper writer and explorer who had made many expeditions in search of material for his writings. After a search of several months Stanley found Livingstone. The two men explored together for a time; then Stanley returned to England, bringing Livingstone's journal with him. Some years later Stanley made other explorations in Africa, and he is given credit for discovering the course of the Congo River and for bringing about the establishment of the Congo Free State.
>
> The section of Africa and the period of time referred to in the following selection are about the same as those described by Jules Verne in "Five Weeks in a Balloon." The name of James Gordon Bennett is familiar to the public today in connection with the James Gordon Bennett Cup, an annual prize for air racers.

ONE of the heroes of Nakivingi* was a warrior named Kibaga, who possessed the power of flying. When the king warred with the Wanyoro,* he sent Kibaga into the air to ascertain the whereabouts of the foe, who, when discovered by this extraordinary being, were attacked on land in their hiding-places by Nakivingi, and from above by the active and faithful Kibaga, who showered great rocks on them, and by these means slew a vast number.

It happened that among the captives of Unyoro, Kibaga saw a beautiful woman, who was solicited by the king in marriage. As Nakivingi was greatly indebted to Kibaga for his unique services, he gave Kibaga this woman as wife, with a warning, however, not to impart the knowledge of his power to her, lest she should betray him. For a long time after the marriage his wife knew nothing of his power; but suspecting something strange in him from his

[1] From "Through the Dark Continent."

84 *Romance of the Airman*

repeated sudden absences and reappearances at his home, she set herself to watch him. One morning as he left his hut she was surprised to see him suddenly mount into the air with a burden of rocks slung on his back. On seeing this she remembered that the Wanyoro complained that more of their people were killed by some means from above than by the spears of Nakivingi; and, Delilah-like,* loving her race and her people more than she loved her husband, she hastened to her people's camp, and communicated, to the surprise of the Wanyoro, what she had that day learned.

To avenge themselves on Kibaga, the Wanyoro set archers in ambush on the summits of each lofty hill, with instructions to confine themselves to watching the air and listening for the brushing of his wings, and to shoot their arrows in the direction of the sound, whether anything was seen or not. By this means on a certain day, as Nakivingi marched to the battle, Kibaga was wounded to the death by an arrow; and upon the road large drops of blood were seen falling, and on coming to a tall tree the king detected a dead body entangled in its branches. When the tree was cut down, Nakivingi saw to his infinite sorrow that it was the body of his faithful warrior Kibaga.

Words and Phrases

To aid in understanding this selection

Nakivingi: king of the Uganda region. Stanley called him the Charlemagne of Uganda.

Wanyoro: the name of an African tribe.

Delilah-like: Delilah learned from her husband, Samson, that his strength lay in his hair, and while he slept she clipped his long locks and thus betrayed him to his enemies. The story is told in the Old Testament, Judges xvi.

The Airman Dreams 85

Exercises and Topics related to your Other Subjects

Subjects for oral themes

Stanley discovers Livingstone.
Stanley as an Explorer.
Geographical Facts about Uganda.

Written theme

The Biography of Henry Morton Stanley.

Other Readings

In this book

"A Balloon Flight across Africa," page 71.

From other sources

"How I Found Livingstone," by Henry Morton Stanley.
"My Kalulu," by Henry Morton Stanley.
"Story of Henry M. Stanley," by Vautier Golding.

Darius Green and his Flying Machine

J. T. TROWBRIDGE

Explanatory Note. John T. Trowbridge, the author of "Darius Green and his Flying Machine," was born in 1827 in a frontier settlement of New York. He taught school for a time, but then decided to devote himself to literature. In Boston he became widely known as a writer of stories and sketches under the pen name of "Paul Creyton." In his first book, "Father Brighthopes," Mr. Trowbridge caught the fancy of the boys of that day, and with a long series of volumes he held juvenile interest unabated through the succeeding generations. The following poem, written in 1870, proved that he was unconsciously a prophet. Happily, Mr. Trowbridge lived to see his prophecy come true.

IF EVER there lived a Yankee lad,
Wise or otherwise, good or bad,
Who, seeing the birds fly, didn't jump
With flapping arms from stake or stump,
    Or, spreading the tail
    Of his coat for a sail,
Take a soaring leap from post or rail,
    And wonder why
    He couldn't fly,
And flap and flutter and wish and try —
If ever you knew a country dunce
Who didn't try that as often as once,
All I can say is, that's a sign
He never would do for a hero of mine.

An aspiring genius was D. Green:
The son of a farmer, — age fourteen;
His body was long and lank and lean, —
Just right for flying, as will be seen;
He had two eyes, each bright as a bean,
And a freckled nose that grew between,

The Airman Dreams

A little awry, — for I must mention
That he had riveted his attention
Upon his wonderful invention,
Twisting his tongue as he twisted the strings,
Working his face as he worked the wings,
And with every turn of gimlet and screw
Turning and screwing his mouth round too,
    Till his nose seemed bent
    To catch the scent,
Around some corner, of new-baked pies,
And his wrinkled cheeks and his squinting eyes
Grew puckered into a queer grimace,
That made him look very droll in the face,
    And also very wise.

And wise he must have been to do more
Than ever a genius did before,
Excepting Dædalus of yore
And his son Icarus, who wore
    Upon their backs
    Those wings of wax
He had read of in the old almanacs.
Darius was clearly of the opinion
That the air is also man's dominion,
And that, with paddle or fin or pinion,
    We soon or late
    Shall navigate
The azure as now we sail the sea.
The thing looks simple enough to me;
    And if you doubt it,
Hear how Darius reasoned about it.

    "Birds can fly,
    An' why can't I?

Romance of the Airman

Must we give in,"
Says he, with a grin,
"'T the bluebird an' phœbe
Are smarter'n we be?
Jest fold our hands an' see the swaller
An' blackbird an' catbird beat us holler?
Does the leetle, chatterin', sassy wren,
No bigger'n my thumb, know more than men?
Jest show me that!
Er prove 't the bat
Has got more brains than's in my hat,
And I'll back down, an' not till then!"

He argued further: "Ner I can't see
What's th'use o' wings to a bumblebee,
Fer to git a livin' with, more'n to me; —
Ain't my business
Important's his'n is?
That Icarus
Was a silly cuss, —
Him an' his daddy Dædalus.
They might 'a' knowed wings made o' wax
Wouldn't stan' sun-heat an' hard whacks.
I'll make mine o' luther,*
Er suthin' er other."

And he said to himself, as he tinkered and planned:
"But I ain't goin' to show my hand
To mummies that never can understand
The fust idee that's big and grand.
They'd 'a' laft an' made fun
O' Creation itself afore 'twas done!"
So he kept his secret from all the rest
Safely buttoned within his vest;

The Airman Dreams

89

And in the loft above the shed
Himself he locks, with thimble and thread
And wax and hammer and buckles and screws,
And all such things as geniuses use; —
Two bats for patterns, curious fellows!
A charcoal-pot and a pair of bellows;
An old hoopskirt or two, as well as
Some wire and several old umbrellas;
A carriage cover for tail and wings;
A piece of harness; and straps and strings;
    And a big strong box,
    In which he locks
These and a hundred other things.

His grinning brothers, Reuben and Burke
And Nathan and Jotham and Solomon, lurk
Around the corner to see him work, —
Sitting cross-legged, like a Turk,
Drawing the waxed end through with a jerk,
And boring the holes with a comical quirk
Of his wise old head, and a knowing smirk.
But vainly they mounted each other's backs,
And poked through knot holes and pried through
    cracks;
With wood from the pile and straw from the stacks
He plugged the knot holes and calked the cracks;
And a bucket of water, which one would think
He had brought up into the loft to drink
    When he chanced to be dry,
    Stood always nigh,
    For Darius was sly!
And whenever at work he happened to spy
At chink or crevice a blinking eye,
He let a dipper of water fly.

Romance of the Airman

"Take that! an' ef ever ye get a peep,
Guess ye'll ketch a weasel asleep!"
    And he sings as he locks
    His big strong box:

"The weasel's head is small an' trim,
An' he is leetle an' long an' slim,
An' quick of motion an' nimble of limb,
    An' ef yeou'll be
    Advised by me
Keep wide awake when ye're ketchin' him!"
    So day after day
He stitched and tinkered and hammered away,
    Till at last 'twas done, —
The greatest invention under the sun!
"An' now," says Darius, "hooray fer some fun!"

    'Twas the Fourth of July,
    And the weather was dry,
And not a cloud was on all the sky,
Save a few light fleeces, which here and there,
    Half mist, half air,
Like foam on the ocean went floating by:
Just as lovely a morning as ever was seen
For a nice little trip in a flying machine.
Thought cunning Darius: "Now I sha'n't go
Along 'ith the fellers to see the show.
I'll say I've got sich a terrible cough!
An' then, when the folks 'ave all gone off
    I'll hev full swing
    For to try the thing,
An' practyse a leetle on the wing."
"Ain't goin' to see the celebration?"
Says Brother Nate. "No; botheration!

The Airman Dreams 91

I've got sich a cold — a toothache — I —
My gracious! — feel's though I should fly!"

Said Jotham, "Sho!
Guess ye better go." But Darius said, "NO!
Shouldn't wonder 'f yeou might see me, though,
'Long 'bout noon, ef I git red
O' this jumpin', thumpin' pain 'n my head."
For all the while to himself he said:
    "I'll tell ye what!
I'll fly a few times around the lot,
To see how't seems, then soon's I've got
The hang o' the thing, ez likely's not,
    I'll astonish the nation,
    And all creation,
By flyin' over the celebration!
Over their heads I'll sail like an eagle;
I'll balance myself on my wings like a sea gull;
I'll dance on the chimbleys; I'll stan' on the steeple;
I'll flop up to winders an' scare the people!
I'll light on the libbe'ty pole, and crow;
An' I'll say to the gawpin' fools below,
    'What world's this 'ere
    That I've come near?'
Fer I'll make 'em believe I'm a chap f'm the moon!
An' I'll try a race 'ith their ol' bulloon."
    He crept from his bed;
And, seeing the others were gone, he said,
"I'm a-gittin' over the cold 'n my head."
    And away he sped
To open the wonderful box in the shed.

His brothers had walked but a little way
When Jotham to Nathan chanced to say,

Romance of the Airman

"What on airth is he up to, hey?"
"Don'o, — the's suthin' er other to pay,
Er he wouldn't 'a' stayed to hum today."
Says Burke, "His toothach's all 'n his eye!
He never'd miss a Fo'th-o'-July
Ef he hedn't some machine to try.
Le's hurry back and hide in the barn,
An' pay him fer tellin' us that yarn!"
"Agreed!" Through the orchard they creep back,
Along by the fences, behind the stack,
And one by one, through a hole in the wall,
In under the dusty barn they crawl,
Dressed in their Sunday garments all;
And a very astonishing sight was that,
When each in his cobwebbed coat and hat
Came up through the floor like an ancient rat.
  And there they hid;
  And Reuben slid
The fastenings back, and the door undid.
  "Keep dark!" said he,
"While I squint an' see what the' is to see."

As knights of old put on their mail, —
  From head to foot
  An iron suit,
Iron jacket and iron boot,
Iron breeches, and on the head
No hat, but an iron pot instead,
  And under the chin the bail, —
I believe they called the thing a helm;
And the lid they carried they called a shield;
And, thus accoutered, they took the field,
  Sallying forth to overwhelm
The dragons and pagans that plagued the realm; —

The Airman Dreams 93

So this modern knight
Prepared for flight,
Put on his wings and strapped them tight;
Jointed and jaunty, strong and light;
Buckled them fast to shoulder and hip, —
Ten feet they measured from tip to tip!
And a helm had he, but that he wore,
Not on his head like those of yore,
But more like the helm of a ship.

"Hush!" Reuben said,
"He's up in the shed!
He's opened the winder, — I see his head!
He stretches it out,
An' pokes it about,
Lookin' to see'f the coast is clear,
An' nobody near; —
Guess he don'o' who's hid in here!
He's riggin' a springboard over the sill!
Stop laffin', Solomon! Burke, keep still!
He's climbin' out now — of all the things!
What's he got on? I van, it's wings!
An' that t'other thing? I vum, it's a tail!
An' there he sets like a hawk on a rail!
Steppin' careful, he travels the length
Of his springboard, and teeters to try its strength.
Now he stretches his wings, like a monstrous
        bat;
Peeks over his shoulder, this way an' that,
Fer to see'f the' 's anyone passin' by;
But the' 's on'y a ca'f an' a goslin' nigh.
They turn up at him a wonderin' eye,
To see — the dragon! he's goin' to fly!
Away he goes! Jimminy! what a jump!

Romance of the Airman

Flop — flop — an' plump
To the ground with a thump!
Flutt'rin an' flound'rin, all in a lump!"
As a demon is hurled by an angel's spear,
Heels over head, to his proper sphere —
Heels over head, and head over heels,
Dizzily down the abyss he wheels, —
So fell Darius. Upon his crown,
In the midst of the barnyard, he came down,
In a wonderful whirl of tangled strings,
Broken braces and broken springs,
Broken tail and broken wings,
Shooting stars, and various things!
Away with a bellow fled the calf,
And what was that? Did the gosling laugh?
'Tis a merry roar
From the old barn door,
And he hears the voice of Jotham crying,
"Say, D'rius! how de yeou like flying?"
Slowly, ruefully, where he lay,
Darius just turned and looked that way,
As he stanched his sorrowful nose with his cuff.
"Wall, I like flyin' well enough,"
He said; "but the' ain't sich a thunderin' sight
O' fun in't when ye come to light."

MORAL

I just have room for the moral here;
And this is the moral: Stick to your sphere.
Or if you insist, as you have the right,
On spreading your wings for a loftier flight,
The moral is, Take care how you light.

The Airman Dreams 95

Words and Phrases

To aid in understanding this selection

This poem, written in a dialect of the uncultured, has words spelled in unusual ways. For example,

I'll make mine o' luther,
Er suthin' er other.

Luther means "leather"; *er*, spelled correctly, is "or"; *suthin'* means "something"; *o'* is the contraction of "of."

Informal Test (Multiple-Choice)

All tests of the multiple-choice type have several answers, only one of which is correct. In each part of the exercise, read the entire sentence, selecting the answer which makes the sentence a correct statement. On your test paper, number as many lines as there are parts to the exercise (in this test there are five). Write after each number the section of the answers in black type which you consider correct. *Example:* Darius did not go to the Fourth of July celebration because **he wanted to take a trip in his flying machine.** The words in black type complete the sentence correctly.

1. Darius did not go to the Fourth of July celebration because **he had a bad cough** **he wanted to take a trip in his flying machine** **he had a toothache** **his brothers decided not to go**

2. He decided not to show anyone his plan, for **he did not want to be laughed at** **he was ashamed of his machine** **he thought someone might try to imitate it** **his brothers might try to fly his machine**

3. When he tried to fly, Darius **killed himself by the fall** **successfully flew to the celebration** **wrecked his machine and made his nose bleed** **never left the springboard**

4. The moral of the poem is **Do not attempt to fly at all** **See that your machine is easily controlled** **Be careful where you alight** **Put on plenty of armor like a knight**

5. Darius Green was **a handsome boy** **an aspiring genius** **an unobserving lad** **a boy who didn't mind being laughed at**

96 *Romance of the Airman*

Exercises and Topics related to your Other Subjects

1. List all the descriptive words that tell what sort of boy Darius was.

2. Write a description of the flying machine that was "the greatest invention under the sun."

3. Examine the biographies of some of the heroes of the air and see if you can fit any one of them to the description of Darius Green.

4. Add another chapter to the poem and tell us what Darius had accomplished by the time he was twenty-one years old.

Other Readings

In this book

"Dædalus and Icarus," page 11.

Argosies of the Air

ALFRED, LORD TENNYSON

Explanatory Note. These lines are from the poem "Locksley Hall," written by Alfred, Lord Tennyson, in 1842. It is said that he spent about six weeks writing this poem. Locksley Hall is an imaginary place on the coast of Lincolnshire. A considerable number of phrases and lines of this deservedly popular poem have become familiar quotations. Read the poem and consider how many. of Tennyson's prophecies have come true.

MEN, my brothers, men the workers, ever reaping some-
    thing new;
That which they have done but earnest* of the things that
    they shall do.
For I dipt into the future, far as human eye could see,
Saw the Vision of the world, and all the wonder that would
    be;
Saw the heavens fill with commerce, argosies* of magic
    sails,
Pilots of the purple twilight, dropping down with costly
    bales;
Heard the heavens fill with shouting, and there rained a
    ghastly dew
From the nations' airy navies, grappling in the central
    blue;
Far along the world-wide whisper of the south wind rushing
    warm
With the standards of the peoples plunging through the
    thunderstorm;
Till the war drum throbbed no longer, and the battle
    flags were furled,
In the Parliament of man, the Federation of the world.*

98 *Romance of the Airman*

Words and Phrases

To aid in understanding this selection

earnest: here, anything serving as a pledge of what is to follow.

argosies: large merchant vessels that carry rich freight.

In the Parliament of man, the Federation of the world: Tennyson, no doubt, expresses a hope that all nations will send representatives to confer with one another, to the end that friendly relations among all countries may prevail.

Exercises and Topics related to your Other Subjects

1. Use as a topic for a theme "Some Interesting Events in the Life of Alfred, Lord Tennyson."

2. Find some familiar quotations in the poem "Locksley Hall."

3. Memorize one of the quotations found.

4. Look up the Briand-Kellogg Peace Pact in the *Congressional Digest*, Volume VII, page 338, "Provisions of Treaty Explained," by the Honorable Frank B. Kellogg.

5. Compare the political and economic conditions of the English people in 1842 with their political and economic conditions today.

Other Readings

From other sources

"Conquering the Air," by A. Williams.

II. The Airman Experiments

To become a Winged Man was the Dream of Early Experimenters

See him from Nature rising slow to art!
To copy instinct then was reason's part;

Thus then to Man the voice of Nature spake —
"Go, from the creatures thy instruction take:
Learn of the birds. . . ."

                    ALEXANDER POPE, "Essay on Man"

Early Scientific Experimenters

FOR many generations mankind has been attempting to emulate the flight of birds. Because he is naturally a land animal, man first learned to travel over the surface of the ground. Gradually he has learned to travel over the surface of the water, to burrow deep beneath the surface of the earth, to explore the depths of the ocean, and finally to conquer the atmosphere. The following is a very brief account of some of the early experimenters whose attempts were, each in turn, steps toward man's success in attaining "the way of an eagle in the air."

Roger Bacon

Almost three hundred years before Columbus discovered America, Roger Bacon foresaw the possibilities of aërial navigation. This philosopher originated the *hollow-globe theory* about the middle of the thirteenth century. He wrote, "The machine must be a large hollow globe of copper or other suitable metal wrought extremely thin so as to have it as light as possible, and it must be filled with ethereal air * or liquid fire."

Bacon, who was one of the most profound and original thinkers of his day, was intimately acquainted with experimental science, geography, and astronomy. He wrote an encyclopedia of knowledge which he called "Opus Majus." Ignorant people thought that much of what they observed in nature was due to magic and that any attempt to give scientific explanations was sacrilegious. Bacon was punished and thrown into prison because of his teachings. His ideas on aviation were not accepted, and therefore they were lost to the world. Not until recently has it been known that he experimented with balloons.

Leonardo da Vinci

At the time that Columbus was exploring the unknown seas in an attempt to find a new route to India, another Italian, Leonardo da Vinci, artist, sculptor, engineer, and architect, was absorbed in writing the *first treatise on mechanical flight* and in demonstrating the principle of the parachute. When his writings on aviation were translated into English in 1925, they revealed that he had made many valuable contributions to science. Read the selection in this book entitled "Da Vinci Did it First."

John Wilkins

In 1648 John Wilkins, a brother-in-law of Oliver Cromwell, published a work entitled "Mathematical Magic," in the second part of which he discusses various novel suggestions for artificial locomotion. There are two chapters on the art of flying. He declares that there are four ways by which it might be possible to achieve flight: *first*, there is the manner successfully practiced by the saints and angels, but this line of approach is outside the field of scientific inquiry; *secondly*, men might learn to harness the birds of the air; *thirdly*, they might devise wings after the manner of Dædalus; *fourthly*, they might build a flying chariot. The flying chariot large enough to carry a number of persons seemed to him the most practicable suggestion. Wilkins writes:

But the fourth and last way seems to me altogether as probable and much more useful than any of the rest; and that is by a flying chariot, which may be so contrived as to carry a man within it; and though the strength of a spring might perhaps be serviceable for the motion of this engine, yet it were better to have it assisted by the labor of some intelligent mover. And, therefore, if it were

The Airman Experiments 103

made big enough to carry sundry persons together, then each of them in their several turns might successively labor in the causing of this motion; which thereby would be much more constant and lasting than it would otherwise be if it did wholly depend on the strength of the same person.

Wilkins believed that it should be "easy to frame an instrument wherein anyone may sit and give such motion unto it as shall convey him aloft through the air." He adds:

There is not any imaginable invention that could prove of greater benefit to the world or glory to the inventor. Therefore it may justly deserve the inquiry of those who have both the leisure and means for such experiment. But unless a man be able to go to the trial of things, he will perform but little in these practical studies.

He believed that the force of gravity would cease to operate at a certain altitude. His work lacked precision. He never got down to technical details, but he did contribute much by way of proclaiming that the seemingly impossible is in reality not impossible — that only lack of knowledge holds men back from achievements and triumphs of which as yet they scarcely dream.

Francesco Lana

As early as 1670 a Jesuit father,* Francesco Lana of Italy, published a book in which he outlined the design for an airship supported by four hollow globes twenty feet in diameter and directed by oars and sails. He later learned that the sails would not be of any use in steering and that no metal thin enough to be buoyed up could withstand the enormous pressure of the air.

Lana said that there was only one obstacle in the way of success.

I do not foresee any other difficulty that could prevail against this invention, save one only, which to me seems the greatest of them all, and that is that God would never surely allow such a machine to be successful, since it would create many disturbances in the civil and political governments of mankind. Where is the man who can fail to see that no city would be proof against surprise, when the ship could at any time be steered over its squares, or even over the courtyard of dwelling houses, and brought to earth for the landing of its crew? Iron weights could be hurled to wreck ships at sea, or they could be set on fire with fireballs and bombs; nor ships alone, but houses, fortresses, and cities could thus be destroyed with the certainty that the [air] ship could come to no harm, as the missiles could be hurled from a vast height.

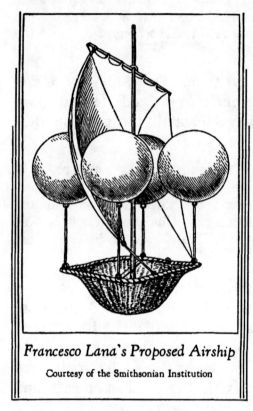

Francesco Lana's Proposed Airship
Courtesy of the Smithsonian Institution

Bartholomew Laurence de Gusman

The most fantastic account of a flying device is that of the Brazilian friar * Bartholomew Laurence de Gusman, who in 1709 petitioned the king of Portugal to grant him exclusive rights to one of the strangest contrivances ever committed to paper in the name of aëronautics. Two loadstones were to draw this flying ship after them. Amber beads strung on an iron net were to help to keep it aloft

The Airman Experiments   105

"by a secret operation," and the heat of the sun was to cause the straw mats lining the bottom of the boat to be drawn toward the beads. Everything was labeled, including "the artist," who was shown intelligently gazing through a telescope and taking up an inconsiderate portion of the room designed "for convenience of ten or eleven men besides the artist."

So impressed was the Portuguese monarch with the advantages of this ship for the transaction of the royal business that he agreed to order the death of any "transgressors," appointed Bartholomew "First Professor of Mathematics" at the University of Coimbra, and promised him the first vacancy at the College of Barcelona, with an annual pension of six hundred thousand reis (about six hundred dollars.)

Sir George Cayley

The father of British aëronautics, Sir George Cayley, a wealthy Englishman, wrote much on the subject of aviation and, without doubt, well deserves the veneration he receives.

In 1796 he made a successful model of a helicopter, a type of machine of which he was one of the first to realize the advantages. Many attribute to him the inauguration of the curved wing, and suggestions for methods by which an aëroplane may be made stable in the air. He advised the use of the tail and the rudder and of the angle at which the wings of an aëroplane are set — the dihedral angle — for lateral stability.

It is particularly to the credit of Sir George Cayley that he actually anticipated the coming of the *internal-combustion machine* when he stated that with the steam engine, as it was in his day, flight in a heavier-than-air machine was impossible. He was the first to point out the

106 *Romance of the Airman*

true path to scientific progress in the study of aëronautical problems, and he established certain principles which are now commonplaces.

Cayley contributed these three things to the study of aëronautics:

1. He derided the idea that man could ever fly by wing-flapping movements.

2. He insisted on harnessing some form of mechanical power.

3. He enunciated the basic principle of the aëroplane; namely, "that every pound of resistance that is done away with will support thirty pounds of additional weight without any additional power."

William Samuel Henson

The first monoplane was built by Henson in 1840. In 1842 he entered a patent that described a machine which is not very far from the monoplane of today in the general principles of its construction. The materials suggested for its construction were spars of bamboo and hollow wood, with wire bracing. The plane was to have a total lifting surface of forty-five hundred square feet, with a triangular tail of fifteen hundred square feet. The engine was to be one of twenty-five or thirty horse power, driving two six-bladed propellers.

John Stringfellow

About this time in aviation history Henson became associated with John Stringfellow, who, when Henson later abandoned further experiment, carried on alone. A large model aëroplane, which actually flew, was constructed by Stringfellow between 1846 and 1848. It had

The Airman Experiments 107

a span of ten feet and a total sustaining area of fourteen square feet. The two propellers were driven by a small steam engine, and the total weight of the model was eight pounds. The tail was set at too great an angle the first time the machine flew, so that it climbed too rapidly; and ultimately the work on this particular model was defeated by a crash.

As early as 1866 the Aëronautical Society of Great Britain was founded, and Stringfellow, who had allowed his experiments to lapse, once more entered the field. In 1868 he showed at the Crystal Palace a model of a tri-plane which boasted a supporting surface of twenty-eight square feet and, with engine, boiler, and fuel, weighed twelve pounds. At this time Stringfellow was awarded £100 in English currency for the construction of a steam engine with the highest ratio of power to weight.

At his death this pioneer in aviation left a name which has been remembered in aviation history. He fully realized the advantages of the curved wing, and it is certain that had the internal-combustion engine been in existence in his day he would have anticipated the remarkable achievement of the Wright brothers.

John J. Montgomery

As early as 1883 John J. Montgomery built a flapping-wing machine, and followed it in 1884 with gliders having curved surfaces. Stability was also of prime importance to Montgomery, and he made many models to obtain the information he desired. He tells us: "These models were tested by dropping them from a cable stretched between two mountain tops, with various loads, adjustments, and positions. And it made no difference whether the models were dropped upside down or in any other conceivable position — they always found their equilibrium immediately and glided safely to earth."

As a result of his experiments Montgomery had full-sized gliders made and launched them from balloons, he and his assistants making some very remarkable glides. The flights were brought to an end by the death of one of his assistants while gliding from a height of two thousand feet. He himself was finally killed in 1911 while carrying out further gliding experiments. Before his death, however, Montgomery realized that man had at last conquered the air.

Sir Hiram S. Maxim

Sir Hiram S. Maxim, of machine-gun fame, built the first airplane which actually succeeded in lifting human beings into the air. After some years of experimentation with propellers, lighting surfaces, and the air resistance of struts of different sections, Sir Hiram constructed a boiler and engines capable of developing great power for their weight. From the beginning he realized that one of the things which prevented flight was the great weight of the engine as compared with its horse power, and he tried to eliminate that difficulty by building a larger airplane. His machine had a wing surface of four thousand feet.

Maxim's object was not to make a "free" flight. He laid down a steel railway eighteen hundred feet long and of nine-foot gauge for the airplane to run on, and outside this another of thirty-five-foot gauge with reversed rails, against the underside of which flanged wheels at the ends of long outriggers would press if the narrow-gauge wheels rose an inch above their rails, so that the machine would remain captive.

The trip on which the giant machine did lift itself, though the flight was less than a quarter of a mile in

The Airman Experiments 109

length, was made on July 31, 1894, a famous date in aviation history. It meant that on this day man was first lifted into the air on wings by mechanical power. The machine was later wrecked, and Maxim abandoned his experiments after spending more than $125,000 on the project.

Otto Lilienthal

If Lilienthal had known the principles discovered by Leonardo da Vinci, the secret of mechanical flight might have been revealed to man earlier. In 1889 this careful student published a treatise on "Bird Flights as a Basis of Aviation." When he was a lad of thirteen he succeeded in making many gliding flights. He built many gliders which appear ludicrous today; yet the elementary principles of wings attached to man formed the fundamentals of present-day flight. Again and again the Wright brothers speak of Lilienthal's assistance to them. The selection entitled "Otto Lilienthal, Inspirer of the Wright Brothers" gives a fuller account of his contribution.

Samuel P. Langley

Professor S. P. Langley, at one time secretary of the Smithsonian Institution, is a most interesting figure in aviation. He experimented several years with his model planes until in 1896 he flew a model over three thousand feet. Thus encouraged, he worked on a plane of man-lifting size; and on October 7, 1903, he was ready to demonstrate his larger machine, which was equipped with a fifty-horse-power engine and two propellers.

The launching device was so defective that the machine plunged into the Potomac River. At the second trial the

The Langley Aërodrome which the Inventor demonstrated October 7, 1903

Courtesy of the Smithsonian Institution

machine was wrecked. It must be remembered that two and a half months later the Wright brothers made their successful flight at Kitty Hawk, North Carolina. Had it not been for the defective launching device of Professor Langley's machine, he, and not the Wright brothers, might have been proclaimed the "Father of Flight."

Thus we see that at the dawn of the twentieth century much time, money, and talent had been spent in serious thought about the possibility of mechanical flight. The work and study of Bacon, Lana, Lilienthal, Cayley, Maxim, and others formed the foundation for the triumphs of those who persevered in their experiments while their fellows scoffed.

The Airman Experiments

111

Words and Phrases

To aid in understanding this selection

ethereal air: very light air resembling that of the upper regions of space.

Jesuit father: a Jesuit is a member of a Roman Catholic religious order (the Society of Jesus) founded in 1534. *Father* is a title of reverence applied to monks, priests, and other Church dignitaries.

friar: from the Latin word meaning "brother." In the Roman Catholic Church it is applied to a member of certain religious orders.

To add to your vocabulary

emulate	inauguration	equilibrium
gravity	enunciate	fantastic
obstacle	sundry	veneration
missile		spar

Technical terms

aërial	angle	loadstone	aëronautics
dihedral	triplane	helicopter	

Informal Test (Multiple-Choice)[1]

1. The father of British aëronautics is   **Sir George Cayley   William Henson   John Stringfellow   Roger Bacon   John Williams**

2. Leonardo da Vinci's writings on aviation were translated into English in   **1910   1895   1916   1904   1925**

3. The first monoplane was built by   **Leonardo da Vinci   John J. Montgomery   Sir Hiram Maxim   William Henson   Bartholomew de Gusman**

4. The first successful aëroplane was invented by   **Lilienthal   Langley   the Wright brothers   Montgomery   Maxim**

[1] For directions, see page 95.

112 *Romance of the Airman*

5. Leonardo da Vinci was   **an Englishman   an Irishman an American   a Swede   an Italian**

6. The model of a triplane was first exhibited in   1850   1875   1860   1868   1863

7. Stringfellow was   **a pioneer in aviation   a writer of books on aviation   an inventor   a lecturer   a mechanic**

Informal Test (Matching)[1]

1. Roger Bacon
2. The Wright brothers
3. Leonardo da Vinci
4. John Wilkins
5. Francesco Lana
6. Sir George Cayley
7. Bartholomew de Gusman
8. William Henson
9. John Stringfellow

parachute
Jesuit father
"Opus Majus"
"Mathematical Magic"
"Father of Flight"
first monoplane
model triplane
"Father of British Aëronautics"
"First Professor of Mathematics" at the University of Coimbra

Exercises and Topics related to your Other Subjects

1. Take an outline map of Europe and write, on the country in which he experimented, the name of each experimenter mentioned in this selection.

2. List on the map the special things that each did and the year in which their experiments were made.

3. Look up in your reference books accounts of each of the men mentioned in this selection.

4. Find from your histories and stories of scientists and discoverers the names of successful people whose advanced ideas were ridiculed, but who are now praised because of their contributions to society.

[1] For directions, see page 9.

The Airman Experiments 113

Other Readings

In this book

"Da Vinci Did it First," page 114.
"Otto Lilienthal, Inspirer of the Wright Brothers," page 124.

From other sources

Any encyclopedia or reference book giving an account of the lives of the men mentioned in this selection.

"Da Vinci Did it First"

EDWIN W. TEALE

Explanatory Note. The manuscripts of Leonardo da Vinci were bequeathed to a friend who carefully guarded them until he died, fifty years after Da Vinci; they were then scattered over various parts of southwestern Europe. In modern times practically all these have been located, and in 1925 an English translation of his work on aviation was made by Ivor B. Hart, of the University of London. This material was first presented in the *Journal of the Royal Aëronautical Society* and later in a book entitled "The Mechanical Investigations of Leonardo da Vinci."

One manuscript of Da Vinci's is entitled "On the Flight of Birds." In this he gives elaborate drawings and explanations of a machine based on principles of flight which he had learned from his study of the movements of birds. He spent thirty years in perfecting his plans for this heavier-than-air machine. He might have anticipated modern lighter-than-air science had he turned his investigations in that direction; for we know that he was aware of the fundamental principle of this phase of aviation and that he demonstrated it to astonished onlookers by causing strange figures of thin wax filled with warm air to soar upward.

THE whir of the Byrd and Wilkins airplane propellers in the Antarctic in recent months has directed fresh attention to a remarkable genius of four centuries ago. When alchemy and astrology were still regarded as exact sciences, he designed a flying machine embodying principles used in present-day aircraft and invented the propeller; and when others had barely ceased thinking of the Strait of Gibraltar as the Portals of the Unknown, he included Antarctica in his map of the world!

All of us know Leonardo da Vinci as the painter of "Mona Lisa," "The Last Supper," and "La Belle Ferronnière." His fame as a painter has obscured his reputation as a great trail blazer of science. Yet he stated scientific laws that four centuries of experiment have not

The Airman Experiments 115

altered, and many of his simplest inventions have become part of our daily lives. The spiral-spring hinge that shuts your screen door is a product of his mind. He invented the wheelbarrow, the rotating smokestack that turns with the wind, and the flexible roller chain used on bicycle sprockets and other chain-drive mechanisms.

Every child in school doing problems in addition and subtraction is helped by this genius of long ago, who is said upon competent authority to have devised the plus and minus signs used the world over!

Leonardo was born in 1452 in a fortified hill village in Tuscany, Italy, the son of a Florentine notary. A strong, amiable, beautiful child, he early showed a gift for music and drawing. At seventeen he became the pupil of the famous artist Andrea del Verrocchio. A year later Verrocchio allowed him to paint a single angel in a large picture of "Christ's Baptism." So superior was this small bit of work that, according to the story, Verrocchio acknowledged the genius of the eighteen-year-old boy by laying down his brushes and never touching them again.

For the next ten years Leonardo painted under the favor of Lorenzo the Magnificent in Florence. His days were spent in incessant painting and study. They were too full of work for roistering, and he led a singularly upright life in the dissolute court. His physical strength was so great that he could bend iron bars over his knee and twist horseshoes. He rode unbroken horses for sport and is said to have been able to disarm any adversary and to have had no equal in running, wrestling, and swimming. Yet his nature was so gentle that he used to go about Florence buying caged birds in order to give them their freedom.

While he was winning recognition as a painter, sculptor, and architect, his active mind was seeking "the soul of

116   *Romance of the Airman*

things" in all branches of learning. He kept lists of people who possessed knowledge and of books he wished to consult, and made long journeys to see them. In his manuscripts are often such notes as "A grandson of Angelo the painter has a book on water which belonged to his father."

The most gifted and brilliant man of his age, he worked harder than anyone around him. His oft repeated maxim was: "Stagnant water loses its purity; even so does inaction sap the vigor of the mind." Leonardo never published a line. But when he died thousands of pages of manuscript, which had accumulated during his life, recorded the harvest of his active intellect. Because he wrote from right to left in the Oriental manner, these manuscripts could be read only with the aid of a mirror.

Many pages were found to be filled with notes on soaring birds, and sketches of proposed flying machines. Some of these notes indicate that he invented the parachute and also designed a toy utilizing the balloon principle two and a half centuries before the brothers Montgolfier, who are credited with the invention of the balloon in 1783.

The first bat-winged machine that he designed was to be made of bamboo, pine, and taffeta, starched to make it air-tight. It was to have flapping wings operated by hand. Later he designed a craft to be lifted by a propeller run by a spring motor. There is no authentic record that Leonardo ever made a trial of his proposed machines; but after studying the plans, John William Lieb, an American mechanical engineer, has said, "Leonardo da Vinci stopped just short of practical results owing to the lack of a modern motor."

The story of how Leonardo became fascinated with the idea of flying throws light upon the extravagant spirit of his time. For a festival he had designed a huge golden

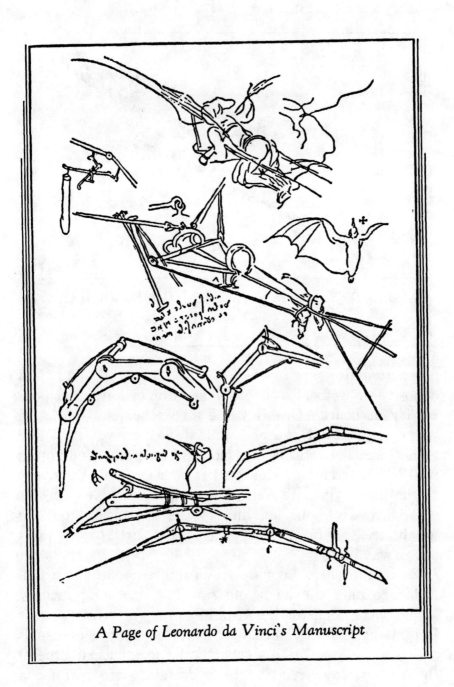

A Page of Leonardo da Vinci's Manuscript

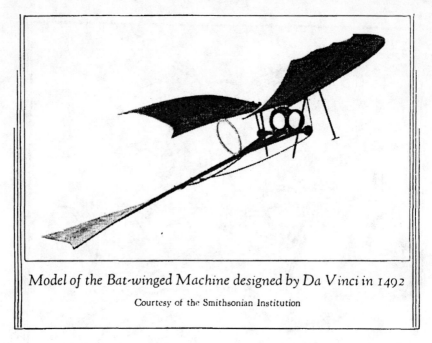

Model of the Bat-winged Machine designed by Da Vinci in 1492
Courtesy of the Smithsonian Institution

lion actuated by springs to walk up to honored guests and deposit flowers before them. This brought him great popularity at court. One day the idea occurred: "What a sensation I could cause if I flew over crowds at a fête in hot weather, sprinkling snow taken from a mountain top!" The result of this bizarre idea was his discovery of the law of gravitation. For, long before Newton, his aërial investigations led him to the conclusion that "a weight seeks to fall to the center of the earth by the most direct way."

From Florence, Leonardo was invited to the court of Milan to play the harp and sing his own compositions. While there, as a further tribute to his versatility, Cæsar Borgia made him military engineer in charge of canals and waterways. In this capacity he formulated some of the earliest laws relating to hydraulics. He planned a canal from Pisa to Florence, diverting the waters of the

The Airman Experiments 119

Arno. Two hundred years after Leonardo's death this canal was constructed exactly as he had projected it.

To speed the work of canal construction, he designed a unique "ox-shovel." At one end of a rope over a pulley on the framework of the machine was attached a huge basket; on the other end, a platform. The basket was lowered into the excavation, the platform rising to the level of the canal bank. When the basket was full of earth an ox was led on the platform. As it sank under his weight the basket rose and was swung out and dumped on the canal bank, much as a modern steam shovel operates. The ox walked up an incline to repeat the process.

As military engineer Leonardo's original mind planned a huge armored car similar to the modern tank, and suggested placing vanes at the rear of projectiles as is done with aircraft bombs of the present. His design for a steam cannon, in which the ball was to be ejected by a piston operating in a cylinder, was the direct forerunner of James Watt's steam engine.

Mechanics he called the "paradise of sciences." Tired from his painting, he continually found relaxation in his tools and in devising new machines. One of his most ingenious inventions was a spit for roasting meat before a fire. A fan mechanism that turned the spit was moved by the hot air rushing up the chimney. Thus the spit automatically turned rapidly when the fire was hot and the meat in danger of burning, and more slowly when the heat died down.

No human being could carry out all the designs of Leonardo's untiring brain. He planned much that he never had opportunity to try. But time has revealed that invariably his ideas were steps in the right direction.

One of his drawings shows a proposed automobile which was to be run by a spring motor. Another reveals a div-

120 *Romance of the Airman*

ing suit in which air was to be supplied to the occupant by a tube, as in modern suits. He designed a life belt which could be inflated in an instant in case of shipwreck. Wire rope was suggested by him, and he thought of using jewels for bearings. His "camera obscura" mechanism forms the basis of all cameras. Machine shops everywhere fight friction by means of roller bearings, first thought of by Leonardo. Such were the products of his hours of "leisure."

Early in the sixteenth century he drew a map of the globe, said to be the first to include America, and also showing an antarctic continent. It was this type of map that was used by Magellan and other early navigators. Even before Columbus sailed from Spain, Leonardo not only maintained that the earth was round but calculated its diameter to be more than seven thousand miles. The actual diameter, as now accepted, is roughly seventy-nine hundred miles!

Fossils, which he picked up on the mountain sides, were called unusual mineral formations by his friends. He correctly declared them to be skeletons of animals. His theories as to wave motion and ocean currents have been shown to be largely correct.

Leonardo had more exact knowledge about the human body than any other man of his day. In preparation for his paintings he dissected bodies and plumbed the secrets of the human organs until he was able to write clear dissertations on the theory of nutrition, on nerve cells, on blood vessels, and on hardening of the arteries. Before Harvey, he understood about the circulation of the blood.

Most botanists now agree that the age of a tree can be told by counting the rings in a cross section of the trunk. Leonardo's sharp eyes are said to have been the first to discover that fact. Another important discovery he made in the field of botany was the principles of phyllotaxis, or the laws governing the distribution of leaves on an axis.

Before Copernicus, Leonardo wrote, "The sun does not move!" and proclaimed that the earth rotates about it. A century before Galileo's time he proposed a telescope, making this note on his manuscript: "Construct glasses so as to see the moon magnified." Before Bacon, he propounded the important law of inductive reasoning, saying, "Without experience, there can be no certainty." Two hundred years before the time of Amontons he formulated laws relating to friction. It has been truly said that "Leonardo da Vinci discovered twenty laws, a single one of which has sufficed for the glory of his successors."

Leonardo da Vinci

During his last years the constant warfare of Renaissance * Italy exiled Leonardo to France, where he was received with honor at the court of King Francis I. When he died in 1519, at the age of sixty-seven, a clause was found in his will that reflected that thoughtful kindness which had characterized his life. It provided that sixty poor men should be hired to act as candle bearers at his funeral.

Up to his last days he was busy painting and studying. This was as he had wished. "As a well-spent day brings happy sleep," he had often said, "so life well used brings happy death."

122   *Romance of the Airman*

Words and Phrases

To aid in understanding this selection

Renaissance: a period of revival of the learning and art of the past.

To add to your vocabulary

alchemy	dissolute court
roistering	bizarre

Technical term

propeller

Informal Test

Below is a list of a number of items. On a sheet of paper write the numbers of the ones invented, discovered, or understood by Da Vinci.

1. Law of gravitation	14. Alarm clock
2. Spring-roller window shade	15. Automobile
3. Propeller	16. Monkey wrench
4. Rotating egg-beater	17. Rubber eraser
5. Plus sign	18. Life belt
6. Coal-oil lamp	19. Pulmotor
7. Spiral-spring hinge	20. Wire rope
8. Wheelbarrow	21. Modern diving suit
9. Mowing scythe	22. Rubber raincoat
10. Rotating smokestack	23. Camera
11. Talking machine	24. Microscope
12. Heating stove	25. Jeweled bearings
13. Parachute	26. Roller bearings

27. Flexible roller chain on a bicycle sprocket
28. Principle of the hot-air balloon
29. Principle of the modern steam shovel
30. Number of miles in the earth's diameter
31. Number of miles to the moon

The Airman Experiments 123

32. Movement of ocean currents
33. Circulation of the blood
34. Function of the liver
35. Movement of the earth around the sun
36. Telescope
37. Determination of the age of trees

Exercises and Topics related to your Other Subjects

Give in one sentence the most significant work of the following men :

Newton	Harvey
James Watt	Copernicus
Galileo	

Subjects for themes

Leonardo da Vinci the Artist.
The Controversy over "La Belle Ferronnière." (See the *Popular Science Monthly* for May, 1929, pages 42–43.)
A Fifteen-Jeweled Watch.

Other Readings

In this book

"A Peruvian Aviator of the Eighteenth Century," page 136.

Suggestion for the Student

You are going to read many stories of people who have made significant contributions to the development of aviation. Start a notebook on aviation that you will enjoy keeping. In this you can keep pictures and clippings that you find in newspapers from time to time. Start now to keep a section called "Who's Who in the Development of Aviation." The scheme below is a suggestion.

Name	Nationality	Date	Contribution
Leonardo da Vinci	Italian	1452–1519	Planned a flying machine Invented the parachute

Otto Lilienthal, Inspirer of the Wright Brothers

C. C. TURNER

> *Explanatory Note.* It is interesting to note that Lilienthal did practically the same work that Leonardo da Vinci had done nearly four hundred years earlier. Undoubtedly aviation was retarded because Da Vinci's work was not published. To Lilienthal is due much credit for the success of the inventors of the airplane. Many times the Wright brothers refer to Lilienthal's observations, which form the foundation on which their invention was built.

PARTICULAR honor belongs to those who believed in the possibility of mechanical flight when all of the world was against them; not the visionaries who believed in it because they hoped for it merely, but those who by sheer force of intellect perceived the means by which it would be accomplished and directed their experiments along the right path. The name of Otto Lilienthal is now among the most honored, but curiously his own countrymen were the last to recognize the value of his work.

Otto Lilienthal was born at Anklam on the twenty-fourth of May, 1848. He and his brother Gustav experimented for many years together, and in 1889 published the results of their labors in the epoch-making book "Bird Flights, the Basis of the Flying Art." This work contained the discovery that the curved surface has greater efficiency than the plane in gliding flight. The Lilienthals had studied the flight of birds and had come to the conclusion that the kind of flight that was possible of imitation mechanically was not by flapping-wing, but was the soaring and gliding methods of certain birds that with wings outstretched and apparently rigid move horizontally and sometimes even in an upward direction. Lilienthal's

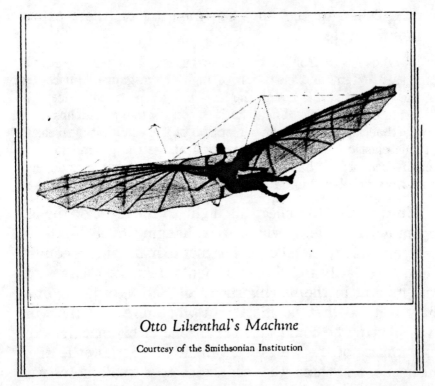

Otto Lilienthal's Machine
Courtesy of the Smithsonian Institution

machine consisted of an arched surface with an area of about one hundred and sixty square feet, made by stretching thin fabric over a light wooden frame. Its weight was forty pounds. In the center was an aperture for the experimenter's body, and the contrivance was held in position by his arms. In running down a gentle slope against the wind, sufficient velocity was acquired to lift the machine off the ground. "The feat," wrote Lilienthal, "requires practice. In the beginning the height should be moderate, and the wings not too large, or the wind will soon show that it is not to be trifled with." His first jumps were from a springboard about four feet in height, and he slowly increased the height of this take-off, eventually gliding from the slope of a hill and not landing until a distance of two hundred and fifty yards had been

126 *Romance of the Airman*

accomplished in the air. Commenting on these experiments he wrote:

To those who from a modest beginning and with gradually increased extent and elevation of flight have gained full control of the apparatus it is not in the least dangerous to cross deep and broad ravines. It is a difficult task to convey to one who has never enjoyed aërial flight a clear perception of the exhilarating pleasure of this elastic motion. The elevation above the ground loses its terrors because we have learned by experience what sure dependence may be placed upon the buoyancy of the air.

He was able to deflect his flight to the right or the left by moving his legs, which were hanging freely from the seat, and he depended upon instinct to maintain his equilibrium. To facilitate his experiments he made a large conical mound in the neighborhood of Berlin, of a height of fifty feet, so that no matter in what direction the wind was blowing he could face it. In one of his machines the extremities of the wings were made of a series of featherlike sails, and these were connected to a small motor near the operator's body and set in motion by the pressure of a knob. This motor was, however, not at all satisfactory on account of the weight. In the year 1896 Lilienthal's experiments had attracted the attention of scientific men everywhere, and in England, France, and America there were a few people who believed in him. His gliding experiments became more and more daring, and he sought to go up in high winds and to be carried along with them. Often he only saved himself by the exercise of quick, dexterous movements, and there is no doubt that he began to develop wonderful skill and knowledge of aërial conditions. He substituted for the one large framework two smaller ones placed one over the other, in reality a biplane, and he found that, using this with a wind velocity of eighteen feet per second, he was carried in a nearly hori-

The Airman Experiments

zontal direction against the wind without having to take a run to get off the ground. Sometimes he found himself in the air at a standstill at a higher altitude than he had been at the starting point. "At these times," he wrote, "I feel very certain that if I leaned a little to one side and so described a circle, and further partook of the motion of the lifting air around me, I should sustain my position. The wind itself tends to direct this motion; but then it must be remembered that my chief object in the air is to overcome this tendency of turning to the left or the right, because I know that behind or under me lies the hill from which I started, and with which I would come in rough contact if I allowed myself to attempt this circular sailing. I have, however, made up my mind by means of either a stronger wind or by flapping the wings to get higher up and farther away from the hill, so that sailing round in circles I can follow the strong uplifting currents and have sufficient air space around and under me to complete with safety a circle, and, lastly, to come up against the wind to land."

Unfortunately the predictions of the skeptics were verified. On August 11, 1896, while experimenting at Gross-Lichtenfelde, near Berlin, and having flown for a distance of about twenty yards, a gust of wind suddenly caught and carried him upward; he lost control of the machine and fell to the ground, breaking his spine, and died soon afterwards. . . .

So valuable were Otto Lilienthal's works that it will be useful to give here his own summarized conclusions. He wrote:

Artificial flight may be defined as that form of aviation in which a man flies at will in any direction by means of an apparatus attached to his body, the use of which requires personal skill. Artificial flight by a single individual is the proper beginning for

128 *Romance of the Airman*

all species of artificial flight, as the necessary conditions can most easily be fulfilled when a man flies individually.

The increasing size of the apparatus makes the construction more difficult in securing lightness in the machine; therefore the building of small apparatus is to be recommended.

The difficulty of rising into the air increases rapidly with the size of the apparatus. The uplifting of a single person, therefore, is more easily attained than that of a large flying machine loaded with several persons.

The destructive power of the wind increases rapidly with the size of the apparatus. A machine intended to serve for the flight of but a single person is most easily governed in the air.

The employment of small patterns of flying machines does not permit of any extended observation, because stable flight cannot be maintained for any length of time automatically. Therefore experiments in actual flight will only be instructive when a man participates in the flight and maintains stable equilibrium at will.

Experiments in gliding by a single individual following closely the model of bird gliding is the only method which permits us, beginning with a very simple apparatus and in a very incomplete form of flight, to gradually develop our proficiency in the art of flying.

Gradual development of flight should begin with the simplest apparatus and movements, and without the complication of dynamic means.

The sailing flight of birds is the only form of flight which is carried on for some length of time without the expenditure of power.

With simple wing surfaces similar to those of the bird, man also can carry out limited flights without expending work, by gliding through the air from elevated points in paths more or less descending.

The peculiarities of wind effects can best be learned by such exercises.

The contrivances which are necessary to counteract the wind effects can only be understood by actual practice in the wind.

The supporting powers of the air and of the wind depend on the shape of the surfaces used, and the best forms can only be evolved by free flight through the air.

The Airman Experiments   129

The maintenance of equilibrium in forward flight is a matter of practice, and can only be learned by repeated personal experiment.

Experience alone can teach us the best forms of construction for sailing apparatus so that it may be of sufficient strength, very light, and most easily managed.

By practice and experience a man can (if the wind be of the right strength) imitate the complete sailing flight of birds by availing himself of the slight upward trend of some winds, by performing circling sweeps, and by allowing the air to carry him.

The efficiency of sailing flight upon fixed wings may be increased by flapping the wings or portions of the wings by means of a motor.

With a proper apparatus, which may be simultaneously used for sailing and rowing flight, a man may obtain all the advantage of bird flight for a certain duration of flight, and may extend his journey in any direction with the least expenditure of power devisable.

Actual practice in individual flight presents the best prospects for developing our capacity until it leads to perfected free flight.

Words and Phrases

To add to your vocabulary

exhilarating	dexterous
premature	skeptics
facilitate	

Technical terms

aperture	biplane
conical	dynamic

Informal Test (Multiple-Choice)[1]

1. Lilienthal depended upon   **instinct   poise   balance   nerve**   to maintain his equilibrium.

2. The sailing flight of birds is the only form of flight which is carried on for any length of time without   **extra exertion   expenditure of power   extra work   work at all**

[1] For directions, see page 95.

130 *Romance of the Airman*

3. The peculiarities of wind can best be learned by **experimentation   study   observation   reading about the wind**

4. Lilienthal found that the **curved   squared   smooth   irregular**   surface has greater efficiency than the plane in gliding flight.

5. He got his ideas for flying from **the clouds   the winds   the birds   books**

6. Lilienthal died from **the effects of illness   the effects of an automobile accident   the effects of a flying accident   old age**

7. Lilienthal's flying machine consisted of **an arched surface with an area of 160 square feet made by stretching thin fabric over a light wooden frame ˙ a smooth surface with an area of 50 square feet made over a steel frame   an even, level surface with an area of 300 square feet made over an iron frame   a curved surface with an area of 100 square feet made over an aluminum frame**

8. Lilienthal used **the water   the hilltops   the trees   the airport**   as the place of his take-off.

Exercises and Topics related to your Other Subjects

1. Make a map showing the region in which Lilienthal tried his flights.

2. Make a miniature model of his plane from beaver board.

3. Draw a bird in flight and show how Lilienthal utilized these motions in his attempted flights.

4. Compare Lilienthal's flights, plane, and ideas with those of his contemporaries.

Other Readings

In this book
"Da Vinci Did it First," page 114.

From other sources
"The Romance of Aëronautics," by C. C. Turner.
"Mechanical Investigations of Leonardo da Vinci," by Ivor B. Hart.

The First Official Recognition of Aviation[1]

ADRIAN VAN MUFFLING

THE first official recognition ever given by a government to the inventor of a flying machine was granted to one Bartholomeo de Guzmao by the king of Portugal; and when we remember that even today some very absurd and unpractical ideas are patented, we need not wonder that this first aëronautical patent was granted to what is perhaps the strangest and weirdest idea of them all. For this invention consisted of a ship built of iron and filled with chopped straw, over the deck of which there stretched a horizontal sail or canopy. Ascensional force was to be derived by three distinct methods:

1. A current of air was to be generated by bellows within the hold to blow upwards against the canopy.
2. Two large globes of loadstone, or magnetic iron, mounted on deck were to attract the metal body of the ship.
3. A number of pieces of amber suspended above the deck were to be heated by torches, and thus, by a well-known principle of static electricity, cause the straw in the hold to rise toward them.

These are three perfectly good ways, so to speak, of lifting oneself by pulling one's own bootstraps.

The original patent granted by John V of Portugal is interesting as a document showing that the value of aircraft to any nation possessing it was well realized; also as an example of the thoroughness with which exclusive privileges were granted and what dire penalties were incurred by the hapless infringer. It is of sufficient interest to quote it here in its entirety from a French translation.

[1] Reprinted from the May, 1927, issue of the *Annals of the American Academy of Political and Social Science*, Volume CXXXI, pages 1–6.

132   Romance of the Airman

Note how well the advantages of flying which we enjoy today were understood at the time.

WE THE KING [titles follow] make known that Father Bartholomeo Lourenzóu de Guzmao has addressed a petition wherein he declares that he has discoyered an instrument designed to navigate in the airs in the same manner as on the ground and waters with far greater speed, covering a distance of two hundred leagues a day. By this instrument one can deliver important messages to distant countries and troops almost at the same instant in which they are prepared, which interests us more than it does other sovereigns on account of the great extent of our possessions; one can avoid thereby the great distances of colonies, the news from which we always receive too late; and furthermore, we can obtain all the necessities from said colonies much sooner and with greater speed; business men can exchange documents and capital with the same speed; all the beleaguered places can be assisted, with men as well as with provisions, at any moment; those who desire can be taken out from them without interference from the enemy; and one can discover the lands adjoining the two poles of the earth.

The glory of this discovery shall revert to the Portuguese nation, a discovery which foreign nations shall vainly attempt to imitate. The real longitudes of the entire world shall be known, for the errors on geographical maps are the cause of many shipwrecks; and furthermore, other advantages shall be useful to the world and shall merit our royal attention; as in connection with this useful invention many problems will present themselves, many crimes will be committed, and other crimes facilitated through the certainty of evading justice by flying into other lands.

The above shall be avoided if the use of it be reserved to one person to whom all orders connected with said transport shall be given, and forbidding its employ to all other under penalty of punishment. Because it is just to remunerate the author of such an important invention, he has asked us for the exclusive privilege to operate said invention, so that no one else can avail himself of it, at any time, in this Kingdom and its colonies, under any pretext whatsoever without the permission of the author or his heirs,

The Airman Experiments 133

under penalty of forfeiting all his possessions, one half of which shall go to the author of the petition and the other half to the denouncer; and under all other penalties that it shall please us to apply, which shall be enforced as soon as it shall be known that any other person is building a similar instrument, even if he has not used the same, unless the culpable one has placed himself beyond jurisdiction by escape.

In consideration of his proposals I accord to the author of said petition the privilege of the execution of his invention to any other's exclusion, who cannot make use of said invention under the penalties as above specified. Only the author of the petition shall have the right to the use of this invention, as is requested in said petition.

This patent shall be privileged and effective in all its provisions beyond the term of one year, in spite of the contrary provisions in Chapter IV, Book II, of our Ordinances.

There has been paid to the treasurer of the court 2 francs 50 cent. as provided on page 160, Vol. I. Registered on page 149, Vol. I. Jose Maria de Faria wrote this patent the 19th day of April, 1709. Manoel de Castro Guimaraes has revised and re-written it.

Received 2 fr. 50.   (Signed) THE KING

According to well-authenticated reports Guzmao is actually known to have made a flight in a machine of his construction shortly after the granting of the patent, in the presence of the court and a vast crowd. Details are lacking, but an eyewitness relates about "*a globe containing fire which he himself had lighted.*" It is evident that the original idea had been abandoned and that the inventor intrusted himself to a hot-air balloon. But it was a deed miraculous for all that; even the good graces of the king were unable to save him from the charge of sorcery, and in 1717 Guzmao was brought before the dreaded Holy Tribunal. All papers relating to the invention were publicly burned, including accounts of the flight that were discovered while the unfortunate inventor was

134 *Romance of the Airman*

condemned to a dungeon, and not only his mistress but all the women he had ever been known to speak to were accused of witchery. Eventually he succeeded in escaping to Spanish territory, where he died shortly afterwards.

Words and Phrases

To add to your vocabulary

culpable well-authenticated

Technical term

aëronautical

Informal Test (Completion)[1]

1. The king of Portugal recognized the following uses for the flying machine :

a. _____

b. _____

ç. _____

d. _____

e. _____

f. _____

g. _____

h. _____

2. He recognized as a danger the use of the machine by _____.

3. He urged, as a prevention of this danger, _____.

4. As a result of this proposal Guzmao was _____.

Exercises and Topics related to your Other Subjects

1. Consult maps of 1700 and find out what the colonial possessions of Portugal were at that time.

2. How many miles would the machine go at the rate of two hundred leagues a day?

[1] For directions, see page 14.

The Airman Experiments 135

Other Readings

In this book

"A Peruvian Aviator of the Eighteenth Century," page 136.

"Early Scientific Experimenters," page 101.

From other sources

"The Flying Island," from Jonathan Swift's satire "Gulliver's Travels," Part III, Chapter III (a story of an island held in the air by a loadstone).

A Peruvian Aviator of the Eighteenth Century

F. P. FARRAR

Explanatory Note. In 1533 Francisco Pizarro, a cruel and treacherous Spaniard, finally conquered the Incas of Peru. The Incas were a powerful people, possessing fabulous quantities of gold and silver. The story of their conquest is one of the most fascinating stories of the New World. Lima, "the City of Kings," was founded by Pizarro. The Peruvians obtained their freedom from Spanish rule in 1824.

INCREDIBLE as it may seem, the history of Peruvian aviation dates from the middle of the eighteenth century. In theory if not in practice, a citizen of Lima anticipated in 1761 the achievements of Orville Wright one hundred and forty years later. It is true that this descendant of Icarus never flew in actual fact; but, if we are to believe him, this was not from lack of desire, but from shortness of funds, the same obstacle which has proved the ruin of many another inventor since the dawn of time. Poverty, as he himself tells us, kept him back and robbed him of the honors which were his due. In place of the hero worship which he would have gleaned had he lived in the twentieth century, his meed was obloquy and ridicule. Instead of being acclaimed in columns of press publicity, he narrowly escaped lynching at the hands of a Lima mob.

Santiago de Cárdenas was born out of date. Not for him were the honors of Lindbergh. His reward was to sink into an unknown grave, unhonored if not unsung. His epitaph might have been

> The time is out of joint: O cursed spite,
> That ever I was born to set it right!

The Airman Experiments 137

"El Volador," * as he afterwards contemptuously came to be known, was born in Lima in 1726 of humble parents. On the death of his father he was sent to sea at the age of ten as cabin boy on a sailing vessel plying between Callao and Valparaiso. From his earliest days, as he tells us in his own pathetic story, he had always been more interested in flying kites than in whipping tops; and in those tedious trips along the Chilean coast he spent the little leisure which falls to a cabin boy in studying the flights of the sea birds which followed in the wake of the vessel. His seafaring days ended with the wreck of his ship in the great tidal wave which overwhelmed Callao in 1746. Thereafter he was free to follow his life's bent.

With his scanty savings Santiago de Cárdenas built himself a hut in the *quebrada* * of Amancaes and devoted himself to the study of the flight of the condors, then more commonly to be seen in the neighborhood of the Cerro San Cristóbal than they are today. For twelve years he led a lonely, disregarded life, spending his days climbing up and down the spur of hills which stretches from Lima to the valley of Chillon, and lying naked on the rocks and feigning death to attract the attention of the *gallinazos*.* His patience was rewarded. He solved, or he believed that he had solved, the mystery of flight. That was in November, 1761; and his great discovery came at an opportune hour. The accursed Englishmen had recently seized the port of Egmont in the Falkland Islands and from that center were raiding at their pleasure His Most Catholic Majesty's trading ships. Communication between Argentine and Peru was threatened, and the mails often fell into the hands of the enemy. It was a propitious moment for De Cárdenas, and he besought an audience of the Viceroy in order to explain his theory and to solicit funds to build a flying machine, with which he guaranteed

138   *Romance of the Airman*

that he would be in a position to carry dispatches between Lima and Buenos Aires.

The Viceroy of those days was an unusually open-minded man as viceroys go. Although his name is more commonly associated with La Perricholi than with more serious matters, Manuel de Amat y Junient had the welfare of Peru at heart, and his court was always open to those who had new ideas to propose. He was the nearest approach to a Roy Soleil* that Lima had ever known.

Amat was sufficiently interested in what De Cárdenas had to say to pass his appeal to the consideration of the Real Audiencia,* who in its turn instructed Doctor Cosme Bueno, *Catedrático de Prima de Matemática* * and the leading mathematician in Lima, to make a report.

In the meantime the public had begun to take cognizance of this Bird Man who had lived all these years unnoticed in one of the folds of the Amancaes valley, less than three miles from the heart of the city. But publicity proved disastrous. Scarcely a week had elapsed since the visit to the Viceregal Palace before the rumor spread abroad that Santiago was about to make a flight from the top of Cerro San Cristóbal to the Plaza des Armas. How the report spread is uncertain; news was always winged in Lima. Santiago himself tells us that the entire population assembled on the housetops and balconies and climbed to the towers of the churches to see the strange sight. The only possible foundation for the story was that De Cárdenas had that afternoon ridden on his mule to the top of the hill, whence he was plainly visible to the crowds below. The wind was blowing strongly and ballooned out the skirts of his riding cloak in such a manner as to give the impression of wings. Instantly shouts were raised: *Ya vuela! Ya vuela!* *

Nothing happened. The innocent cause of the popular

The Airman Experiments 139

excitement rode back to the city to encounter a furious mob, who insisted on a flight. "Either you fly," they shouted, "or we'll stone you." De Cárdenas had to take refuge in the Cathedral to escape the wrath of the disappointed Limeñans, from whose tender mercies he was with some difficulty rescued by a detachment of soldiers sent from the Palace. Thereafter popular enthusiasm for aviation and the aviator gradually waned, and was only kept alive through the medium of a popular song, *La Pava*,* which lampooned the public authorities in so indecent a manner that the Holy Office had to forbid that it should be sung in public.

In due course Dr. Bueno made his report. It is a measured and weighty dissertation befitting a scientist of European reputation; and those who are interested in the attitude of science to aviation in the eighteenth century may read the document for themselves in the Biblioteca Nacional.*

In his *Disertación sobre el Arte de Volar** Dr. Bueno begins by giving an account of Santiago de Cárdenas, whom he describes as "an individual of low character but of no small intelligence and skill"; and he then proceeds to deal with the subject of aviation without giving the slightest hint of the manner in which De Cárdenas proposed to fly or the theories which he had produced to support his claim that he could carry the royal mails from Lima to Buenos Aires by — to use the modern word — airplane. Indeed, it would seem that the worthy doctor was more concerned to show his own wisdom than to set forth the case of the man upon whom he was called upon to pass judgment.

The professor divides his dissertation into two parts. In the first, to show his open-mindedness, he weighs the reasons why man should be able to fly. We imitate the

140 *Romance of the Airman*

fishes in swimming under the sea, he argues; why should we not be able to compete with the birds in the realm of air? A condor's wings can sustain a weight of thirty-two pounds; cannot man invent wings capable of carrying a weight of one hundred and fifty pounds? Moreover, man has flown. In mythical times Dædalus was followed in the air by his son Icarus. More recently there was Rigiomortano, a celebrated astronomer and Bishop of Ratisbon, who manufactured an artificial eagle, capable of carrying a man's weight, with which he carried out successful experiments in the presence of the Emperor Frederick IV. Again, in 1700, a Portuguese flew in a machine of his own invention at a height of from three to four feet above the palace grounds at Lisbon, though unfortunately he ended by falling and smashing himself and his machine. And yet again, there was Juan Bautista Dante, who flew over the town of Perugia in Italy in the fifteenth century, finally falling on the top of a church and breaking his leg. A priest, too, flew over Plasencia and was killed. All these instances, says Dr. Bueno, prove that man can fly for short distances. Why, then, should he be incapable of sustained flights? The answer is not very definite. But the worthy professor is satisfied that in Peru, at least, distance flights are physically impossible. In attempting to fly over the Andes a man would meet his death either from asphyxiation or from cold.

Having shown so far that his mind is not biased in its attitude to aviation, Dr. Bueno proceeds to crush the poor little human fly who had dared to claim that he could outrival the birds of the air. In the first place, he unmasks a battery of great mathematical names to support his contention that man is physically incapable of flying, and, more important still, was never intended by the Divine Creator to fly. Father Kirke, Gaspar Scot, Tosco, Fran-

The Airman Experiments 141

cisco Bayle, San Aubin, Leibnitz — we may know little today of the genius represented by these illustrious names, but they bore weight, no doubt, in the eighteenth century. Mere hallucination is their verdict; a moral impossibility; flying in the face of Providence. "Alfonso Borelli, in his great work *De Motu Animalium*, proves conclusively from the flight of birds the impossibility that man should fly." It might conceivably be possible, says Dr. Bueno, to imitate the wings of a bird, but what about the tail? True, a few men have claimed short flights — or, rather, they have glided through the air. In this manner some have flown, or rather have fallen. To make any further claim than that would be a mortal presumption.

Finally, the pious spirit of the age — and possibly a hint from the Holy Office — gets the better of science. First and last, it is not God's will that man should fly. That suffices.

The conclusion of the whole matter is so characteristic that it merits to be quoted in full; the more so because it anticipates some of the terrors which aviation — in war, at least — has brought in its train:

If man had the means of daring the air, no door would be closed to concupiscence * or vengeance. Homes would become the scenes of assassinations and robberies. How should we escape our enemies when day and night they would have it in their power to surprise us? To surprise would be added cruelty, and to artifice fury. What security would there be in the land, even the most sacred?

It seems to me that if anyone should ever achieve this impossible thing, he should be cast out of the world before propagating an art so fatal and so pernicious.

There were many who in the World War might well have wished the same.

But Dr. Cosme Bueno sees no cause for alarm.

There is no reason to fear, because God in His Wisdom has placed us in our own element and the birds in theirs, an invul-

142 Romance of the Airman

nerable wall which will never be broken. Let us be content with the place which the Supreme Creator has given us and not essay foolish and impossible undertakings. Those who attempt the impossible reveal their senselessness and their illusions.

So Dr. Bueno; and we cannot but feel that according to his lights he was an honest if a bigoted man. But assuredly he was no prophet.

But not one whit was Santiago de Cárdenas dismayed by this most emphatic condemnation of his experiments. The war with England was causing a continuous interruption of communications with Spain and great annoyance to the public authorities. Santiago El Volador embraced the opportunity to present a second memorial to the Viceroy. It is a remarkable document for the age in which it was written, and proves that, in theory at least, he was well in advance of his times. He proposes — indeed, undertakes — to do what aviators today are trying to do and have not yet wholly succeeded in doing: he offers to carry the mail in three days' flight from Lima to Madrid. This is his schedule:

Lima to Porto Bello, one day.
Porto Bello to Havana, one day.
Havana to Madrid, one day.

Pathetically he confesses that this is *mucho tiempo**; but he adds, "If I could succeed in flying like the condor at eighty leagues an hour, less than a day would be needed to get to Europe."

The Viceroy Amat disappoints the hopes which we had entertained of him. Perhaps with everlasting injury to the cause of aviation in Peru, he turned the appeal down with the laconic *No hay lugar,** which has on so many occasions been the death knell to great hopes. Had he yielded a willing ear, had he opened the regal exchequer, who may say but that the name of Santiago de Cárdenas

The Airman Experiments 143

might not have ranked with Edison and Bell and the Wright brothers in benefits to the cause of science and human progress?

Once more Santiago El Volador rises superior to discouragement. He will stand before Cæsar's Judgment Seat; he will appeal to Cæsar himself. He is not without friends who in jest or earnest are willing to support him. With better faith than faces the Pinillos and the Cornejos of today, there were merchants in Lima who were willing to advance money to enable him to build a machine. But no. The king of Spain must hear his cause; and there is not lacking a relative of His Catholic Majesty, the Duke of San Carlos, who promises to put the memorial in the king's own hands.

And so, patiently and in a fair clerkly hand, he proceeds to set down in writing the cause which he seeks to plead before the eyes of the distant representative of Majesty. The original manuscript may be studied in the Biblioteca Nacional, a human document written with the pen of hope and inscribed with the ink of enthusiasm. In the course of time the ink has faded to a pale brown, so faint in parts that only with much patience and some acquaintance with archaic penmanship may it be currently read.

The manuscript is illustrated with the author's own drawings, one of which shows him with the wings of a condor in his hand and the pathetic inscription:

I had the skill to fly through space,
had not poverty held me back.

Other illustrations show condors at rest and in flight, and sections of the structure of their wings.

But it is sad to relate that, unless a great part of the manuscript is missing, — it ends abruptly at page 147, — Santiago de Cárdenas does nothing to enlighten us on the

144 *Romance of the Airman*

manner in which he proposed to navigate the air or the type of machine he proposed to construct. The greater part of his space is devoted to the story of his life and his studies of the flight of birds. He also deals at length, as Bueno had done, with the pros and cons of flying. But the great secret, the secret which was to have won for him the honor of the first transatlantic flight, is buried with him in the grave. The manuscript, so beautifully written on such thick handmade paper, never passed into the hands of the king of Spain. The Duke of San Carlos left Lima before *El Nuebo Sistema de Nabegar por los Aires** was completed. Perhaps it was never finished. The author himself died in 1766, and his name passed into the eternal oblivion of those who have tried and failed.

The whole course of the world's history would have been changed had a Peruvian in 1762 proved that man can conquer the air as surely as he rules the sea. Santiago de Cárdenas died the laughing-stock of his countrymen. He was a prophet without honor in his own country. But he was a true prophet.

Words and Phrases

To aid in understanding this selection

El Volador: the Flyer.

quebrada: ravine.

gallinazos: kites or other scavenger birds; as, buzzards. Here the term refers to condors.

Roy Soleil: Sun King, a title sometimes given to brilliant or generous rulers.

Real Audiencia: Court of Royal Judges.

Catedrático de Prima de Matemática: professor of mathematics in the university.

Ya vuela: already he is flying.

La Pava: The Turkey Hen.

The Airman Experiments 145

Biblioteca Nacional: the National Library.

Disertación sobre el Arte de Volar: Dissertation on the Art of Flying.

concupiscence: any inordinate desire.

mucho tiempo: much time.

No hay lugar: the petition is denied; more literally, not the opportune time.

El Nuebo Sistema de Nabegar por los Aires: The New System of Sailing by Air.

To add to your vocabulary

obloquy	cognizance	regal exchequer
condor	asphyxiation	archaic penmanship
viceroy	hallucination	

Informal Test (Multiple-Choice)[1]

1. Santiago expressed his plan of human flight in **1492 1533 1761 1856**

2. When he was ten years old he **went to school in Lima worked in the fields of Peru became a cabin boy on a sailing vessel**

3. As a boy he especially enjoyed **whipping tops sailing boats reading books flying kites**

4. He studied the flight of the condors for **twenty years twelve years thirty years five years**

5. At the time he made his discovery there was trouble with **the Dutch the French the English the Portuguese**

6. He guaranteed that he could carry dispatches from Lima to **Panama Buenos Aires Lisbon the Falkland Islands**

7. The viceroy was **tyrannical unapproachable open-minded courageous**

8. The matter was turned over to **the priests the king of Spain a professor of mathematics the prime minister**

[1] For directions, see page 95.

146 *Romance of the Airman*

9. When the mob demanded that Cárdenas fly, he took refuge in the Cathedral the Viceregal Palace the Amancaes valley

10. Dr. Bueno reported that Cárdenas was a man of low character and considerable intelligence and skill low intelligence and cunning small intelligence and skill

11. Dr. Bueno's final conclusion was that man would fly soon in a few centuries never when a lighter metal was discovered

12. In the second request which Cárdenas presented to the viceroy he proposed to carry the mail to Madrid in one week three days one day ten days

13. Merchants in Lima were willing to advance money to build the machine considered Cárdenas insane sent a petition to the king of Spain

14. The manuscript was never presented to the king because the relative died the king died the relative left Lima too soon

Exercises and Topics related to your Other Subjects

1. Locate on the map Lima, Callao, Valparaiso, and the Falkland Islands.

2. From your history find out what was going on in the colonies of North America and in Europe at the time of Cárdenas'(look for the Seven Years' War in Europe and for the French and Indian wars in America).

Subject for oral theme

The Work of Cárdenas compared with that of Leonardo da Vinci.

Other Readings

In this book

"Da Vinci Did it First," page 114.

"The First Official Recognition of Aviation," page 131.

From other sources

"Francisco Pizarro," in "American Explorers," by W. F. Gordy.

Benjamin Franklin as a Patron of Aviation

BENJAMIN FRANKLIN (1706–1790) was a great American statesman and diplomat and one of the signers of the Declaration of Independence. As a representative of the United States he was also instrumental in making a treaty with France in 1783. In spite of his great services to the country as a diplomat, however, Franklin found time for many other interests.

From his earliest years he appears to have had a fondness for scientific subjects. He invented the Franklin stove in 1742, a device to provide for the recirculation of heat from the fireplace in order to warm the entire room. This invention was a great boon to the people of his day. There were no furnaces, no stoves, — nothing but a "place to make a fire which warmed the face and hands while the cold air nipped at one's back and heels." Franklin might have made a fortune from this invention; but he refused to take the patent offered him by the governor of the province, saying, "As we enjoy great advantages from the invention of others, we should be glad of an opportunity to serve others by any invention of ours."

Franklin's most important discoveries are connected with electricity, but every branch of natural science was of interest to him. He wrote about light, heat, fire, air, sun spots, the stars, the tides, the wind, waterspouts, rainfall, ventilation, sound, and many other things.

The invention of the balloon in 1782, by the Frenchman Montgolfier, interested Franklin greatly, and he not only subscribed liberally toward the advancement of the new science of aviation, but watched the experiments with

148 *Romance of the Airman*

keen delight. "The progress made in the management of balloons," he wrote to a friend, "has been rapid. Yet I fear it will hardly become a common carriage in my time, though, being easiest of all *voitures* [vehicles], it would be extremely convenient to me, now that my malady forbids the use of old ones over a pavement."

Many other letters written by Franklin, and many written to him, show the interest he felt in the subject of aviation and also the store of information he had on the subject. Even when he was well past seventy years of age and deeply engaged in the affairs of the nation, he still found time for his pursuit of the new developments in aviation, and his letters show that he appreciated the importance and practicability of air transportation.

One of his many English friends writes in the following letter of the experiments being made in England.

From Sir Joseph Banks to B. Franklin

Ascent of a Balloon

Soho Square, 28 November, 1783

Dear Sir,

I am in truth much indebted to you for the favor you have done me in transmitting the copy of the *procès verbal** on Montgolfier's experiments, which I have this moment received. The experiment becomes now interesting in no small degree. I laughed when balloons, of scarce more importance than soap bubbles, occupied the attention of France; but when men can with safety pass and do pass more than five miles in the first experiment, I begin to fancy that I espy the hand of the master in the education of the infant of knowledge, which so speedily attains such a degree of maturity, and do not scruple to guess that my old friend, who used to assist me when I was younger, has had some share in the success of this enterprise.

On Tuesday last a miserable taffeta balloon was let loose here under the direction of a Mr. Zambeccari, an Italian nobleman, as

The Airman Experiments 149

I hear. It was ten feet in diameter, and filled with inflammable air made from the filings of iron and vitriolic acid. The silk was oiled, the seams covered with tar, and the outside gilt. It had been shown for several days floating about in a public room, at a shilling for the sight, and half a crown for the admission when it should be let loose.

The day was fine; the wind a gentle breeze from the north. At a few minutes after one o'clock it set out, and before night fell at a small village near Petworth in Sussex, having run over about forty-eight miles of country. The countryman who first saw it observed it in its descent. It appeared at first small, and, increasing fast, surprised him so much that he ran away. He returned, however, and found it burst by the expansion of the contained fluid. . . .

JOSEPH BANKS

Francis Hopkinson, of the Philadelphia Philosophical Society, writes to Franklin in May, 1784, telling him of the interest that some of his friends have in balloons, and suggests the possibility of the invention of a machine that will give them a progressive motion.

We have been diverting ourselves with raising paper balloons by means of burnt straw, to the great astonishment of the populace. This discovery, like electricity, magnetism, and many other important phenomena, serves for amusement at first; its uses and applications will hereafter unfold themselves. There may be many mechanical means of giving the balloon a progressive motion, other than what the current of wind would give it. Perhaps this is as simple as any. Let the balloon be constructed of an oblong form, something like the body of a fish, or of a bird, or a wherry,* and let there be a large and light wheel in the stern, vertically mounted. This wheel should consist of many vanes or fans of canvass, whose planes should be considerably inclined with respect to the plane of its motion, exactly like the wheel of a smoke-jack.* If the navigator turns this wheel swiftly round by means of a winch, there is no doubt but it would (in a calm, at least) give the machine a progressive motion, upon the same principle that a boat is sculled through the water.

150 *Romance of the Airman*

Richard Price, of the English Parliament, writes to Franklin in October, 1784, telling of the progress of aviation in England:

We have at last begun to fly here. Such an ardor prevails that probably we shall soon, in this instance, leave France behind us. Dr. Priestley, in a letter which I have just received from him, tells me that he is eager in pursuing his experiments, and that he has discovered a method of filling the largest balloons with the lightest inflammable air in a very short time and at a very small expense.

Franklin exercises the precaution credited to a man of his years when he attempts to dissuade a friend from attempting to cross the English Channel in a balloon:

Passy,* 20 June, 1785

Dear Sir,

I have just received the only letter from you that has given me pain. It informs me of your intention to attempt passing to England in the car of a balloon. In the present imperfect state of that invention, I think it much too soon to hazard a voyage of that distance. It is said here by some of those who have had experience that as yet they have not found means to keep up a balloon more than two hours; for that, by now and then losing air to prevent rising too high and bursting, and now and then discharging ballast to avoid descending too low, these means of regulation are exhausted. Besides this, all the circumstances of danger by disappointment, in the operation of *soupapes*, etc. etc., seem not to be yet well known, and therefore not easily provided against. For on Wednesday last M. Pilatre de Rosier,* who had studied the subject as much as any man, lost his support in the air by the bursting of his balloon, or by some other means we are yet unacquainted with, and fell with his companion from the height of one thousand *toises*, on the rocky coast, and were both found dashed to pieces.

You, having lived a good life, do not fear death. But pardon the anxious freedom of a friend, if he tells you, that, the continuance of your life being of importance to your family and your

The Airman Experiments 151

country, though you might laudably hazard it for their good, you have no right to risk it for a fancy. I pray God this may reach you in time, and have some effect toward changing your design; being ever, my dear friend, yours affectionately,

B. FRANKLIN

The probable importance of balloons and the knowledge Franklin had of the details of the construction of the Montgolfier balloons are revealed in a letter which he wrote from Passy, France, to John Ingenhousz, a physician to the emperor of Austria, on the sixteenth of January, 1784. It reads in part as follows:

It appears, as you observe, to be a discovery of great importance, and what may possibly give a new turn to human affairs. Convincing sovereigns of the folly of wars may perhaps be one effect of it; since it will be impracticable for the most potent of them to guard his dominions. Five thousand balloons, capable of raising two men each, could not cost more than five ships of the line; and where is the prince who can afford so to cover his country with troops for its defense, as that ten thousand men descending from the clouds might not in many places do an infinite deal of mischief, before a force could be brought together to repel them? It is a pity that any national jealousy should, as you imagine it may, have prevented the English from prosecuting the experiment, since they are such ingenious mechanicians, that in their hands it might have made a more rapid progress toward perfection, and all the utility it is capable of affording.

The balloon of Messrs. Charles and Robert was really filled with inflammable air. The quantity being great, it was expensive, and tedious filling, requiring two or three days and nights constant labor. It had a *soupape*, or valve, near the top, which they could open by pulling a string, and thereby let out some air when they had a mind to descend; and they discharged some of their ballast of sand when they would rise again. A great deal of air must have been let out when they landed, so that the loose part might envelope one of them; yet, the car being lightened by that one getting out of it, there was enough left to carry up the other rapidly. They had no fire with them. That is used only in

152 *Romance of the Airman*

M. Montgolfier's globe, which is open at bottom, and straw constantly burnt to keep it up. This kind is sooner and cheaper filled; but must be of much greater dimensions to carry up the same weight, since air rarefied by heat is only twice lighter. M. Morveau, a famous chemist at Dijon, has discovered an inflammable air that will cost only a twenty-fifth part of the price of what is made by oil of vitriol poured on iron filings. They say it is made from sea coal. Its comparative weight is not mentioned.

After his long and useful career as a diplomat in France and his return to America, Franklin, then eighty-one years old, expressed his desire to own a balloon. He writes the following from Philadelphia under the date of April 18, 1787, to M. Alphonsus Le Roy of Paris:

Your account of the progress made in the art of ballooning, by the acquisition of a tight *enveloppe* and the means of descending and rising without throwing out ballast, or letting out air, is very pleasing. I am sorry the artists at Javelle do not continue their experiments. I always thought they were in the likeliest way of making improvements, as they were remote from interruption in their experiments. I have sometimes wished I had brought with me from France a balloon sufficiently large to raise me from the ground. In my malady it would have been the most easy carriage for me, being led by a string held by a man walking on the ground.

Franklin's interest in aviation is proof of his standing as a scientist of his day. He was always observing, collecting facts, and writing out his conclusions.

The public business in which he was constantly employed and his long years of diplomatic service in England and France were serious interruptions of the scientific researches which may well be called the great passion of his life. If he had not been claimed to serve his country as a political leader, he might have been the greatest scientist of all time, and practical aviation might have been a reality a hundred years earlier.

The Airman Experiments 153

Words and Phrases

To aid in understanding this selection

procès verbal: official report.

wherry: a kind of light rowboat for carrying passengers and freight on rivers.

smokejack: an apparatus for turning a rod used in holding meat to be roasted before a fire.

Passy: the name of the village that Franklin selected for his residence. It is about two miles from the heart of Paris and not far from the court at Versailles.

M. Pilatre de Rosier: a Frenchman who made the first successful flight in a balloon.

Technical term

soupape

Informal Test (Multiple-Choice)[1]

1. Benjamin Franklin was a contemporary of **Columbus Grant Washington Lincoln**

2. Franklin's ideas concerning aviation were recorded **in his "Autobiography" in "Poor Richard's Almanac" in his letters in his scientific monographs**

3. Franklin was **31 51 71 81** when he expressed his wish to own a balloon.

4. Among the inventions of Franklin was **a stove an electric fan a telephone an automatic gun**

5. Franklin believed that the invention of the balloon would **be ignored by the public contribute to human progress retard progress be a financial drain upon the country**

Exercises and Topics related to your Other Subjects

1. The many-sided Franklin. Consult your history textbook to learn how many different political offices Franklin held.

2. Franklin, editor and author. From a recent issue of the *Saturday Evening Post* learn of Franklin as an editor. From "Poor

[1] For directions, see page 95.

154   Romance of the Airman

Richard's Almanac" learn the topics that were discussed in his day. Compare these with the topics offered by modern publications.

3. Treaties with other nations. Learn from your civics all the facts you can concerning treaties between nations. Learn from your history the treaties made between the United States and France that were negotiated by Franklin.

4. Quotations and maxims. Make a list of Franklin's maxims that pertain to thrift.

5. Franklin's environment. From any source possible collect facts concerning the historic places made memorable by Franklin and his associates that you might see if you were to visit Boston and Philadelphia today.

Other Readings

From other sources

"The True Benjamin Franklin," by S. G. Fisher. J. B. Lippincott Company.

"Benjamin Franklin," by E. L. Dudley. The Macmillan Company.

Franklin's "Autobiography."

Alexander Bell's Contribution to Aviation

DR. ALEXANDER GRAHAM BELL, the inventor of the telephone, should be named among the early patrons of aviation. His scientific knowledge and the financial aid given by both him and his wife made possible thousands of experiments with heavier-than-air flying machines. The windy hillsides of "Beinn Bhreagh,"* the Bell summer estate in Nova Scotia, furnished an excellent place for trying out the numerous kites with which Dr. Bell and his associates made their experiments.

Four friends worked constantly with Dr. Bell, one of whom was Professor Samuel P. Langley, at that time secretary of the Smithsonian Institution in Washington. Professor Langley believed so firmly that sustained flight was not only possible but also practical that he had persuaded Congress to appropriate $50,000 with which he might make experiments. Closely associated with him and Dr. Bell were Hiram Maxim, Octave Chanute, and Augustus Herring, all pioneers in aëronautics. These five men worked patiently on, despite the fact that most of the men of science of the time were either indifferent to all experimentation with flying machines or definitely opposed to it.

Dr. Bell's interest in aërial flight dated back to his boyhood days. Always a precocious child, he early showed a mind so original and of such an inventive turn that his chums recognized it by making him leader and chief "lecturer" of their "Society for the Promotion of Fine Arts among Boys"; and experimental kite-flying was merely one phase of numerous interesting and sometimes startling experiments into which he led these boyhood friends.

His enthusiasm for aëronautics grew as he reached man-

155

Romance of the Airman

hood, and it became his fondest hope that he might do something really valuable as a contribution to the science of aviation. His position as the successful inventor of the telephone had already been firmly established in the scientific world. Many of his friends, fearing that his interest in the subject of flying machines would endanger his standing as an inventor, attempted to persuade him to give up what they considered a foolish enthusiasm and to turn his attention to inventions more worth while. But it was hopeless; instead he became the sponsor of the Aërial Experimental Association, the purpose of which was to bring into closer relationship all experimenters in aviation.

All heavier-than-air machines are built on the kite principle. Every schoolboy knows that his kite flies best when it is held by a string against the wind. If there is no wind, the boy may create an artificial current by running across the field with the kite. In the modern airplane the boy and the string are replaced by a motor and a propeller that drive the kite forward to create the wind which will support it. Many forms of kites have been used by experimenters; but Dr. Bell and his friends chose as their models the huge tetrahedral, or four-sided, box type* that Hargrave first devised.

Larger and larger grew the Beinn Bhreagh kites; frames were made by the hundreds, and yards and yards of silk were sewed into winged cells. These kites taught their experimenters much about the possibilities of power-driven machines. The smoothest and best place for a take-off was a lake in the center of the Bell estate; but as this lake was frozen over only a part of the year, pontoons were devised to replace the skids used in the winter. Thus the first successful take-off from water was accomplished, and the use of the pontoons was the first step toward the development of the present hydroplane.

The Airman Experiments

Alexander Graham Bell's Tetrahedral Aërodrome
Courtesy of the Smithsonian Institution

Many interesting and amusing stories have been told of the experimenters and their work. One concerns the largest of all the kites built. When completed, it was so big that nothing short of a hurricane could move it. It was months before Dr. Bell was able to try it. Finally, a southeast gale raged all one night and part of the next day. The howling wind, which brought terror to everyone else, was music in the ears of the impatient inventor. He went to bed that night with great plans for a successful tryout the next morning. Morning came, but no workmen! Too late the experimenter remembered that the day was a holiday. To the impatient Dr. Bell the nonappearance of his men was unpardonable. He locked himself in his laboratory and posted a notice that it was closed permanently. Given a little time to think it over, however, the really kind-hearted and sensible inventor realized his folly; what to him was a tragedy was to his men merely

158 *Romance of the Airman*

an incident in the day's work. The laboratory was re-opened, and the work went on.

After many kites had been made and experimented with, it was agreed that each member of the Aërial Experimental Association should submit a design of his own. These machines the association would build in turn and try out for the inventor. Then arose the discussion of a suitable name for such machines. Dr. Bell favored the name *aërodrome**; others objected or offered substitutes. Dictionaries were consulted and editors of magazines appealed to, but finally Dr. Bell's name was accepted. Thus the term *aërodrome* first meant a "flying machine," not a "hangar," its accepted meaning today.

Lieutenant Selfridge's design was the first one built. He was a student of Otto Lilienthal's, and his machine resembled the type built by the earlier inventor. It was a biplane of cloth stretched on a flat frame. It weighed five hundred pounds, and was called *Red Wing*. On March 12, 1908, it flew three hundred and nineteen feet in what is claimed as the first public demonstration of a flying machine. *White Wing* was built next, a plane similar to the first one, but with various improvements. It made five flights totaling nearly two thousand feet. The next machine built was *June Bug*. This one, the work of Glenn H. Curtiss,* marks the beginning of his long and successful career as a designer and builder of aircraft. To explain the name, he says that the machine was begun in June, finished in June, and first flown in June, and that everybody knows he is a "bug" about flying. This was the machine which won the *Scientific American* cup, the first prize ever won by a flying machine in America. The contest took place at Hammondsport, New York, when the *June Bug* flew one and one-fourth miles and landed within a few feet of its starting place.

The Airman Experiments 159

Even while engaged in his own experimental flights, Dr. Bell maintained a keen interest in what the Wright brothers were doing. He paid for the making of photographs of their flights and insisted on the preservation of all their records, which he said would some day be recognized as making aviation history. As a regent of the Smithsonian Institution he used his influence to secure for them the Langley Medal, which was presented to the Wrights at a public gathering of distinguished guests. The presentation was made by President Roosevelt.

Thus we see that although Dr. Bell did not succeed in his desire to have his own name linked with any special achievement in the field of aviation, he was the means of bringing success to many other inventors and formulated many laws necessary for the further development of the science of aëronautics. He himself probably never realized what is evident today: that his greatest contribution to the development of aviation was the lending of his name and influence to it at the time when most men of his position were indifferent to this new development. By doing this, he removed flying and flying-machines from the realm of impractical things and placed the new science on a firm basis.

Words and Phrases

To aid in understanding this selection

Beinn Bhreagh: Gaelic term for "beautiful mountain." The estate of Dr. Bell is on beautiful Cape Breton, in Canada, and resembles many Scottish homesteads.

The Hargrave box kite was first devised by Laurence Hargrave, an Australian. Hargrave gave a fresh impetus to scientific kite-flying by the introduction of a new principle and the invention of what is known as the "cellular construction of kites." In 1903 Dr. Bell wrote, "I have had the feeling that a properly constructed flying machine should be capable

160 *Romance of the Airman*

of being flown as a kite; and, conversely, that a properly constructed kite should be capable of use as a flying machine when driven by its own propellers." In 1907 Dr. Bell experimented with a large man-lifting kite called the *Cygnet*. It was more than forty feet long and lifted Lieutenant Selfridge to a height of one hundred and sixty-eight feet, remaining in the air seven minutes. The speed plane of today is a first cousin of the kite.

aërodrome: here the word means a flying machine. It has undergone several changes in meaning. At one time it referred to an aviation course; now it is applied to a hangar. In some future time, when boys and girls read of Bell's aërodrome circling the air they will think that this great experimenter had a flight of fancy.

Glenn H. Curtiss: president of the Curtiss Aëroplane Company. He began work as a newsboy and later became a mechanic. He has won many international prizes for his accomplishments in aëronautics.

Technical term

tetrahedral

Informal Test (Multiple-Choice)[1]

1. Alexander Graham Bell was a native of   **Canada   Scotland   the United States   Mexico**

2. Scientific men of the nineties regarded experimentation in the field of aviation as   **promising fruitful results   impractical something to be encouraged   outside the field of legitimate research**

3. The words that best describe Bell's temperament and disposition are   **rigidly scientific   mercenary   generous   practical   untiring worker   spasmodic   easily influenced   sensitive   indifferent to the opinion of others**

4. Bell's friends thought that his standing as an inventor **would be endangered   would be strengthened   would be unaffected**   by his experiments with kites.

[1] For directions, see page 95.

The Airman Experiments 161

John Domenjox of Old Orchard, Maine, invented and piloted this Sail Glider

Exercises and Topics related to your Other Subjects

1. Look up in an encyclopedia some facts in regard to the Smithsonian Institution.

2. Read in your general-science literature what you can about the invention of the telephone.

3. From the reference books at hand find out the prizes that are awarded annually for contributions to science.

4. Learn from a biography of Alexander Graham Bell other interests that he had.

Other Readings

From other sources

"Alexander Graham Bell," by Catherine MacKenzie.
"Famous Leaders of Industry," by E. Wildman.
"Masters of Science and Invention," by F. L. Darrow.

III. The Airman Invents

United States Army Air Corps

The invention all admired, and each how he
To be the inventor miss'd; so easy it seem'd
Once found, which yet unfound most would have thought
Impossible.

MILTON, "Paradise Lost"

From Foot to Flying Machine

HENDRIK VAN LOON

> *Explanatory Note.* Hendrik Van Loon is an American journalist. He was born in 1882. He has been a professor of history in several American universities and has gained distinction as a writer of history for young readers. In 1923 his book "The Story of Mankind" was given the first Newbery Medal, an award made annually for the best juvenile book by an American writer. His "Story of the Bible" is another book that has been enjoyed by hundreds of boys and girls.
>
> The following selection is taken from Van Loon's "Man the Miracle Maker." In this book he shows how man has increased his natural powers by the invention of mechanical devices. The powers of the voice are increased by the megaphone, the telephone, and the radio; the power of the eye, by the telescope and the microscope; the power of the hand, by simple tools and power-driven machines; the power of the foot, by carts, wagons, boats, automobiles, and flying machines. The book is written for boys and girls, but is delightful reading for people of all ages. The many clever drawings add much to its attractiveness.

FROM the beginning of time people had envied the birds. Their freedom of movement had filled their hearts with justifiable envy. The birds were independent of roads and bridges. Rivers and seas meant nothing to them. They had even solved the problem of cold and heat by migrating from north to south and from south to north with the changes of the seasons. Attempts to imitate the birds in one form or another, therefore, were almost as old as the human race itself, and we find kites mentioned in Chinese histories of forty centuries ago.

But nothing shows quite so clearly how much man wanted to fly as the fact that in every mythology the gods are blessed with the gift of soaring through space.

Nothing, however, was done in a practical way until late in the Middle Ages, when the problem of substituting wings for feet was studied quite seriously by our old friend

166 *Romance of the Airman*

Leonardo da Vinci. He even went so far as to construct a number of flying machines which worked beautifully on paper, but which invariably refused to leave the earth whenever they were exposed to a practical test.

Nowadays we know why Leonardo was bound to fail. There was nothing the matter with the body of his artificial birds. But the human hand was not strong enough to lift these overgrown kites from the ground. And nothing could be done until the hand should have acquired a thousand times more power than it had in the sixteenth century.

The problem, however, continued to interest people. During the latter half of the eighteenth century a firm of French paper manufacturers buttoned together a number of sheets of tissue paper, made them into a balloon, filled the thing with hot air, and sent it up to the skies before a gaping multitude who promptly attacked the monster when it came down again and dispatched it with their pitchforks. But although man was now on his aërial way, he was unable to control the direction in which he was going.

With a favorable wind he sometimes could use a balloon to travel from one country to another. He even crossed the English Channel. But once in France or Great Britain, he had no means at his disposal to return whence he had come.

The same was true of the soaring machines, which were almost as old as the Chinese kites, but which were not made a subject of scientific investigation until about fifty years ago, when steam navigation and railroad trains seemed to have reached the end of their development and when there was another attack upon the skies.

The bird-shaped dinguses with which people began to slide through space in the seventies and the eighties of the last century could keep afloat for quite a long while, but a sudden gust of wind might cause their occupants to break their necks. Furthermore, it was hard to get them started,

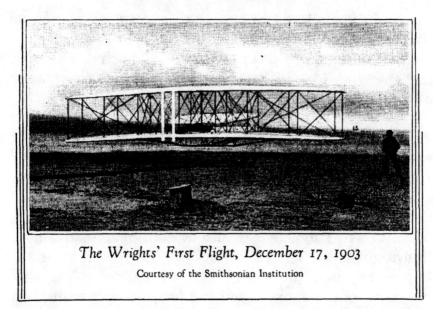

The Wrights' First Flight, December 17, 1903
Courtesy of the Smithsonian Institution

and it was even more difficult to force them to land where one actually wanted to go. And winged man remained an idle dream until the manufacturers of those multiplied hands, known as motors, had reduced their product to such small proportions and had made them so reliable that they could be used without any risk of sudden collapse or an abrupt descent to the fields below.

The Wright brothers, so it seemed, were the first to fly. Their first journey lasted only fifty-nine seconds,* but the thing had been done, and the rest was comparatively easy.

The inevitable cross-Channel voyage followed soon afterwards, and when Bleriot flew from Calais* to Dover* the whole world was convinced that now at last those old enemies of the human race, space and distance, had been successfully defeated, and that the people of the earth, united into one glorious brotherhood, would forever after live in peace and harmony.

The purring propellers of the Zeppelins, crossing and recrossing the same English Channel with their deadly

168 *Romance of the Airman*

cargo of dynamite and poison gas, once more warned us that the human foot, like the human hand, is an instrument that can be used for evil quite as much as for good, and that the Road of Progress takes strange turns, many of which run through the cemetery.

As for the future of the multiplied foot, whether in a modified form, of which as yet we have no conception, it will ever allow us to escape from our planetary prison, that I indeed do not know. But it does not appear to be outside the limits of imminent possibilities. We may have to know a little more about the laws of gravity than we do at present; we may have to discover a great many more things about our nearest stellar neighbors than we know at present; but when we realize in what miraculous way the power of the human hand and foot has been multiplied during only one short century, there is no reason why we should despair and feel that we are doomed to spend all of our days on one and the same speck of dust.

Remember one thing: we may seem to have traveled pretty far during the last five decades, but we are still terribly new at the business of using our brains. And few members of the human race have reached the point where they have the courage of their mathematical convictions.

But give them time.

Words and Phrases

To aid in understanding this selection

> **fifty-nine seconds:** the last of the four trials mentioned in the selection in this book entitled "The Experiments of a Flying Man." The first of these lasted twelve seconds.
> **Calais:** the French port nearest England.
> **Dover:** the English port nearest France.

To add to your vocabulary

> imminent   planetary prison   stellar neighbors

The Airman Invents 169

Informal Test (Completion)[1]

1. _____ were mentioned in Chinese stories forty centuries ago.

2. _____ constructed a flying machine in the late Middle Ages.

3. _____ flew from Calais to Dover.

4. We must know more about laws of _____ before we fly to other planets.

5. In the eighteenth century a firm of paper manufacturers made a _____.

6. The winged man remained an idle dream until the invention of _____.

7. The Zeppelins crossed the English Channel with cargoes of _____.

Exercises and Topics related to your Other Subjects

1. Prepare a short talk entitled "The Road of Progress sometimes turns through the Cemetery," using concrete illustrations, such as the use of the motor car in a bank robbery or the airplane in war.

2. Write a brief account of the Newbery Medal and the awards that have been made.

Other Readings

In this book

"Da Vinci Did it First," page 114.
"A Peruvian Aviator of the Eighteenth Century," page 136.
"Bleriot crosses the English Channel," page 257.

From other sources

"The Story of Mankind," by Hendrik Van Loon.
"Picturesque Chinese Kites," *Scientific American*, Volume LXXXIX, page 408.

[1] For directions, see page 14.

The Montgolfier Brothers, Inventors of the Balloon

C. C. TURNER

Explanatory Note. Note that the patent as granted by Louis XVI of France to the Montgolfier brothers carried with it a distinct social standing, as it put them in the ranks of the nobility. But it gave them no protection against imitation by unscrupulous persons. In America the national government offers protection to all inventors, but grants no social standing whatsoever.

It is a coincidence worth noting that just as the invention of the heavier-than-air machines is associated with two brothers, Wilbur and Orville Wright, so to two brothers, Stephen and Joseph Montgolfier, is generally accredited the invention of the lighter-than-air machine.

THE two brothers Stephen and Joseph Montgolfier were members of an ancient paper-manufacturing family. One of their ancestors introduced paper into the Holy Land,* and the father of the balloon inventors was the first to make vellum paper in Great Britain. The famous brothers resided in the town of Annonay,* in Auvergne.

The story goes that on a November night in 1782 they were sitting together over the fire, and while watching the smoke curl up the chimney one of them exclaimed, "Why should not smoke be made to raise bodies into the air?" There may or may not be literal truth in this story; but in a paper read before the Academy of Lyons the elder brother stated that they owed their inspiration to reading a French translation of Priestly's "Experiments relating to the Different Kinds of Air," which was, he said, "like light in darkness." From that moment they conceived the possibility of navigating the air.

Their own trade gave them the idea of a suitable material with which to make experiments, and they made a large paper bag which they filled with smoke by holding

The Airman Invents 171

it over a chafing dish. The bag distended, became buoyant, and floated to the ceiling. While they were making this experiment the widow of a neighbor who had had business transactions with them, seeing smoke escaping from the room, ran in and stood watching them. Noticing that they had some difficulty in holding the bag over the dish, she suggested that they should tie the dish onto the bag. They followed her advice, and found that it made the work much simpler. The same experiment was repeated in the open air, when the smoke-filled bag ascended to a great height. Then a bag of about six hundred cubic feet capacity was made and filled with smoke, with the result that it broke away the strings holding it down and floated away to a great distance.

It must not be supposed that the brothers Montgolfier were under any delusion as to the reason for this phenomenon, or that they ascribed any particular virtue to smoke. They probably knew that it was the hot air that possessed the lifting power, and that the smoke was only an unavoidable circumstance of the experiment. They proceeded to make a linen and paper bag 35 feet in diameter and with a capacity of about 23,000 cubic feet. When filled, this balloon rose to a height of 1000 feet and traveled a distance of a mile.

After this success they decided to give a public exhibition; and rumors of their wonderful discovery having already traveled abroad, enormous interest was aroused by the announcement that on the fifth of June the large balloon already made would be sent up into the air. Invitations to witness the experiment were sent to the State Assembly of Vivarais, then in session at Annonay, and on the appointed day an immense crowd assembled in the market place, in the midst of which stood the two brothers and their assistants. The waiting crowd had eyes

172 *Romance of the Airman*

only for the swelling balloon, a huge ball tied down over a hole in the ground into which straw and wool had been thrown for the furnace. The furnace needed the services of two men only, but to hold the impatient balloon down took up the energies of eight assistants. The bag and its frame weighed three hundred pounds. Most of the crowd were frankly cynical and refused, until they saw, to believe the declaration of the Montgolfiers that when the bag was sufficiently filled with hot air it would of its own accord ascend into the sky. Everything went on according to the program, and at a given signal the balloon was loosed. At once it shot upwards, climbing higher and higher until its altitude was estimated at about six thousand feet. It traveled a mile and a half in a horizontal direction before it came to earth.

Great public excitement and enthusiasm was caused by the news of this event, and in Paris a subscription was raised to defray the cost of further experiments with "inflammable air." The manufacture of hydrogen gas was expensive. One thousand pounds of iron filings and four hundred and ninety-eight pounds of sulphuric acid were necessary to fill a balloon of twenty-two thousand cubic feet capacity. This an experimenter named Charles resolved to do, and this, by the way, was the first occasion on which a contrivance of the kind was called a "balloon." On the twenty-third of August, 1783, the filling of the new balloon commenced in the Place des Victoires. Bulletins were published daily as to its progress, but as the crowd grew to vast proportions the balloon was moved during the night of the twenty-sixth to the Champ de Mars. A description by an eyewitness was as follows:

No more wonderful scene can be imagined than the balloon being thus conveyed, preceded by lighted torches, surrounded by

The Word "Balloon" was First applied to Charles's Invention made in 1783

Courtesy of the Smithsonian Institution

174 *Romance of the Airman*

a cortège, and escorted by a detachment of foot and horse guards; the nocturnal march, the form and capacity of the body carried with so much precaution, the silence that reigned, the unseasonable hour, all tended to give a singularity and mystery truly imposing to all those that were unacquainted with the cause. The cab drivers on the road were so astonished that they were impelled to stop their carriages and to kneel humbly, hat in hand, whilst the procession was passing.

The ascent was an imposing business. This occurred on the twenty-seventh of August in the presence of a vast concourse of people kept in order by thousands of troops. The event took place at 5 P.M., and was signalized by the firing of cannon. The balloon rose to a height of over three thousand feet in a few seconds, when it vanished into the clouds. After remaining in the air for three quarters of an hour it safely descended in a field near Gonesse, fifteen miles distant. The astonishment of the villagers may be imagined. A contemporary writer described it as follows:

On first sight it is supposed by many to have come from another world; many flee; others more sensible think it an enormous bird. After it has alighted, there is yet motion from the gas it contains. A small crowd gathers courage from numbers and approaches by gradual steps, hoping meanwhile that the monster will take flight. At length one bolder than the rest takes his gun, aims carefully within range, fires, witnesses the monster shrink, gives a shout of triumph, and the crowd rushes in with flails and pitchforks. One tears what he thinks to be the skin, and so causes a poisonous stench; again all retire; shame no doubt urges them on, and they tie the cause of alarm to a horse's tail, who gallops across the country tearing it to shreds.

The government deemed it advisable at this stage to issue the following proclamation:

A discovery has been made which the Government deems it right to make known so that alarm may not be occasioned to the people. On calculating the different weights of inflammable and

The Ascent of François Pilâtre de Rozier and the Marquis d'Arlandes in a Lighter-than-Air Machine invented by the Montgolfier Brothers in 1783

Courtesy of the Smithsonian Institution

176 *Romance of the Airman*

common air it has been found that a balloon filled with inflammable air will rise toward heaven till it is in equilibrium with the surrounding air; which may not happen till it has attained to a great height. Anyone who should see such a globe, resembling the moon in an eclipse, should be aware that far from being an alarming phenomenon it is only a machine made of taffetas or light canvas covered with paper, that cannot possibly cause any harm and which will some day prove serviceable to the wants of society.

As to the Montgolfiers, so highly were they esteemed that Louis XVI issued the following "letter patent":

To the Sieur Pierre Montgolfier,* December, 1783:

Louis, by the grace of God King of France and of Navarre, to all present and to come, greeting:

The aërostatic machines invented by the two brothers, the Sires Étienne-Jacques and Joseph-Michel Montgolfier, have become so celebrated, the experiment made before us on the nineteenth of September by the said Étienne-Jacques Montgolfier, and those that have followed, have had such success, that we have no doubt but that this invention will cause a memorable epoch in physical history; we hope also that it will furnish new means to increase the power of man, or at least to extend his knowledge.

Persuaded that one of our chief duties is to encourage persons who cultivate the sciences, and to show the effects of our good wishes to those who succeed in enriching them by happy discoveries, we have thought that this ought more especially to draw our attention to the two enlightened naturalists who share the glory of the discovery.

We have learnt that the Sieur Pierre Montgolfier, their father, is of ancient and honorable family, and that having received from his ancestors a paper manufactory situated at Annonay, in Vivarais, he has rendered it by his care and intelligence one of the most important in the kingdom, so that three hundred people are there employed. We are also informed that the said Sire Pierre Montgolfier was the first to make vellum paper, and that in 1780 the States of Languedoc, wishing to imitate the Dutch manufacture, entrusted to him the commission, by which he gave so much satisfaction, that many manufacturers copied his produc-

The Airman Invents   177

tions. These circumstances relating to the Sire Pierre Montgolfier are sufficient to place him among those large manufacturers who by their zeal, their activity, and their talents, can hope to receive the most flattering and distinguished honor we are able to accord — that of being raised to the rights and prerogatives of the nobility. But what has caused us to bestow it at once on the Sire Pierre Montgolfier is, that it may be (both) a reward worthy of the labors of the father and of the beautiful discovery of aërostatic machines, entirely owing to the knowledge and researches of his two sons.

For these causes, by our especial grace, full power, and royal authority, we have ennobled, and by these present signed by our hand do ennoble the said Sire Pierre Montgolfier, and we have honored and do honor him with the title of Squire and we wish and it pleases us that he be enrolled and addressed, as we have enrolled and addressed him, Noble, at all times, together with his children and descendants, male and female, born and to be born in legitimate marriage; that they may and like him at all times and in all places be ranked as squires, and be enabled to arrive at all degrees of chivalry and other dignities, titles, and qualities, reserved for our nobility, that they shall be inscribed in the list of squires, and that they shall enjoy all rights, privileges, and prerogatives that are reserved to them.

LOUIS

The news of the discovery of the balloon swept through the world and brought with it joy and jubilation. In England it seemed to excite envy and malice; for at that period there was little love lost between the two countries, and the people of each had the grossest misconceptions of the other. In the English periodicals of the time, claims were made that the Montgolfier discovery was really due to English experiment and research. Again, when the news reached St. Petersburg and got to the ears of the aged scientist Euler, who had himself been experimenting toward the invention of an aërostat, it is said that he had a fit and died. He had, be it said, labored under terrible physical affliction, and had been dictating to his sons a

178 *Romance of the Airman*

treatise on aërostatical globes. The news of the success of the Montgolfiers was, no doubt, a bitter disappointment.

Clearly the next step was the taking of a human being into the air by this new machine. Who would volunteer to risk his life in the cause of science?

Words and Phrases

To aid in understanding this selection

Holy Land: Palestine. It is called the Holy Land because it was the scene of Christ's birth, ministry, and death.

Annonay: a town in southern France. One of its most important industries today is the manufacture of paper. The citizens of the town have erected a monument to their distinguished citizens Stephen and Joseph Montgolfier.

Sieur Pierre Montgolfier: father of the Montgolfier brothers. *Sieur* is the French word for "lord."

To add to your vocabulary

vellum	phenomenon
contemporary	inflammable
treatise	

Technical term

aërostat

Informal Test (Multiple-Choice)[1]

1. The Montgolfier brothers were **English   Russian   French   American** scientists.

2. They lived during the **twentieth   eighteenth   sixteenth   nineteenth** century.

3. They knew it was the **hot air   smoke   material of the bag   wind** that possessed the lifting power.

4. The inhabitants were **uninterested   unexcited   fearful   very enthusiastic** over the experiments made by the Montgolfiers.

[1] For directions, see page 95.

The Airman Invents   179

5. The government issued a proclamation so that   alarm may not be occasioned to the people   the people may know of the progress made by the Montgolfiers   there may be an immense crowd in the market place when the balloon ascends   science may be encouraged

6. The patent given by the king granted to the scientists' father protection from imitation   social standing   a large sum of money a place in the lawmaking body

7. The news of the success of the balloon was received in England   with joy and jubilation   with envy and malice   with bitter disappointment   with indifference

8. Louis XVI was the king of   Italy   England   Germany France   during the   sixteenth   nineteenth   eighteenth twentieth   century.

Exercises and Topics related to your Other Subjects

1. Choose as a topic in oral English the theme "Paper-making." Study the subject in the reference books; then consult your local newspaper office as to the different kinds of paper used in printing. Learn other uses of paper.

2. Assume that you need to secure a patent to protect an invention you have made. Learn from your reference books the form of the application, to whom it should be addressed, the description of the patent, the oath that must be taken, the fee that must be paid, and the protection guaranteed by the patent. Make an application for this patent, and present it to your teacher for approval.

3. The story of the career of Louis XVI of France, from the time he became king, at the age of eleven, to the day he was beheaded, is most interesting. Read of his life.

4. Note that the French government encouraged inventions of aircraft. Find out what the United States government has done to increase interest in aviation (see "The Wright Brothers, the First Successful Flyers," page 185).

5. Compare the story of James Watt and his observations of the steam from the teakettle with that of the Montgolfier brothers as told in this selection.

180 *Romance of the Airman*

6. An experiment: Blow up a football or a basket ball as full as possible. Weigh it carefully. Allow all the air to escape; then weigh it again. Calculate the weight of the air the ball held.

7. One cubic foot of air weighs one thirteenth of a pound. How much would the air weigh in a balloon the cubic content of which is the same as your schoolroom?

Other Readings

In this book

"The Wright Brothers, the First Successful Flyers," page 185.

"The First Flyers," page 181.

"The First Dirigible to circumnavigate the Globe," page 381.

From other sources

"Marvels of Aviation," by C. C. Turner.

"Heroes of the Air," by Chelsea Fraser.

The First Flyers

FLORENCE BOYCE DAVIS

Explanatory Note. When the Montgolfier brothers were making their experiments with balloons, they made a test flight with animals, to find out whether man could breathe in the higher atmosphere. The flight referred to in this poem took place on September 19, 1783. Benjamin Franklin wrote from Paris that these first flyers returned from the balloon ascent without the loss of a bit of wool or a single feather. Other animals have taken flights. In the first crossing of the Atlantic by Alcock and Brown, two black cats accompanied their masters as mascots; on the round-the-world cruise of the *Graf Zeppelin* (1929) Lady Drummond Hay carried her dog with her.

THE brothers Montgolfier built a balloon, —
'Twas in seventeen hundred and eighty-three,
The first of its kind for the world to see, —
And it sailed like a runaway moon,
Up — and up — and up — and away,
Over the crowds at Annonay.
Those who had come to look and laugh
Were filled with awe as they watched it fly —
A globe afloat in a summer sky,
And it rode a mile and a half!

They marveled much at the sight they saw:
The linen bag of enormous size,
Slowly inflated before their eyes
Over a fire fed with straw;
Straining the cords that held it there,
Fretting to mount to the upper air,
Till, freed of its leash, 'twas off with a bound,
Hunting the sky like a winged hound.
Very excited they were that day
In the old French town of Annonay.

182 *Romance of the Airman*

The young inventors were well content
With their aërostatic experiment;
Said Joseph to Jacques: "We have tried it out
And proved she can fly beyond a doubt;
But now the thing we must make her do
Is carry a passenger or two;
Even our critics would then give heed."
Said Jacques to Joseph, "They would, indeed!"

Summer time passed; on bank and wall
Ripened the vintage* of early fall.
Versailles* was wearing a festive air;
The king, the queen, and the court were there,
And crowds that gathered, on pleasure bent,
To witness another balloon ascent.
Joseph and Jacques Montgolfier
Were this time taking a passenger —
Or two, or three, as the case might be —
On the perilous journey in the air;
No wonder the crowds were gathered there!
Ornamented with figures and foils
Strikingly done in the brightest of oils,
The big balloon was a sight to see!
Wildly they cheered it on its way
As it rose from earth that autumn day
Carrying travelers three —
Bold adventurers, skyward bound.
The welkin* rang for miles around
As over the heads of the merry crowds,
Up — and up — and into the clouds
Went the swinging cage with the gilded lock —
Bearing a sheep, a duck, and a cock!

Two miles out, in Vaucresson Wood,
They landed safely, as fliers should.

The Airman Invents 183

How the sheep, of a courage never the best,
Regarded the strange, aërial test,
Or whether the duck looked sadly back
And rent the heavens with raucous* quack,
Or the cock emitted a lusty crow
At finding the weather changing so,
Are things we shall never rightly know;

But this we may quite depend upon:
In the years to come, and the years that have gone,
Whoever has flown, or whoever may fly
As the cycles of time go wheeling by,
First of them all were they who went
On this famous trip to the firmament,
Away in the clouds their tryst* to keep —
A cock, a duck, and a woolly sheep!

Words and Phrases

To aid in understanding this selection

vintage: the grape harvest.
Versailles: a city in France near Paris.
welkin: the sky.
raucous: hoarse.
tryst: an appointment to meet.

Informal Test (Completion)[1]

1. It has been _____ years since the Montgolfier brothers built their balloon.

2. The balloon was made of _____.

3. The air that filled the balloon was heated by a fire made of _____.

[1] For directions, see page 14.

184   *Romance of the Airman*

4. The three travelers who made up the first party of flyers were _____, _____, and _____.

5. Among those who witnessed the first flight were the _____, the _____, and the _____.

Exercises and Topics related to your Other Subjects

Read to the class Tom Sawyer's explanation of the meaning of the word *welkin* (see "Tom Sawyer Abroad," Chapter V).

Other Readings

In this book

"The Montgolfier Brothers, Inventors of the Balloon," page 170.

The Wright Brothers, the First Successful Flyers

D. THOMPSON WHITE

> *Explanatory Note.* Americans are now proud of the inventors of the heavier-than-air flying machine, but they were unsympathetic toward their initial efforts and slow to recognize their final triumph. France seemed a much more appreciative country and proclaimed the Wright brothers geniuses of a high order. It is to be regretted that the original Wright plane is in a museum in England rather than in an American museum. It is often referred to as the "Wright plane in the wrong place." In December, 1928, just twenty-five years after the first flight, which lasted a little more than twelve seconds, the entire world celebrated the event with exhibitions, dinners, and speeches in which words of eulogy were profuse. Delegates from many lands attended the International Civil Aëronautics Conference and took part in the triple conferences at Dayton, Washington, and Kitty Hawk. Congress voted the Distinguished Flying Cross to the inventors. During the ceremonies in America, Frenchmen across the sea gathered to lay a wreath upon the monument to Wilbur Wright at Le Mans, where he had given the Old World its first view of the New World's invention. In London, on December 17, 1928, a historic date in the annals of aviation, a banquet was set for one hundred persons in the Science Museum beneath the widespread wings of the machine in which the first flight had been made at Kitty Hawk.

AND now, through the succession of attempts and failures, each brings its bit of information on this triumph of man over the air and leads the world to the Wright brothers, famed far and wide as the first men to fly a machine, mechanically propelled, in a free flight. December 17, 1903, at Kitty Hawk, North Carolina, on a little incline called Kill Devil Hill, the Wright brothers realized their dream of carrying a man aloft in a mechanical machine.

Before relating the scientific advances made by the Wright brothers, it is interesting to note the early life which the brothers lived in preparation for their tremendous achievement. Wilbur Wright was born near Newcastle, Indiana, on the sixteenth of April, 1867, and his brother Orville at Dayton, Ohio, on August 19, 1871. There were two other brothers in the family, and a sister, Katherine. The Wright brothers received a great deal of encouragement from Katherine, their success being speeded by her efforts. Fortunate indeed were these famous brothers in having a father who was a liberal man of broad views who encouraged original thought. At the age of seventeen Orville, following the early inclination of both brothers toward journalism, started the publication of a local weekly newspaper, of which his brother Wilbur was the editor. This publication was followed by an evening newspaper and a weekly magazine, for which Wilbur Wright wrote extensively. An evidence of the mechanical, as well as imaginative, minds which the Wright brothers possessed is the fact that they formed and successfully operated the Wright Cycle Company.

Orville Wright, standing beside the Tablet that marks the Place of the First Successful Flight in a Heavier-than-Air Machine

The first display of active interest in flying on the part of the Wrights dates back to the time of Lilienthal's untimely death. In 1901 Wilbur Wright said:

> My own active interest in aëronautical problems dates to the death of Lilienthal in 1896. The brief notice of his death which appeared in the telegraphic news at that time aroused a passive

The Airman Invents 187

interest which had existed from my childhood and led me to take down from the shelves of our home library a book on "Animal Mechanism," by Professor Marey, which I had already read several times. It seems to my brother and myself that the main reason why the problem had remained so long unsolved was that no one had been able to obtain any adequate practice. We figured that Lilienthal in five years of time had spent only about five hours in actual gliding through the air.

Unlike the others who had experimented with the all-absorbing problem of flying, the Wright brothers decided that one could not learn to fly, or build a mechanically powered flying machine, by building something that would glide. They built countless gliders, it is true, but these activities were solely for the purpose of testing out the conclusions of their predecessors. They found during the course of their early work that many of the statements and figures given in books were very far from the truth, and they decided that the only way to be certain was to obtain figures for themselves.

That the two brothers were fully aware of the difficulties which they were bound to encounter is evidenced by the statement of Wilbur, in which he says:

There are only two ways of learning to ride a fractious horse: one is to get on him and learn by actual practice how each motion and trick may be best met; the other is to sit on a fence and watch the beast awhile, and then retire to the house, and at leisure figure out the best way of overcoming his jumps and kicks. The latter system is safer, but the former, on the whole, turns out the larger proportion of good riders.

It is very much the same [in] learning to ride a flying machine: if you are looking for perfect safety you will do well to sit on a fence and watch the birds, but if you really wish to learn you must mount a machine and become acquainted with its tricks by actual trial. The balancing of a gliding or flying machine is very simple in theory. It merely consists of causing the center of pres-

188 Romance of the Airman

sure to coincide with the center of gravity. But in actual practice there seems to be an almost boundless incompatibility of temper which prevents their remaining peaceably together for a single instant, so that the operator, who in this case acts as peacemaker, often suffers injury to himself while attempting to bring them together.

Marveling at the results which Lilienthal had produced in the short space of five hours in the air, the Wright brothers determined that practice was the essential factor in learning the secret of flying. Accordingly, they worked out a scheme whereby they might practice by the hour. Wilbur Wright said:

It seemed feasible to do this by building a machine which would be sustained at a speed of eighteen miles per hour, and then finding a locality where winds of this velocity were common. With these conditions, a rope attached to the machine to keep it from floating backward would answer very nearly the same purpose as a propeller driven by a motor, and it would be possible to practice by the hour and without any serious danger, as it would not be necessary to rise far from the ground, and the machine would not have any forward motion at all.

It was for this reason that Kitty Hawk, North Carolina, was chosen for the aërial pursuits of the brothers. They chose this little settlement on the strip of land which separates Albemarle Sound from the Atlantic Ocean. In the summer of 1900 they took up their quarters there and proceeded to construct a glider with one hundred and sixty-five square feet of supporting surface.

Their first glider brought disappointment to the brothers; for they found that the lift was not nearly so great as they had anticipated. So they immediately set out to secure greater lifting power by the construction of a new glider with an entirely different camber and greater lifting surface. This new glider, the largest ever built up to that time

The Airman Invents 189

by any experimenter, had an area of three hundred and eight square feet. The results of their experiments with the glider were the discovery that control could be maintained through the use of a small surface set in front of the main planes, a rudder, and the twisting of the wings.

Laborious work followed with the glider; but the brothers were determined to fly, and they were also convinced that no time was wasted in learning every possible angle of gliding, for in that way only could they accustom themselves to being in the air. They would not attempt to fly a mechanically driven plane until they had secured all possible data to insure success.

In the following year, in September and October, 1902, nearly one thousand flights were made, many of them over six hundred feet in length, and in winds of over twenty miles per hour. After these successful journeys off the earth, the brothers started to discuss the possibilities of putting an engine in the glider and using a propeller to drive it forward.

An idea of the diverse difficulties which the brothers encountered when they first considered this problem is aptly expressed by Wilbur and Orville in 1908, in reminiscing about their then past problems. They said:

What at first seemed a simple problem became more complex the longer we studied it. With the machine moving forward, the air flying backward, the propellers turning sidewise, and nothing standing still, it seemed impossible to find a starting point from which to trace the various simultaneous reactions. Contemplation of it was confusing. After long arguments we often found ourselves in the ludicrous position of each having been converted to the other's side, with no more agreement than when the discussion began.

So through a period of studying, arguing, trying, and experimenting, the brothers built their plane, and at last were ready to make the first trial flight.

This took place, as has been said, December 17, 1903,

190 *Romance of the Airman*

at Kitty Hawk, North Carolina. There were only five people present to witness this startling inauguration of a new era in the history of the world. No newspaper reporters, cameramen, or motion-picture photographers recorded the event. The five people who witnessed the flight were John T. Daniels, W. S. Dough, A. D. Etheridge, W. D. Brinkley, and John Ward.

An interesting item about the first flight and the manner of choosing which of the brothers should fly the plane comes to light. On December 14 the brothers were ready for the trial flight, and they flipped a coin for the privilege of flying the plane. Wilbur won. Bad weather had set in; but they pushed the plane along the track runway, and the plane, after a 40-foot run, rose a few feet and stalled. That was the end of that attempt; so the next turn belonged to Orville.

On the seventeenth, the day of the successful flight, Orville was flying the plane, Wilbur running along the side to balance the machine on the 150-foot runway, which they had constructed up the side of the hill on a nine-degree slope. After a 40-foot run the plane lifted. The course of the flight up and down was erratic, due to irregularity of the air and lack of experience in handling the machine. A sudden rise would take the plane up about ten feet; then a quick downward dart would start it groundward. A sudden drop at the end of a 120-foot flight ended the first successful entrance of man into the air. This feat lasted twelve seconds.

This first flight simply began the flying difficulties of the brothers, although they realized that their ideal had been actually accomplished. They could fly, — they knew that now, — but they must now learn to maneuver the plane in circles, in turns, and in all the exigencies of flight. During the preliminary flights the plane had been flown

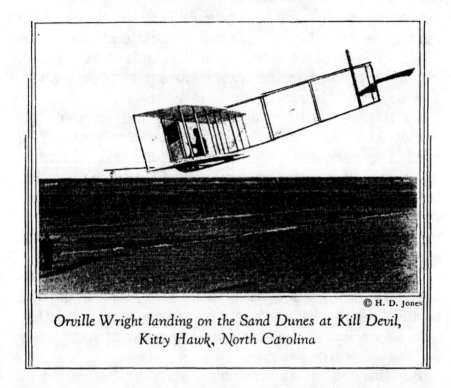
Orville Wright landing on the Sand Dunes at Kill Devil, Kitty Hawk, North Carolina

in a straight line. But this was impractical, for it necessitated landing every time the pilot wished to turn around.

The problem of turning the plane in the air was mastered by the brothers after careful thought and study. The circling was carried out by means of the patented interlocking of the wires which warped the wings and controlled the vertical rudder. When it was required to circle to the left, for example, the vertical rudder was moved to the left, and the right wing was warped slightly upwards and the left wing slightly downwards. This made the machine tilt so that the left wing was lower than the right, and the machine began to slip to the left. In doing so, however, the air struck the vertical rudder at a greater angle than was necessary to compensate for the

192 Romance of the Airman

difference in resistance of the right and left wings. This caused the tail to lag behind; and so the lateral movements of the main airplane sidewise, as the result of the tipping, became combined with a rotary movement about its vertical axis, and the machine flew in a circle.

In 1904 about one hundred flights were carried out, during which the machine left the ground only about ten feet. The disadvantage of thus flying low was that when an uncontrollable position was reached the machine landed before the method of regaining control could be found. Actually the cause of the trouble was loss of flying speed in most cases, and the trouble was correctly diagnosed and allowed for later.

The work of the Wright brothers at this time came to the attention of the United States government, and the brothers received a contract to produce a machine that would fly a hundred and twenty-five miles at forty miles an hour and carry two men.

Practically the same machine that had been used in 1905, which had flown eleven, twelve, fifteen, and twenty-four miles, was used for the government. The framework of the machine was of larchwood, and its span was forty feet. The motor developed twelve to fifteen horse power and weighed two hundred and forty pounds. The wings were covered with ordinary good-quality muslin, and the chassis consisted of skids or runners like those of a sleigh. The total weight of the machine was nine hundred and twenty-five pounds, including the motor.

At this same period attempts to fly were being made in France and other countries. Captain Ferber, in 1899, began a series of gliding experiments at the Military School at Fontainebleau, and in 1905 he made his first attempt to fly in a power-driven airplane. The unfortunate death of the captain in an airplane accident in 1909 was a great

The Airman Invents 193

loss to aëronautics, for, like the Wrights, he was a scientific investigator of distinction.

Henri and Maurice Farman, Santos Dumont, Hubert Latham, Bleriot, Voisin, and a host of others were contemporaries of Captain Ferber.

The peculiar type of machine designed by Voisin was cellular in construction, like a series of boxes fastened together. His machines were biplanes with four vertical panels between them. The propeller was behind the main planes, and the tail, also of boxlike construction, was carried on outriggers. Voisin has the credit for founding the first airplane factory in the world.

Henry Farman followed up the experiments of Voisin and designed a plane of his own with which Paulhan won the London-to-Manchester flight.

Three years after the Wrights had flown, the first officially recorded flight in Europe occurred. Santos Dumont, on the twenty-third of October, 1906, won a prize for the first flight, which was one hundred and sixty-four feet long. Only a year previously the Wrights had flown twenty-four miles, but the world was not ready to believe in their achievements.

Space does not permit an account of all the feverish flights that occurred within the next period in the history of flight, but it suffices to say that aviation was one of the paramount topics of the day.

In August, 1908, despite the fact that the Wrights had been flying for five years, the world really recognized the great achievement of the brothers. All the world knew of the Wrights by now, and all eyes were focused on the brothers and their machine. It was then that Wilbur Wright made his first flight over European soil. He remained in the air only one minute and forty-seven seconds, but that was sufficient to silence the doubters and critics forever.

194   *Romance of the Airman*

On September 21 Wilbur Wright astounded everyone by remaining in the air for over an hour and a half and flying sixty-one miles. The progress made by aviation during 1908 was due to the inspiring example of Orville and Wilbur Wright.

A hazardous undertaking in 1909 further stimulated aviation activity and interest, for in that year Bleriot flew the English Channel. Everyone was talking about aviation — everyone was keen for flying; but there were two men, the two who had done the most, who did not talk. Wilbur and Orville Wright, in the words of Wilbur, maintained the attitude that "the bird which talks most is the parrot, and it is the bird which flies least."

Flying had ceased to be a joke. It was reality. The Wright brothers and Dr. Samuel P. Langley in America, Lilienthal in Germany, Bleriot and others in France and in other countries, had started man up into the air.

In the past quarter of a century aviation has developed into one of the world's greatest industries, and it is only at the pinnacles of imagination that the world can conceive of the strides that it will take in the future.

While at the present time the public is most familiar with the airplane as a mail, express, and passenger carrier, it is used in a wide variety of pursuits, such as aërial photography, dusting of crops, forest-patrol work, scientific studies, aërial advertising, geographical study, spotting schools of fish, observing traffic congestion, searching for lost persons, surveying, map-making, representation of properties, engineering surveys, carrying supplies to inaccessible regions, first aid to devastated cities, and in many other ways.

The airplane has proved its mettle, and it is here to save time, to help in emergency, and to speed the business of the world. There is one other thing that the airplane does

The Airman Invents 195

and will continue to do, and that is to give man the triumphant exhilaration of the conquest of the air. Now man has wings; he can fly with the birds.

All honor and veneration to the pioneers who gave their intelligence, their time, and many of them their lives to the cause of aviation!

Words and Phrases

To add to your vocabulary

        erratic   decorum

Technical term   camber

Informal Test (Completion)[1]

1. Wilbur Wright was born at _____ _____ in the year _____.

2. Orville Wright was born at _____ _____ in the year _____.

3. There were _____ members in the Wright family, _____ boys and _____.

4. Orville and Wilbur operated the _____.

5. Their experiments in flying were made at _____ _____ on a hill called _____ _____.

6. The inventors were inspired by _____ _____.

7. Wilbur Wright compared learning to fly with riding a _____ _____.

8. The inventors were sure that progress in aviation had been retarded by lack of _____.

9. There were _____ men that witnessed the first successful flight made by the Wright brothers.

10. The method of determining which of the brothers should make the first flight was by _____ _____.

11. The first flight was _____ _____ long, and it lasted _____ _____.

[1] For directions, see page 14.

196 *Romance of the Airman*

12. Wilbur Wright made his first flight on European soil in the year _ _ _ _ _ _ _.

13. In the year _ _ _ _ _ _ Bleriot flew across the English Channel.

14. Five uses of the airplane are

a. _

b. _

c. _

d. _

e. _

15. Katherine Wright _ _ _ _ _ _ her brothers in their experiments with flying machines.

16. The two types of flying machines are the heavier-than-air and the lighter-than-air. The Wright brothers experimented with the _ _ _ _ _ _ _ _ _ _ _ _ _ _ _ _ _ _ type.

Exercises and Topics related to your Other Subjects

1. Consult some magazine that gives plans for building airplane models or gliders (*The Popular Science Monthly* for March, 1929, is an excellent issue) and make a plane. Study the principles of flight as you experiment.

2. Plan a talk to give in assembly on the anniversary of the first successful flight (December 17). Use as your subject "The Greatest Contribution made to Aëronautics during this Year."

3. Collect from magazines pictures of the Wright brothers and their inventions; also pictures of the inventions made by Lilienthal, Bleriot, Langley, and other contemporaries of the Wrights. Make an aviation scrapbook.

Other Readings

In this book

"Otto Lilienthal, Inspirer of the Wright Brothers," page 124.
"The Experiments of a Flying Man," page 197.

From other sources

"The Romance of Aëronautics," by C. C. Turner.
"The Big Aviation Book for Boys," by J. L. French.

The Experiments of a Flying Man

WILBUR WRIGHT

> *Explanatory Note.* It is interesting to read in the editor's note that prefaced this article when it was published in *The Independent*, February, 1904, that "recently scientists and the public generally were surprised to read a report in the daily papers that the air has been successfully navigated by a device which covered a distance of about three miles without the aid of a balloon attachment. While the distance was somewhat exaggerated, it was demonstrated that the flying machine had actually gone over half a mile before accidentally touching the ground." Contrast this with the longest nonstop flight on record today.

THE person who merely watches the flight of a bird gathers the impression that the bird has nothing to think of but the flappings of its wings. As a matter of fact, this is a very small part of its mental labor. If I take a piece of paper and, after placing it parallel with the ground, quickly let it fall, it will not settle steadily down as a staid, sensible piece of paper ought to do, but it insists on contravening every recognized rule of decorum, turning over and over, darting hither and thither in the most erratic manner, much after the style of an untrained horse. Yet this is the style of steed that men must learn to manage before flying can become an everyday sport. The bird has learned the art of equilibrium, and learned it so thoroughly that its skill is not apparent to our sight. We only learn to appreciate it when we try to imitate it.

Lilienthal's experiments in balancing began where others left off, and thus saved the many thousands of dollars that it had been customary to spend in building and fitting expensive engines to machines which were uncontrollable when tried. He built a pair of wings of a size suitable to sustain his own weight, and made use of gravity as his motor. This motor not only cost him nothing to begin

198   *Romance of the Airman*

with, but it required no expensive fuel while in operation, and never had to be sent to the shop for repairs. It had one serious drawback, however, in that it always insisted on fixing the conditions under which it would work. These were that the man should first betake himself and the machine to the top of a hill and fly with a downward as well as a forward motion. Unless these conditions were complied with, gravity served no better than a balky horse — it would not work at all. Although Lilienthal must have thought the conditions were rather hard, he nevertheless accepted them until something better should turn up; and in this manner he made some two thousand flights, in a few cases landing at a point more than a thousand feet distant from his place of starting. Other men, no doubt, long before had thought of trying such a plan. Lilienthal not only thought but acted, and in so doing probably made the greatest contribution to the solution of the flying problem that has ever been made by any one man. He demonstrated the feasibility of actual practice in the air, without which success is impossible.

From this I was led to read more modern works; and as my brother soon became equally interested with myself, we passed from the reading to the thinking, and finally to the working, stage. The wonder was not that he had done so little, but that he had accomplished so much. It would not be considered at all safe for a bicycle rider to attempt to ride through a crowded city street after only five hours of practice spread out in bits of ten seconds each over a period of five years; yet Lilienthal with this brief practice was remarkably successful in meeting the fluctuations and eddies of wind gusts. We thought that if some method could be found by which it would be possible to practice by the hour instead of by the second, there would be hope of advancing.

The Airman Invents

We found, according to the accepted tables of air pressures on curved surfaces, that a machine spreading two hundred square feet of wing surface would be sufficient for our purpose, and that places could easily be found along the Atlantic coast where winds of sixteen to twenty-five miles were not at all uncommon. Our next work was to draw up the plans for a suitable machine. After much study we finally concluded that tails were a source of trouble rather than of assistance, and therefore we decided to dispense with them altogether. It seemed reasonable that if the body of the operator could be placed in a horizontal position instead of the upright, as in the machines of Lilienthal, Pilcher, and Chanute, the wind resistance could be very materially reduced, since only one square foot instead of five would be exposed. As a full half horse power could be saved by this change, we finally arranged to try at least the horizontal position.

We began our experiments on the Atlantic coast at Kitty Hawk, North Carolina, in 1900, trying the machine as a kite. The results were very satisfactory; yet we were all well aware that this method of testing is never wholly convincing until the results are confirmed by actual gliding experience.

Our attention was next turned to gliding; but no hill suitable for the purpose could be found near our camp at Kitty Hawk. This compelled us to take the machine to a point four miles south, where the Kill Devil sand hill rises from the flat sand to a height of more than one hundred feet. Its main slope is toward the northeast and has an inclination of ten degrees. On the day of our arrival the wind blew about twenty-five miles an hour, and as we had had no experience at all in gliding we deemed it unsafe to attempt to leave the ground. But on the day following, the wind having subsided to fourteen miles per hour, we

200 Romance of the Airman

made about a dozen glides. It had been the original intention that the operator should run with the machine to obtain initial velocity, and assume the horizontal position only after the machine was in free flight. When it came time to land he was to resume the upright position and light on his feet, after the style of previous gliding experimenters. But on actual trial we found it much better to employ the help of two assistants in starting, which the peculiar form of our machine enabled us readily to do, and in landing we found that it was entirely practicable to land while still reclining in a horizontal position upon the machine. Although the landings were made while moving at speeds of more than twenty miles an hour, neither machine nor operator suffered any injury. The control of the machine proved even better than we had dared to expect, responding quickly to the slightest motion of the rudder. With these glides our experiments for the year 1900 closed.

Our 1902 pattern was changed to a double-deck machine having two surfaces, each 32 feet from tip to tip and 5 feet from front to rear. The total area of the main surface was about 305 square feet. The front rudder spread 14 square feet additional, and the vertical tail about 12 square feet, which was subsequently reduced to 6 square feet. The weight was $116\frac{1}{2}$ pounds. Including the operator the total weight was from 250 to 260 pounds. It was built to withstand hard usage, and in nearly a thousand glides was injured but once. It repeatedly withstood without damage the immense strains arising from landing at full speed in a slight hollow, where only the tips of the wings touched the earth, the entire weight of the machine and operator being suspended between.

The practice ground at the Kill Devil hills consists of a level plain of bare sand, from which rises a group of detached hills or mounds formed of sand heaped up by the

The Double-deck Glider built by the Wright Brothers in 1902
Courtesy of the Smithsonian Institution

winds. The three which we used for gliding experiments are known as the Big Hill, the Little Hill, and the West Hill, and have heights of one hundred feet, thirty feet, and sixty feet respectively. In accordance with our custom of beginning operations with the greatest possible caution, we selected the Little Hill as the field of our first experiments, and began by flying the machine as a kite.

The kite experiments having shown that it ought to be possible to glide on the seven-degree slope, we next proceeded to try it. Although on this first day it was not considered advisable to venture upon any absolutely free flights, the machine soon demonstrated its ability to glide with this angle of descent. At a later period we made more than a hundred flights the full length of this slope, and landed a short distance out on the level ground. On the second day the machine was taken to the Big Hill, and

Romance of the Airman

regular gliding was commenced. The wind was somewhat brisk. In one flight the wind struck the machine from the left and began lifting the left wing in a decidedly alarming manner. Owing to the fact that in the new machine changes had been made in the mechanisms operating the rudders, so that the movements were exactly reversed, it was necessary to think a moment before proceeding to make the proper adjustment. But meanwhile the left wing was rising higher and higher. I therefore decided to bring the machine to the ground as quickly as possible, but in my confusion forgot the change that had been made in the front rudder, and instinctively turned it the wrong way. Almost instantly it reared up as though bent on a mad attempt to pierce the heavens. But after a moment it seemed to perceive the folly of such an undertaking and gradually slowed up till it came almost to a stop, with the front of the machine still pointing heavenward. By this time I had recovered myself and reversed the rudder to its full extent, at the same time climbing upward toward the front so as to bring my weight to bear on the part that was too high. Under this heroic treatment the machine turned downward and soon began to gather headway again. By the time the ground was reached it was under fair control; but as one wing touched first, it swung around in landing and came to rest with the wind blowing in from the rear. There was no unusual shock in landing, and no damage at all resulted.

In the next trials my brother Orville did most of the gliding. After a few preliminary flights to accustom himself to the new method of operating the front rudder, he felt himself ready to undertake the management of the lateral control also. Shortly afterwards he started on a flight with one wing slightly higher than the other. This caused the machine to veer to the left. He waited a mo-

The Airman Invents 203

ment to see whether it would right itself, but, finding that it did not, then decided to apply the control. At the very instant he did this, however, the right wing most unexpectedly rose much worse than before, and led him to think that possibly he had made a mistake. A moment of thought was required to assure himself that he had made the right motion, and another to increase the movement. Meanwhile he had neglected the front rudder by which the fore and aft balance was maintained. The machine turned up in front more and more till it assumed a most dangerous attitude. We who were on the ground noticed this in advance of the navigator, who was thoroughly absorbed in the attempt to restore the lateral balance, but our shouts of alarm were drowned by the howlings of the wind. It was only when the machine came to a stop and started backward that he at length realized the true situation. From the height of nearly thirty feet the machine struck the ground. The unlucky aëronaut had time for one hasty glance behind him, and the next instant found himself the center of a mass of fluttering wreckage.

This little misadventure, which occurred almost at the very beginning of our practice with the new machine, was the only thing approaching an accident that happened during these experiments, and was the only occasion on which the machine suffered any injury. The latter was made as good as new by a few days' labor, and was not again broken in any of the many hundred glides which we subsequently made with it. By long practice the management of a flying machine should become as instinctive as the balancing movements a man unconsciously employs with every step in walking, but in the early days it is easy to make blunders. For the purpose of reducing the danger to the lowest possible point we usually kept close

204 *Romance of the Airman*

to the ground. Often a glide of several hundred feet would be made at a height of a few feet, or even a few inches sometimes. It was the aim to avoid unnecessary risk. While the high flights were more spectacular, the low ones were fully as valuable for training purposes.

In October last we resumed the trials on the Kill Devil practice ground with the machine which we had used during the previous year, and succeeded in making flights in which the operator remained in the air over a minute, at one time being suspended 1 minute $11\frac{4}{5}$ seconds. While carrying on the experiments our power machine was under construction. In dimensions it measures a little over 40 feet from tip to tip of the wings, of which there are a pair. Its length fore and aft, to use a nautical phrase, is about 20 feet, and the weight, including that of the operator, as well as the engine and other machinery, is slightly over 700 pounds. We designed the machine to be driven by a pair of aërial screw propellers placed just behind the main wings. One of the propellers was set to revolve vertically and intended to give a forward motion, while the other, underneath the machine and revolving horizontally, was to assist in sustaining it in the air.

We decided to use a gasoline motor for power, and constructed one of the 4-cycle type, which, revolving at a speed of 1200 revolutions a minute, would develop 16 brake horse power. It was provided with cylinders of 4-inch diameter and having a 4-inch stroke and intended to consume between 9 and 10 pounds of gasoline an hour. The weight of the engine, including the wheel, is 152 pounds.

We had calculated that this amount of mechanical power would be sufficient to maintain the machine in the air, as well as to propel it, the calculations being the result of gliding experiments, which showed that when the wind

The Airman Invents 205

was blowing at a rate of 18 miles an hour the power consumed in operation was equal to $1\frac{1}{2}$ horse power, while with a wind of 25 miles an hour it represented 2 horse power, being capable of sustaining a weight of 160 pounds per horse power at the 18-mile rate.

After the motor device was completed, two flights were made by my brother and two by myself on December 17 last. The apparatus had been placed on a single-rail track built on the level, the track supporting it at a height of 8 inches from the ground. It was moved along the rail by the motor, and after running about 40 feet ascended into the air. The first flight covered but a short distance. Upon each successive attempt, however, the distance was increased until at the last trial the machine flew a distance of a little over a half-mile through the air by actual measurement. We decided that the flight ended here, because the operator touched a slight hummock of sand by turning the rudder too far in attempting to go nearer to the surface. The experiments, however, showed that the machine possessed sufficient power to remain suspended longer if desired. According to the time taken of each flight a speed varying from 30 to 35 miles an hour was attained in the air.

We should have postponed these trials until the coming season but for the fact that we wished to satisfy ourselves whether the machine had sufficient power to fly, sufficient strength to withstand the shock of landing, sufficient capacity to control. Winter had already set in when the last trials were made; but these facts were definitely established, and we know that the age of the flying machine has come at last.

206 *Romance of the Airman*

Words and Phrases

To add to your vocabulary

decorum	velocity
erratic	fluctuating
equilibrium	

Technical terms

gliding	propellers
leeward	rudder
aëronaut	

Informal Test (Multiple-Choice) [1]

1. Lilienthal probably made the greatest contribution to the solution of the flying problem by **thinking about flying trying to fly talking about flying giving up trying to fly**

2. The Wrights began their experiments at **Kitty Hawk Dayton West Hill Charleston**

3. Orville Wright had the little misadventure because **he was unaccustomed to the control he neglected the front rudder one wing was higher than the other the slope was too steep**

4. The flyers stayed close to the ground because **the flights were more spectacular they wanted to reduce the danger to the lowest possible point the low flights were more easily made the wind was in the wrong direction**

5. The power machine was an improvement in flying machines because **it used a gasoline motor for power it weighed seven hundred pounds it was driven by a pair of aërial screw propellers placed behind the main wings it had sufficient power to fly it had sufficient strength to withstand the shock of landing and sufficient capacity to control**

Exercises and Topics related to your Other Subjects

1. Work out and dramatize the conversation between Wilbur and Orville Wright in which Orville is explaining why he met with the misadventure.

[1] For directions, see page 95.

The Airman Invents 207

2. Americans regret that the original Wright machine is not in a museum in this country. Find from your reference book how it came to be placed in a museum in England.

3. From your knowledge of general science tell why the Wrights were able to say with accuracy that the age of the flying machine had come.

Other Readings

In this book

"Otto Lilienthal, Inspirer of the Wright Brothers," page 124.

From other sources

"Masters of Science and Invention," by F. L. Darrow.

The Story of Zeppelin's Early Projects

C. C. TURNER

> *Explanatory Note.* Count Ferdinand von Zeppelin, born in Constance, Baden, in 1838, was one of the foremost aëronauts of his time. On July 8, 1913, he celebrated his seventy-fifth birthday by steering his twentieth airship on its maiden voyage. The greatest factory that makes lighter-than-air craft is named in his honor. It is the Zeppelin works at Friedrichshafen, Germany. It was in this factory that the *Los Angeles*, now owned by America, and the *Graf Zeppelin*, the first airship to circumnavigate the globe, were built.

No MATTER what the future has in store for aëronautical science, no matter what discoveries are made revolutionizing present methods, the name of Zeppelin will always hold a big place in its annals. His is one of the great heroic figures in aëronautical progress. The devotion of his life and the tremendous character of his projects and achievements surround his name with extraordinary interest.

Ferdinand von Zeppelin acquired his taste for ballooning during the American Civil War. He was a young officer in a volunteer German corps on the Union side, and while attached to the Army of the Mississippi he made a few ascents in captive observation balloons. On returning to Germany he soon saw service again in the war against Austria in 1866, in which he served with distinction. Four years later, in the war against France, he had a company of Württemberg cavalry. Again he won distinction, this time by riding with three or four comrades far into French territory and obtaining valuable information. He was the only survivor. On retiring from the colors he devoted himself to his pet project of airship construction, spending his own money freely in experiments and starting a company for the purpose of raising further money when his own failed. Zeppelin was able to begin work on an airship in 1898, and it was ready for trial ascents in July, 1900.

From the moment of the first trial of this enormous airship Zeppelin had the hearts of his fellow countrymen. From that instant he became one of the most conspicuous figures in his time, and his gigantic battle with misfortune, which came in the shape of accident and disaster to successive airships which he built, was watched with fascination. His history is a long record of misadventure and disaster interspersed with occasional triumph.

Count Ferdinand von Zeppelin
Courtesy of Luftschiffbau Zeppelin

Zeppelin's first balloon was the largest that had ever been made, and it differed from previous dirigible balloons in being of the rigid type.

In the first Zeppelin airship the gas containers, of which there were sixteen, having a total capacity of 400,000 cubic feet, were inclosed in a long aluminum framework covered with linen and silk. The interior was divided into sections, each of which contained one of the gas bags. The total length was 420 feet, and its diameter was 38 feet. There were two cars, each carrying a motor of 16 horse power; and each motor drove two four-bladed screw pro-

Romance of the Airman

pellers. A sliding weight was used to raise or lower the front of the balloon, so that when in motion it would be driven slightly up or down, apart from the equilibrium obtained by the buoyancy of its gas.

The construction of the outer envelope was a matter of supreme importance. It provided a smooth surface, protected the gas envelope from injury, and, above all, maintained the shape of the balloon. In the non-rigid and semi-rigid types loss of gas or the contraction of gas due to cold is accompanied by the shrinkage of the envelope, when the pressure against the atmosphere makes a huge "pocket" in the balloon, and it becomes impossible to make any headway. In these circumstances the airship becomes helpless in the wind. Within certain limits the ballonet employed in non-rigid and semi-rigid airships obviates this difficulty; for by pumping air into the ballonet, which is inside the gas envelope, the space caused by shrinkage of the gas is taken up and the outward form of the balloon is maintained.

The weight of Zeppelin's rigid framework was a serious drawback. It necessitated a balloon of unprecedented size in order that there might be a sufficient margin of lifting power to carry it. Even so, it could not be made of any great thickness, and was so weak, in fact, that Maxim pointed out that the retention of its shape was largely dependent upon the retention of the full amount of gas in the envelopes. As the gas envelopes lost gas, said Maxim, the resisting power of the aluminum case became less.

The building of this monster divided aëronauts into two schools, the pro-Zeppelins* and the anti-Zeppelins.* Surcouf, the famous French airship builder, declared that the rigid frame was an absurdity. . . . Both he and Maxim, on the day before the trial of one of Zeppelin's later airships, predicted disaster, and their prophecy was fulfilled. . .

1909 Zeppelin Model
Courtesy of Luftschiffbau Zeppelin

The first ascent was made in July, 1900, when the winch that worked the sliding weight was broken, and the whole balloon was so bent that the propellers could not be properly worked. The maximum speed attained was only eight and one-half miles per hour, and it was impossible to steer, as the ropes used for this purpose became entangled. On descending to Lake Constance, where the balloon had its floating shed, further injury was sustained by running on a pile. On October 31 a further attempt was made, when a speed of twenty miles an hour was reached. This exceeded that obtained on any previous dirigible balloon, and accordingly Zeppelin was hailed throughout Germany as the conqueror of the air and as the inspired

212 *Romance of the Airman*

inventor who was to give his Fatherland the world-wide dominion which the patriotic desired.

From that time Zeppelin's career consisted of alternate disappointment and success, disaster and triumph. No one man, with the exception of Santos-Dumont, had made so many airships as Zeppelin, and the Brazilian's little fleet consisted of comparatively insignificant vessels, its aggregate value not equaling that of one Zeppelin.

The cost of a Zeppelin airship was, indeed, heavy, and it took all the funds he was able to raise, helped by the fact that German factories supplied him with materials at cost price, to construct the second airship, with which a first flight was made in January, 1906. On that occasion the weather favored the ascent; yet within a few minutes a gusty wind sprang up which tested the endurance of the airship and the stability and the skill of the aëronaut to the utmost. It managed, however, to make a safe descent, but only to be destroyed during the night by a gale.

Words and Phrases

To aid in understanding this selection

> **pro-Zeppelins:** those who believed, as did Zeppelin, that the rigid type of airship would prove the most successful.
>
> **anti-Zeppelins:** those who believed that Zeppelin's ideas were unpractical.
>
> **Santos-Dumont:** Santos-Dumont was born in Brazil, was educated in France, and resided in Paris after his father's death. His first attempt at flying was made in Paris in 1897 in a spherical balloon.

To add to your vocabulary

retention	stability	aggregate	annals

Technical terms

ballonet	buoyancy	winch	balloon
aëronaut	propeller	dirigible	semi-rigid

The Airman Invents
213

Informal Tests (Multiple-Choice and Completion)[1]

1. Zeppelin was born in **France Germany the United States Austria Holland**

2. The Zeppelin is a dirigible of the **rigid non-rigid semi-rigid** type.

3. Zeppelin's pet project was _____ _____.

4. Zeppelin will always hold a place in the annals of _____ science.

5. Zeppelin made his first balloon ascension in · **Germany France the United States Austria Italy**

6. Zeppelin's first airship was completed in the year _____.

7. _____ and _____ predicted disaster before the trial of one of Zeppelin's airships.

8. During his lifetime Zeppelin was **loved disliked tolerated denounced rejected** by the people of his country.

9. _____ was a famous French airship-builder of this period.

10. The speed made per hour by Zeppelin's first balloon was **ten miles five and one-half miles twenty miles eight and one-half miles seventeen miles**

Informal Test (Matching)[2]

Match the names of the men with the country where each was born.

1. **Maxim**	Germany
2. **Santos-Dumont**	the United States
3. **Zeppelin**	France
4. **Surcouf**	Brazil

Exercises and Topics related to your Other Subjects

1. Write a biography of Ferdinand von Zeppelin.

2. Tell of the use made of the Zeppelins during the World War.

3. Describe the first Zeppelin.

[1] For directions, see pages 95 and 14.
[2] For directions, see page 9.

214 *Romance of the Airman*

4. Make a booklet containing pictures of the first Zeppelins made and of those made recently and now in use.

5. Read an account of a trip in a modern Zeppelin. Report on this reading to the class. Use a map to make the route.

Other Readings

In this book

"My First Balloon Ascent," page 217.

From other sources

"Crossing the Ocean by Zeppelin," by H. Allen, *The Living Age*, June, 1929.

"Inside the *Graf Zeppelin*," by C. C. Rosendahl, *Scientific American*, March, 1929.

"Zeppelins and Super-Zeppelins," by R. P. Hearne.

"Aviation," by A. E. Berriman.

"Artificial and Natural Flight," by H. S. Maxim.

"My Airships: a Story of My Life," by Alberto Santos-Dumont.

"History of Aëronautics," by A. Rotch.

IV. The Airman becomes a Pathfinder

© Byrd Antarctic Expedition

Cloudless skies and windless streams,
Silent, liquid, and serene;
As the birds within the wind,
As the fish within the wave,
As the thoughts of man's own mind
Float through all above the grave,
We make there our liquid lair,
Voyaging cloudlike and unpent
Through the boundless element.
                    SHELLEY, "Prometheus Unbound"

My First Balloon Ascent

ALBERTO SANTOS-DUMONT

Explanatory Note. Alberto Santos-Dumont, an aëronaut and designer of dirigible balloons, was born in Brazil in 1873. He was the son of a rich coffee planter. From an early age he was interested in mechanics and engineering and especially in the literature of aëronautics. In 1897 he made his first ascent at Paris. Soon afterwards he constructed a spherical balloon in which new and original ideas were embodied, and he was the first to succeed in applying a gasoline engine and a screw propeller to an airship. After building a series of airships in which he made flights, Santos-Dumont, in his sixth balloon, succeeded on October 19, 1901, in making a trip from Saint-Cloud to and around the Eiffel Tower and back to the starting point in thirty minutes forty and one-half seconds. The trip won the coveted prize of 100,000 francs offered to the aëronaut who should make the journey in thirty minutes.

The selection given here describes his experiences on his first ascent.

At 11 A.M. all was ready. The basket rocked prettily beneath the balloon, which a mild, fresh breeze was caressing. Impatient to be off, I stood in my corner of the narrow wicker basket with a bag of ballast in my hand. In the other corner M. Machuron gave the word: "Let go, all!"

Suddenly the wind ceased. The air seemed motionless around us. We were off, going at the speed of the air current in which we now lived and moved. Indeed, for us there was no more wind; and this is the first great fact of all spherical ballooning. Infinitely gentle is this unfelt movement forward and upward. The illusion is complete: it seems not to be the balloon that moves, but the earth that sinks down and away.

At the bottom of the abyss which already opened almost a mile below us, the earth, instead of appearing round like a ball, shows concave, like a bowl, by a peculiar phenome-

218 *Romance of the Airman*

non of refraction whose effect is to lift up constantly to the aëronaut's eyes the circle of the horizon.

Villages and woods, meadows and châteaux,* pass across the moving scene, out of which the whistling of locomotives throws sharp notes. These faint, piercing sounds, together with the yelping and barking of dogs, are the only noises that reach one through the depths of the upper air. The human voice cannot mount up into these boundless solitudes. Human beings look like ants along the white lines that are highways; and the rows of houses look like children's playthings.

While my gaze was still held fascinated on the scene, a cloud passed before the sun. Its shadow cooled the gas in the balloon, which wrinkled and began descending, gently at first and then with accelerated speed, against which we strove by throwing out ballast. This is the second great fact of spherical ballooning — we are masters of our altitude by the possession of a few kilos of sand!

Regaining our equilibrium above a plateau of clouds almost two miles high, we enjoyed a wonderful sight. The sun cast the shadow of the balloon on this screen of dazzling whiteness, while our own profiles, magnified to giant size, appeared in the center of a triple rainbow! As we could no longer see the earth, all sensation of movement ceased. We might be going at storm speed and not know it. We could not even know the direction we were taking, save by descending below the clouds to regain our bearings!

A joyous peal of bells mounted up to us. It was the noonday Angelus, ringing from some village belfry. I had brought up with us a substantial lunch of hard-boiled eggs, cold roast beef and chicken, cheese, ice cream, fruits and cakes, champagne, coffee and chartreuse. Nothing is more delicious than lunching like this above the clouds in a spherical balloon. No dining-room can be so marvelous in

The Airman becomes a Pathfinder 219

its decoration. The sun sets the clouds in ebullition,* making them throw up rainbow jets of frozen vapor like great sheaves of fireworks all around the table. Lovely white spangles of the most delicate ice formation scatter here and there by magic, while flakes of snow form moment by moment out of nothingness, beneath our very eyes, and in our very drinking-glasses!

I was finishing my little glass when the curtain suddenly fell on this wonderful stage-setting of sunlight, cloud billows, and azure. The barometer rose rapidly five millimeters, showing an abrupt rupture of equilibrium and a swift descent. Probably the balloon had become loaded down with several pounds of snow, and it was falling into a cloud.

We passed into the half-darkness of the fog. We could still see our basket, our instruments, and the parts of the rigging nearest us; but the netting that held us to the balloon was visible only to a certain height, and the balloon itself had completely disappeared. So we had for a moment the strange and delightful sensation of hanging in the void* without support — of having lost our last ounce of weight in a limbo of nothingness, vaporous, somber, and portentous!

After a few minutes of fall, slackened by throwing out more ballast, we found ourselves under the clouds at a distance of about one fifth of a mile from the ground. A village fled away from us below. We took our bearings with the compass and compared our route-map with the immense natural map that unfolded below. Soon we could identify roads, railways, villages, and forests, all hastening toward us from the horizon with the swiftness of the wind itself!

The storm which had sent us downward marked a change of weather. Now little gusts began to push the balloon

220 *Romance of the Airman*

from right to left, up and down. From time to time the guide-rope — a great rope dangling one hundred yards long below our basket — would touch earth; and soon the basket too began to graze the tops of trees.

What is called "guide-roping" thus began for me under conditions peculiarly instructive. We had a sack of ballast at hand; and when some special obstacle rose in our path, like a tree or a house, we threw out a few handfuls of sand to leap up and pass over it. More than fifty yards of the guide-rope dragged behind us on the ground; and this was more than enough to keep our equilibrium under the altitude of one hundred yards, above which we decided not to rise for the rest of the trip.

This first ascent allowed me to appreciate fully the utility of this simple part of the spherical balloon's rigging, without which its landing would usually present grave difficulties. When, for one reason or another, — humidity gathering on the surface of the balloon, a downward stroke of wind, accidental loss of gas, or, more frequently, the passing of a cloud before the face of the sun, — the balloon came back to earth with disquieting speed, the guide-rope would come to rest in part on the ground, and so, unballasting the whole system by so much of its weight, stopped, or at least eased, the fall. Under contrary conditions any too rapid upward tendency of the balloon was counterbalanced by the lifting of the guide-rope off the ground, so that a little more of its weight became added to the weight of the floating system of the moment before.

Like all human devices, however, the guide-rope, along with its advantages, has its inconveniences. Its rubbing along the uneven surfaces of the ground — over fields and meadows, hills and valleys, roads and houses, hedges and telegraph wires — gives violent shocks to the balloon. Or it may happen that the guide-rope, rapidly unraveling the

The Airman becomes a Pathfinder   221

snarl in which it has twisted itself, catches hold of some asperity of the surface or winds itself around the trunk or branches of a tree. Such an incident was alone lacking to complete my instruction.

As we passed a little group of trees a shock stronger than any hitherto felt threw us backward in the basket. The balloon had stopped short and was swaying in the wind-gusts at the end of its guide-rope, which had coiled itself around the head of an oak. For a quarter of an hour it kept us shaking like a salad-basket; and it was only by throwing out a quantity of ballast that we finally got our-selves loose. The lightened balloon made a tremendous leap upward and pierced the clouds like a cannon ball. In-deed, it threatened to reach dangerous heights, considering the little ballast we had remaining in store for use in descend-ing. It was time to have recourse to effective means — to open the maneuver valve and let out a portion of our gas.

It was the work of a moment. The balloon began de-scending to earth again, and soon the guide-rope again rested on the ground. There was nothing to do but to bring the trip to an end, because only a few handfuls of sand remained to us.

He who wishes to navigate an airship should first prac-tice a good many landings in a spherical balloon; that is, if he wishes to land without breaking balloon, keel, motor, rudder, propeller, water-ballast cylinders, and fuel-holders.

The wind being rather strong, it was necessary to seek shelter for this last maneuver. At the end of the plain a corner of the Forest of Fontainebleau was hurrying toward us. In a few moments we had turned the extremity of the wood, sacrificing our last handful of ballast. The trees now protected us from the violence of the wind; and we cast anchor, at the same time opening wide the emergency valve for the wholesale escape of the gas.

Romance of the Airman

Alberto Santos-Dumont Dirigible No. 9, built in 1903
Courtesy of the Smithsonian Institution

The twofold maneuver landed us without the least dragging. We set foot on solid ground, and stood there, watching the balloon die. Stretched out in the field, it was losing the remains of its gas in convulsive agitations, like a great bird that dies beating its wings.

Words and Phrases

To aid in understanding this selection
    château: the French word for *castle*.
    ebullition: the act of boiling up.
    hanging in the void: hanging in an empty space.

To add to your vocabulary

| infinite | abyss | accelerated | humidity |

Technical terms

| ballast | keel | rudder | propeller |

The Airman becomes a Pathfinder 223

Informal Test (Multiple-Choice)[1]

1. To the passengers in the balloon the earth appeared **round concave flat**

2. The shadow from the cloud cooled the gas, causing the balloon to **ascend stop descend**

3. The guide-rope touching the uneven surfaces of the earth causes the balloon to **rise descend receive a shock**

4. He who wishes to navigate an airship should first practice **landing taking off the mechanics of flying**

Informal Test (Completion)[2]

1. The throwing out of ballast causes the balloon to _ _ _ _ _ _.

2. When the passengers could no longer see the earth, the movement of the balloon seemed to _ _ _ _ _ _.

3. Without the _ _ _ _ _ _ the landing of a balloon would usually present grave difficulty.

4. When the emergency valve is opened, the balloon _ _ _ _ _ _.

5. In landing, the balloon was protected from the wind by the _ _ _ _ _ _.

Exercises and Topics related to your Other Subjects

1. Draw a map of France, showing the place where the balloon took off and where it landed. Use the scale of miles and measure the distance between the two points.

2. Construct a toy balloon that will represent the one in the story. Show the guide-rope and the location of the ballast. Be able to tell briefly how and when each is used.

3. Paint one of the scenes described in the story, showing the balloon in the air. See if your classmates can tell which paragraph you have illustrated.

[1] For directions, see page 95. [2] For directions, see page 14.

224 *Romance of the Airman*

4. Are balloons of commercial value? Prove your answer by giving up-to-date facts.

5. What men besides Santos-Dumont have helped to make air travel possible?

Other Readings

In this book

"The Montgolfier Brothers, Inventors of the Balloon," page 170.

From other sources

"My Airships," by Alberto Santos-Dumont.

A Record-breaking Balloon Voyage

HENRY HELM CLAYTON

> **Explanatory Note.** In 1885 Professor A. Lawrence Rotch founded the Blue Hill Meteorological Observatory, just outside Boston. Here he carried on careful scientific investigations until his death in 1912, when the observatory and grounds became the property of Harvard University.
>
> The international balloon contest of 1907 was the second held to compete for the James Gordon Bennett Cup. The cup had been won the previous year by two Americans of the United States Weather Bureau, representing the National Geographic Society. Their record had been four hundred and two miles.

Why the Voyage was Made

IN SOME moment of rest or recreation in the open air everyone must have looked into the blue sky, seen the snowy masses of cloud, and wondered to what unknown haven they were drifting. For me the study of the sky and the weather has an irresistible fascination. In my youth I watched the clouds with eager interest; and in my manhood I have spent many years in observing and pondering over the meanings of their various shapes and motions, because I believe they hold secrets of great interest to the human race. Stop the vast flow of invisible vapor of which the cloud is but a visible symbol, and within a single year every wheel of industry would cease to turn, and our own busy land would be as silent and tenantless as the great Sahara; the summer sun would no more woo the fields to verdure; and the trees of our groves and forests would be but bare and lifeless trunks. Fortunately no such grand catastrophe is likely to occur; but the variations of rainfall from month to month and year to year have a very great influence on our lives and

226   *Romance of the Airman*

comfort, and a knowledge of the laws of these changes will aid much in increasing the good, and decreasing the evil, of their effect. I have hoped to aid in wresting these secrets from nature; but the study of the clouds has also had for me another interest, because I believe that the air is one day to be the highway of human travel, and a knowledge of its currents will aid in making its navigation safe and rapid.

The Blue Hill Meteorological Observatory, with which I am connected, has won a place among the leading observatories of the world for its researches concerning the conditions of the upper air, and the director, Professor A. Lawrence Rotch, is widely known in Europe. For this reason, when the interested aëronauts of the great nations of Europe began to make arrangements for the first international balloon contest, to be held in America, naturally they sought information from the observatory in regard to the conditions likely to be met here. All the contestants had studied the problem of the balloon and its equipment, and had provided themselves with the best balloons and instruments that the present state of the art permits. The pilots were all experienced men, and all had given much thought to the use of favorable air currents in ballooning. The Germans, particularly appreciative of scientific knowledge and the advantages of expert advice, invited the director of the Blue Hill Observatory to go as aide in one of their balloons. Not finding it convenient to go himself, the director asked me to represent the observatory in this voyage. And so it happened that I was to undertake to map out the best air currents for a balloon to take, in order to reach the greatest distance from its starting point at St. Louis, and to put into actual practice what I had often planned in imagination.

The Airman becomes a Pathfinder 227

Provided with heavy wraps for the balloon voyage, I arrived at St. Louis on October 20, the morning before the race. Already the air was full of eager preparation and expectancy. The newspapers contained full accounts of receptions given to the visiting aëronauts, pungent paragraphs concerning the characteristics of the individuals, and vivid descriptions of the preliminary trial trips in the balloons. Most of the aëronauts had come from far-distant lands, and some of them had only a limited command of English. Under the inspiration of the Aëro Club of St. Louis many thousands of dollars had been contributed toward the promotion of this unique race, a section of the city's gas plant had been reserved for the purpose of making a light gas especially for the balloons, and about three hundred soldiers had been detailed from the United States army to aid in protecting and launching the balloons. All this careful preparation assured the filling and dispatching of the balloons with exemplary promptness. On the afternoon of my arrival I was called to meet the officials conducting the race and the contestants for the prize. At this meeting the rules of the contest were discussed and agreed upon. It was decided that whenever any contestant came to the ground voluntarily and landed, the race was over for him — he would not be allowed to rise again; but much discussion arose in regard to the time that might be given for a contestant to free himself if his trail-rope became entangled with objects below. It was agreed that fifteen minutes were to be allowed in case of such an accident, at the end of which time, if he had not freed himself, he was to be considered as having landed. It was decided that the distance should be measured in a straight line from St. Louis to the point of landing.

228 Romance of the Airman

Preparations for the Voyage

The morning of the race found me busy in aiding my German friends in the preparation of the balloons for a start. All the balloons were spread out, each on a large sheet of canvas, with the valve uppermost and the mouth next the gas main. Next, the various lines were attached: first, a line for operating the valve and allowing the gas to escape when necessary; second, a line for ripping open the top of the balloon and thus letting out all the gas at once. This line was to be used only at the moment of landing. Its employment is comparatively new, and it is one of the most useful of the various devices for rendering ballooning safe. So secure did the pilot of our balloon, the *Pommern*, feel in its use that the anchor usually carried was dispensed with.

In order to place these ropes properly, a man had to crawl down through the empty balloon and come out at its mouth. After the arrangement of these details, the net to which the basket is attached when in place was quickly spread over the balloon under the skillful guidance of our pilot, Mr. Erbsloeh.

Before noon all the balloons were ready to receive the supply of gas which was to carry them aloft, and within less than two hours afterwards, the gas main being connected with all the balloons simultaneously, they became swelling globes, some twenty-five or thirty feet in diameter, towering above the ground and gently oscillating in the breeze.

As a check on the movements of the contestants and to provide material for a study of the race afterwards, the Aëro Club at St. Louis gave each contestant a sealed, self-recording barometer which traced on a sheet every movement of the balloon in a vertical direction, and thus showed

The Airman becomes a Pathfinder   229

at what height it was sailing at each moment in its course, making it impossible for any contestant to descend to earth without a record of the event. These packages were placed in the baskets of the balloons by the judges themselves, with instructions that they were to be returned with the seal unbroken immediately after landing.

In addition to these instruments we had recording barometers of our own, thermometers of a delicate kind for recording temperature, and compasses of various sizes and shapes. In use the thermometers are whirled outside of the basket of the balloon as far as one can reach, in order that the temperature may be obtained away from the balloon and not be affected by the temperature of the observers' bodies.

The rules of the contest were that the balloons should ascend following one another in rapid succession. That in which I was to aid, and of which Oscar Erbsloeh was the pilot, was assigned by lot the first place in the list. We were provided with red envelopes by the committee, with instructions to throw them overboard at the end of each two hours and as near as possible to towns, so that they might more readily be found. We also had a number of blanks placed in envelopes addressed to various newspapers, which we were requested to fill out and throw overboard, giving our position and speed at the time.

Before all this preparation was complete, throngs had begun to gather to see the race. Nearly an hour before the time of our departure the streets immediately around the balloon field were dense with people. During this last hour crowds came streaming in from every direction. All the surrounding towns and cities contributed to the gathering, and some sightseers had come from as far as Boston and New York. Before the ascent of the first balloon every seat on the stands erected for ticket-holders was taken, and

Ready for the Departure at a Gordon Bennett Race

a crowd, estimated by the newspapers at three hundred thousand, surrounded the field of operations to witness the first race of this kind ever held in America.

The Beginning of the Voyage

Five minutes before the time of starting, Mr. Glidden, the timekeeper, began to call off the elapsing minutes and then, during the last minute, the elapsing intervals of ten seconds. This was a hurried period of final preparation; sand bags for ballast were hung all around our basket, which was the smallest of the nine, until its dimensions seemed nearly doubled. Finally, after several bags of ballast had been added and removed, the balance was adjusted so as to give only a slight excess of lift, and the

The Airman becomes a Pathfinder 231

Pommern was ready to carry Mr. Erbsloeh and myself on our long journey. A few seconds after four o'clock the order to depart was given. We grasped the hands of our friends in a final farewell, the restraining hands of the soldiers were removed, and slowly the earth began to recede from us. A wild, tumultuous cheer burst from the waiting thousands, and I waved my hat in return to the waving hats and handkerchiefs below. The balloon was rising and moving northward without the slightest jar or jolt, such as one ordinarily associates with motion, and it was difficult to realize that we were not stationary and the world spinning beneath us. Soon the great city of St. Louis lay spread out below us as on a map. The houses and street cars looked like toys, and the men like creeping ants.

The upper currents of the atmosphere in the United States almost always move toward some point between northeast and southeast, usually nearly east. We had discussed our course the previous evening at dinner, and Mr. Erbsloeh, deferring to my opinion about the best current to take, agreed to seek this upper current immediately after leaving St. Louis, and to make directly for the Atlantic coast, going south of the lake region. We wished to reach the coast as far north as possible, because in that direction the land stretched to the greatest distance from St. Louis, and it was agreed that we should ascend or descend as was necessary during the voyage in order to find favoring currents. About half an hour before the ascent of our balloon one of the small sounding balloons* which were then being liberated daily from St. Louis by Mr. S. P. Fergusson for Professor Rotch, was set free, somewhat in advance of the usual hour, for the purpose of aiding the balloonists. The air currents near the earth's surface were toward the north or northwest; but this small balloon showed that the eastward upper current

232 *Romance of the Airman*

which we sought was to be found at a height of about one mile and a half, and, throwing out sufficient ballast, we rose at once to find it. This maneuver rendered our balloon one of the most conspicuous in the race, as is shown by the following remarks from the St. Louis *Republic* on the morning following the race:

The *Pommern* first, and then the *America*, made the brightest marks in the sky. Experts said the *Anjou* held the most gas, but the German far and away was the most conspicuous in the heavens. High and far she soared, and far and high went the others, but always was the *Pommern* the most majestic. Long after the business-like *United States* had swept out of sight, lost in the murk of haze to the northwest, the pride of the Teutons hung a sapphire sun in an opalescent sky, high in the north. "It is magnificent, but not good ballooning," said a veteran; "the others are sailing lower and making more distance." Nevertheless was the *Pommern* a sight good for the eye.

A Night in the Sky

This remark of the veteran, confirmed by all the experts with whom I have discussed the matter since, showed that Mr. Erbsloeh, with the audacity of youth and confidence in his ability as a balloonist, and I, with the audacity of my ignorance of ballooning, but desirous of utilizing the air currents to the best advantage, had broken the tradition of long-distance ballooning, which is to keep near the earth, at least during the first night out. At the height of about a mile and a quarter we found a current moving toward the northeast with a speed of about twenty-two miles an hour. Here the ascent of the balloon was checked, and at this level we prepared to spend the night. It was now past sunset. In finding our course we had crossed the lower Missouri near its mouth and then the Mississippi near the city of Alton, Illinois. The sun had set in a deep

The Airman becomes a Pathfinder 233

haze, a glowing ball of fire; but the adjustments necessary to beginning our journey had prevented much note of this, our first sunset. It was about 6 P.M. when we passed the twin cities of Alton and Upper Alton, their brilliant electric lights sparkling in the gathering dusk like swarms of fireflies on a summer evening.

We watched these glowing lights amid a silence more profound than any I have ever known. After we left St. Louis the roar of the city sank to a soft murmur and then ceased, and now not a sound was to be heard, not even the rustle of the wind, because we were moving with the wind and hence in a dead calm. One often speaks of "the silent wood," but in the midst of the wood are heard the rustlings of the leaves and the myriad voices of nature; only in a balloon far above the earth is absolute silence to be found, a silence as of death. Onward we drifted through the night, past the twinkling lights of various towns, and the scenery below us, bathed in the mellow moonlight, was like a fairyland of toy gardens and glistening brooks.

As we passed over towns, we threw overboard the notices provided for giving the press information of our progress. In order to cause these notices to be more easily found, I bought a number of small rubber balloons from a peddler on the ground, and at the appointed time a package of notices was attached to one of them and it was set free. The balloon, thus weighted, descended rapidly, and I thought it would serve to attract the attention of anyone who passed near it after it had reached the earth.. However, I have as yet no knowledge whether or not this device assisted in the finding of our notices.

About 3 A.M. the brilliant lights of a large city brightened the haze of the lower air like a coming dawn. This was Lafayette, Indiana, and we were soon passing over its northern suburbs, now wrapped in profound slumber. The

234   *Romance of the Airman*

throbbing and whistling of locomotives which reached our ears, showed, however, that all was not dead, but that even in the dead of night some life was astir to carry on the activities of a busy world. Here we crossed the Wabash (moving softly toward the southwest), and soon afterwards we had an adventure often enjoyed by balloonists — that of a race with a locomotive, in which, I regret to say, the locomotive won. It was evidently a swift midnight express for the East, and when our courses finally diverged, the train was already several miles ahead of us.

From Dawn to Twilight

The balloon had now sunk to within three fourths of a mile of the earth's surface, and we first became aware of approaching dawn, not by the appearance of the sky, but by the awakening life below. There came to our ears, out of the depths, first the faint, shrill bugle calls of chanticleers, then the barking of dogs, and finally the soft, muffled rumble of a wagon on its early trip to the city. As if not to disappoint the expectant life below, there soon appeared a rosy flush on the eastern sky, and the whole heavens, both east and west, were then suffused with pink. The sunrise was not more brilliant than I have seen below, but the unobstructed view in every direction and the strange surroundings gave it an unusual beauty. The landscape was now seen clearly for the first time, and there spread out below us a scene so picturesque that it is difficult to describe. We were crossing the headwaters of the Wabash, whose bed was covered with a broad river of fog far more beautiful than the river itself; while into it flowed smaller streams of mist, and here and there a lakelet of fog in a basin between the hills reflected faintly, from the crests of its snowy billows, the colors of the rosy dawn.

The Airman becomes a Pathfinder   235

While we were directly over the valley of the Wabash an electric car, with glaring headlight, rushed along on its early morning trip like some submarine monster at the bottom of a wide river of fog.

The cause of this fog is the great cooling of the surface of the earth by radiation. The air, more transparent than glass, is but little heated by day or cooled at night by radiation, so that, at heights exceeding a half-mile, there is very little daily change in its temperature, and it is scarcely more than one degree warmer during the day than at night. On the other hand, the earth's surface is much heated by day and much cooled at night, causing a large daily change in the temperature of the ground and in the air which comes in contact with the ground. This cooling of the lower air does not extend to a height of more than five hundred feet above level ground, so that a balloon floating along near that altitude is in air almost as warm as that of the day. As a consequence balloonists like to seek this height, if there are not other reasons why it is desirable to go higher; because, except near the ground at night, the air grows colder as one goes higher, and at heights of five or six miles the cold is more intense than that of the coldest part of the earth's surface.

The balloon is like a little earth : it absorbs and radiates heat very powerfully. At night the balloon is continuously cooling, and we had to throw out ballast at intervals to keep from sinking to the earth on account of the cooling and shrinking of the gas, as well as on account of a slow loss of gas through the envelope of the balloon. This ballast was in the form of little scoopfuls of sand taken from a bag.

On the other hand, when the sun rose that first morning, a dazzling, brilliant orb, the balloon was heated in a surprisingly few minutes. Its gas, expanding and growing

236 *Romance of the Airman*

lighter, caused us to ascend rapidly, and we were soon again at a height of about eight thousand feet. Had it not been for an opening at the bottom of the gas-bag, made for that purpose, the balloon would have ascended many miles, — in fact, until the expanding gas burst the envelope asunder and allowed it to fall to earth a lifeless mass. I knew all this; but I knew also that many years of experience had adapted the balloon to meet these demands, and I had not the slightest fear. In fact, I watched with intense pleasure the grand panorama unfolding in all its detail by the light of day. Apparently quite unconscious of our existence, the busy world of man awoke and began its daily routine. Its inhabitants were microbes, creeping along the ground, or riding noiselessly on almost microscopic vehicles at a pace which seemed so slow that even a snail might envy it. How strange it all was! The whole visible world below was like a garden divided into innumerable plots of green and brown, with the lines of small separation running always east and west or north and south, and thus rendering the use of the compass unnecessary for obtaining directions. Those garden plots were farms, broad acres in extent. The untamed rocks alone stood weirdly out from the general culture. So strange did they appear that it was not until I had consulted my companion that I felt sure these were indeed rocks, standing out like little irregular volcanic cones above the general level of the prairie. All day we were crossing the great state of Ohio, so splendidly cultivated as to be almost a garden, with hardly an interval of waste land from one end to the other. We passed over or near the cities of Dayton, Springfield, Columbus, Newark, and Zanesville. When we reached Columbus it was already past noon, and we were hungry. Reclining in our basket, and shielding ourselves as best we could from the sun, we

The Airman becomes a Pathfinder   237

ate our midday meal. At the height of two miles the sun shines with fierce intensity unknown below, where the dust and the denser air scatter the rays which, thus diffused, lose their intensity while illumining every nook and corner of our houses. At heights exceeding five miles this diffused light is mostly gone, and the sun shines a glowing ball, sharply outlined in a sky of which the blue is so dark as to approach blackness. At the outer limits of the atmosphere the sun would appear a brilliant star of massive size among other stars; and if one stepped from its burning rays into shadow he would enter Egyptian darkness. At the height of a mile and a half we found it necessary to shelter our faces to prevent sunburn, although the air around us was but little warmer than that of the previous night, being about forty-five degrees. As the afternoon wore on and the balloon began to cool and sink, we were obliged to throw out much sand, casting it away a scoopful at a time; and just after sunset it was even necessary to empty two or three bags at once.

In preparation for a long trip in the air I had provided myself with an instrument for taking latitude and longitude from the balloon in the same way that a ship determines its position at sea; but, owing to some error in observation and to unsatisfactory maps, we lost our bearing in eastern Ohio, and consequently, shortly after sunset, in order to make inquiries we allowed our balloon to settle within about two hundred feet of the ground near a lonely farmhouse. The inhabitants of the farm did not see us until we were close upon them, and then consternation reigned supreme. In the barnyard, pigs, chickens, geese, and sheep rushed frantically in every direction for cover, hopping over and under one another and turning every conceivable angle. The chickens had no doubt seen hawks before in their time, but a monster twenty-five feet

238 *Romance of the Airman*

in diameter probably baffled the imagination of the most daring of their tribe. In the midst of this commotion and noise a woman appeared at the door of the house, and, gazing motionless from wonder, fear, or other emotion, could not reply to our oft-repeated inquiry as to the name of the nearest town.

In a brief time we had swept past her little domain on to that of a farmer who responded to our inquiry by the query "Where did you come from?" and then "Where are you going?" Before we could get this matter settled to his satisfaction, we were out of hearing; and, passing over a small cluster of houses, we learned from some boys that we were over the town of Otsego. As my knowledge of geographical names had limits, and I was not quite sure whether we had yet passed out of Ohio into Pennsylvania, I asked what state the town was in. It took the boys some minutes to overcome the shock of their surprise that these wanderers in the air did not even know what state they were in. They evidently thought that we were in a state of supreme ignorance; but finally we learned that the town was in Ohio, between Zanesville and Port Washington. Freeing ourselves from the boys, who had seized our trail-rope, we now rose several hundred feet and continued our journey toward the northeast. Soon the sun set once more amid a brilliant glow of red. In the gathering dusk the Ohio River was flowing below us grand and silent on its journey to the sea, but by a route far more indirect than that we sought. We crossed about twenty miles north of Wheeling, West Virginia. From out of the darkness below a voice came up to us with the familiar demand, "Where are you going?" and then, in insistent repetition, "Where are you going?" I was considering whether I should say to New York or Boston; but reply was unnecessary, for, not getting an immediate

The Airman becomes a Pathfinder 239

response, he gave us a warm invitation to a much hotter and more wicked place than either of those I had in mind! It seemed a strange behest to an occupant of the skies, but it is said that even angels may fall.

From Pittsburgh to Philadelphia

At 7.20 P.M. we passed over the city of Pittsburgh, with its glowing furnaces and innumerable lights. Over all this region there was a tinge of smoke indicating the center of the great coal industries and making it difficult to see clearly the objects beneath us. I was much impressed by the weird beauty of these glowing furnaces as seen from above; and it did not occur to me to connect these and the smoky air with the invitation earlier in the evening until I related the incident to an audience of young men at a university a few weeks later. We were now traveling northeastward well along the path we had planned to follow from St. Louis. But we were approaching mountains with which neither of us was familiar; and as the balloon was now within a distance of about one thousand feet of the ground, it seemed desirable to rise in order to avoid becoming entangled in the forests on the mountain side.

We threw over ballast and rose to a height of about a mile. We were soon crossing the ridges of the Appalachian Mountains, which showed dusky gray outlines in the moonlight, while between them lay black, abysmal valleys. There were suggestions of awful precipices and bottomless depths which made me shudder involuntarily as I looked into them, although up to that time I had felt as safe and as free from fear as if I had been taking a voyage on an ocean liner above the depths of the great ocean of water. About 2 A.M. we saw the brilliant lights of Harrisburg to the north, and passed directly over the city of Carlisle,

240 *Romance of the Airman*

where long lines of lights stretched at right angles to each other. We were now within about two thousand feet of the ground, and I listened for signs of life, but the sleeping city was as quiet as the dead. We crossed the Susquehanna River near the rapids, at a height of less than one thousand feet, and could hear the gurgling murmur of the waters long before they came in view, and after they were lost to sight. We crossed a railroad-siding, where a puffing engine was waiting with a train of cars, and called through our megaphone, hoping to attract the notice of the engineer; but our voices were drowned by the hissing steam. Some factories, or foundries, were passed, where the wheels of industry evidently turn by night as well as by day, for we could hear the throb of engines and the voices of men.

Even before the first signs of dawn appeared in the east, we were hailed with a cheerful "Good morning" by some early riser, and in response to our inquiries he informed us that we were then thirty-seven miles from Philadelphia and moving directly toward that city. At this time and until we reached Philadelphia at sunrise, the air below us was entirely calm; fogs and mists filled the valleys and hollows, and there was not the slightest noise or rustle of the wind amid the trees. The air in which we floated was moving over the calm air below, as over a soft cushion, at a speed of about thirty miles an hour. So smoothly did we glide that a glass of water filled to the brim would not have spilled a drop. We were going with the speed of the wind, and not a breath of air rustled through the balloon. It was ideal traveling, — no smoke, no dust, no jar, no noise; we were out in the open, fresh morning air at a comfortable temperature of about fifty-five degrees, and watching an unfolding panorama of surpassing beauty. We were approaching Philadelphia, over the suburban homes, flower gardens, and beautiful estates of its wealthier citizens.

The Airman becomes a Pathfinder 241

Floating at a height of between five hundred and one thousand feet above the earth, we exchanged morning greetings and bits of information with people below, hearing them as distinctly as if only separated from them by the width of a street, so easily does sound travel upward to this height. We talked through a megaphone and were easily understood.

As the balloon passed over a railway station where an early morning train had stopped, the passengers clambered out to see us, and I heard afterwards that it was with much difficulty the conductor got them in again, so as not to delay the train. Presently we crossed the Schuylkill, and then came a wilderness of factories with tall chimneys belching sparks. As the balloon was now within a few hundred feet of the earth, and there was a possibility of sparks reaching it, a small scoopful of ballast was thrown overboard, which sent us upward about fifty or a hundred feet. Some workmen, noticing this, supposed that we had thrown something at them — so I read afterwards in a newspaper.

Down after Forty Hours

Before we had reached the center of Philadelphia the warming rays of the rising sun touched the balloon, and we shot upward to a height slightly exceeding two miles, where the temperature was found to be a few tenths of a degree below the freezing point. This maneuver of the balloon was in accordance with our wishes, because the ocean was now near, and if we were to continue our voyage, for which we had ample gas and provisions, it must be in the direction of New York and New England. The lower currents were moving east-northeast; but these would have carried us a little south of our desired goal, and we wished to know whether there might be a more favorable

242 *Romance of the Airman*

current within a reasonable distance of the earth's surface. At the height of two miles the state of New Jersey lay spread out below us like a map. Looking eastward we could see the bays and inlets of the shore line for fully fifty miles on either hand, while the great ocean lay before us glistening in the morning sun with a silver sheen. We did not find a favorable current. It became evident that we must descend, and Mr. Erbsloeh requested me to pack everything secure because the balloon might strike the earth with a shock.

I pulled the valve-rope and down we came, two miles in a few minutes. When within several hundred yards of the earth's surface, we emptied two bags of sand, checking the downward speed of the balloon; and a few additional scoopfuls of sand thrown overboard brought us into equilibrium within a short distance of the ground, over which we continued to glide rapidly toward the northeast, traversing the state of New Jersey diagonally in about an hour and a half. We crossed the head of a bay and could see the waves of the ocean breaking on the shore beyond. It was high time to descend, and, selecting an open place in the suburbs of Asbury Park, we opened our valve and approached the ground. Suddenly our flight was arrested. We had encountered some telegraph wires amid which the basket was entangled, while the great mass of the balloon above was tugging to free us. The emptying of two more bags of ballast, a combined push against the wires, and the balloon was free once more, ascending rapidly. It now became necessary to act quickly: the valve was reopened and, in addition, a small hole was torn in the side of the balloon with the ripping cord. This was effective, and we touched the ground; then, with a long vigorous pull of the ripping-cord, the balloon lay to the leeward of the basket, an empty bag, and the race was

The Airman becomes a Pathfinder 243

over. In forty hours we had traversed the greatest distance in a straight line ever traveled by a balloon in America, and had won the race. In an air line from St. Louis, the distance is 872 miles; but in making this distance, since the course was not perfectly straight, we had traveled 932 miles at a speed varying between 17 and 31 miles an hour and averaging 23.3 miles an hour. In all this distance we had found it necessary to inquire as to our geographical position only once.

Although we had traveled this great distance, there remained plenty of provisions, gas, and ballast for another day's journey in the air. Out of the forty-one original bags of ballast we had twelve remaining, — a larger number, as it developed afterwards, than any other contestant.

Our first question to the people who immediately surrounded us was in regard to the latest news from the others in the race.

We were informed that the balloon *United States* had landed near Lake Ontario, but that the others were still in the air. We had no definite news of the others until late in the evening.

We were most hospitably received by the citizens of Asbury Park. The mayor made a speech extending to us a cordial welcome and giving us the freedom of the city. The leading citizens also provided us with an ample dinner. The news-gatherers came early, and after getting the information they wanted they left us to finish our journey in a more commonplace manner, and seek a much-needed rest.

Life in a Basket

During the forty hours that we were in the air we lived in a basket two and a half by three feet. In these narrow quarters there was not much room for freedom of motion;

244 *Romance of the Airman*

yet neither of us felt greatly cramped for room, on account
of the excitement and novelty of the voyage and the fact
that we were much engaged with the details of the management of the balloon and with the problem of keeping track
of its course. This latter was accomplished by means of
our instrument for determining latitude and longitude and
by means of maps which we carried, one for each state,
plotted on a large scale. From these maps the names of
the towns and rivers over which the balloon passed were
determined by their appearance on the maps. We were
also busied in trying to keep informed of the direction and
speed of the air currents above and below us.

One of the methods which I devised for doing this was
to suspend a small plumb bob by a slender cord far below
the basket of the balloon, and by another cord to suspend
a very light silk banner. This banner swung nearly the
same length below the basket as did the plumb bob, and the
slightest difference in the speed or direction of any current
below the balloon, as far down as we could let this device,
was determined by the swinging of the banner away from
the bob. For finding the motion of currents farther below
us we threw out light objects, such as pieces of paper,
from the car and watched their motion while descending.
In this way we kept fairly well informed of the movements
of the currents below us without having to waste our gas
and ballast in ascending or descending. The determination
of the motions of the currents above us was more difficult.
But we were aided to some extent in doing this by the few
clouds which we saw. On account of our own motion it
was difficult to tell exactly in which directions the clouds
were going; we could tell only whether they were moving
to the right or left of the balloon. Plenty of exercise was
obtained in drawing up the fifty-pound bags of ballast
over the sides of the basket, where they were suspended

The Airman becomes a Pathfinder 245

from small rings, and afterwards in throwing out the sand as it was needed in order to maintain our position in the air. There was no provision for sleep; but we ate our three regular meals in the air just as if we had been on the ground. There was no dressing for breakfast or dinner, except to exchange our shoes for slippers, and to add or remove wraps as the temperature demanded. For food we carried such provisions as rolls, mutton chops, mutton stew, fried chicken, eggs, crackers, and sausage. The last we did not taste. It was a concentrated food reserved in case the balloon might drop in some out-of-the-way place, as in the fastnesses of the mountains or in the wilds of Cànada, where we would be several days in finding our way out to civilization. For drinks we carried some dozen or so bottles of Apollinaris water, a bottle of coffee, a bottle of tea, and two or three bottles of wine.

In order to supply the blood with the necessary oxygen, the heart beats automatically much more rapidly at great altitudes, where the air is rare, than it does at the earth's surface, and for this reason it is best not to use stimulants. Already the brain is surcharged with blood, and there is a feeling of exhilaration.

For bathing one of us would pour slowly on the hands of the other a bottle of Apollinaris water. This was an expensive bath, perhaps, but it answered the purpose admirably, serving for both water and soap, because the free carbon dioxide in the water acted as a cleansing agent.

After having been in the air so many hours, with the earth apparently swimming along beneath the balloon, that condition had come to seem the normal one, and when we had landed I felt for an hour as if something wrong had happened to the earth, which lay so quiet and still beneath the feet.

246   *Romance of the Airman*

Result of the Race

In making the air a domain for human travel, the conquest of which seems almost in sight, a competitive race like this is a trial of methods, materials, and men to the utmost possibilities; and although the results of one race cannot settle the matter, the results of many races determine the best of these appliances and also open the door to new inventions and new methods. Another advantage of such a contest is that it adds much to our knowledge of the movements of the atmosphere. The various tracks followed by the balloons map out the motions of the air and enable the meteorologist to follow its spiral motion toward the storm center and to note the daily waves of oscillation from side to side of the general course followed by the air.

In the distances traveled this balloon race from St. Louis proved to be one of the greatest ever undertaken. Seven of the nine contestants crossed the Allegheny Mountains and landed near the Atlantic coast, while one landed in the region of the Great Lakes about six hundred miles from the starting point.

This result is so impressive that it has aroused the imagination of the American people and set them wondering as to the possibilities of this novel method of navigation. Aëro clubs have sprung into existence in almost every large city; the Signal Corps of our army is considering the building of several airships, and Congress will be asked for a large appropriation for further experiments; the officers of our navy are discussing the possibilities of launching flying machines from naval vessels or of sending up men in captive balloons from the ships for the purpose of reconnoitering; and a horde of inventors are at work on improvements of present appliances and on new machines

The Airman becomes a Pathfinder 247

for navigating the air. It seems safe to predict that the next year or two will witness an enormous activity in this matter in America.

In Europe the question of navigating the air has been longer a matter of public interest, and there the balloon has been brought to its present state of development. There exist well-organized clubs for using the balloon in sport and in recreation, and ascents for this purpose are very frequent in summer. Elongated or cigar-shaped balloons have been devised and driven through the air with a speed increasing as light motors of greater power have been invented, until now these elongated balloons navigate the air by their own power at velocities of twenty-five to thirty miles an hour, making long excursions and returning to their starting points. Monster airships of this kind some three hundred feet in length are already in commission in the war departments of every great nation in Europe, and hundreds of thousands of dollars are being expended in their further improvement.

The flying machine, or the machine which without gas will navigate the air, as does the bird, was first successfully used in America. After centuries of human effort Wilbur and Orville Wright of Dayton, Ohio, were the first to fly with wings (or aëroplanes) in a motor-driven machine without gas. The machines of this class are those on which the greatest amount of thought is being spent by inventors at present, for it seems probable to thoughtful men that these will be the machines which in the future will swiftly carry men and messages through the air. But long after these machines have been perfected, the balloon will still retain a place in sport and recreation, just as does the sailing boat, since its rival, the steam-driven craft, has largely displaced it for business and for war.

248 *Romance of the Airman*

The world seems on the point of realizing that vision of Tennyson, who wrote more than half a century ago,

For I dipt into the future, far as human eye could see,
Saw the Vision of the world, and all the wonder that would be;
Saw the heavens fill with commerce, argosies of magic sails,
Pilots of the purple twilight, dropping down with costly bales;
Heard the heavens fill with shouting, and there rained a ghastly dew
From the nations' airy navies grappling in the central blue.

Words and Phrases

To aid in understanding this selection

> **sounding balloons:** this experiment was begun during the World's Fair in St. Louis in 1904. Seventy-six of these small balloons, with registering devices, were sent up in order to study the condition of the air several miles above the earth.

To add to your vocabulary

pungent	Teutons
oscillating	abysmal
tumultuous	plumb bob
opalescent	reconnoitering

Technical term ballast

Informal Test (Completion)[1]

1. The race was from _____.

2. This balloon was owned by _____.

3. To keep an accurate record of the movements, each balloon was provided with _____.

4. When the lots were drawn, this balloon received _____ place.

5. The upper currents of the air in the United States nearly always move in an _____ direction.

[1] For directions, see page 14.

The Airman becomes a Pathfinder   249

6. As they passed towns they threw overboard _____.
7. The balloon landed in the state of _____.
8. The journey had lasted _____ hours.

Exercises and Topics related to your Other Subjects

1. On an outline map of the United States trace the balloon voyage. Wherever the author notes the time of passing a particular place, mark the time on that place.

2. Consult your science books and reference books and explain
a. How a self-recording barometer works.
b. Why the thermometer was whirled outside the balloon.
c. Why throwing sand bags out would make the balloon go higher.

3. Read the first two paragraphs of Irving's "Legend of Sleepy Hollow" and compare his description of "one of the quietest places in the world" with this author's description of "absolute silence," page 233.

4. Re-read carefully the author's description of dawn and then make a collection of other literary descriptions of the same subject. Read the best ones to the class. In "The Boat on the Serchio," by Percy Bysshe Shelley, is one of the best pictures of daybreak.

5. Prepare to read before the class five passages from this selection that give what you consider the five most beautiful pictures.

Other Readings

In this book

See "Explanatory Note" on "The Flying Warrior of Uganda" (page 83) for a reference to James Gordon Bennett.

From other sources

"Wonderful Balloon Ascents," by F. Marion.

Andrée's Polar Expedition

CHARLES C. TURNER

Explanatory Note. Salomon August Andrée was born in Sweden in 1854. He was educated as an engineer and had broad experience in engineering, both as a practical worker and as a teacher. He spent some years experimenting with balloons and made several interesting flights. In 1895 he presented to the Academy of Science a project for a balloon trip to the North Pole. The money was raised by national subscription. The king of Sweden gave almost a fourth of the total amount.

An enormous balloon was made in Paris for the expedition. The car of the balloon was equipped with a food supply for four months, and with all tools and supplies necessary for any emergency that might arise. Andrée, with two companions, Nils Strindberg and Dr. Ekholm, planned to start in the summer of 1896; but the wind was not favorable, and the adventure was postponed until the following year.

For thirty-three years no more was known of the fate of the expedition than is told in the following account. In August, 1930, the bodies of Andrée, Strindberg, and Frankel were discovered on White Island, Fridjof Nansen Land, by a Norwegian sealing vessel. The remains of a temporary camp indicated that the party had made a long march over snow and ice, and had finally perished from the cold. Among the ruins of the camp was found Andrée's diary, the pages of which held the secrets of the mystery that had so long baffled the world.

ON MAY 28 of the following year (1897) they started again for Dane's Island. Frankel and Svedenborg accompanied Andrée and Strindberg, as Dr. Ekholm had retired from the expedition. From May 30 to July 11 they waited, and then, with a wind somewhat west of south, they started on the ill-fated voyage. The departure was described by Machuron* as follows:

The entire crew of the *Svensksund* are present, and also the crews of the three Norwegian whaling vessels anchored in Virgo Bay. There is profound silence at this minute; we hear only the whistling of the wind through the woodwork of the shed, and the flapping of the canvas which hangs over the upper part of the south side.

The Airman becomes a Pathfinder   251

Among the cordage of the car are seen the three heroes, standing admirably cool and calm. Andrée is always calm, cold, and impassible. Not a trace of emotion is visible on his countenance; nothing but an expression of firm resolution and an indomitable will. He is just the man for such an enterprise, and he is well seconded by his two companions.

At last the decisive moment arrives.

One! Two! Cut! cries Andrée in Swedish.

The three sailors obey the order simultaneously, and in one second the aërial ship, free and unfettered, rises majestically into space, saluted with our heartiest cheers.

We rush to the doors to get out of the shed. I have the chance of getting out first through a secret opening I have made in the woodwork, so as to be able to rush to my photographic apparatus and have time to take a few snapshots at this stupendous moment.

Being encumbered with the heavy cordage that it takes with it, the balloon does not rise to a height of one hundred meters. It is dragged by the wind. Behind the mountain that is sheltering us, stormy winds are raging, and a current of air sweeps down from the summit and attacks the balloon, which for a moment descends rapidly toward the sea. This incident, which we had foreseen before the departure, but the natural cause of which struck few of the spectators at the moment, produces great excitement amongst some of us. The sailors rush to the boats to be ready to lend assistance to the explorers, whom they expect to see engulfed in the waves. Their alarm is of short duration; the descending movement soon becomes slower, and the car just touches the water and ascends again immediately.

Unfortunately the lower parts of the guide-ropes, which were made so as to become detached if they should be caught in the ground, have remained on the shore. At the start the ropes were caught in some rocks on the shore, and the screws for separating the parts worked loose. But Andrée is well provided against this loss, so that this accident is not likely to have serious consequences.

At the edge of the water, on the beach studded with rocks and large stones, we all stand, breathlessly watching the various phases, rapidly following one upon another, of the commencement of this stirring and unprecedented aërial journey.

252 *Romance of the Airman*

The balloon, which has now righted itself at about one hundred and sixty-four feet above the sea, is rapidly speeding away; the guide-ropes glide over the water, making a very perceptible wake, which is visible from its starting-point, like the track made by a ship. The state of affairs seems to us on the shore to be the best that could be hoped for. We exchange last signals of farewell with our friends; hats and handkerchiefs are waved frantically.

Soon we can no longer distinguish the aëronauts, but we can see that they are arranging their sails, as these latter are displayed in succession on their bamboo mast; then we observe a change of direction. The balloon is now traveling straight to the north. It goes along swiftly, notwithstanding the resistance that must be offered by the dragging ropes. We estimate its speed at from eighteen to twenty-two miles an hour. If it keeps up this initial speed and the same direction, it will reach the pole in less than two days.

The aërial globe seems now no bigger than an egg. On the horizon an obstacle appears in the route; this is the continuation of a chain of mountains about one hundred meters high, right in the path of the balloon, which seems very close to the obstacle, and some of the sailors round me, who have never before seen a balloon start on its trip, seem in great terror. They think the balloon will be hopelessly wrecked. I reassure them, telling them that the balloon is still far away from the hills, which will be easily surmounted, without there even being any necessity to throw out ballast.

The balloon travels on, maintained at the same altitude by the guide-ropes. In the neighborhood of the hills there is an upward current of air; the balloon will follow this; it would risk striking against the obstacle only if the movement were downwards, which is not the case. Moreover, the guide-ropes first rest upon the rocks and thus lighten the balloon, which gradually rises. We see it clear the top of the hill, and stand out clearly for a few minutes against the blue sky, and then slowly disappear from our view behind the hill.

Scattered along the shore, we stand motionless, with hearts full, and anxious eyes, gazing at the silent horizon. For one moment then, between two hills, we perceive a gray speck over the sea, very, very far away, and then it finally disappears.

The Airman becomes a Pathfinder 253

The way to the pole is clear, no more obstacles to encounter; the sea, the ice-field, and the Unknown!

We look at one another for a moment, stupefied. Instinctively we draw together without saying a word. There is nothing, nothing whatever in the distance to tell us where our friends are; they are now shrouded in mystery.

Farewell! Farewell! Our most fervent prayers go with you. May God help you! Honor and glory to your names!

On July 22 one of Andrée's pigeons was killed by some fishermen near Spitsbergen. It carried the following message:

The Andrée Polar Expedition to the *Aftonbladet*,* Stockholm. July 13, 12.30 P.M., 82 degrees 2 minutes north latitude, 15 degrees 5 minutes east longitude. Good journey eastwards, 10 degrees south. All goes well on board. This is the third message sent by the pigeon. ANDRÉE

On August 31 a buoy* was picked up bearing the message:

Buoy No. 4. First to be thrown out. 11th July, 10 P.M., Greenwich mean time. All well up till now. We are pursuing our course at an altitude of about 250 meters. Direction at first northerly 10 degrees east; later, northerly 45 degrees east. Four carrier pigeons were despatched at 5.40 P.M. They flew westwards. We are now above the ice, which is very cut up in all directions. Weather splendid. In excellent spirits. Andrée, Strindberg, Fraenkel. [Postscript later on] Above the clouds, 7.45, Greenwich mean time.

The Anthropological and Geological Society at Stockholm later received the following telegram from a shipowner at Mandal:

Captain Hueland, of the steamship *Vaagan*, who arrived there on Monday morning, reports that when off Kola Fjord, Iceland, in 65 degrees 34 minutes north lat., 21 degrees 28 minutes west

254 *Romance of the Airman*

long., on May 14th, he found a drifting buoy, marked "No. 7." Inside the buoy was a capsule, marked "Andrée's Polar Expedition," containing a slip of paper, on which was given the following: "Drifting buoy No. 7. This buoy was thrown out from Andrée's balloon on July 11, 1897, 10.55 P.M., Greenwich mean time, 82 degrees north lat., 25 degrees east long. We are at an altitude of 600 meters. All well, Andrée, Strindberg, Fraenkel."

In December, 1909, an extraordinary story was published on the authority of a missionary who had devoted many years of his life to work among the Eskimos. The missionary reported to his bishop that in the course of his wanderings in the extreme north of Canada he came across an unknown tribe of Eskimos, who had come from the farthest north. According to what they told him they had a strange experience at a period which must have been some years ago. They said that they were one day astonished to see a "white house" in the sky coming down toward the earth. In it they found two half-starved white men; but though their vitality was to a certain extent restored by meals of reindeer flesh, they were so weak that they died shortly afterwards. The Eskimos stated that they used the "white house" as a storeroom for the ropes, of which there were a great number attached. They still had with them several ropes, all well-made and remarkably strong.

Many other reports have appeared regarding alleged discoveries of traces of Andrée and his expedition, but on investigation they have proved to be without foundation.

One of these stories suggests that Andrée and his companions were slain by the Eskimos. Another relates to the finding of a lonely grave marked by a wooden cross with the word "Andrée." But "Andrée" is a very common name; and, indeed, none of these reports was ever verified.

The Airman becomes a Pathfinder 255

Words and Phrases

To aid in understanding this selection

Machuron and Lachambre: the authors of a book called "Andrée and his Balloon," from which the quotations in this selection are taken.

Aftonbladet: A Stockholm newspaper.

buoy: Andrée took twelve dispatch buoys, each consisting of a sphere of cork, about seven inches in diameter, inside of which was a capsule in which messages could be sealed. These spheres were weighted with lead at the bottom, and at the top were copper stoppers bearing the inscription "Andrée's Polar Expedition, 1896" and a number. A little Swedish flag of thin metal surmounted each buoy. A thirteenth buoy, larger than the others, was to be left at that point of the route nearest to the geographical pole which could be reached by the balloon.

To add to your vocabulary

indomitable will alleged discoveries verified

Technical term aëronauts

Informal Test (True-False)[1]

1. Andrée showed great emotion at the start of his voyage.

2. The balloon rose at first to a height of a hundred meters.

3. The sailors expected to see the three explorers engulfed in the waves.

4. The loss of the ropes was of no serious consequence to Andrée.

5. When the balloon was last seen its speed was estimated to be forty miles an hour.

6. Loud cheers went up as the balloon disappeared from sight.

7. Three carrier pigeons returned with messages from Andrée.

8. Only two of Andrée's buoys were found.

[1] For directions, see page 54.

256 *Romance of the Airman*

9. The last message from the expedition reported the crew in great distress.

10. The missionary tale was not published until nineteen years after Andrée's flight.

11. The Eskimos had nothing with them to prove their story of the "white house."

12. All the reports concerning the fate of Andrée were verified.

Exercises and Topics related to your Other Subjects

1. Locate on your map the following:
a. Dane's Island.
b. Virgo Bay.
c. Andrée's location on July 11.
d. Andrée's location on July 13.
e. Where Buoy No. 7 was found.

2. How many feet high was Andrée when he reported six hundred meters?

3. Give the height of the mountain range in feet.

4. Give a short talk on the carrier pigeon.

5. Make a map showing Dane's Island, White Island, and the North Pole.

Other Readings

In this book

"Byrd's Flight to the North Pole," page 275.

From other sources

"Andrée's Balloon Expedition in Search of the North Pole,"
by Henri Lachambre and Alexis Machuron.

Bleriot crosses the English Channel

LOUIS BLERIOT of France, one of the most experienced pioneers in aviation, began his experiments in building and flying airplanes about the same time that the Wright brothers began to attract the attention of Americans to their successes; that is, about 1900.

The type of plane first built by Bleriot was the flapping-wing model. This was soon abandoned for the biplane glider, which in turn was laid aside for the monoplane. In quick succession seven planes were built and crashed, but Bleriot each time escaped with slight injuries. His enthusiasm did not wane because of his failures. As soon as one plane was wrecked he promptly built a better one. His eighth plane brought him great joy. It remained in the air for eight and one-half minutes! No doubt the day of this trial flight, July 6, 1908, was a red-letter day in Bleriot's life.

As workers in all fields of industry and service meet others striving to attain the same goals, so the pioneers in aviation competed with each other. The success of one worker stimulated others to excel. It was no wonder that when successful flights over land were made, many should hunger for more daring ventures and attempt to fly the English Channel. When handsome prizes, of several thousand dollars, were offered for this feat, and Bleriot had built his eleventh plane, he and his rivals vied with each other to be first in crossing to England.

The English Channel had been crossed by air more than a hundred years before Bleriot made his memorable flight. Jean Pierre Blanchard and Dr. Jeffries, an American physician, were the first to venture on this hazardous journey. It was in the month of January, 1785, that these two young men started in a balloon from Dover to "somewhere on

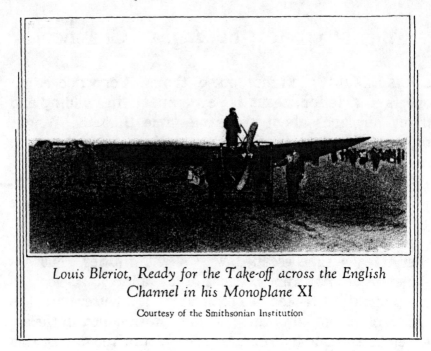

Louis Bleriot, Ready for the Take-off across the English Channel in his Monoplane XI

Courtesy of the Smithsonian Institution

the other side." It is recorded that when they were about one third of the way across, their balloon began to descend and they were forced to throw out everything in their car or boat. When their journey was about three fourths completed, they began to go down again and were forced to throw out their anchor and even to strip off part of their clothing in order to keep in the air. Their approach to land was a spectacle, as they described an arc* high over the land and descended in the forest of Guines, in northern France.

To attempt to fly this arm of the sea, either side of which was edged with cliffs hundreds of feet high, was a hazardous undertaking that few would venture. The fact that Latham and others had been rescued by a torpedo-boat destroyer and safely transported to shore a few days before did not dishearten Bleriot. Many who knew of Bleriot's plans

The Airman becomes a Pathfinder

Louis Bleriot crossing the English Channel July 25, 1909
Courtesy of the Smithsonian Institution

asked: "Could the boat travel as fast as the plane?" "Would it be in the right place in case the motors failed?" "If it were not, would the weight of the machine cause all to be swallowed up by the sea?"

None of these questions daunted the determined and strong-hearted Bleriot. He rose early — at 3 A.M. — on Sunday, July 25, 1909, and found weather conditions just right. He tested his machine with a fifteen-minute trial flight and landed on a cliff near Calais, France, from which he was to start. At 4.35, as the sun rose, he started his motor at full speed and soon was on his way toward the English coast. The torpedo-boat destroyer *Escopette*, which was several miles at sea ready to come to Bleriot's rescue, was soon left behind. How anxious Mme.* Bleriot must have been as she and the other passengers on the *Escopette* saw her husband leave them in the distance!

260 *Romance of the Airman*

The *Escopette* arrived in time for Mme. Bleriot to add her congratulations to those of the hundreds that gave the distinguished Frenchman an early-morning reception as soon as he ended his memorable flight. Not all Englishmen rejoiced when the early caller was announced. Gulliver's invasion of the dominion of the Lilliputians* could not have been more exciting than Bleriot's arrival. The feat was considered by some an invasion comparable to that of Cæsar himself. Great Britain, they thought, was safe because it was an inaccessible island. They now moaned, "The impregnability* of Britain has passed away!"

The triumphant flight of Louis Bleriot across the English Channel, accomplished in thirty-seven minutes in his monoplane *XI*, flying at the rate of forty miles per hour on July 25, 1909, goes down in the annals of aviation as the first successful cross-Channel flight in a heavier-than-air machine.

If you visit England today you will find as a memorial to this aviator a monoplane, carved in stone, planted on the spot where he landed in a meadow behind Dover Castle.

Words and Phrases

To aid in understanding this selection

described an arc: traced the outline of an arc, or curve.
Mme.: abbreviation for the French word *madame*, used as we use *Mrs.*
domain of the Lilliputians: in Swift's satire "Gulliver's Travels" an imaginary island inhabited by very tiny men.
impregnability: ability to resist an attack by enemies.

To add to your vocabulary

transported   hazardous

Technical terms

monoplane   biplane   car

The Airman becomes a Pathfinder 261

Informal Test (Completion)[1]

1. Bleriot began his experiments about the year _ _ _ _ _ _.

2. The type of plane first built by Bleriot was the _ _ _ _ _ _.

3. Bleriot was most successful with the _ _ _ _ _ _ type of machine.

4. The first crossing of the English Channel by Bleriot was on the _ _ _ _ _ _ day of the month of _ _ _ _ _ _ in the year _ _ _ _ _ _.

5. The first balloon to cross the English Channel was driven by _ _ _ _ _ _ in the year _ _ _ _ _ _.

Informal Test (Multiple-Choice)[2]

1. Bleriot flew across the English Channel in **twenty-seven thirty-seven forty-seven fifty-seven** minutes.

2. Bleriot's monoplane *XI* flew at the rate of **20 40 60 80** miles per hour when making the cross-Channel flight.

3. Bleriot started across to England from **Spain Germany France Holland**

4. Bleriot was **strong-hearted and determined vain and foolhardy weak and cowardly conservative and cautious**

Exercises and Topics related to your Other Subjects

1. On an outline map of western Europe find Calais and Dover.

2. List all the features of a monoplane that make it superior to a biplane.

3. Read in your history about the invasion of Britain by Cæsar.

4. Find out what you can about some of Bleriot's rivals in aviation, such as Henry Farman, M. Latham, and Santos-Dumont.

Other Readings

From other sources

"Sky High," by E. Hodgins and F. A. Magoun.

[1] For directions, see page 14.   [2] For directions, see page 95.

The Amundsen-Ellsworth Polar Flight

ROALD AMUNDSEN AND LINCOLN ELLSWORTH

Explanatory Note. The explorers set off from King's Bay, Spitsbergen, May 21, 1925, expecting to be back in a few days. The selection given here, taken from Ellsworth's account in "Our Polar Flight,"[1] gives the story of the first several days of their hardships. They were forced to abandon the *N–24*; but after great difficulties they were able to extricate the *N–25* and fly safely back to the North Cape, where they were taken in tow by a sealing tub and brought back to King's Bay. The entire trip consumed twenty-eight days.

So LONG as the human ear can hark back to the breaking of waves over deep seas; so long as the human eye can follow the gleam of the Northern Lights over the silent snow fields; then so long, no doubt, will the lure of the unknown draw restless souls into those great Arctic wastes.

I sit here about to set down a brief record of our late polar experience, and I stop to try to recall when it was that my imagination was first captured by the lure of the Arctic. I must have been very young, because I cannot now recall when first it was. Doubtless somewhere in my ancestry there was a restless wanderer with an unappeasable desire to attain the Farthest North; and, not attaining it, he passed it on with other sins and virtues to torment his descendants.

The large blank spaces surrounding the North Pole have been a challenge to the daring since charts first were made. For nearly four generations that mysterious plain has been the ultimate quest of numberless adventurers.

Before this adventure of ours, explorers had depended upon ships and dogs. Andrée and Wellman planned to reach the Pole with balloons, but theirs were hardly more

[1] Copyright, 1925, by Dodd, Mead and Company, Inc.

The Airman becomes a Pathfinder 263

than plans. Andrée met with disaster soon after leaving Spitsbergen. Wellman's expedition never left the ground.

What days they were — those ship and dog days! What small returns came to those men for their vast spending of energy and toil and gold! I am filled with admiration for the courage and the hardihood of the men who cut adrift from civilization and set out with dogs or on foot over the trackless ice fields of the Far North. All honor to them!

No doubt the men who have been through it best realize what a hopeless, heartbreaking quest it was. Peary's land base at Camp Columbia was only 413 miles from the Pole, yet it took him twenty-three years to traverse that 413 miles.

Curiously enough, Peary was the first man with whom I ever discussed the matter of using an airplane for polar work. That was shortly before his death, and he was enthusiastic about the project. Eight years later, in 1924, Captain Amundsen arrived in New York. He had already announced his belief that the Polar Sea could be crossed in a plane, and for those eight years my mind had not freed itself of the idea. We had a long talk, and as the result I brought Amundsen and my father together. My father too became enthusiastic and agreed to buy us two flying boats. Thus the adventure began.

The island of Spitsbergen, lying just halfway between Norway and the North Pole, is ideally situated to serve as a base for polar exploration. Besides its nearness to the Pole — ten degrees, or six hundred nautical miles* — a warm current, an offshoot of the Gulf Stream, follows along the western and northern coasts of the island, and has the effect of producing ice-free waters at the highest latitude in the world. These were the principal reasons which prompted Captain Amundsen and myself to choose Spitsbergen as a base for our aëroplane flight to the Pole.

264 Romance of the Airman

We wanted to be on the ground early in the spring and to make our flight before the summer fogs should enshroud the polar pack and hide from view any possible landing place beneath us, for it was our intention to descend at the Pole for observations. From April 19 to August 24 (one hundred and twenty-seven days) the sun never sets in the latitude of King's Bay, Spitsbergen, where we had established our base. Here one may find growing during the long summer days one hundred and ten distinct species of flowering plants and grasses. But from October 26 to February 17 is another story: the long Arctic winter is at hand, and the sun never shows above the horizon. Many houses have been built along the Spitsbergen coast during the last twenty years by mining companies who annually ship about three hundred thousand tons of coal, and King's Bay boasts of being the most northerly habitation in the world.

May 21, 1925, is the day we have long awaited, when, with two Dornier-Wal flying boats, we are ready to take off from the ice at King's Bay to start into the Unknown. We are carrying 7800 pounds of dead weight in each plane. As this is 1200 pounds above the estimated maximum lift, we are compelled to leave behind our radio equipment, which would mean an additional 300 pounds. Our provisions are sufficient to last one month, at the rate of two pounds per day per man. The daily ration list per man is:

Pemmican	400 gr.
Milk chocolate	250 gr.
Oatmeal biscuits	125 gr.
Powdered milk	100 gr.
Malted-milk tablets	125 gr.

At 4.15 P.M. all is ready for the start. The 450-horsepower Rolls-Royce motors are turned over for warming up. At five o'clock the full horse power is turned on. We

The Airman becomes a Pathfinder 265

move. The *N-25* has Captain Amundsen as navigator. Riiser-Larsen is his pilot, and Feucht mechanic. I am navigator of the *N-24*, with Dietrichson for pilot, and Omdal my mechanic. Six men in all.

The first two hours of our flight, after leaving Amsterdam Islands, we ran into a heavy bank of fog and rose one thousand meters to clear it. This ascent was glorified by as beautiful a natural phenomenon as I have ever seen. Looking down into the mist, we saw a double halo in the middle of which the sun cast a perfect shadow of our plane. Evanescent and phantom-like, these two multicolored halos beckoned us enticingly into the Unknown. I recalled the ancient legend which says that the rainbow is a token that man shall not perish by water. The fog lasted until midway between latitudes eighty-two and eighty-three. Through rifts in the mist we caught glimpses of the open sea. This lasted for an hour; then, after another hour, the ocean showed, strewn with small ice floes, which indicated the fringe of the polar pack. Then, to quote Captain Amundsen, "suddenly the mist disappeared and the entire panorama of polar ice stretched away before our eyes — the most spectacular sheet of snow and ice ever seen by man from an aërial perspective." From our altitude we could overlook sixty or seventy miles in any direction. The far-flung expanse was strikingly beautiful in its simplicity. There was nothing to break the deadly monotony of snow and ice but a network of narrow cracks, or "leads," which scarred this white surface and was the only indication to an aërial observer of the ceaseless movement of the polar pack. We had crossed the threshold into the Unknown! I was thrilled at the thought that never before had man lost himself with such speed — seventy-five miles per hour — into unknown space. The silence of ages was now being broken for the first time by the roar of our motors.

266 *Romance of the Airman*

We were but gnats in an immense void. We had lost all contacts with civilization. Time and distance suddenly seemed to count for nothing. What lay ahead was all that mattered now.

> Something hidden. Go and find it.
> Go and look behind the Ranges —
> Something lost behind the Ranges,
> Lost and waiting for you. Go!

On we sped for eight hours, till the sun had shifted from the west to a point directly ahead of us. By all rights we should now be at the Pole, for our dead reckoning showed that we had traveled just one thousand kilometers (six hundred miles) at seventy-five miles per hour; but shortly after leaving Amsterdam Islands we had run into a heavy northeast wind, which had been steadily driving us westward. Our fuel supply was now about half exhausted; and at this juncture, strangely enough, just ahead of us was the first open lead of water that was large enough for an aëroplane to land in that we had encountered on our whole journey north. There was nothing left now but to descend for observations to learn where we were. As Captain Amundsen's plane started to circle for a landing, his rear motor back-fired and stopped, so that he finally disappeared among a lot of ice hummocks,* with only one motor going.

This was at 1 A. M. on the morning of May 22. The lead ran east and west, meeting our course at right angles. It was an awful-looking hole. We circled for about ten minutes, looking for enough open water to land in. The lead was choked up with a chaotic mass of floating ice floes, and it looked as if someone had started to dynamite the ice pack. Ice blocks standing on edge or piled high on top of one another, hummocks and pressure-ridges, were all that greeted our eyes. It was like trying to land in the Grand Canyon.

The Airman becomes a Pathfinder 267

We came down in a little lagoon among the ice floes, taxied over to a huge ice cake, and, anchoring our plane to it, jumped out with our sextant and artificial horizon to find out where we were. Not knowing what to expect, I carried my rifle; but after our long flight I was a bit unsteady on my legs, tumbled down into the deep snow, and choked up the barrel. Our eyes were bloodshot, and we were almost stone deaf after listening to the unceasing roar of our motors for eight hours, and the stillness seemed intensified.

Looking around on landing, I had the feeling that nothing but death could be at home in this part of the world, and that there could not possibly be any life in such an environment, when I was surprised to see a seal pop up his head beside the plane. I am sure he was as surprised as we were, for he raised himself half out of the water to inspect us and seemed not at all afraid to approach, as he came almost up to us. We had no thought of taking his life, for we expected to be off and on our way again toward the Pole after our observation. His curiosity satisfied, he disappeared, and we never saw another sign of life in those waters during our entire stay in the ice.

Our observations showed that we had come down in latitude 87 degrees 44 minutes north, longitude 10 degrees 20 minutes west. As our flight meridian was 12 degrees east, where we landed was, therefore, 22 degrees 20 minutes off our course. This westerly drift had cost us nearly a degree in latitude and enough extra fuel to have carried us to the Pole. As it was, we were just 136 nautical miles from it. At the altitude at which we had been flying just before descending, our visible horizon was 46 miles, which means that we had been able to see ahead as far as latitude 88 degrees 30 minutes north, or to within just 90 miles of the North Pole. We had left civilization, and eight hours

268 Romance of the Airman

later we were able to view the earth within 90 miles of the goal that it had taken Peary twenty-three years to reach. Truly "the efforts of one generation may become the commonplace of the next."

When we had finished taking our observation, we began to wonder where the *N–25* was. We crawled up on all the high hummocks near by and with our field glasses searched the horizon. Dietrichson remarked that perhaps Amundsen had gone on to the Pole. "It would be just like him," he said. It was not until noon, however, of the twenty-second that we spotted them from an especially high hill of ice. The *N–25* lay with her nose pointing into the air at an angle of forty-five degrees, among a lot of rough hummocks and against a huge cake of old blue Arctic ice about forty feet thick, three miles away. It was a rough-looking country, and the position of the *N–25* was terrible to behold. To us it looked as though she had crashed into this ice.

We of the *N–24* were not in too good shape where we were. We had torn the nails loose on the bottom of our plane when we took off from King's Bay, so that she was leaking badly; in fact, the water was now above the bottom of the petrol tanks. Also, our forward motor was disabled. In short, we were badly wrecked. Things looked so hopeless to us at that moment that it seemed as though the impossible would have to happen ever to get us out. No words so well express our mental attitude at that time as the following lines of Swinburne's:

> From hopes cut down across a world of fears,
> We gaze with eyes too passionate for tears,
> Where Faith abides, though Hope be put to flight.

That first day, while Dietrichson and I had tried to reach the *N–25*, Omdal had been trying to repair the motor. We dragged our canvas canoe up over hummocks and

The Airman becomes a Pathfinder 269

tumbled into icy crevasses until we were thoroughly exhausted. The snow was over two to three feet deep all over the ice, and we floundered through it, never knowing what we were going to step on next. Twice Dietrichson went down between the floes, and only by hanging on to the canoe was he able to save himself from sinking. After half a mile of this we were forced to give up and return.

We pitched our tent on top of the ice floe, moved all our equipment out of the plane into it, and tried to make ourselves as comfortable as possible. But there was no sleep for us and very little rest during the next five days. Omdal was continually working on the motor, while Dietrichson and I took turns at the pump. Only by the most incessant pumping were we able to keep the water down below the gasoline tanks.

Although we had located the *N–25*, they did not see us till the afternoon of the second day, which was May 23. We had taken the small inflated balloons which the meteorologist had given us with which to obtain data regarding the upper air strata, and after tying pieces of flannel to them set them loose. We hoped that the wind would drift them over to the *N–25* and so indicate . . . in which direction to look for us. But the wind blew them in the wrong direction, or else they drifted too low and got tangled up in the rough ice.

Through all that first day the wind was blowing from the north, and we could see quite a few patches of open water. On the second day the wind shifted to the south, and the ice began to close in on us. It was as though we were in the grasp of a gigantic claw that was slowly but surely contracting. We had a feeling that soon we would be crushed.

On the third day, May 24, the temperature was −11.5°C., and we had trouble with our pump freezing. The two

270 *Romance of the Airman*

planes were now slowly drifting together, and we established a line of communication, so that we knew each other's positions pretty well. It is tedious work, semaphoring, for it requires two men: one with the flag, and the other with a pair of field glasses to read the signals. It took us a whole hour merely to signal our positions, after which we must wait for their return signals and then reply to them.

On this day, after an exchange of signals, we decided to try to reach Amundsen. We packed our canvas canoe, put it on our sledge, and started across what looked to us like mountainous hummocks. After only going a few hundred yards we had to give up. The labor was too exhausting. With no sleep for three days, and only liquid food, our strength was not what it should have been. Leaving our canvas canoe, we now made up our packs of fifty pounds each, and pushed on. We might or might not return to our plane again.

According to my diary we traveled the first two miles in two hours and fifteen minutes, when we came upon a large lead that separated us from the *N–25* and which we could see no way to cross. We talked to them by signal and they advised our returning. So after a seven-hour trip we returned to our sinking plane, having covered perhaps five and one-half miles in about the same length of time it had taken us to fly from Spitsbergen to latitude 87 degrees 44 minutes. Arriving at our plane, we pitched camp again and cooked a heavy pemmican soup over our Primus stove.

All our energies were now being bent in getting the *N–24* up onto the ice floe, for we knew she would be crushed if we left her in the lead. The whole cake we were on was only about two hundred meters in diameter, and there was only one level stretch on it of eighty meters. It

The Airman becomes a Pathfinder   271

was laborious work for Dietrichson and myself to try to clear the soggy, wet snow, for all we had to work with was one clumsy homemade wooden shovel and our ice anchor. As I would loosen the snow by picking at it with the anchor, Dietrichson would shovel it away.

Looking through our glasses at the *N–25*, we could see the propellers going and Amundsen pulling up and down on the wings, trying to loosen the plane from the ice, but she did not budge. On the morning of May 26 Amundsen signaled to us that if we couldn't save our plane to come over and help them. We had so far succeeded in getting the nose of our plane up onto the ice cake; but with only one engine working, it was impossible to do more. Anyway, she was safe now from sinking, but not from being crushed, should the ice press in on her. During the five days of our separation the ice had so shifted that the two planes were now plainly in sight of each other and only half a mile apart. During that time the ice had been in continual movement, so that now all the heavy ice had moved out from between the two camps. We signaled to the *N–25* that we were coming; and making up loads of eighty pounds per man, we started across the freshly frozen lead that separated us from our companions. We were well aware of the chances we were taking, crossing this new ice, but we saw no other alternative. We *must* get over to the *N–25* with all possible speed if we were ever to get back again to civilization.

With our feet shoved loosely into our skis—for we never fastened them on here for fear of getting tangled up, should we fall into the sea—we shuffled along, slowly feeling our way over the thin ice. Omdal was in the lead, myself and Dietrichson — who had recovered from his slight attack of snow blindness the next day — following in that order. Suddenly I heard Dietrichson yelling be-

272   *Romance of the Airman*

hind me; and before I knew what it was all about, Omdal, ahead of me, cried out also and disappeared as though the ice beneath him had suddenly opened and swallowed him. The ice under me started to sag, and I quickly jumped sideways to avoid the same fate that had overtaken my companions. There just happened to be some old ice beside me, and that was what saved me. Lying down on my stomach, partly on this ledge of old ice and partly out on the new ice, I reached the skis out and pulled Dietrichson over to where I could grab his pack and partly pull him out onto the firmer ice, where he lay panting and exhausted. Then I turned my attention to Omdal. Only his pallid face showed above the water. It is strange, when I think that both these Norwegians had been conversing almost wholly in their native tongue, that Omdal was now crying in English, "I'm gone! I'm gone!" — and he was almost gone too. The only thing that kept him from going way under was the fact that he kept digging his fingers into the ice. I reached him just in time to pull him over to the firmer ice. I reached him just before he sank, and held him by his pack until Dietrichson could crawl over to me and hold him up while I cut off the pack. It took all the remaining strength of the two of us to drag Omdal up onto the old ice.

Our companions could not reach us, neither could they see us, as a few old ice hummocks of great size stood directly in front of the *N–25*. They could do nothing but listen to the agonizing cries of their fellow men in distress. We finally succeeded in getting over to our companions, who gave us dry clothes and hot chocolate, and we were soon all right again, except for Omdal's swollen and lacerated hands. Both men had lost their skis. In view of the probability of being forced to tramp to Greenland, four hundred miles away, the loss of these skis seemed a calamity.

The Airman becomes a Pathfinder 273

I was surprised at the change only five days had wrought in Captain Amundsen. He seemed to me to have aged ten years. We now joined our companions in the work of freeing the *N–25* from her precarious position.

Words and Phrases

To aid in understanding this selection
  nautical mile: 6080.27 feet.
  hummock: a ridge of ice.

To add to your vocabulary

void	skis
evanescent	chaotic mass

Technical terms

taxied	artificial horizon
sextant	semaphoring

Informal Test (Completion)[1]

1. The flying boats for the expedition were paid for by _ _ _ _ _ _.

2. The summer was undesirable for the flight owing to _ _ _ _ _ _.

3. From April to August _ _ _ _ _ _ species of flowers and grasses grow around King's Bay.

4. Mining companies ship _ _ _ _ _ _ from King's Bay.

5. Because of being heavily loaded the expedition had to leave the _ _ _ _ _ _ behind.

6. The navigator for the *N–25* was _ _ _ _ _ _.

7. The navigator for the *N–24* was _ _ _ _ _ _.

8. The only sign of life observed in the waters during the entire stay was _ _ _ _ _ _.

9. The explorers were within _ _ _ _ _ _ miles of the North Pole.

10. Peary had taken _ _ _ _ _ _ years to travel this same distance.

[1] For directions, see page 14.

274 *Romance of the Airman*

11. The planes landed about _____ miles apart.

12. The walk of five and a half miles required _____ hours' time.

13. The occupants of the two planes were separated for _____ days.

14. The great loss on the trip to Amundsen's plane was that of _____.

Exercises and Topics related to your Other Subjects

1. Locate on your map the point of the landing, latitude 87 degrees 44 minutes north and longitude 10 degrees 20 minutes west. In the same way locate the most northern point visible at this location.

2. Make a brief report to the class about Swinburne, author of the lines quoted in this selection.

3. How many feet high was the plane at one thousand meters?

4. How many feet in diameter was the cake of ice two hundred meters in diameter?

5. Consult your science books and arithmetics and explain the difference between a Fahrenheit and a centigrade thermometer. When the thermometer reading was $-11.5°$ C., what would it be by a Fahrenheit thermometer?

Other Readings

In this book

"Andrée's Polar Expedition," page 250.

"*Gjoa* — To Amundsen," page 431.

From other sources

"Our Polar Flight," by Roald Amundsen and Lincoln Ellsworth.

"My Life as an Explorer," by Roald Amundsen.

Byrd's Flight to the North Pole

CHELSEA FRASER

SINCE Peary discovered the North Pole in 1909, after spending twenty-three years in the quest, other ambitious explorers have been eager to verify his observations, or else disprove them, by attaining the same goal, as some of these chapters go to show. To add to the incentive, scientists have declared it their belief, from observation and study of the polar tides and the migrations of Arctic birds, that unknown land, if not a continent itself, must exist in that mystic region which Peary gave only a cursory visit.

Great glory, of course, would be the man's who could be second in reaching the Pole. A still greater fame would rest upon his head should he return with proofs of the existence of a new continent.

So, since Peary's return many polar expeditions have been planned. Some of these have never gone any further than the planning, but others have faced the bitter cold and confusing fogs of the ice-pack in a futile attempt to accomplish their objective. Ships and dog sleds have conveyed some, while others have depended on the modern airplane to bring quicker results; but misfortune always attended the expeditions, irrespective of how carefully they had been conducted, up to the year 1926.

Yet, in spite of these failures, interest in the mysteries of the Northland increased until in the spring of 1926 it was at such a fever heat that no less than nine expeditions were being equipped for exploration by various nations. Of these, two accomplished their purpose before the remainder had even left their bases of operations, so quickly did they get away, dart into the very heart of the great

275

276 *Romance of the Airman*

unknown, and return once more to the mainland. Used as the public was to speed in transportation, it gasped to see it actually applied to accomplishment in polar work. In fact, one gasp followed another in quick succession; for, in less than twenty-four hours after Byrd's airplane had returned, wireless news was received from the dirigible flown by Amundsen, Ellsworth, and Nobile that they too were passing over the North Pole!

It is with these two expeditions, involving the first airplane and the first dirigible ever directed across the frozen wastes of the Pole, that this chapter has to deal. An American operated the airplane, and a Norwegian, an American, and an Italian handled the dirigible.

The Flight of the *Josephine Ford*

When only twelve years old Richard Byrd begged his mother so insistently to allow him to make a trip around the world, all by himself, that she consented, thinking he would be back, like most boys with the wanderlust in their blood, before he had been away from home more than two or three nights.

But little Dick was different from most boys, just as he is different from most men today. He had no idle curiosity to see the country, but a serious purpose — one looking toward his ultimate usefulness to the world in general. So he did not come back until he had accomplished his errand — just as he did not come back to Spitsbergen after leaving it until, as a man, he had likewise performed his task.

Yes, he kept going. At twelve he left his home at Richmond, Virginia, a city founded by his forefathers, went overland to San Francisco, and earned his way to the Philippines by doing chores on a steamer. Then he

The Airman becomes a Pathfinder   277

traveled on coasting vessels from one Asiatic port to another, finally returning to America when he was fifteen.

While he was at school he became greatly interested in tales of Arctic exploration, so much so that he determined to make an effort to discover the North Pole himself when he was through with his studies. Four years later, however, while he was a student at the Naval Academy, he received the discouraging news that Peary had robbed him of the contemplated glory.

"Well, if I can't be the first to see the Pole, then I'll be the second to see it," was Richard Byrd's determination. Patiently he continued his studies. To the audacity and self-reliance which marked his boyhood trip around the world, he added the attributes of science, technical skill, and the experience of important service to his country — all of which combined to fit him most efficiently for the trip he meant to make some day to the hub of the universe.

After going through the navy routine, Byrd's interest in aviation caused him to transfer to the Naval Air Service, whereupon he gave a great deal of special study to the instruments used in aërial navigation. This resulted in several very clever inventions, which revolutionized old processes and put aviation on a much safer basis.

One of these inventions was the so-called "bubble sextant," which enables flyers to obtain an artificial horizon and to calculate positions while in flight. Another device was the "sun compass," and still another a "drift indicator," the latter instrument proving of the utmost value to him in his subsequent polar dash.

As the result of these and other accomplishments, in 1919 Byrd was assigned to the duty of developing aërial navigational methods and providing equipment for the successful transatlantic flight of the *NC–4*, detailed in another portion of this volume. He volunteered to fly from

278 *Romance of the Airman*

England to this country in the dirigible *ZR-2*, and was waiting in England when that craft was wrecked.

When, in 1924, Roald Amundsen, noted Arctic explorer, asked the United States to lend him a pilot for his airplane expedition, Richard Byrd was the first man to volunteer, but the Navy Department rejected him because he was a married man. However, they allowed him to go with MacMillan* the following year; and although the expedition was a failure in so far as reaching the Pole went, Byrd flew over three thousand miles in the frozen regions and secured much valuable data for the scientific world.

Unsatisfied with the results of his 1925 flight with MacMillan, Lieutenant Commander Byrd succeeded in enlisting the financial aid of Edsel Ford, John D. Rockefeller, Jr., and others in promoting another flight in the spring of 1926. Neither money nor talent was spared. The result was that Byrd was furnished with just the kind of plane he wanted, a commercial three-engined Fokker, which he proceeded to christen the *Josephine Ford* in honor of the daughter of Edsel Ford.

This machine was designed to make a sixteen-hundred-mile nonstop flight, if required. Commander Byrd's first plans were to make Peary Land, five hundred miles from the Pole, his key-base; to dash out to the Pole and directly back again . . . would certainly not be endangering his fuel supply.

But when the good ship *Chantier*, leaving New York April 6, with the dismantled airplane and its crew aboard, reached King's Bay, Spitsbergen, on April 29, a further study of matters convinced Byrd and his mechanic, Floyd Bennett,* that a great deal of time could be saved by flying directly out from King's Bay itself. Besides, it was problematical whether a safe landing could be found on Peary Land.

The Airman becomes a Pathfinder

Byrd's Plane, the *Josephine Ford*, at King's Bay

"Considering the fact that there are other expeditions on the point of leaving and likely to snatch the honors away from us at any moment," said Byrd to Bennett, "I am more than willing to fly for the Pole without unnecessary delays. In fact, as you know, our rivals, Amundsen, Ellsworth, and Nobile, are already here with their dirigible, and who knows just how soon they will take it into their heads to depart on the same errand as ourselves?"

"The sooner we leave the better, I'm thinking, too," agreed Bennett, who had had considerable Arctic experience and was a first-class pilot as well as a mechanic.

So preparations were made with every possible speed. The *Josephine Ford* was assembled, gasoline and oil run into her tanks, and the flying instruments taken aboard. Among these instruments were four compasses. Two were

280 *Romance of the Airman*

of the ordinary magnetic type, the third was a Bumstead sun compass, and the fourth was an earth induction compass.

In the Arctic seas the sun is in sight during the entire twenty-four hours. Elevated a little above the rim of the horizon, it travels around the Pole in a complete circle. The sun compass is devised to accord with this regular movement. It is really a sundial combined with a clock mechanism which causes a hand to move around the dial once in twenty-four hours. At the same time the movement of the sun causes the shadow of the pin to travel in a circle about the dial once in twenty-four hours. The slowly moving shadow of the sun is thereby caused to fall on the slowly moving hand of the dial. As long as the shadow continues on the dial, the pilot is sure that he is on his course.

The induction compass consists of a revolving coil driven by a small motor. Electrical current is set up the moment the airplane is off its course, and when on its course there is an utter absence of current. The amount of deviation on the part of the craft is calculated by the varying strength of the electricity.

It was realized that the two magnetic compasses would not be perfectly reliable. For one thing, the metal of the plane body would affect them somewhat, and, for another thing, they were certain to give aberrations due to the fact that they would be influenced by the Magnetic Pole rather than the North Pole, the former being on Bootha Island, twelve hundred miles south of the latter. Yet, by making allowances for these known variations, a fairly accurate estimate of position was possible; so the magnetic instruments were carried along in case the others failed. No reasonable precaution should be overlooked.

Physically, Commander Byrd was unusually well fortified to stand the rigors of the trip. Not only did he and

The Airman becomes a Pathfinder 281

Bennett wear heavy, fur-lined flying suits and helmets and gloves, but Byrd had inured his body to severe cold and sudden changes of temperature by going about all winter long without underwear, gloves, or overcoat for several years past. He was as hardy and tough as a polar bear, and as cheerful under the lash of bitter winds as any Eskimo or Laplander.

Although Commander Byrd's flight from Peary Land had been set for May 15, the change in his plans made it possible for him to fly from King's Bay six days ahead of schedule. By Sunday, May 9, everything was ready for the take-off, and at 12.30 A.M., Greenwich time, the big monoplane, with its three sturdy engines roaring, arose from the ground and started off toward the North Pole, going as straight as a bird flies.

The sun was shining, there were no bothering head winds, and not a sign of fog loomed ahead. It was a most promising start, and the hearts of both men beat high with hope and stirred with sporting excitement.

In the pilot's seat sat Commander Byrd, looking steadfastly ahead, his hands ever busy with the controls and instruments, while his companion listened intently for squeaks or other noises betokening motor trouble. Up, up, they shot, gradually gaining altitude, until they were flying fully two thousand feet above the sea.

Below gleamed a dark mass of water which later merged into the white squares of the pack ice. Byrd looked hard for some sign of life, but there was none — not a polar bear, not a seal, not even a bird.

Every hour the two flyers alternated at the wheel, to avoid fatigue. When he was not piloting, Bennett busied himself filling the gas tanks from the supply cans and in gauging the constantly diminishing quantity left in them. And when Byrd was not at the wheel, he was incessantly

282 Romance of the Airman

navigating, and applying every ounce of his mind into making their course so straight that they were unlikely to deviate a half-mile from the imaginary line leading them on toward their goal.

After they had been out several hours, both men began to feel hungry and drank several cups of hot tea from their thermos bottles. At that time they were flying along at a rate of over a mile and a half a minute, and the air was so keen that when Byrd stood up to consult the sun compass, the bitter wind struck his exposed cheeks and nose and severely frost-bit them. Only by the briskest kind of rubbing was he able to restore circulation to the affected parts and prevent them from freezing. Indeed, several times he found his hands growing numb through his sealskin gloves, and he had to beat his fingers against the cockpit in order to save them.

Presently Commander Byrd detected an oil leak * in the right-hand motor. He relieved Bennett of the wheel and asked him to examine the leak and advise him as to its seriousness. Bennett wrote a note stating that the leak was very bad; that it might be well for them to land on their skis and try to repair it. But, as they were within an hour's run of the Pole at the time, Byrd decided to go on, and throttled down the starboard motor to check its inclination to leak.

At the end of the hour the Commander took fresh calculations and gave vent to an exclamation of joy. They were at the Pole! It was 9.04 Greenwich time, on the morning of May 10, and just about the minute he had figured he would strike his objective.

The two flyers looked solemnly at one another, then shook hands without a word. Although American flags had been taken aboard for the purpose of dropping one or more in just such an event as the present, Commander

The Airman becomes a Pathfinder   283

Byrd suddenly decided that the act would be inappropriate, since Peary, another American, had planted the Stars and Stripes some seventeen years previously.

So they flew on, going several miles farther, then circled back over the great expanse of ribbed ice which lay about the Pole and took a number of still pictures of the scene, as well as some motion views.

As they hovered over the inspiring spot, Commander Byrd thought of a little coin that he carried pinned to his shirt — the same coin that Peary himself had worn when he visited the place. For the second time that small coin had reached the top of the world, just as both explorers had hoped it might!

Now Byrd and Bennett began to concern themselves with their return. What would they do about the leaky oil tank? Much writing with numbed fingers went back and forth on little pads between the two flyers. Bennett still advocated a landing, if a promising one appeared; Byrd maintained that it was too risky so long as the oil held out.

The Commander finally set a course for Gray Hook, Spitsbergen, a few miles east of Amsterdam Island. Bennett took the wheel for his usual stint, and Byrd busied himself comparing the variations of the magnetic compasses with the sun compass. In so doing he made the important discovery that he could tell how much they were drifting by the amount the magnetic instrument differed from the sun instrument. From that moment on he felt no further fear of the airplane's greatest enemy, fog, and continued the homeward flight with renewed confidence.

The wind began to freshen and change direction after they had left the Pole, and in another hour they were making more than a hundred miles an hour. In the vast,

284 Romance of the Airman

white area about them, as still as a graveyard except for the startling roar of their motors, they felt no larger than a pin point, as lonely as one can imagine, and as detached from the universe as a star. Here in another world, far from the haunts of their own kind, the passions and petty meannesses of civilization fell from their shoulders. What wonder that they felt no emotion of achievement or fear of death while in the midst of both!

Three hours after leaving the North Pole they had re-entered the explored regions. Fully ten thousand miles of territory had been transferred by them from the unknown sections of maps to the known. This service to future generations was well worth feeling proud over.

In the meanwhile the motor attached to the leaking oil tank was still pounding away without a hitch, and the flyers had hopes that the supply would hold out until their arrival at King's Bay. If it should not, however, they felt no great alarm now, for they were confident that they could make their destination on two motors if not three. As a matter of fact, the tank did not exhaust itself, which was owing to the oil being of a heavy type, with a slow feed.

In the meantime the *Chantier* was lying quietly at anchor in the harbor at King's Bay, and the huge envelope of the *Norge*, the airship of Amundsen and Ellsworth, was tugging lazily at her moorings in the big hangar on the hillside. Up until four o'clock that morning of the ninth of May, wireless messages had been received reporting the progress of the Fokker as she advanced; but after that hour nothing was picked up, and a feeling of uneasiness had assailed the numerous friends of Byrd and Bennett.

About six o'clock in the afternoon Captain Amundsen, Lincoln Ellsworth, Colonel Nobile, and others of the rival

The Airman becomes a Pathfinder   285

crew were ranged about the big table in the *Norge's* mess hall, finishing their soup and discussing the portent of the *Josephine Ford's* silence, when suddenly there was a cry of "Byrd is coming!"

Sure enough, high over the hills on the other side of the bay, a tiny speck of birdlike shape, but too large to be a bird, showed itself in the sky. The experienced airmen recognized it at once as the blue Fokker plane. Even the hum of the motors could be heard faintly, still whirring smoothly and tirelessly after fifteen hours and fifty-one minutes of steady going, during which an exploit had been accomplished which many scientific men had said could never be done.

As the plane rapidly drew closer, it turned southward over the bay, making huge circles over the glaciers, then swerved back northward over the mountains.

People began to gather on the hillsides, excitedly pointing toward the machine. The steam whistle aboard the *Chantier* shrieked out a noisy welcome, was tied open, and continued its wild blast in a roaring, continuous stream of sound. Figures appeared on the ship's deck, scrambled down the rope ladder, and made for the shore.

For several minutes Commander Byrd continued to circle over the town, just to prove that he had plenty of gas left after his visit to the North Pole. Then he slowly swooped downward and landed.

Captain Amundsen, rival though he was, was one of the first to reach Byrd's side. He came panting up the hill, threw his long arms around the American flyer, hugged him, and kissed his cheek in the European fashion of greeting a friend, and exclaimed feelingly:

"You have been to the Pole! It is magnificent! It is wonderful! You have beaten us, but my men are full of admiration, sir!"

286 *Romance of the Airman*

It was a gracious, noble thing for Amundsen to say, on the very eve of his own planned departure for the same goal, after years of vain effort to attain it. Nor was Ellsworth, his American partner, nor Nobile, far behind him. These leaders also offered their hearty congratulations to the triumphant flyers of the *Ford*.

After the hand-shaking was over, Byrd and Bennett, very tired from sitting so long in the cramped cockpits, stretched their arms and legs. The eyes of both men were heavy from loss of rest and intense strain; but before going aboard the *Chantier*, Commander Byrd insisted upon sending a telegram of his safe arrival to his anxious mother in Virginia, to his wife in Boston, and to President Coolidge.

As they approached the *Chantier*, those on deck cheered hoarsely and the band played "The Star-Spangled Banner." And when they were actually on deck the entire crew, many of whom were hardly rested from their labors in getting the airplane off, danced about them in childish joy at this quick ending of their work.

Words and Phrases

To aid in understanding this selection

MacMillan: Donald B. MacMillan's party made scout flights from Etah, Greenland, in two navy amphibian planes in August, 1925.

Floyd Bennett: Byrd, in speaking of Bennett as his companion for the expedition to the North Pole, said, "I would rather have Floyd with me than any other man in the world."

oil leak: a leak caused by a rivet's jarring loose. When the oil got down below the rivet hole, it stopped leaking.

To add to your vocabulary

cursory	inured
deviation	swerved
aberrations	

The Airman becomes a Pathfinder 287

Technical terms

airplane	sun compass
dirigible	magnetic compass
aërial navigation	induction compass
bubble sextant	drift indicator

Informal Test (Completion)[1]

1. Peary spent _ _ _ _ _ _ years in reaching the Pole.

2. In the spring of 1926 there were at least _ _ _ _ _ _ expeditions in preparation for the polar dash.

3. The *Norge* reached the Pole less than _ _ _ _ _ _ hours after Byrd.

4. Byrd's plane was named _ _ _ _ _ _.

5. Byrd started on his first trip round the world when he was _ _ _ _ _ _ years old.

6. While he was a student at _ _ _ _ _ _, he learned that Peary had reached the Pole.

7. Byrd invented _ _ _ _ _ _.

8. Byrd volunteered as a pilot for the polar expedition of _ _ _ _ _ _.

9. He went on the polar expedition of _ _ _ _ _ _.

10. Byrd's polar expedition was financed by _ _ _ _ _ _.

11. His companion during the trip to the Pole was _ _ _ _ _ _ _ _ _ _ _ _.

12. The only trouble they had with their motors was _ _ _ _ _ _.

13. Byrd carried with him _ _ _ _ _ _ that Peary had carried to the Pole.

14. The first person to greet Byrd on his landing was _ _ _ _ _ _ _ _ _ _ _ _.

15. The band on the *Chantier* welcomed them with _ _ _ _ _ _ _ _ _ _ _ _.

[1] For directions, see page 14.

288 *Romance of the Airman*

Exercises and Topics related to your Other Subjects

1. Make a map showing Byrd's route.

2. Locate on the map the following:
a. Peary Land.
b. The Magnetic Pole.
c. Gray Hook.

3. Byrd reached the Pole at 9.04 A.M., Greenwich time. What time was that by his mother's clock at Richmond, Virginia? What time was it at San Francisco, California?

Subjects for oral themes

The Sun Compass was for Byrd what the Magnetic Compass was for Columbus.
Superstitions about "Lucky Pieces." (Alcock carried a kewpie doll and two little yarn figures as lucky omens on the first transatlantic flight.)
Peary's Trip to the Pole.
MacMillan's Polar Expeditions.

Other Readings

In this book

"Floyd Bennett laid to Rest as the Elements Rage," page 426.
"Bisecting the Arctic," page 289.

From other sources

"Skyward," by Richard E. Byrd.
"Little America," by Richard E. Byrd.
"A Tenderfoot with Peary," by G. Borup.
"Heroes of the Farthest North and Farthest South," by J. Kennedy MacLean.
"MacMillan's Flight in Quest of a New Polar Land," from "Heroes of the Air," by Chelsea Fraser.
"Four Years in the White North," by D. B. MacMillan.

Bisecting the Arctic

F. RAMM

Explanatory Note. General Umberto Nobile of Italy and Captain Roald Amundsen each had conceived a plan of reaching the North Pole by means of a dirigible. They finally decided to join forces and to make the expedition in the dirigible *Norge,* which was purchased from the Italian government. The expedition set off from Rome in April, 1926, and was ready for the dash to the Pole from Spitsbergen on May 10.

The cruise from the Pole to Teller was filled with thrilling incidents. The crew were greatly interested in their first sight of Eskimos on the coast of Bering Strait. They learned afterwards that these people had taken the *Norge* for a flying seal, a whale, or even the devil himself. In Nobile's own account of the voyage he gives a dramatic, almost poetical, description of the deflation of the huge dirigible at the end of her journey.

ON THURSDAY morning at 8.55 A. M. the *Norge* rose with a cargo of twelve tons, including fuel, from King's Bay, Spitsbergen. Before we left Amsterdam Island we corrected our compass by solar observations and wireless signals, so that, in order to facilitate our later radiogoniometric tests, we might follow close to the meridian that passes through the King's Bay wireless station. We navigated through broad sunshine except for the last hour before we reached the Pole. This part of our journey offered nothing of especial interest, since all the land we sighted had already been flown over by the Amundsen-Ellsworth expedition * last year. Our course was constantly regulated by radiogoniometric checks, and by observations of longitude whenever the sun was in a favorable position.

By half past two next morning we were able to ascertain by a successful solar observation that we had arrived over the Pole. Our vessel descended to a lower elevation. We throttled down the motors, and Amundsen, Ellsworth,

The Norge leaving King's Bay for its Transpolar Flight

and Nobile threw over the national flags of their respective countries. These were attached to sharp-pointed steel staffs, which stuck upright in the ice and remained there. During this ceremony the crew of the *Norge* stood with bared heads. The fluttering banners on the glistening ice below made a wonderful picture.

We circled over the Pole and turned in the direction of Point Barrow. Everyone was on the alert to discover land, for we were crossing a tract of the globe's surface more than twelve hundred miles long which had never before been seen by human eye. About seven o'clock we reached the Ice Pole, which is regarded as the most difficult point of access on the earth's surface, and shook hands joyously over our achievement.

Soon afterwards a dense fog compelled us to ascend to a great elevation, but frequent apertures in the cloud blanket enabled us to see large stretches beneath. We were unable to make out any land. Heavy clouds gathered above us, and gradually sank down until they mingled with the fog below, compelling us to continue blindly through the mist.

This was the beginning of the most anxious part of our journey. We sank to a lower elevation, but encountered a snowstorm. When we ascended to get out of that, frost gathered on the cordage and outer metal portions of the airship and rapidly accumulated into a thick ice coating. The bank of clouds was so high that we could not ascend above it without too great a sacrifice of gas. We kept experimenting, however, with different altitudes, keeping a sharp eye on the temperature and on the ice accumulation, but found no level where we escaped this impediment entirely, and so continued on our course as best we could.

Colonel Umberto Nobile and his Faithful Dog

The ice that had gathered on our cordage and on the outside of the motor gondolas fell off in pieces, striking the propellers, which batted it against the vessel's side. Other ice, which had formed on the propellers themselves, was likewise hurled in all directions. Consequently we passed several hours of extreme anxiety, during which the whole crew was constantly on the watch to repair holes in the outer skin and the gas bags. Luckily the gas bags had been made extra strong in contemplation of this very possibility; but we could never be sure that they would hold out. We no longer scanned the pack ice beneath us with purely Platonic feelings, but with a lively appreciation of the fact that it might become our only highway to safety. Finally atmospheric conditions improved somewhat, and we were able to take a course beneath the clouds which was comparatively free from moisture.

Our magnetic compass exhibited erratic variations because the deviation kept changing. Now and then, however, the sun would pierce the clouds and enable us to take an observation. Our sun compass, which was fastened outside the gondola, had become a block of ice and was useless. Just as we crossed the Alaska coast a little west of Point Barrow, however, we were able to determine a north-and-south course by solar observations; but we did not know our latitude, because the fog had prevented our seeing the earth below to estimate our speed. Consequently, about forty-eight hours after leaving King's Bay, we took a course approximately parallel with the Alaska coast. A rising wind from behind increased our speed, but it was very misty, and the deep snow concealed the contour of the land; so we rose to a higher elevation, hoping to sight more favorable atmospheric conditions farther south. Nothing resulted from this, and we later descended closer to the ground, although at some risk of driving headlong into a mountain side through the dense fog.

We continued navigating more or less blindly in this manner until finally a lucky solar observation indicated that we were directly over Bering Strait. We now struck a moist air current which deposited ice rapidly on the

The Airman becomes a Pathfinder 293

outer envelope of the airship. This was a much greater danger than it had been a few hours before, because we had already exhausted our patching materials.

It was therefore decided to land at the first opportunity. We headed directly toward the east, but soon discovered that this carried us over open water and then across an ice field. Conditions seemed no better farther south. We therefore steered a little more to the northward, where ice conditions seemed to be better, but we made slow progress.

During the last night of our journey we signaled constantly, hoping to ascertain our position from some wireless station, but in vain. Finally we found ourselves again over land, and saw several Eskimo huts. We attempted to descend in order to inquire our position, but violent squalls prevented. Thereupon we ascended through the clouds to an elevation where we could ascertain our latitude [1] by a solar observation. In doing so we drifted a considerable distance inland, so that we required a full hour to regain the coast after descending to a lower level.

The fog was now exceedingly dense, but we began to hear the wireless apparatus at Nome receiving signals from some other station, and were able to ascertain our approximate position from that. Conjecturing that we were about over Cape Prince of Wales, we turned northwest, following the coast line; but the wind from the mountains was exceedingly violent and tossed us about incessantly, so that our barograph needle danced around like that of a seismograph* during an earthquake. Again we lost our exact position, for the violent tossing of the vessel did not permit us to descend low enough to see the earth through the mist. As the wind continued to increase in force, we finally decided to land at Teller and not to try to reach Nome, as the terrain seemed to be fairly good at

[1] Latitude 71° N.; longitude between 157° and 158° W.

294 Romance of the Airman

the former point. But we all knew what it meant to moor our vessel in such weather without assistance from the earth, and were prepared for the worst.

Our first supper in Teller was an unforgettable event. The hot coffee tasted like ambrosia, for every member of the *Norge's* crew had suffered intensely from the cold for hours at a time, especially when the fog was the worst and the air was filled with moisture. The moment we opened a cabin window to make an observation a dank, chill mist would pour in and fill the cabin, making the work of the observers, who had to manipulate their instruments with bare hands, exceedingly difficult.

No sooner was our ship safely on land than we tried to get into connection with the wireless station at Nome, in order to notify the world that we were safe. But the Teller station had not been working for two years, and we signaled for several hours without result. It was not until we had repaired our own sending apparatus, twenty-four hours later, that we established a connection. It was rather exciting during the interval to keep picking up signals calling for the *Norge*, showing that we were supposed to be drifting over the ocean farther south.

Amundsen, Ellsworth, and Wisting * immediately left Teller, and will await the other members of the expedition at Nome. We leave as soon as the airship is completely dismantled. Amundsen and his two companions drove out over the ice with dog sleds for more than twenty miles before they reached open water. A big three-ton motor boat which is to take them to Nome had to be hauled the same distance by dog sleds.

During our flight every member of the crew was so busy with his duties, navigating, steering, and attending to the wireless and the motors, that no one had time to think of danger. We now realize how narrowly we escaped de-

The Airman becomes a Pathfinder   295

struction, and how largely we owe our safety to a combination of good luck and wise prevision. Probably we were in greatest danger when we were crossing Alaska at a low altitude in a violent northwestern storm and nearly lost our course. The big ship was carried along only one hundred or one hundred and fifty feet above the ground at a rate of nearly sixty miles an hour. The ice-and-snow-covered landscape flew past us as rapidly as it does through the windows of an express train.

Before Amundsen left us every member of the expedition offered him his services for a new exploration. Our leader answered: "When I was a young man I made up my mind to travel over the whole world, to reach both Poles, and to make the Northwestern and Northeastern Passages. I have done all that. Another generation can now take a hand." *

We have been hard at work taking the vessel to pieces and packing it in boxes to be shipped back to Rome, where it will be reassembled. It received only minor injuries during the landing, and can easily be rebuilt. But the first day was spent resting up from our seventy-one hours of arduous labor.

Riiser Larsen, to whom was confided the difficult task of navigating the vessel, steered her safely over an unknown course through fog and snow, and against violent head winds, and, although he had but fragmentary observations to guide him, was able to report to Amundsen and Ellsworth, forty-six hours after we left King's Bay, that Point Barrow on the coast of Alaska was in sight.

Colonel Nobile watched with tireless attention every maneuver of the vessel and every movement of its complicated machinery. The result of the flight fully justified the wise provisions he had made for a winter journey. He had foreseen with remarkable prescience * the very dif-

296 *Romance of the Airman*

ficulties and dangers that we actually encountered. For example, had he not anticipated the possibility that ice from the propeller would be thrown against the side of the vessel, and strengthened the gas bags of that section of her hull to provide against this, we should probably have been forced to land on the polar ice.

Wisting, the quartermaster of the *Norge*, had but four hours' sleep during our whole period in the air. Gottwaldt, Storm, and Johnsen, our radio operators, were almost continuously at their apparatus, taking meteorological observations and trying to pick up messages from wireless stations. As long as our antennæ and generators were free from ice we were in continuous touch with land stations and knew precisely where we were. The Italian members of our crew — Cecioni, Arduino, Caratti, Poella, and Alessandrini — and also Omdal were in almost constant attendance on our motors, utilizing the brief periods when they were off duty to assist in patching the vessel's skin.

Our provisions consisted of buttered bread, hard-boiled eggs, meat, and cake, all of which froze solid. Indeed, even the coffee and tea in our thermos flasks were cold.

Words and Phrases

To aid in understanding this selection

the **Amundsen-Ellsworth expedition:** an unsuccessful flight for the Pole in 1925.

seismograph: an instrument for recording graphs that denote the period, extent, and direction of each of the vibrations of an earthquake.

Wisting: Captain Wisting of this crew had been with Amundsen when he discovered the South Pole in 1911. When the *Norge* reached the North Pole, Amundsen and Wisting were the only two men who had seen both poles. Byrd's flight to the South Pole in 1929 added a third name to the list of those who had seen both the top and the bottom of the world.

The Airman becomes a Pathfinder   297

Another generation can now take a hand: Amundsen sums up his life work in the quotation given by Ramm. He spoke truer than he knew. Two years later he made his last expedition in an effort to rescue Colonel Nobile, whose airship *Italia* had been wrecked on its way to the North Pole. Colonel Nobile and Amundsen had had a bitter quarrel; but when the former was lost in the Arctic seas, Amundsen headed one of the searching expeditions sent out for him. Nobile was rescued by another party; but Amundsen was lost, presumably somewhere off the Norwegian coast.

prescience: foresight.

To add to your vocabulary

apertures	terrain
erratic	ambrosia
contour	dank
conjecturing	

Technical terms

barograph	gondola

Informal Test (Completion)[1]

1. The flags were supported by _ _ _ _ _ _.

2. When the *Norge* sank to a lower elevation, the crew encountered _ _ _ _ _ _.

3. When they rose higher, there was trouble from _ _ _ _ _ _.

4. The whole crew was engaged constantly on the watch for _ _ _ _ _ _.

5. The sun compass had become _ _ _ _ _ _.

6. The landing was necessary because of the exhaustion of _ _ _ _ _ _.

7. The men who left Teller at once were _ _ _ _ _ _.

8. They traveled the first twenty miles from Teller by _ _ _ _ _ _.

9. They went on in _ _ _ _ _ _.

[1] For directions, see page 14.

298 Romance of the Airman

10. The crew had not realized how dangerous the flight was because _____.

11. Amundsen said he would leave further explorations to _____.

12. The navigator for this trip was _____.

13. Wisting slept only _____ hours on the whole flight.

Exercises and Topics related to your Other Subjects

Locate on a map Cape Prince of Wales and the place on the Alaskan coast indicated by the latitude and longitude given in the footnote on page 293.

Compare what "Land!" meant to Nobile with what it meant to Columbus. (Nobile said that when the officer on watch cried "Land!" as they sighted the coast of Alaska, he realized what the feelings of Columbus must have been nearly four and a half centuries ago.)

Subject for oral theme

The Eyes of Three Nations watch the Flags drop at "the Top of the World."

Other Readings

In this book

"The Amundsen-Ellsworth Polar Flight," page 262.
"Byrd's Flight to the North Pole," page 275.

From other sources

"My Life as an Explorer," by Roald Amundsen.
"The Tragedy of the *Italia*," by Davide Giudici.
"Navigating the *Norge*," by General Umberto Nobile, *National Geographic Magazine*, August, 1927.
"The Last Voyage of the *Karluk*," by R. A. Bartlett and R. T. Hale.

Crossing the Atlantic

WHEN Robert L. Ripley published in his "Believe It or Not!" pictures the statement that Lindbergh was the sixty-seventh man to make a nonstop transatlantic flight, his announcement was received by an incredulous public — one might say a defensive public — unwilling to have its young hero's laurels shared by sixty-six other men.

Crossing the Atlantic by air had been a dream of a half-century at least. In 1873 three venturous spirits — William H. Donaldson, Alfred Ford, and George A. Lunt — planned a transoceanic flight in a balloon. Their balloon, the *Graphic*, hopped off boldly on this hazardous undertaking from Brooklyn, New York, on October 7, 1873. Fortunately for the three men in the basket, a storm drove them down safely on land in New Canaan, Connecticut.

The news of this first attempted flight was read in America by a public that had been put in a state of expectancy by certain fictitious stories of Atlantic crossings. A quarter of a century before this the New York *Sun* had carried the startling headlines

---

THE ATLANTIC CROSSED IN THREE DAYS!

Signal Triumph of Mr. Monck Mason's Flying Machine!

This was followed by a detailed account as vivid as that given by the metropolitan papers to the *Graf Zeppelin's* spectacular cruise around the world in August, 1929. But, alas, the readers learned after a few days' suspense that

300 *Romance of the Airman*

they had been the victims of a hoax by that master story-writer Edgar Allan Poe. Not to be outdone by this earlier writer, Mark Twain, in "Tom Sawyer Abroad," pictures Tom, accompanied by the faithful Huck and Jim, sending Aunt Polly word of his trip across the ocean. The letter is dated "In the *Welkin*, approaching England," and is signed "From Tom Sawyer, the Erronort." The ink was scarcely dry on this fictitious account when the newspapers published the news of the first real attempt.

During the war the United States navy had started the construction of flying boats that would be able to cross the Atlantic, but it was not until the spring of 1919 that the preparations were complete for the trial flight. The plan was to take off from Trepassey Bay, Newfoundland, for Lisbon, Portugal, with a stop at the Azores. From Portugal a flight was to be made to Plymouth, England, to return the visit which the *Mayflower* had made three centuries before.

Three seaplanes, the *NC–1*, *NC–3*, and *NC–4*, took off on May 16 over a route made safe to the Azores by watchful destroyers of the United States navy and equally safe from the Azores to Lisbon by the guardianship of the British navy. The *NC–4*, under the command of Lieutenant Commander A. C. Read, was the only plane to get across. The total flying time to Lisbon was 26 hours and 45 minutes. The feat had been accomplished! The Atlantic had been crossed! The *NC–4* now reposes in the Smithsonian Institution at Washington, D.C., a monument to another significant American achievement in aviation.

But before the *NC–4* had completed her crossing, three other expeditions were under way for a nonstop transatlantic flight, stimulated by the offer of a $50,000 prize from the London *Daily Mail*, Lord Northcliffe's paper.

The NC-4 at the Azores in May, 1919
Courtesy of the Smithsonian Institution

Two British flyers, Hawker and Grieve, left St. John's, Newfoundland, for a nonstop flight to Ireland on May 18. A week went by, and nothing was heard from the flyers. All England mourned them as dead, when word came that they had been rescued by the Danish steamer *Mary*, after a forced landing. England was wild with joy, and it accorded a welcome to the defeated flyers such as few heroes have received. King George bestowed upon them the Royal Air Force Cross for their bravery, and Lord Northcliffe presented them with a consolation prize of $25,000!

About an hour after the Hawker and Grieve start, a second pair of British competitors for the prize attempted to take off from the same place. Raynham and Morgan broke an axle before they cleared the ground. While they awaited repairs the successful flight was made.

A third British entry in the race was the Vickers-Vimy bomber of Captain John Alcock and Lieutenant Arthur

The Vickers-Vimy, the Plane in which Alcock and Brown made their Transatlantic Flight on June 14, 1919

Courtesy of the Smithsonian Institution

Brown. On June 14 they made a hurried take-off from St. John's, leaving a rival behind who was intent on assembling his Handley-Page machine. A short distance out their wireless apparatus was torn away by winds, and they were forced to find their way unaided. Soon they were in a dense fog. Night came on with neither moon nor stars. A heavy sleet covered the plane with ice. All the long night they struggled on with no guide but their compass. Morning dawned, the sun peeped through the clouds, and they were able to check their compass course with the sun compass. The sun-reading showed they were almost exactly on their path. Then Clifden came in view, and in a few minutes the plane was landed, nose down, in a bog. The prize was won, and the first nonstop flight was ended more than eight years before Lindbergh's crossing. They wired the following report to London:

The Airman becomes a Pathfinder 303

Landed at Clifden at 8.40 A.M. Greenwich mean time, 15th of June, 1919, Vickers-Vimy Atlantic machine, leaving Newfoundland coast at 4.28 P.M. Greenwich mean time, 14th of June. Total time, 16 hours, 12 minutes.

ALCOCK and BROWN

England again was wild with joy, and made a second ovation for returned heroes. Winston Churchill, Secretary of State for War, in a speech of welcome to them said that while Columbus, four hundred years before, had crossed the Atlantic in ninety days, Alcock and Brown had crossed in sixteen hours. He continued, "How different were those two voyages in all except two conditions — the peril and the pluck!" The king of England knighted these men who had brought such glory to the British nation. But Americans claimed some of the glory; for Brown, although in the king's service, was born of American parents.

Meantime the lighter-than-air craft *R–34* was preparing for an east-west crossing. In 1910 a non-rigid airship, *America,* commanded by Walter Wellman, had attempted to fly the Atlantic, but had met disaster when about a thousand miles out from Atlantic City, the starting point. The *R–34* was the largest British dirigible, a huge rigid airship carrying five cars. Under the command of Major H. G. Scott the voyage was made from East Fortune, Scotland, to Mineola, Long Island, in 108 hours and 12 minutes. The plan was to land on July 4, but unfavorable winds prolonged the trip until the morning of July 6. There were thirty-one men aboard, including Lieutenant Commander Zachary Lansdowne, later commander of the ill-fated *Shenandoah,* who had been invited to represent the air corps of the United States army, and who thus gained the distinction of being the first American citizen to make a nonstop Atlantic crossing. After being

R-34, a British Dirigible that covered 3200 Miles, from Scotland to Mineola, New York, in One Hundred and Eight Hours and Twelve Minutes

fêted for four days in America the *R-34* turned homeward with Major W. N. Hensley, Jr., this time, representing the air corps. As the British ship sailed away she complimented her hosts by flying the American flag. The return journey was made in 74 hours and 56 minutes. On the way home the following message was sent back.

TO THE AMERICAN OFFICERS, ROOSEVELT FIELD:

Good-by, America! We thank you for your hospitality, and we hope the good relations of the two countries will continue forevermore.

Crew of the *R-34*

According to the provisions of the treaty that closed the World War, Germany was to build for the United States a dirigible at the great Zeppelin works at Friedrichshafen. When this ship, the *ZR-3*, was finished, it was brought to America under the command of Dr. Hugo Eckener, president of the Zeppelin works, and a crew of thirty-two. They landed at Lakehurst, New Jersey, on October 15, 1924, after a nonstop voyage of 81 hours and 17 minutes.

The Airman becomes a Pathfinder   305

When the passengers of this vessel disembarked, the number of men who had made a nonstop flight numbered sixty-six. The German flag was replaced by the Stars and Stripes, and the name *ZR-3* was changed to *Los Angeles*.

Then came the spring of 1927, with a second great race across the Atlantic for another prize, $25,000, offered this time by Raymond Orteig. Two gallant young Frenchmen, Nungesser and Coli, met their death in attempting an east-west crossing in early May. In the few weeks following that tragedy, Lindbergh, Chamberlin, and Byrd made their successful crossings in rapid succession, and the air path from America to Europe was made.

Words and Phrases

To add to your vocabulary

      hoax   welkin   bog

Technical term   dirigible

Informal Test (Matching)[1]

1. "The Balloon Hoax"
2. The first plane to fly the Atlantic
3. The commander of the first plane
4. The $50,000 prize
5. The $25,000 prize
6. Hawker and Grieve
7. Raynham and Morgan
8. The first nonstop transatlantic flight
9. The first east-west nonstop flight

ZR-3
Landsdowne
broken axle
Raymond Orteig
Alcock and Brown
Hawker and Grieve
R-34
Friedrichshafen
Charles Lindbergh
Clifden
lost flyers
Lord Northcliffe
A. C. Read

[1] For directions, see page 9.

306 *Romance of the Airman*

10. The American representative on the first east-west crossing   *NC–4*

11. The ship given as reparations   Edgar Allan Poe

12. The winner of the Orteig prize   St. John's

13. The recipients of the $25,000 consolation prize   Mark Twain

14. The landing place of the first nonstop flight   flying boats

15. The take-off of the first nonstop flight   Roosevelt Field

16. The Zeppelin works

Exercises and Topics related to your Other Subjects

1. On an outline map of the Atlantic Ocean, mark the flights told of in this selection.

2. Alcock and Brown landed at Clifden, Ireland, at 8.40 A.M., Greenwich time. What time was it by the clocks in Chicago? by the clocks in your town?

Subject for oral theme

Contrast the voyage of the *Mayflower* with that of the *NC–4*.

Subject for written theme

The Zeppelin Works

Other Readings

In this book

"Nungesser and Coli fly to Death in the *White Bird*," page 307

From other sources

"Tom Sawyer Abroad," by Mark Twain.

"The Balloon Hoax," by Edgar Allan Poe.

"They Did it First," from "Skylarking," by Bruce Gould.

"Skyward," by Richard E. Byrd, Chapter XII.

"Record Flights," by Clarence Chamberlin.

"20 Hrs. 40 Min.," by Amelia Earhart.

"We," by Charles Lindbergh, Chapter X.

"The Log of the H. M. A. *R–34*," by E. M. Maitland.

Nungesser and Coli fly to Death in the *White Bird*

IRVING CRUMP

> *Explanatory Note.* When Europe had once more settled back into peaceful pursuits after the World War, Raymond Orteig, a prominent and wealthy hotel owner, offered a large sum of money to the man who should successfully complete a nonstop flight between New York and Paris. This prize of $25,000 was offered with the hope that it would hasten the time when a commercial air route between America and France would be definitely established. Many daring aviators tried their luck, and either were rewarded with victory and renown or went to their deaths somewhere on the journey across. The tragic story of two of the most daring flyers is told here.

COFFIN, candles, skull and crossbones — a grisly emblem was Nungesser's. He had it painted on the side of the *White Bird*, and was proud of it — the sign of death.

But he did not put it there because he thought his airplane was doomed to go down under the waves on the transatlantic flight. No, indeed, for he was confident that he would be the first man in history to get all the way across, and that thus he would add to the glory of France.

Nungesser put his insignia there to flout death. It was defiance — defiance from a man who had braved death innumerable times over the lines of the enemy during the World War. He had been wounded many times, but had always recovered the best of health, and as a result he had the feeling that he simply could not die.

Not that his wounds were not serious. They were; in fact, some were so serious that in the beginning his life was despaired of. In many parts of his body the bones were so cruelly hurt that they had to be removed and aluminum substituted in their place. One of his knees had been fitted with a joint, and the same applied to an

308 *Romance of the Airman*

elbow and his jaw, and it was even said that part of his skull had been replaced by this metal.

And that was the Nungesser who on Sunday, May 8, 1927, hopped off for New York City from Le Bourget Air Field in Paris, and has never been seen or heard of since. That was the dearly beloved ace of the French air forces, that "Prince of Pilots," who in his latest endeavor to bring glory to his country sacrificed his life, for there is no doubt about his having met his death somewhere on his journey across.

Charles Nungesser and François Coli, his navigator — they were the two who electrified the world on that day, and who threw France into a frenzy of mourning when, as one day succeeded another, no news was received of them. Noble, heroic men! Let us trace their dramatic story from beginning to end, or as near to the end as it is possible to come, for their fate remains a mystery.

Nungesser, all his life, was in search of adventure. In his early youth he went to the pampas regions in the Argentine, where he became a cowboy and where his greatest diversion was hunting wild game. He became a crack shot with pistol and rifle, and was in excellent physical condition when the first guns of the World War were fired and his beloved native land was in danger of being throttled.

He dropped all of his interests and returned to France as rapidly as possible to join her military forces. He was assigned to the Second Hussars, but that regiment was not active enough for him. He had crossed the seas to get into the fray, so he had himself transferred to the 148th Infantry, where he encountered more thrilling events.

One day the Germans completely surrounded his company. The French commanding officer was unable to see any way of escape without reënforcements, and he chose

The Airman becomes a Pathfinder 309

young Nungesser to attempt the perilous task of running the German fire and obtaining the aid they needed.

After dark, Nungesser, with one companion, jumped into an automobile and rushed past the German rifle and machine-gun fire. The two men held their heads down as they speeded along; but all was not to be well, for a machine-gun bullet disabled their engine and forced their machine to stop. Nungesser and his companion immediately jumped out and, protected by the darkness, found refuge in a clump of underbrush by the roadside. When the enemy soldiers came up to take possession of the machine and to make its passengers prisoners, they found, of course, only the automobile.

Proceeding warily toward their destination, the two French soldiers discovered a German automobile approaching, and, barricading the road so that it could not pass, they waited for it. The car contained three or four enemy officers; but, nothing daunted, Nungesser stepped out and began to shoot. The officers surrendered, and Nungesser and his companion took possession of the machine in return for the one the other German soldiers had ruined and captured. They made the rest of their journey in this motor, being forced many times to run the gauntlet of enemy rifle fire. Several times the car was hit; but the engine was not injured, and the men were not once wounded. They were almost exhausted when they reached their post and delivered the message. Their gallantry, however, had saved their company.

There is a story going the rounds of the French army that when Nungesser arrived at his destination with his message the commanding officer said to him:

"You are a Hussar, and your automobile is a car of death; from now on you will be known as the Hussar of Death."

310 *Romance of the Airman*

Nungesser, the legend says, always cherished those words, and there are those who say that it was that thought which made him almost believe that he bore a charmed life. Whether or not this is true, the fact remains that from that time on he adopted as his insignia the white coffin and a black background, with a candle on each side of the head of the coffin and beneath them the skull and crossbones — the coat of arms of the Hussar of Death.

The noted pilot, for his exploits in the war, had received before the armistice every possible decoration the French government could bestow, and some of the decorations, where the law of the land did not prohibit it, had been awarded to him more than once. It is on record that he was thus awarded forty-six separate medals.

He brought down during the war forty-five enemy planes, and was known in the air service as the "Prince of Pilots." His Croix de Guerre contained twenty-eight palms and two stars.

The young lieutenant had a penchant for disregarding his wounds, and it is said of him that more than once he fled the hospital and was up in his plane before anyone could halt him. To tell of all his exploits in the World War would be most interesting, but there will not be space to deal with them here. Suffice it to say that he set the groundwork for his career as an aviator through his training and exploits in the army.

Major Coli, his flight companion, also had a notable career in the army, where he enlisted as a private and worked himself up from the ranks. He lost one eye from wounds received in battle and was awarded the cross of the Legion of Honor for his valor.

For many years prior to the war, Coli had been an officer in the Merchant Marine service, and had been

The Airman becomes a Pathfinder 311

refused a commission in the French navy because of his ill health. It was after this disappointment that he joined the army. After the war he became greatly interested in civilian aviation, and he was selected by Nungesser as his flight companion because of his profound knowledge of navigation.

After making their plans together for many months in secret, Nungesser and Coli, on March 26, 1927, announced that they were going to attempt to make the flight from Paris to New York. About this time there were many internationally known airmen preparing to accomplish the feat, but patriotic Nungesser felt that he should fly for the glory of France. Although he announced himself as an entry for the Orteig prize, there is no doubt that his attempt was made not for the money, but for the glory — the glory of France — and the personal satisfaction to himself.

France, always jealous of her supremacy in the air, rejoiced when Nungesser announced that he and Major Coli were going to attempt the flight, and the populace was thrilled day after day as the details of the building of the huge plane the *White Bird* were given out.

Nungesser again became the national hero, as he had been during the war, and there was scarcely one of his countrymen who would not neglect everything else to talk about the great ace, the man who was to fly across the seas for France.

Late in April, Nungesser announced that he was about ready to start; then the tragic death of Commander Noel Davis and his assistant, Lieutenant Wooster, was flashed around the world. They had been killed in their test flight just before their projected attempt to cross the seas from west to east, and that accident greatly sobered the French nation. They were indeed sorrowful over the deaths of

312 Romance of the Airman

the gallant Americans, and many of them implored Nungesser and Coli to be cautious so that they should not meet a like tragic fate.

The French flyers did profit by lessons learned from the deplorable accident, and in bulletins assured the French public that they would not attempt the flight until the weather was auspicious; they even went so far as to say that from day to day there would be postponements and that the people must bear with them in their effort to be cautious.

While they were waiting for favorable weather reports, Nungesser and Coli devoted their time to getting themselves into excellent physical condition for the effort. While both men, in the early days, had been very muscular, and Nungesser had enjoyed a great reputation as an athlete, their experiences in the war had taken from them a great deal of their natural physical resistance. But, in good health or poor, neither of the two feared the effort.

About the first week in May the restless birdmen, they who had urged the French people to be patient, became most restive, and could not resist taking their plane on a test flight over Paris from Villacoublay, where their machine had been in the hangar. Their previous announcement that they would not take their machine aloft again until they were ready to hop off for the transatlantic flight set abroad rumors that the two were on their way, and Paris, once again, went into a frenzy over it. We in America, who do not understand the enthusiastic temperament of the Latin races, sometimes are not able to understand their moods. As a matter of fact the projected flight had France in its grip, and every action of the principals was important to the people. For four hours the two pilots stayed aloft, and there is even now some doubt as to whether they had not intended to hop off

The Airman becomes a Pathfinder 313

that evening. However that may be, they were prevented by a terrific thunderstorm, which made flight impossible.

But the test whetted the appetites of the people, and they no longer urged patience. They had exhausted that virtue, and wanted their heroes to fly. The aviators were ready to start the next day, April 7, but the storms were persistent, and the meteorological conditions over the ocean were much more menacing.

The eventful day finally came, on Sunday, May 8. The aviators had spent all of the night, as well as almost all of the preceding day, analyzing the weather reports, which were being relayed to them from all possible sources. The conflict between many of these caused them much anxiety, but they were impatient to be off. Accordingly they accepted the favorable weather reports and rejected those at variance with them. They were set for the flight, and said so; and from that time on, events moved speedily.

Their *White Bird*, rolled outside its hangar, was filled with fuel, which brought the weight of their Levasseur craft up to five tons. The rations were stowed in the cockpit, consisting of caviar and bananas with a quantity of cold coffee and other liquids sufficient to sustain them through forty hours of the laborious vigil.

It was a few minutes after five o'clock in the evening, and the holiday crowds at Le Bourget and on the boulevards of Paris received word of the impending take-off as if by magic. In hordes they went to the field in motors and by surface cars, busses, and the Métropolitain, the Paris subway. By the time the engines were fully warmed up, the spectators numbered thousands, and soldiers had to augment the work of the police in keeping the crowds back from the hangar and away from the runway along which the *White Bird* was about to taxi in order to attain her flying speed.

314 *Romance of the Airman*

Tears were shed; some of the people became hysterical when they realized that the national idol was about to leap from the earth on a perilous trip from which he might never return. Even Nungesser, busy as he was, perceived the change in the mood of the crowd, and, before hiding himself in the cockpit, he said to those near him: "This is for the glory of France. It must be done. But don't let anyone worry or fret. We certainly are not going to our deaths."

The take-off was a work of art. The plane sailed out slowly at first and then gained speed very rapidly. It rose from the ground in a manner befitting its name. *White Bird* she was called; and white bird she looked.

Beautiful curves were described as Nungesser brought her back over the field before flying west — and the crowd cheered and shouted its good wishes to the two.

As Nungesser headed the plane toward the sea, four other planes took off and became his escort. They flew with him until they were outdistanced. So Nungesser and Coli sailed on through the clouds into a mystery which probably never will be solved. No word has ever been heard from them.

When America knew that the flight had been started, watches were set all along the Atlantic coast and at all of the air fields, so that the plane could be sighted the instant it came into view. It was known that the flyers had discarded their landing gear as soon as they had attained the air. This was to reduce the weight of the machine, but it would spell danger to them when they tried to land. The aviators had decided to alight in New York waters, and felt sure they would be rescued — and that was just what America was waiting to do.

While France had seen the last of the *White Bird* and her passengers, the craft was sighted several times over

The Airman becomes a Pathfinder 315

cities and villages in Ireland. Ships at sea, waiting to receive messages from the plane, failed in their effort. The signal light of the *White Bird* was never seen, and she carried no radio.

It is known, however, that the plane, immediately after passing Ireland, ran into treacherous weather over the ocean. Rain was falling so heavily that visibility was slight. It was a beating rain and one that might almost force a heavily laden plane to the surface of the seas.

Added to this, farther out, on a lane that the two men must travel, heavy fogs had set in; and off the coast of Newfoundland, which the *White Bird* was to reach in the course of twenty hours, there were sudden hailstorms that might easily down [the most] intrepid men.

It will be remembered that similar storms off the coast of Newfoundland almost compelled Lindbergh to turn back; it is doubtful if he could have weathered the storms if they had lasted an hour longer.

Nungesser and Coli also had to contend with terrific head winds. These, continuing steadily, would cause them to use much more of their fuel than they had anticipated, and that circumstance alone might have caused their deaths. Indeed, they had a most cruel combination of weather conditions against them.

The United States Weather Bureau issued many bulletins after the flight of the *White Bird* had commenced, which indicated that if the flyers had succeeded in passing Newfoundland they would have run into raging storms of such severity that they would not have been able to go farther.

Before he left France, it will be remembered, Nungesser dropped his landing gear, as he had decided to land in the waters near New York. In fact, he had said to those seeing him off, "I shall land as near the Statue of Liberty as I can."

316 *Romance of the Airman*

For that reason the United States government had assigned several tugs to stand by the statue to await the arrival of the plane, and these were joined by others until there was a virtual fleet waiting to rescue Nungesser and Coli. But the plane never arrived. All the precautions taken on the American side of the ocean were useless, for somewhere between Ireland and New York the pilots had met with a mishap.

In New York the people were more than convinced of this when the plane had not been heard of by the following Tuesday, May 10. In France the people refused to believe that Nungesser, their idol, could be lost. Then, as the days wore on, and they felt that some mishap had befallen the plane and probably had killed the aviators, the people of France, particularly of Paris, went into a frenzy of grief.

A few began to rave unjustly against America. They alleged that this government had misled the flyers with false information as to weather conditions. Others said that America had refused to give them any weather information. Of course these statements, made in the heat of grief, were erroneous, and were quickly corrected by the people of Paris when they had recovered their poise.

America, as a matter of fact, felt the loss of the flying men very keenly. This government sent out destroyers and naval planes to search the seas along the route the *White Bird* was known to have taken. But there never was a clue to them found. . . . Great Britain and France also had their naval vessels take up the search, and they too were unsuccessful.

Daniel Guggenheim, a noted American philanthropist, expended a huge sum of money out of his personal fortune to send an airplane through certain regions of Canada from which rumors had come that the men or their plane had been seen there. This plane too came back unsuccessful.

The Airman becomes a Pathfinder 317

From time to time, for months, there were rumors that traces of the two gallant Frenchmen had been seen here or there, but all of them proved to be groundless. One telegraph operator in the wild, unpopulated sections of Canada sent out a report that the missing men had sent up flares and that they were even then in the hands of friendly Eskimo or Indian tribes; but when this report was investigated, it was found to be an imaginary story. When the operator was confronted with the proof that he had been fabricating, he admitted it.

Nungesser and Coli were lost. The world agreed on that — and France was broken-hearted.

Words and Phrases

To add to your vocabulary

transatlantic navigator augment

Technical terms

hangar landing gear

Informal Test (Multiple-Choice) [1]

1. Nungesser attempted the transatlantic flight because of his love of adventure because he wished to be the first to make a commercial air route because of his desire to glorify France

2. François Coli helped Nungesser in his flight as radio operator mechanic pilot navigator

3. The *White Bird* was a Wright machine Curtiss plane Levasseur type of airplane

4. Nungesser chose his emblem because of its unusual design because it represented danger because it was significant of defiance

5. The internationally known airport Le Bourget is located in England Germany France America

[1] For directions, see page 95.

318 *Romance of the Airman*

Exercises and Topics related to your Other Subjects

1. Draw a map of Europe. On it locate the distance covered by Nungesser and Coli before all trace of them was lost.

2. Make a list of the most important airports in the United States and Europe. Be able to locate the largest ones in the United States.

3. Make a drawing of a hangar. Give the dimensions of some of the largest ones in the United States.

4. Find pictures illustrating the different types of aircraft used today. Write a short description of the one you are most interested in.

5. Who was the first inventor of the airplane? Read an account of his life and be able to report on it.

Other Readings

Read accounts of other prominent aviators who have attempted transatlantic flights.

An Airman drops in on a German Farm[1]

CLARENCE D. CHAMBERLIN

> *Explanatory Note.* At the time that Lindbergh was preparing to set off across the Atlantic in the *Spirit of St. Louis*, there were two other competitors for the Orteig prize: Clarence Chamberlin with the *Columbia*, and Commander Byrd with the *America*. The three expeditions were each scheduled to set off during the last week of May, but were detained by unfavorable weather.
>
> Chamberlin's Bellanca monoplane was owned by Mr. C. A. Levine, who was a passenger when the plane was finally able to take off on June 4. Since Lindbergh had won the transatlantic flight, their plan was now to make a nonstop distance record. Their goal was Berlin, but they were forced down for fuel one hundred and ten miles from their destination. After refueling they set out for Berlin, but missed the way and landed sixty-five miles beyond the city.

WE CLIMBED stiffly out of the plane and stamped about, trying to bring our cramping legs and kinked muscles back to life. The solid soil of Germany felt unreal beneath our feet. I was unable to balance myself, unless I kept on the go, and staggered around drunkenly whenever I tried to stand still. Mr. Levine was hopping and skipping like a prize fighter jumping his rope, but, however glad we were to have Old Mother Earth under us again, our legs took to the unaccustomed experience strangely. We stretched our arms and backs and rubbed our muscles; it was a great relief to have room to move once more, even if the most of my moving was in erratic circles; and if the wheat field had been dry instead of drenched, I, for one, would have stretched out luxuriously there on the ground and slept.

We were, it seemed, as much alone here on this Saxon farm as we had been out there over the ocean or high

[1] Printed from "Record Flights," by Clarence D. Chamberlin, by permission of Dorrance and Company, Publishers, Philadelphia.

320 *Romance of the Airman*

above the clouds. Except for the few words we said to each other we were in a funeral-quiet and deserted land. Not a soul was in sight, and it was nearly half an hour before a middle-aged woman and two boys appeared walking across the field toward us. News that we had started to fly to Germany probably had not yet penetrated to this remote rural district, and to them the *Columbia* was just an airplane — a German airplane, of course — which had mashed down a lot of wheat. They were not highly pleased.

The woman spoke to us in German, and I attempted to answer her. Her look of wrath changed to one of amazement, then sudden fear. The boys too seemed suddenly frightened, and all three turned precipitately and ran, leaving us in utter bewilderment. Of course we had not slept or shaved for two days, but our appearance scarcely warranted such a reception. Not until long after my return to America was I to learn, through letters and newspaper clippings sent me from Germany, that the poor woman had mistaken us for a band of notorious kidnapers who had been terrorizing this region. We probably looked the part, and I suppose she thought the airplane was just a new and up-to-date method of carrying off our victims.

Within an hour fifteen or twenty men, women, and children, coming out from the villages to work in the fields, had assembled about our plane and were inspecting both the *Columbia* and her crew with frank curiosity. The woman and her two boys, either deciding their first estimate of us had been wrong, or convinced that there was safety in numbers, returned to the scene and began to complain about their trampled wheat. No one paid much attention to them; they were too busy trying to understand our questions.

My own German hadn't been called into play since my Iowa school days and proved not only rusty but of the

Clarence Chamberlin and C. A. Levine standing in Front of the Columbia

most elementary sort. Mr. Levine had assured me that he could talk "well enough to get by" when we got to Germany, but I soon learned that his German was better understood in New York than in Germany. However, we made out fairly well by supplementing with signs the few words we could muster in halting German. Gradually we began to make ourselves understood and to get some information.

We had landed, they said, on a farm near the village of Mansfeldt, which in turn was near the town of Eisleben. The latter place, being larger, took all the credit in the news dispatches, and poor Mansfeldt was crowded almost entirely out of the headlines. There was open skepticism when we said we had flown all the way from

322 *Romance of the Airman*

New York — "Von New York gekommen?"* The farm folk and villagers shook their heads, unable to grasp such talk. Then we pointed to the words *New York* painted on the *Columbia's* fuselage. Still they were doubtful; and we gathered from the conversation that they thought Mr. Levine was from some other part of Germany, but were unable to account for me, unless I really was an American or possibly an Englishman.

They managed to understand finally that we needed fuel for our motor, and one of the boys of the woman in whose field we had landed now volunteered to ride four miles on his bicycle and have ninety liters of benzol sent out to us. The closest place where it could be obtained was the town of Eisleben, which is probably the one that I wanted to land near in the first place. I tried my best to tell the kid to bring us a map of Germany when he came back, but neither Levine nor I could think of the word for map — *Landkarte*. We wished afterward that we had drawn one with a stick in the wheat field or taken some crude but effective means of making him understand.

Our chief thought was to refuel as quickly as possible and to fly on to Berlin. Neither of us had eaten very much on the way from New York, and still we were not hungry. While we were waiting for the benzol, we each sucked one of the oranges left in the plane, but that was all. We were more concerned about getting off again than about such unimportant matters as food.

A truck drove up finally with the fuel aboard, ninety liters, or about twenty gallons. The driver had brought along a funnel; but we could not use this on the cabin tank, and those in the wings had been sealed shut at Roosevelt Field so that our flight would stand as an official record. This caused more delay while one of the women in the crowd walked a mile across the fields after a tea

The Airman becomes a Pathfinder   323

or coffee pot with a long curved snout which we used as a transfer vessel. It held about a quart or less, so that it was necessary to fill and empty it a hundred times before we had taken all the benzol aboard. I crouched in the cabin on top of the gas tank and "poured," making quite a mess inside the ship by the fuel I spilled. It was a slow, tedious task, and it was more than an hour before we had finished. The teapot that served us so well, I have since heard, has been put in a museum in Holland!

A boy of twelve or thirteen, who spoke passably good English, had now joined the crowd and immediately jumped into local fame by acting as our interpreter. No one living near by had a map, he told us after canvassing those around; we could only get one by sending to Eisleben. This would take time; and as everybody told us Berlin was only a hundred miles away, "in that direction" (pointing), we decided to go on without it rather than to wait.

We found a big piece of brown wrapping paper in the cabin — it had been around some of our clothing or food supplies — and wrote on it a certificate of our landing at Mansfeldt, or Eisleben, which we asked several members of the crowd to sign. About fifteen or twenty put their signatures at the bottom, although I don't suppose one of them knew the meaning in English, except as we told them through the interpreter. There was nothing else to do except to pay for our benzol (twelve dollars for twenty gallons), tell everybody good-by, start up the motor, and go.

This was not as simple as it sounds. The motor had originally had an inertia starter, but this had been left behind to save weight when we took off from Roosevelt Field. It was up to us to get our engine going by the old-fashioned method of throwing the propeller over by hand. There was a chap in the crowd who told us he either was

324 *Romance of the Airman*

an airplane mechanic home on a vacation, or had served as an airplane mechanic during the war, — I couldn't quite make out which, — and I had rather counted on his doing the cranking. He was so awkward at the job when he endeavored to oblige [us] that I was afraid he would fall into the propeller and be killed even if he managed to get it started. Levine had never thrown over an airplane propeller in his life, so he was eliminated for the same reason. It was up to me.

Now, I was so weak I could hardly pull the propeller around to make the cylinders take in a charge of gas, much less give it the quick, snappy throw-over that is the secret of starting gasoline motors. I toiled and sweated there in that wheat field for half an hour while Levine sat in the plane and manipulated switch and throttle at my direction.

At last it "caught," and the motor broke into its familiar popping roar, right then the sweetest sound in all Germany to me. I staggered around to the side of the plane, pulled myself in the windows, and took my place at the controls. With the friendly and helpful farmers holding the *Columbia* back by her struts and tail, I tested the engine with her new fuel until I was satisfied. Then I nodded to them to stand clear, opened the throttle wide, and the Bellanca once more was taking off to Berlin.

Words and Phrases

To aid in understanding this selection
   Von New York gekommen? Come from New York?

To add to your vocabulary
    erratic circle   precipitately   open skepticism

Technical terms
           fuselage   struts

The Airman becomes a Pathfinder 325

Informal Test (True-False)[1]

1. When Chamberlin and Levine stepped out of the plane they could scarcely stand up.

2. In five minutes a crowd had gathered round the plane.

3. The woman who came up was very angry at first.

4. The woman and her boys were frightened because they thought the aviators were supernatural beings.

5. They complained because their vegetable garden had been destroyed.

6. The villagers were expecting the New York flyers.

7. The boy went on horseback to the village to have the benzol sent out.

8. Chamberlin sent him for a map.

9. The aviators ate a substantial meal while they waited for the benzol.

10. The driver of the truck forgot to bring a funnel.

11. The interpreter was a college student home on a vacation.

12. They were told that Berlin was a hundred miles away.

13. They tore a piece of paper from a notebook and secured the signature of fifteen or twenty bystanders.

14. A mechanic in the crowd started the engine for Chamberlin.

Exercises and Topics related to your Other Subjects

1. Prepare a short talk for the class on "The Value of the Study of Foreign Languages to the Young People of Today."

2. Consult reference books and magazines and make a short report on "Life in Rural Germany Today."

Other Readings

From other sources

"Record Flights," by Clarence D. Chamberlin.

[1] For directions, see page 54.

Our Flight in the *Friendship*

AMELIA EARHART

Explanatory Note. This selection is an extract from Amelia Earhart's book entitled " 20 Hrs. 40 Min." Miss Earhart was the first woman to fly across the Atlantic, and this book is her report of the flight. She expected to pilot the plane part of the way, but on account of fogs, clouds, and rain it was necessary for Stultz to drive in order to follow the compass. Her account of the life in the Trepassey Bay village is one of the most interesting parts of the book and should be read by students for the geography of this region.

The Preparations

I LEARNED that the Fokker had been bought from Commander Byrd by the Honorable Mrs. Frederick Guest of London, whose husband had been in the Air Ministry of Lloyd George and is prominently associated with aviation in Great Britain. Mrs. Guest, formerly Miss Amy Phipps of Pittsburgh, financed the expedition from first to last, and it was due entirely to her generosity and sportsmanship that opportunity to go was given me.

The transfer of ownership of the plane from Commander Byrd to Mrs. Guest had been kept secret. It had been her desire to hop off for the Atlantic crossing without attracting any advance attention. When subsequently, for personal reasons, Mrs. Guest herself abandoned the flight she was still eager to have the plans consummated, if possible, with an American woman on board.

A few days later I was told the flight actually would be made and that I could go — if I wished. Under the circumstances there was only one answer. I couldn't say no. For here was fate holding out the best in the way of flying ability in the person of Wilmer Stultz, pilot, aided by Lou Gordon as flight mechanic; and a beautiful ship admirably equipped for the test before it.

The Airman becomes a Pathfinder 327

When I first saw the *Friendship* she was jacked up in the shadows of a hangar at East Boston. Mechanics and welders worked near by on the struts for the pontoons that were shortly to replace the wheels. The ship's golden wings, with their spread of seventy-two feet, were strong and exquisitely fashioned. The red orange of the fuselage, though blending with the gold, was chosen not for artistry but for practical use. If we had come down, orange could have been seen further than any other color.

The plane just then was being equipped, presumably for its use on Byrd's forthcoming Antarctic trip. Stultz and Gordon were supposed to be in Byrd's employ, and Commander Robert Elmer, U.S.N., retired, was directing technical activities.

Our purpose was to keep the plans secret. Once the world knew, we would be submerged in a deluge of curiosity, making it impossible to continue the preparations in orderly fashion. Then, too, it would do no good to aviation to invite discussion of a project which some accident might delay. Actually the pontoon equipment on this type of plane was experimental, and no one definitely could tell in advance whether or not it would prove practicable. Another objection was the possibility of instigating a "race," which no one wanted. Mrs. Guest proposed that the *Friendship*, as she afterwards named the plane, should cross the Atlantic irrespective of the action of others. By our example we did not want to risk hurrying ill-prepared aspirants into the field with possible tragic results.

Only twice did I actually see the *Friendship* during all this time. I was pretty well known at the landing fields, and obviously it might provoke comment if I seemed too interested in the plane. For this reason I had no chance to take part in any of the test flying. Actually the first

328 *Romance of the Airman*

time I was off the water in the *Friendship* was the Sunday morning when we finally got under way.

The preparation of a large plane for a long flight is a complex task. It is one that cannot — or at least should not — be rushed. Especially is that fact true where, as in the case of the *Friendship*, the equipment was of a somewhat experimental nature.

Throughout the operations Commander Byrd kept in close touch with what was being done, with Stultz and Gordon and Commander Elmer, who was overseeing the technical detail. Necessary instruments were installed and gradually tried out; while varying load tests, countless take-offs from the bay, and brief flights around Boston were made. The radio was tested, and the inevitable last-minute changes and adjustments arranged.

With the radio we were particularly fortunate because Stultz is a skillful operator. It is unusual to find a man who is a great pilot, an instrument flyer, navigator, and a really good radio operator all in one.

Finally the ship itself was ready to go, and our problems focused on the weather. At this stage weather is an important factor in all plans of transoceanic flying.

Supplementing the meager reports available from ships to the Weather Bureau, the *Friendship's* backers arranged a service of their own. Special digests of the British reports were cabled to New York each morning, and meteorological data were radioed in from the ships at sea. All this information, supplementing that already at hand, was then coördinated and plotted out in the New York office of the United States Weather Bureau. There we came to feel that no flight could have a better friend than Dr. James H. Kimball, whose interest and unfailing helpfulness were indispensable.

The weather service for a flight such as ours must be

The Airman becomes a Pathfinder 329

largely planned and entirely underwritten by the backers of the flight itself. And, like so much else, it is an expensive undertaking.

Nearly three weeks dragged by in Boston. Sometimes Mr. and Mrs. Layman were there, hoping for an immediate take-off, sometimes Mrs. Putnam. Commander Elmer and Mr. Putnam were on hand constantly. Mrs. Guest's sons, Winston and Raymond, followed the preparations as closely as they dared without risking disclosure of the ownership.

It was during this period that I had the pleasure of seeing something of Commander and Mrs. Byrd, at their Brimmer Street home, just then bursting with the preparations for his Antarctic expedition — a place of tents and furs, specially devised instruments, concentrated foodstuffs, and all the rest of the paraphernalia which make the practical, and sometimes the picturesque, background of a great expedition. There I met "Scotty" Allan, famous Alaskan dog driver, who was advising Byrd as to canine preparations.

The weather remained persistently unfavorable. When it was right in Boston, the mid-Atlantic was forbidding. I have a memory of long, gray days which had a way of dampening our spirits against our best efforts to be cheerful.

In Boston, I remember, a solicitous friend wished to give me a bag for extra clothing.

"There isn't going to be any," I explained.

That appeared to concern him somewhat — certainly much more than it did me. There seems to be a feeling that a woman preparing to drop in on England, so to speak, ought to have something of a wardrobe.

However, I chose to take with me only what I had on. The men on the *Friendship* took no "extras." Pounds —

330 Romance of the Airman

even ounces — can count desperately. Obviously I should not load up with unessentials if they didn't.

I'm told it's interesting to know exactly what the outfit included. Just my old flying clothes, comfortably, if not elegantly, battered and worn. High laced boots, brown broadcloth breeks, white silk blouse with a red necktie (rather antiquated!), and a companionably ancient leather coat, rather long, with plenty of pockets and a snug buttoning collar. A homely brown sweater accompanied it. A light leather flying helmet and goggles completed the picture, such as it was. A single elegance was a brown and white silk scarf.

When it was cold I wore — as did the men — a heavy fur-lined flying suit which covers one completely from head to toe, shoes and all. Mine was lent to me by my friend Major Charles H. Woolley of Boston, who, by the way, had no idea when he lent it what it was to be used for. He suspected, I think, that I intended to do some high flying.

Toilet articles began with a toothbrush and ended with a comb. The only extras were some fresh handkerchiefs and a tube of cold cream. My "vanity case" was a small army knapsack.

Equipment was simple too. Mr. Layman let me take his camera, and Mrs. Layman her wrist watch. Field glasses, with plenty of use in the Arctic behind them, were lent me by G.P.P., and I was given a compact log book.

Besides toothbrushes — generic term — and food, our "baggage" was a book and a packet of messages which some of those associated with the enterprise asked to have carried across to friends on the other side.

The book — perhaps the only one to have crossed the Atlantic by air route — is "Skyward," written by Commander Richard Evelyn Byrd. He sent it to Mrs. Guest.

The Airman becomes a Pathfinder 331

Commander Byrd, of course, had owned the *Friendship* and has outstandingly sponsored the wisdom of utilizing tri-motored ships equipped with pontoons for long-distance over-water flying. So it was appropriate that his book should be taken to the woman who bought his plane and made the transatlantic flight possible.

This copy of his book which I delivered bears the following inscription:

I am sending you this copy of my first book by the first girl to cross the Atlantic Ocean by air — the very brave Miss Earhart. But for circumstances I well know that it would have been you who would have crossed first. I send you my heartiest congratulations and good wishes. I admire your determination and courage.

[Then follows an account of the flight to Trepassey, their two weeks' wait in this quaint fishing village, and finally their hop across the Atlantic.]

Journey's End

There at Burry Port, Wales, — we learned its name later, — on the morning of June 18, we opened the door of the fuselage and looked out upon what we could see of the British Isles through the rain. For Bill and Slim and me it was an introduction to the Old World. Curiously, the first crossing of the Atlantic for all of us was in the *Friendship*. None that may follow can have the quality of this initial voyage. Although we all hope to be able to cross by plane again, we have visions of doing so in a transatlantic plane liner.

Slim dropped down upon the starboard pontoon and made fast to the buoy with the length of rope we had on board for just such a purpose — or, had affairs gone less well, for use with a sea anchor. We didn't doubt that

332 *Romance of the Airman*

tying to the buoy in such a way was against official etiquette and that shortly we should be reprimanded by some marine traffic cop. But the buoy was the only mooring available, and as we'd come rather a long way, we risked offending.

We could see factories in the distance and hear the hum of activity. Houses dotted the green hillside. We were some distance offshore, but the beach looked muddy and barren. The only people in sight were three men working on a railroad track at the base of the hill. To them we waved, and Slim yelled lustily for service.

Finally they noticed us, straightened up, and even went so far as to walk down to the shore and look us over. Then their animation died out, and they went back to their work. The *Friendship* simply wasn't interesting. An itinerant transatlantic plane meant nothing.

In the meantime three or four more people had gathered to look at us. To Slim's call for a boat we had no answer. I waved a towel desperately out the front windows, and one friendly soul pulled off his coat and waved back.

It must have been nearly an hour before the first boats came out. Our first visitor was Norman Fisher, who arrived in a dory.* Bill went ashore with him and telephoned our friends at Southampton while Slim and I remained on the *Friendship*. A vigorous ferry service was soon instituted, and many small boats began to swarm about us. While we waited Slim contrived a nap. I recall I seriously considered the problem of a sandwich and decided food was not interesting just then.

Late in the afternoon Captain Railey, whom I had last seen in Boston, arrived by seaplane with Captain Bailey of the Imperial Airways and Allen Raymond of the *New York Times*.

Owing to the racing tide it was decided not to try to

The Airman becomes a Pathfinder   333

take off, but to leave the plane at Burry Port and stay at a near-by hotel for the night. Bill made a skillful mooring in a protected harbor, and we rowed ashore. There were six policemen to handle the crowd. That they got us through was remarkable. In the enthusiasm of their greeting those hospitable Welsh people nearly tore our clothes off.

Finally we reached the shelter of the Frickers Metal Company office, where we remained until police reënforcements arrived. In the meantime we had tea, and I knew I was in Britain.

Twice, before the crowd would let us get away, we had to go to an upper balcony and wave. They just wanted to see us. I tried to make them realize that all the credit belonged to the boys, who did the work. But from the beginning it was evident the accident of sex — the fact that I happened to be the first woman to have made the Atlantic flight — made me the chief performer in our particular side show.

With the descent of reporters one of the first questions I was asked was whether I knew Colonel Lindbergh and whether I thought I looked like him. Gleefully they informed me I had been dubbed "Lady Lindy." I explained that I had never had the honor of meeting Colonel Lindbergh, that I was sure I looked like no one (and, just then, nothing) in the world, and that I would grasp the first opportunity to apologize to him for innocently inflicting the idiotic comparison. (The idiotic part is all mine, of course.)

[Next day they flew to Southampton.]

As we approached, a seaplane came out to meet us, and we presumed it was to guide us to the landing place. As Bill prepared to follow, Captain Railey discovered that we were not being guided. In the uncertainty of landing amid berthed steamers in a strange place, Bill finally

334 *Romance of the Airman*

picked up the green lights of a signal gun which marked the official launch coming to greet us. Mrs. Guest, owner of the *Friendship* and sponsor of the flight, was there, her son Raymond, and Hubert Scott Payne of the Imperial Airways. My first meeting with the generous woman who permitted me so much was there in Southampton. It was a rather exciting moment despite the fatigue which was creeping upon all of us. On shore we were welcomed by Mrs. Foster Welch, the Mayor of Southampton. She wore her official necklace in honor of the occasion, and we were impressed with her graciousness. Though a woman may hold such office in Great Britain, the fact isn't acknowledged, for she is still addressed as if she were a man.

With the crowd behind, I drove to London with Mr. and Mrs. Scott Payne. The whole ride seemed a dream. I remember stopping to see Winchester Cathedral and hearing that Southampton was the only seaplane base in England and being made to feel really at home by Mrs. Payne, who sat next to me.

London gave us so much to do and see that I hardly had time to think. One impression lingers, — that of warm hospitality, which was given without stint. I stayed with Mrs. Guest at Park Lane. Lady Astor permitted me a glance of beautiful country when she invited me to Cliveden. Lord Lonsdale was host at the Olympic Horse Show, which happened to be in action during our stay. The British Air League were hosts at a large luncheon primarily organized by the women's division, at which I was particularly glad to meet Madame de Landa and Lady Heath. From the latter I bought the historic little *Avro*, with which she had flown alone from Cape Town to London. I was guest too at a luncheon of Mrs. Houghton's, wife of the American ambassador — and many other people lavished undeserved hospitality upon us.

The Airman becomes a Pathfinder

Miss Amelia Earhart, the First Woman to fly across the Atlantic, is looking out of the Door of the Friendship as it takes to a Landing at Southampton

Being a social worker I had, of course, to see Toynbee Hall,* dean of settlement houses, on which our own Denison House* in Boston is patterned. Nothing in England will interest me more than to revisit Toynbee Hall and [to visit] the settlement houses that I did not see.

336 *Romance of the Airman*

But this can be no catalogue of what that brief time in London meant to us. To attempt to say "Thank you" adequately would take a book in itself — and this little volume is to concern the flight and whatever I may be able to add about aviation in general. Altogether it was an alluring introduction to England, enough to make me wish to return and explore what, this time, I merely touched.

Words and Phrases

To aid in understanding this selection

dory: a narrow, flat-bottomed boat used for fishing.

Toynbee Hall: a settlement house in London where members of Oxford and Cambridge universities teach the working classes. In the United States many college settlements have been patterned after Toynbee Hall.

Denison House: the settlement house, in Boston, at which Miss Earhart worked.

To add to your vocabulary

consummated	aspirant
antiquated	itinerant

Technical terms

hangar	fuselage
pontoon	

Informal Test (Multiple-Choice)[1]

1. The plane was first owned by   Stultz   Gordon   Byrd

2. The name of the plane was   *Skyward   Friendship   Columbia   Question Mark*

3. The Welsh called Miss Earhart   **Miss America**   **Lady Lindy**   **Mrs. Stultz**

[1] For directions, see page 95.

The Airman becomes a Pathfinder   337

4. Scotty Allan was at Commander Byrd's to tell him about
ships   planes   dogs

5. The plane was painted orange   **because it would last
longer   because it could be seen farther   because it was
prettier**

Exercises and Topics related to your Other Subjects

1. Draw a map, and on it show the pathway of the *Friendship*
across the Atlantic.

2. Locate Trepassey Bay; Burry Port; Southampton.

3. Find the average number of miles per hour made on the trip.

Other Readings

In this book

"Crossing the Atlantic," page 299.

From other sources

"20 Hrs. 40 Min.," by Amelia Earhart.
"Skyward," by Richard E. Byrd.
"Labrador: the Country and People," by W. T. Grenfell.
"Girls Who Became Famous," by Sarah Bolton.

The *Southern Cross* visits the Fiji Islands

KINGSFORD-SMITH AND ULM

Explanatory Note. The *Southern Cross* made the first flight across the Pacific, starting on May 31, 1928. The total distance of seventy-three hundred miles from Oakland, California, to Brisbane, Australia, was made in eighty-three hours and nineteen minutes with only two stops, at Hawaii and the Fiji Islands. The flight between these two stops broke all previous nonstop records. The pilots, Captain C. E. Kingsford-Smith and C. T. Ulm, are Australians; the navigator, H. W. Lyon, and the radio operator, J. W. Warner, are Americans. The story of their flight is one of the most fascinating stories in the literature of aviation.

WE CAME to a standstill on the oval* at 3.50 P.M. We had mastered the longest hop of the flight. In effect, we had, so to speak, "broken the back" of it. We had covered the 3138 statute miles from Barking Sands* to Suva* in thirty-four hours thirty minutes.

We looked on our air conquest of the Pacific as being complete. We had no qualms about the final and shortest stage to Brisbane.*

Aglow with all the colors of a Persian bazaar was the crowd of people who surged round the little oval in the moist heat of the afternoon. It was a white- and tropical-garbed host that surged in about the *Southern Cross*. An ocean of heads swept back and forth round the plane the moment the three motors stopped after their strenuous and sterling service to us.

They told us the gathering cheered with frantic enthusiasm, and that many a native fled to the security of the vegetation at our approach. Yet we heard nothing but the ceaseless thunder of the motors. Even when they were stopped, their roar kept hammering dully in our ears.

In the wild rush to greet us, the first to fight their way

The Airman becomes a Pathfinder

All Suva had a Holiday to view the Southern Cross after it had completed the Longest Hop of its Transpacific Flight

close to the plane were six or seven old war pilots who had cabled to us at Honolulu, and who had charge of the arrangements for landing. They dashed out from under a tree close to where Smith ground-looped the machine. At their heels ran a rope cordon of Defense Club lads, who encircled the machine with their rope barrier just in time to check the charge of the crowd. Then the Fijian and Indian Police flung their solid frames into the scrum* or succession of scrums that developed about the machine.

As soon as we saw that our propellers were safe we climbed out of the cockpit. Around us swept a frantically excited crowd. A forest of hands shot at us as we appeared on the little ladder below the cockpit. Everyone, European and Fijian, wanted to greet us at the same moment.

Our presence at Suva caused an immense stir among the Fijian population. Thousands of the natives had never seen a plane. They ascribed to us various supernatural qualities, and arrayed themselves in their most colorful raiment, and staged bewildering ceremonies in our honor.

340 *Romance of the Airman*

In fact, the natives exalted us to the stature of demigods, quite without justification. They flocked in from the cane fields and the other plantations to see the Wanga Vuka (the bird-ship). Down through the ravines from the hills, where palms and deep bronze-green and red foliage rioted, they came, in all the bravery of gaudy sashes and headdress that dazzled the eye. Their bards composed ballads to celebrate our achievement, and it was clear that our swoop from the blue had thoroughly stirred the native imagination. They were all ready to help if they could. They were prepared to carry us, or even the *Southern Cross*, wherever we willed. We could have had the help of thousands of native volunteers to carry out service of any kind associated with the bird-ship.

An illustration of how they exalted us to the elevation of the supermen of ancient mythology was given in a story that came across to Suva from the neighboring islands of the Lomaiviti province. There the natives had been told that about June 4 we would call at Suva on our flight to Australia, and that we would be passing very close to their island. It had been suggested that our course would be as near as possible to the route of mail steamers from Honolulu to Suva.

On the morning of June 4 the only European trader on the island told the natives to keep a close lookout for the plane. This they promised to do, and declared, too, that as soon as they saw it they would come to his house and tell him that the plane was in sight.

A great crowd of natives came hurrying through the trees to the trader's home on the morning of June 5. Their faces were grim and serious. They had the puckered brows and the wide-open eyes of people who had been astounded at some amazing sight.

"My word," said Turaga, their spokesman, "we did see

The Airman becomes a Pathfinder 341

the aëroplane last night. It was a wonderful sight; did you not see it, too?"

So did their trader interpret their message. He told them he had not seen the plane, and expressed displeasure at the fact that they had not attempted to call him to see it.

"Yes, we should have called you," Turaga, the native spokesman acknowledged; "but we became so excited that we forgot to call you. It was a wonderful sight to see his plane rest over the island. Yes, he actually rested. He must have been too early to go on to Suva, so he stayed for some time over our island."

Here was mystifying intelligence for the trader. He could not understand the native's references to the plane resting. He was intrigued, and decided to accept their story and question them further.

"Yes," Turaga, the native spokesman, said in his own tongue; "and I will tell you how he actually did it, we saw him so plainly. He found that he must be ahead of time, and that he had to wait till daylight before he went on to Suva. So he decided to have a rest, and he went up to the moon and hooked his plane onto the moon. We saw him hook on with the big hooks, and the plane rested there. It stayed there for an hour. Boss, we saw him stay there, true!"

The trader was more mystified than ever. It was clear that the natives had seen something in the sky. It was clear, too, that they certainly had not seen the *Southern Cross* hook up to the moon.

We have heard of the advice to hitch one's wagon to a star, and we knew too the fox-trot "Keep on sweeping the cobwebs from the moon," but we had never essayed either feat.

Certainly the idea showed a fine imagination in the natives. It would have been a boon to us in those squalls

342 *Romance of the Airman*

that we struck on the night before we got into Suva if we could have flung our grappling iron onto the moon or the tail of a comet for a welcome rest from the storm battering.

But we were not the supermen that the natives believed we were.

The trader pondered over the strange story. Then the solution came to him quite by accident. He discovered in the newspapers that on June 4 there was to be an eclipse of the moon. It was to occur about the time that he asked the natives to watch for the plane.

They had seen the dark shadow on the moon, and had become convinced that it was the *Southern Cross* moored up there to a pinnacle in the moon mountains, swinging lazily on its moorings over the lunar valleys.

It was a most colorful flight of native fancy, but regretfully we had to disclaim the prowess that those swarthy chieftains out there on the hills of Lomaiviti ascribed to us. The trader sent for the natives, and told them that it was not the plane but the eclipse of the moon that they had seen.

They shook their heads in disbelief.

Eclipse of the moon — bah! That was no eclipse of the moon. It was the *Southern Cross* resting quietly on a lunar plateau!

So muttered the old natives, the wise men of the party. They said nothing, but they shook their heads, and their eyes showed how incredulous they were of the eclipse story.

Down through the palm thickets they went, back to their villages, still fondly cherishing that more poetical vision of the *Southern Cross* clinging to the moon. Anyhow, it was a pity that such a colorful fancy should be blasted.

The Airman becomes a Pathfinder 343

Words and Phrases

To aid in understanding this selection

oval: Albert Park Sports Oval was the landing field at Suva.
Barking Sands: a port on the island of Kauai, Hawaii.
Suva: a city in the Fiji Islands.
Brisbane: an important city of Australia.
scrum: scrummage or scrimmage. The first two forms are in common use with the English.

To add to your vocabulary

demigods	cordon	incredulous
bards	pinnacle	
intrigued	lunar valleys	

Informal Test (Completion)[1]

1. The distance from Barking Sands to Suva was _____ miles.

2. The time of the flight was _____ hours.

3. The arrangements for the landing were in charge of _____.

4. The crowd was kept back from the plane by _____.

5. The natives called the plane _____.

6. They came in from _____ to see the plane.

7. The natives who were set to watch for the plane reported that _____.

8. The trader understood what they had seen when _____.

9. When the trader explained to them what they had seen, they _____.

Exercises and Topics related to your Other Subjects

1. Trace the flight of the *Southern Cross* on the map.

2. Explain why there were Indian police in Suva.

3. Select a good passage of description from "The Flight of the *Southern Cross*" and prepare it to read aloud to the class.

[1] For directions, see page 14.

344 *Romance of the Airman*

4. Compare this true story with the imaginative one told by Jules Verne in "Five Weeks in a Balloon."

5. In a description of the flight just before the landing at Suva this sentence is found, "We were indeed in the paradise immortalized by Stevenson." Read a biography of Robert Louis Stevenson and explain the sentence.

Subjects for oral themes

The Fiji Islands.

Brisbane, a Modern City.

Other Reading

In this book

"A Balloon Flight across Africa," page 71.

Lady Heath flies across Africa

LADY MARY HEATH

Explanatory Note. Lady Mary Heath has been one of the women pioneers in aviation. She has attracted especial attention for her solo flying. In her lecture tour in this country in the spring of 1929 she not only flew alone but did her own mechanical work.

I LISTENED on Monday to an account by Mr. Gerald Bowyer of his adventures in traveling from Cape Town to London by motor car — the first time a standard motor car has made this trip. Mr. Bowyer refuses to call Africa the Dark Continent; he calls it the Light Continent. He says that throughout his journey he saw but one leopard, a few buck, a couple of hyena, and an odd jackal or two. Roads, whether they are the better roads of the Uganda, the narrower native tracks of Tanganyika, or the very occasional roads that thread the swamps in North Rhodesia, all bring a certain amount of civilization close to them, for civilization follows the path of transport. But in flying over Africa one is unable, much as one would like to, to stick to the safer lines of civilization and roads, and is obliged to get from landing place to landing place across anything that may lie between, whether it be swamp or forest, or craggy mountain ranges with desolate valleys in between.

Looking back on my flight, I am chiefly impressed by the minute scratches human effort has made on the surface of Africa. Over great areas there is no sign of living habitation. The fever and damps of the swamps make life impossible, and in other closely wooded areas there is depopulation owing to the ravages of sleeping sickness. Even in the more highly civilized parts there are great areas of lonely country — mountainous stretches of veld * in South Africa, and still more mountainous areas of desert to the

346   *Romance of the Airman*

north. . . . From all its coasts Africa slopes upward to a
great central plateau, on which are found, far away from
the ravages of civilization, the lowest forms of animal and
vegetable life. Many pilots have flown this route, and I
have heard one of them say that on the whole trip he saw
no game or anything alive. I can only surmise that this
man did not know what the living things looked like when
he saw them. The natural instinct of game is to stand
stock-still when it hears a suspicious sound, and to remain
still until it discovers the cause and direction of that which
startles it. It is therefore not so easy for one who has
not actually walked and shot over the country to distinguish wild life. For my part, having lived in all three of
the British East African territories, and having traveled
through all our other possessions in that continent, often
with a gun in search of game, my eyes were quick to see
wild animals, and there was an abundance of them.

As far south as Livingstone — twenty miles south of it,
in fact — I saw rhinos in the bush, and flying low over
them was horrified to observe the devoted mother of a
baby rhinoceros run headlong from her charge when she
heard the machine. Other game behaved quite differently.
On the Serengati plains in the west of Kenya the great
herds of buck, numbering often many thousands, ran like
a frightened herd of sheep from the noise of the engine.
But two or three times on the edge of the plains when I
passed over groups of lions, either sunning themselves in
the morning heat or ranging from place to place, I was
surprised to find that they took apparently no notice of
my machine. They probably regarded me, as the natives
did in various wild places in which I landed, as an "act
of God." In the southern Sudan I found the rhinos more
quiescent, the white rhino, a creature peculiar to that region, ignoring my presence completely; and the large

Lady Mary Heath flying her Plane Gypsy Moth

herds of elephants took but little notice. Of the smaller game hidden among the undergrowth I can say little, the tiny buck, guinea fowl, and snakes being altogether hidden from my view. Other birds than the guinea fowl, such as the great eagles which frequent the granite hills rising out of the forest plains, drifted by with complete contempt, sometimes only a few yards off.

I retain wonderful memories of the beauties of Central Africa. On the equator itself there is no great heat, owing to the height of the central plateau; and where there is not forest or swamp there are vast rolling plains of agricultural land, which the white settler is beginning to discover and to exploit. As soon as the powers that be help him by laying down transport and postal facilities — for those are the two things necessary to open up Central Africa — we shall have a great storehouse of mineral and agricultural wealth. A railway runs northward from the

348 *Romance of the Airman*

Cape for five days' journey before it branches off toward the Belgian Congo. Westward a line runs inland through Portuguese East Africa from Beira, and again another line runs from Dar-es-Salaam to Lake Tanganyika. Another line is gradually creeping eastward from Lobito; but in the very center, where there are gold and diamonds, and that still more priceless possession, a rich virgin soil, there is nothing except impossibly bad roads which cannot be used during the rainy season, from March to October. Never shall I forget the beauty of climbing at nine thousand feet over the ridge of the Rungwa Mountains on the southern side of Tanganyika. The drifting white clouds that held the coming of the rains were flecking the sky and gilding the crest of the next range. Underneath them, intersecting the mottled ground of the valleys, were the silver ribbons of watercourses flowing to Lake Rukwa and the semidry swamp which lies to the north. In this valley there are hundreds of white people finding a living by washing the gold from the rivers. A little farther north a new diamond mine has recently been discovered. Two or three hundred miles still farther north, on the shores of Victoria Nyanza, there is an enormous meat-canning industry starting. All these industries are begging for transport facilities to connect them with the Mother Country. Unless the Imperial Government can find means to provide the help that is required, these people will have to go elsewhere, and their industries will be lost to the Empire.

From a navigational point of view, flying over Central Africa is child's play. The visibility is wonderful. One can see fifty or seventy miles with the greatest ease, and in Africa things are built on a big scale. A single range as large as the Pennines, a lake as large as Ireland, a solitary hill as big as Vesuvius, are common occurrences, so that one does not have to concentrate on the details immediately

The Airman becomes a Pathfinder 349

beneath one, such as roads, crossroads, railways, and the twists of tiny rivers, as one does in the small area and perpetually bad visibility of the British Isles. An hour before reaching Lake Bangweota the shining stretches of its waters and the glittering silver of the bend of the Nile can be seen. The extreme beauty and bigness of things make one forget the possibility of a forced landing.

This danger is really an ever-present one, and it is a danger that could be greatly lessened or altogether removed if the governments of Central Africa would combine to provide a chain of wireless stations such as they have in the Sudan and such as the Italian and French colonies so proudly possess. To my mind, Abercorn is the center of Africa, and for five hundred miles to the south there is a single telegraph line which lies on the ground for nine months out of twelve owing to the thefts of wire-loving natives or the pell-mell rush of careless giraffes or the ravages of storms. To the north of Abercorn to Tabora there are four hundred miles of forest and swamp over which the trans-African aviator must fly and through which the trans-African traveler must go, and here there is no line for communication of any kind. To herald one's advent or to warn the villagers of one's coming means a day's job by runner, and one might be lost for weeks in the forest before the country people became aware that it was even necessary to send out a search party. These things must be remedied.

Words and Phrases

To aid in understanding this selection
   veld: a tract of land without forest.

To add to your vocabulary
          quiescent   ravages of civilization

350 *Romance of the Airman*

Informal Test (Multiple-Choice)[1]

1. Traveling by motor through Africa brings one in contact with civilization because **one keeps along the coast one goes only to the larger cities civilization follows the roads**

2. Lady Heath was impressed with **the great development of African industries the high mountains the small amount of work man had done in Africa the long railways**

3. Lady Heath saw many wild animals from her plane because **she had had much experience as a hunter in Africa she was much afraid of wild animals she had a great interest in wild life**

4. When the lions heard the roar of the engine **they ran like a herd of frightened sheep they ran away from their cubs they apparently took no notice of it**

5. The two things needed by the white settler in Central Africa are **machinery and workers medical aid and sanitary conditions transport and postal facilities**

6. The priceless possession of Central Africa is **a rich virgin soil the diamond-mining industry the gold-mining industry**

7. Flying over Africa is hazardous because of **the poor visibility the hot winds the danger of a forced landing**

8. The governments of Central Africa should combine to provide **a system of railways a series of landing fields a chain of wireless stations**

Exercises and Topics related to your Other Subjects

1. Trace Lady Heath's voyage on the map and locate all the places she mentions.

2. Name the three British East African territories and locate the other British possessions in Africa.

3. What governments would be included in Lady Heath's suggestions for a series of wireless stations?

[1] For directions, see page 95.

The Airman becomes a Pathfinder 351

4. Consult your reference books for the work of David Livingstone and Henry Stanley in Africa and write a theme on "Exploring Africa by Foot and by Plane."

5. Compare Lady Heath's flight across Africa with the imaginary ones of Mark Twain and Jules Verne.

Other Readings

In this book

"The Flying Warrior of Uganda," page 83.

From other sources

"The Boys' Trader Horn," by Kenneth P. Hempton.
"Lost in the Jungle," by Paul Belloni Du Chaillu.
"Wild Life under the Equator," by Paul Belloni Du Chaillu.

Preparation for the Antarctic Expedition

COMMANDER RICHARD E. BYRD

Explanatory Note. Byrd's expedition into the Antarctic was the best-equipped polar expedition ever sent out. The base ship, the *Samson*, was a Norwegian vessel fifty years old. It was rechristened with the name *City of New York*. The supplies for the expedition were assembled at Dunedin, New Zealand, during the autumn of 1928. On December 2, 1928, the *City of New York* and the *Eleanor Bolling* left this port for the South Polar regions. A landing was made on the day after Christmas at Discovery Inlet. Explorations were carried on with four airplanes: a Ford tri-motor named in honor of Floyd Bennett, a Fokker, a Fairchild, and a General Aircraft monoplane. By December of the following year the South Pole had been reached and more than thirty-five thousand square miles of new land had been discovered. Congress rewarded Byrd for his explorations by conferring upon him the rank of Rear Admiral in the United States navy.

NAPOLEON, I think, is credited with the famous remark "An army marches on its stomach." He might well have added, "And so does any other expedition."

Particularly is this true of expeditions into regions of extreme temperature. Everyone is familiar with the bad effects of the tropics on white men who have not had time to become thoroughly acclimated to the heat. That long-continued extreme cold may produce the same slowing down of vitality and decreased resistance to disease is not so well known. It is vitally important, however, and has been the subject of study by every explorer interested in keeping his men fit during long polar sieges. Clothing has something to do with it. In the tropics it is possible to dress in a fairly comfortable manner. At the poles quantities of clothing that keep all air from the body and whose weight is a burden must be worn almost continuously. But more important even than clothing is diet. .

For many months now the medical director of the expe-

The Airman becomes a Pathfinder

Martin Rönne making Wind-proof Clothing for the Antarctic Expedition

dition, Dr. Francis D. Coman of Johns Hopkins Hospital in Baltimore, has been studying that question. With him rests the responsibility of keeping all of us healthy during our stay in Antarctica.

On board the *Samson* the food will be much the same as on any other vessel. Tennent, the cook who went with me on the *Chantier* to Spitsbergen in 1926, will be aboard, and I have no doubt will provide the same admirable fare as he did two years ago. From New York to New Zealand, across the tropics from one temperate region into another, there will be little trouble. At Dunedin, New Zealand, fresh supplies will be loaded, and not until the frozen shores of the Bay of Whales are reached, and our village laid down, will the problem of what we must eat become of paramount importance.

Among other things, but perhaps most important of all, we must guard against scurvy. For centuries this disease has attacked sailors long at sea, the inhabitants of beleaguered cities, explorers — everyone who is cut off from fresh food and made dependent on preserved meats, hardtack, and the like. Scurvy has taken a great toll of life in polar exploration. There are many preventives or antiscorbutics* used; one of them, lime juice, has been required in the British navy since 1795, but I have been able to discover only one sure preventive — fresh meat. Fruit and vegetable juices — even vinegar — are supposed to be safeguards against it, but they are not sufficiently sure to be wholly relied on. Dr. Coman is making extensive studies covering all antiscorbutics, and experiments are being carried on with a view to obtaining the scurvy-preventing vitamines in a compressed tablet form. If these are successful the product should prove of the utmost value in many fields of endeavor.

© Byrd Antarctic Expedition

Dr. Francis D. Coman and Chief Cook Tennent examining Dehydrated Food

The cans have been painted, to prevent rust

The Airman becomes a Pathfinder

355

Food and Containers

How our supplies are packed will be almost as important as the supplies themselves. Getting as much as possible into the smallest space will be necessary, of course, but getting it there safely will be equally important. Containers will take up valuable weight and space, and so wherever possible they will be made to answer two purposes. As many as possible of our packing cases will be standardized in size and construction. When they have been landed at the base they will be stacked like the four walls of a house and roofed over. Supplies will be withdrawn from the inner ends of the boxes, leaving a shelter which can be used for storage or workshops.

This will apply only to such goods as may be frozen without serious detriment. The others, reduced to a minimum in quantity, will have to be stored somewhere in the heated huts. After the Bay of Whales is reached we shall not be able to use the ordinary tin can with which every grocery store is filled. In temperatures below − 25° Fahrenheit, tin undergoes a curious change, becoming brittle and falling into powder at the least touch. In the extreme cold of Antarctica the tin plating of the cans would soon fall away, and the bare iron left would rust through in a short time. Substituting glass is out of the question on any extensive scale because of its weight and liability to breakage. Cans made of some such noncorrosive alloy as Monel metal will probably be our solution.

Our tentative provision list has been prepared for eighteen months, so that, if it is necessary to wait until the fall of 1929 to make the flight over the South Pole, there will be no shortage of food.

Twenty-two tons of frozen meats, including mutton, veal, corned beef, corned tongue and shoulder, fresh pork

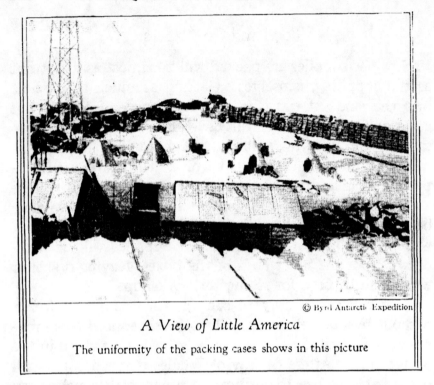

A View of Little America
The uniformity of the packing cases shows in this picture

and pork sausage, smoked ham, bacon, two tons of chicken, and half a ton of frankfurters, as well as many other varieties of meat, will form one of the largest items. In addition to the frozen meats there will be several cases of ox-tongue, deviled chicken and ham, beef extract, chicken and bouillon cubes. The latter, requiring only the addition of water to be ready to use, will be especially valuable on the final flight and on ground work with the dogs. Twenty-five hundred pounds of pemmican will be taken. Elsewhere, on a following page, you will find a list of the other major items of our commissary.

There will be plenty of extras — the little things that make all the difference between real food and what would otherwise seem a bread-and-water diet, no matter how healthful it might be. Sherry, a quarter of a ton of assorted

The Airman becomes a Pathfinder   357

candies, and a great variety of articles like fancy biscuits and tinned plum pudding will supply this welcome variety.

The quantity of flour taken will insure a continuous supply of bread, cakes, and pies. Bread and biscuit will be cooked fresh daily at the main base, assorted cakes every night, and pies three times a week.

Fuel away from the base and in the shelters will be kerosene, but at the main base coal will be the mainstay.

On the sledding expeditions the food supplies will be radically altered, so that every ounce of available space on the dog sleds may be used to best advantage. The sleds will be arranged in trains of two, with seven dogs pulling, and the second sled hitched to the first by crossed chains. The first will carry about eight hundred pounds; the second, four hundred. In this carrying capacity must be stowed one or more tents, whatever equipment for observations or other purposes may be necessary, cooking utensils, food for the dogs, and in the remaining space food for the men.

Naturally, that food must be as concentrated as possible. The great stand-by of all polar explorers has been pemmican, or polar hash, as it has been called. Formulas vary; but the usual composition is dried meat, one or more cereals, suet, lard, or other edible fat, and sometimes raisins or the like. Sometimes fish is substituted for the meat. Personally I prefer pemmican without sweetening, and most of ours will be without it.

Preparing it for use is quite simple. Water or snow is added, and the mixture heated over a kerosene pressure stove into a sort of mush. Any other odds and ends of food on hand may be dropped in, resulting often in a weird and wonderful stew. On a long and bitter trip with food running low and every ounce of energy needed to carry the men on, it is usually necessary to kill the dogs,

358 *Romance of the Airman*

one at a time, feeding skin, bones, and refuse to the other dogs and cooking the rest for food.

At the Bay of Whales we expect to kill a hundred tons of seal, which will be prepared and stored in natural refrigerators. Part of this meat will form the principal food of the dogs, and the rest will be for us the best-known preventive for scurvy. Scurvy is thought of as a disease limited to mankind, but dogs may suffer from it just as seriously as ourselves, and the seal meat will serve this purpose for them also. Seal meat is not particularly appetizing, for the seals feed on fish, and their flesh is apt to be rank and oily; but, liberally doused with sauces, it will not be far different from venison.

Motive Power at the Poles

I have mentioned before the dogs which will go with us in addition to the tractors and planes, to augment our mechanical equipment and supply us with the safest method so far discovered of traveling overland in polar wastes. There will be nearly a hundred altogether; Eskimo dogs for the most part, brought down from Alaska. There will be a nucleus, however, of highly trained halfbreeds, known as Chinooks. These dogs are the result of interbreeding Eskimo and German shepherds, and are the finest sled dogs known. They combine the tremendous brute strength of the Eskimo with the great intelligence of the shepherds, and are so clever that they will be used at the Bay of Whales in breaking in the Eskimos on our particular type of sled work.

Arthur T. Walden, at his farm in Wonalancet, New Hampshire, has been training the Chinooks through the past winter, assisted by three drivers who will accompany him south, and by "Scotty" Allen, one of the country's

The Airman becomes a Pathfinder

A Dog Team on the Trail © Byrd Antarctic Expedition

finest drivers. Arthur Walden himself is a seasoned veteran, trained in the early days in Alaska, when dog sledges were the only means of communication, and the sledge driver had to keep going day or night in all kinds of weather, and over country treacherous with ravines and frozen rivers.

At the head of his group is Chinook,* generally considered the greatest of them all. His grandmother was Polaris, the Eskimo dog which led Peary's team on the expedition that discovered the North Pole, his father a German shepherd rescued from a Massachusetts pound. For strength and intelligence he has few equals.

He and his comrades will be the leaders of our teams, and the finest of them will probably comprise the team to be taken, together with a light sledge, on the plane that makes the final dash for the pole.

360 *Romance of the Airman*

The sledges are now being built at South Tamworth, New Hampshire, of specially selected straight-grain ash and under Mr. Walden's personal supervision. They will be the Alaskan freight-sled type, of basket design, ten feet in length, with a long detachable gee-pole on the front of the left-hand runner, and both double- and single-ended sleds will be included. The gee-pole, carried only on the first sledge of the two-sledge trains, will be used in steering and guiding the dogs. Harnesses and collars are being specially made so that they can be handled with gloved hands in extreme cold, and a mile of rope will go along for lashings and traces. The traces will be simple; the leader is fastened to the end of a long center rope, and behind him are three pairs of dogs, fastened two and two on either side of the central rope. The leather portions of the harnesses will be bitter-tanned to prevent the dogs' eating them.

In driving, the man in charge walks behind the dogs and in front of the sled, the gee-pole in his hand. He has a whip, but it is seldom used, and then never on the leader. The lead-dog must have almost human intelligence; he is in charge of his team in real earnest, and except on the very rare occasions when he gets into a fight he is controlled only by the voice of the driver, and treated as befits his station.

Clothing for Fifty Degrees below Zero

Tramping for twenty miles a day over snow-covered country in a driving blizzard, dressed in heavy furs and sealskin boots, is a task that needs to be tried to be appreciated. One day, with a heated house and warm food at its end, would be enough for any of us under ordinary circumstances, but at the poles it is often necessary to

The Airman becomes a Pathfinder

Building Snow Houses in Little America

repeat the march day after day for weeks, with a mush made of pemmican and an icy tent pitched on the bare snow for comfort at night. The earlier explorers faced this inevitably, but by the use of planes and intermediate bases we hope to avoid some of it.

Some, but not all. Laying the bases will require work with dog sleds; so will short overland exploring trips; so will our forced march, if anything should happen on the way to the pole itself. And our clothing must be planned accordingly. It must be light, and yet warm enough to protect us against blizzards on the ground and the extreme wind and cold of the upper levels of the air when flying. Part of it must be waterproof, particularly our boots, since the surface snow at times melts under the warmth of the summer sun.

In all, one hundred and fifty suits and fifty sleeping-bag outfits will be taken. The suits will consist of pants made

362 *Romance of the Airman*

of reindeer skins with the fur outside, coats or parkas *
made of reindeer skin, with linings of fawn or squirrel skin
with the fur turned inside. *Fawn* is the term given to the
skins of young reindeers, lighter, although less durable,
than that from older animals. For my own use I am taking a pair of bearskin trousers that I wore flying over
the North Pole. They are heavier but no warmer than
reindeer.

Boots are particularly important. Sharp ice wears them
away quickly. Moisture from perspiration, if not guarded
against, will freeze the feet. Above all, they must be large
enough. Tight boots would lead to chilblains and actual
freezing.

Getting them large enough means that space must be
allowed for reindeer socks, worn with the fur inside, one
or more pairs of wool socks, and possibly one pair of silk.
Silk has the great disadvantage of keeping moisture in,
not being absorptive like wool or cotton, although it also
keeps cold air out.

The soles will be made of sealskin, one of the hardest
and toughest leathers known, while the uppers will be of
softer reindeer. Between the sole and the foot will be a
layer of senna grass, to act as an insulating space between
the socks and the boot-sole. This will effectually prevent
moisture from keeping the socks wet during hiking. Sweat
is a most important factor; for if there is nothing to ab-
sorb it, such as the senna grass, it will soon freeze the feet.

Gloves will also be very large, to enable woolen mittens
to be worn underneath, and will be made of both sealskin
and reindeer hide.

In making up all these garments the rule must be remembered that fur outside keeps the cold out, and fur
inside keeps the warmth in. For this reason all outer
garments will be of skins worn as the animals wear them;

The Airman becomes a Pathfinder 363

when they are almost impervious to wind and moisture. The inner garments and linings will have fur on the inside, to conserve the body warmth as much as possible.

The reindeer-skin sleeping-bags will be furred on the inside. On the march it will be necessary to sleep in them completely dressed. In this way the fur will often become saturated with moisture during sleep, causing serious inconvenience and even death if a wet bag is used night after night. The dodge that avoids this is a simple one, but not particularly well known. It consists only in turning the bag inside out, and exposing it to the outside air for a few moments. The moisture freezes almost at once, and may then be brushed away like dust.

Another useful dodge I learned in the Arctic. Often on sled trips a sudden blizzard comes up which must be weathered without putting up tents. The method is simple: crouch in the snow so that the edge of the parka touches the ground, and bank up around it a layer of snow to keep out the wind. The fur hood is pulled closely about the face, and the hands placed Chinese fashion in the long unrolled sleeves of the parka. In this way it is possible to sit out in comparative comfort a blizzard that might otherwise be almost fatal.

In addition to the fur hoods, some sort of mask may be used when flying and in high winds. Colored glasses that filter out the rays of light causing snow blindness will be standard equipment for everyone, protecting the eyes against wind and blowing snow as well.

For repairs to clothing one hundred and nineteen reindeer pelts will be taken, fifty of them being young fawn skins. Martin Rönne, sailmaker on Amundsen's ship, the *Fram*, will have charge of all repairs to clothing and tents. Besides the parkas, boots, and trousers, he will have socks, moccasins, ski boots, wool waterproof ski suits, Burberry

364 *Romance of the Airman*

wind-breakers, heavy underwear, and dozens of other articles of clothing to look after.

Food, clothing, fuel, planes, dogs, and men will take up most of the *Samson's* limited cargo capacity; but in the odd corners will be stowed ukuleles, banjos, guitars, and other stringed instruments, saxophones, a small studio piano, outdoor sporting equipment, a portable motion-picture outfit and assortment of reels, and paraphernalia for the usual indoor games. There will be rifles, shotguns, and ammunition for target practice and sealing, and a great number of books. With these the monotonous routine of a possible winter on the ice will be made more bearable.

The Man Power of the Expedition

In the final analysis men form the real backbone of any expedition. Our preparations, both in thought and materials, have been as thorough as possible, but all of them can be knocked into a heap by some failure in personnel. I anticipate none, but it is a hazard for which there can be little preparation and no defense.

There will be no failure in morale. The men who will comprise the expedition all possess the necessary qualities of mind and brain to endure the long strain of polar work, the loneliness, hardship, and danger. They have been chosen not only for what they know and can do, but for what they are. There is no room here to go into all the complicated details of their selection. Let me only say that the finest pilot or scientist in the world would be less than useless if he had not the quality of keeping up his own morale under strain and of helping others to keep up theirs.

Physical failure is our only fear. Entirely unpredictable, it may crop up in the least expected places. The best-

The Airman becomes a Pathfinder 365

known example of it occurred during Scott's tragic expedition to the South Pole. One of the mainstays of the little party on the final dash was Petty Officer Evans, whom Scott referred to as "our strong man." Yet when the group began to die of exhaustion and exposure, Petty Officer Evans was the first to go, and his death was one of the factors, almost without a doubt, in the final catastrophe.

Gauging a man's physical reaction to hardship and cold is difficult, and hardship and cold, sleeplessness and nerve strain, will be, in greater or less degree, the portion of all of us. The conditions at the poles are so different from anything met with elsewhere that there are no standards to go by; the evidence that a man can stand up under them, until he has proved it on the spot, must be mostly what lawyers term circumstantial. But I believe implicitly that all my companions will come through; with no other belief could I possibly start on such a journey as we contemplate.

The man who was to have gone with me as second in command will not be with us. Floyd Bennett, great aviator, friend, and companion in many a dangerous enterprise, died in line of duty last May. His place in the planes will be taken by Chief Petty Officer Harold I. June, U.S.N., a pilot of skill and long experience. Little known to the public because his flying has been confined to nonspectacular achievements, he is, nevertheless, one of the ablest pilots in the navy. His colleague as pilot-mechanic will be Bernt Balchen, the young Norwegian who returned from Spitsbergen with me and who flew on the transatlantic flight of the *America*. He was at the controls when we landed at Ver-sur-Mer. With myself as pilot-navigator, they will probably form the crew of the Ford tri-motored plane *Floyd Bennett* on the flight to the pole.

Byrd and his Companions the Morning after the America landed at Ver-sur-Mer

The chief engineer of the expedition will be Thomas B. Mulroy, who went with me on the North Pole expedition and did sterling work both in the engine room and on shore.

The Marine Corps will be represented by the two mechanics who will keep the planes and tractors up to par, K. F. Bubier and Victor Czegka. Bubier was assigned by the Marine Corps, and Czegka was granted leave of absence to be able to go with us. On these two men will rest the great responsibility of caring for the sensitive motors of the three planes. The newspapers will give them — to judge by the past — little credit. All the mechanics do is to put the engines in commission, and that is not enough to excite any very general enthusiasm. Who recognizes the

The Airman becomes a Pathfinder 367

name of "Doc" Kinkade today? Probably not one person in a hundred. Yet he is the wizard of the Wright Aëronautical Corporation and the man who tuned up the engines that carried Lindbergh, Chamberlin, and myself across the Atlantic. Without his genius those flights might never have been made, yet he is too modest and self-effacing to crowd — or be pushed — into the limelight. And there are dozens of others like Kinkade. I hope the time will come when they are more generally appreciated.

In charge of our extensive radio equipment will be Malcolm P. Hanson, civilian employee of the Naval Research Laboratory, assigned by the navy to the expedition. Hanson stowed away to go to the North Pole with me, and through continued hard work kept our radio apparatus in perfect condition. He is one of the country's foremost experts on the subject. With him will be associated Leo V. Berkner, assigned by the Department of Commerce, Lloyd K. Grenlie, an ex-marine who was associated with Hanson in the North Pole work, and H. F. Mason, who has been with Wilkins.* The apparatus under their care will be, so far as I know, the most extensive that any polar expedition has ever carried, and all four are even now finding their hands full.

William C. Haynes, otherwise known as "Cyclone" Haynes, meteorologist of the United States Weather Bureau, is our meteorologist. His services are made possible through the generosity of the National Geographic Society. Haynes was another of our North Pole group, and while at Spitsbergen he produced weather as nearly perfect as could be desired. I hope he will be able to do as much on the opposite side of the world.

*Although I expect to do a certain amount of geological work myself, our expert in that line will be L. M. Gould, of the University of Michigan. Since some of the most

368   *Romance of the Airman*

important questions regarding Antarctica turn about geology, his job will be an exacting one.

In addition to these two scientists the Guggenheim Foundation is giving us the services of an aërologist, but at the time this is written he has not yet been chosen.

I wish it were possible to say a word about all of the nearly sixty men with the expedition, but unfortunately lack of space prevents me. All of them will be essential parts of our machine — of our team, I might say, for an expedition has one thing at least in common with a football team: both depend on the perfect functioning of every individual.

I should like to tell you about Richard G. Brophy, business manager of the entire outfit, Doctor Coman Davies, who will be our physicist and glaciologist, and many others, but that is impossible now. Doubtless the newspapers will contain full details later, and to them, if you are interested, I refer you.

The Challenge of the South

Men and equipment, months of forethought and minute preparation, are part of my answer to the challenge of the South — almost the last great challenge left to the explorer. To meet that challenge — and to conquer it — is the purpose of our expedition.

What a better knowledge of the barren Antarctic continent will do for humanity is not for me to say. I believe, for one thing, that it will make the enormously important problem of predicting weather conditions much easier to solve accurately than it is at present; for another, that it will add a great deal to our knowledge of geology, and may possibly open up new supplies of minerals and even coal and oil. These supplies cannot be worked at once;

The Airman becomes a Pathfinder   369

but with the rapid depletion of reserves in temperate climates, the knowledge of the existence of vital necessities elsewhere will be of value in the future.

Such results will be practicable and tangible, but there will be many others not so obviously useful: pages of observations, for instance, that may seem to have no immediate use. Perhaps in the end they will actually prove to have none at all. On the other hand, they may some day supply the missing link in an otherwise insoluble problem.

There are questions of geography to be determined: whether the chain of the Rockies and the Andes runs across the bottom of the world and up through the Australasian islands and the Himalayas, to form an immense world-spanning girdle; whether there are more active volcanoes lost in the polar ice than the two known at present, Mts. Erebus and Terror, and if so, what relation they bear to the formation of Antarctica. There are dozens of other facts to be investigated or discovered, and all of them will have particular interest to some branch of science.

So much for science. The primary purpose of our expedition, as I have told you, is scientific — the study of new lands and new knowledge; but I must confess that the instant when we drop from our plane the flag of the United States, to rest for the first time at the world's farthest south, as it has for so long at the farthest north, will be for me the greatest moment of the expedition.

What a Polar Expedition Eats

A complete list of our proposed supplies would fill the whole of this page, even if printed in very small type. Below you will find some of the largest items. They are calculated for eighteen months. Divide the figures by

370 *Romance of the Airman*

eighteen and compare them with the amounts used in your own home in the course of a month.

44,000 lbs. frozen meats, including mutton, veal, pork, beef, etc.; 4000 lbs. frozen chicken; 1000 lbs. frankfurters; 2500 lbs. pemmican; assorted cases of hot tamales, ox-tongue, deviled meats, meat extracts, preserved soups, and bouillon cubes; 1000 lbs. dry codfish; 50 pails salt mackerel; 700 lbs. fresh fish; 260 cases canned fish; salmon, clams, kippered herring, etc.; 3000 lbs. butter; 3000 lbs. lard; 800 lbs. cheese; 250 cases condensed or dehydrated milk; 150 cases eggs in powdered or dehydrated form; 20,000 lbs. wheat, graham, and buckwheat flour; 1500 lbs. corn meal; 2 bbls. Swedish health bread; 25 cases pilot bread (hard-tack); 4000 lbs. assorted cookies and crackers; 14,000 lbs. granulated, brown, maple, and confectioners' sugar; 500 lbs. assorted candies; 17 cases fresh lemons, apples, oranges, and grapefruit; 80 cases preserved peaches, pineapples, cherries, plums, grapefruit, etc.; 5000 lbs. dried fruits; 20,000 cans assorted vegetables; 5 bbls. sauerkraut; 780 bushels potatoes; 8000 lbs. fresh and dried onions, cabbage, turnips, carrots, and spinach; 4000 lbs. dry navy beans and peas; 2500 lbs. coffee; 200 lbs. tea; 200 lbs. cocoa.

This list is only tentative as yet, and may be very greatly altered before plans are finally completed. It will, nevertheless, give you some idea of the great complexity of provisioning a polar expedition.

Words and Phrases

To aid in understanding this selection

antiscorbutics: preventives of the disease called scurvy.

parka: a fur coat cut like a shirt.

Wilkins: in April, 1928, George Hubert Wilkins, accompanied by Carl B. Eielson, flew from Point Barrow, Alaska, to Spitsbergen and proved that the great continent of the North Polar region was a myth. In December of that year he failed in an attempt to reach the South Pole.

Chinook: the saddest incident of the expedition was the loss of this twelve-year-old lead dog.

The Airman becomes a Pathfinder 371

To add to your vocabulary

nucleus	meteorologist
insulating space	physicist
impervious	glaciologist
dehydrated	

Technical term

aërologist

Informal Test (Completion)[1]

1. The health of polar explorers is more dependent upon _____ than upon clothes.

2. The chief cause of scurvy is _____.

3. Provisions will be taken for _____ months.

4. At the main base the fuel used will be _____.

5. Each train of two dog sleds will be pulled by _____ dogs.

6. The great stand-by for polar food is _____.

7. The food supply will be increased in the Antarctic region by the addition of _____.

8. A Chinook is a cross between a _____ and an _____.

9. The soles of the boots are made of _____.

10. Sleeping-bags are of _____.

11. Clothing will be repaired with _____.

12. The man who was to be second in command was _____.

13. His place will be taken by _____.

14. The number of men on the expedition will be _____.

Exercises and Topics related to your Other Subjects

1. Locate on a map

Dunedin	Mt. Erebus
New Zealand	Mt. Terror
Bay of Whales	Marie Byrd Land

[1] For directions, see page 14.

372 *Romance of the Airman*

2. On a map of Antarctica locate the discoveries and explorations made by Byrd's party.

3. President Eliot's "Five-Foot Shelf" was included in the number of books mentioned by Byrd in this selection. Make a list of these books.

4. A problem in business arithmetic: Consult the market reports and your grocer for prices of the different kinds of foods and foodstuffs that Byrd took with him on his expedition to the Antarctic. Calculate the cost of all the provisions taken.

Subjects for oral themes

Practical Uses of Monel Metal.
The Guggenheim Foundation.
The Daniel Guggenheim Fund for the Promotion of Aëronautics.

Subjects for written themes

The Race between Amundsen and Scott to the South Pole.
The Antarctic Explorations of Shackleton.
The Antarctic Expedition of Sir Hubert Wilkins.

Other Readings

In this book

"Byrd's Flight to the North Pole," page 275.

From other sources

"Voyages of Captain Scott," by R. F. Scott.
"South!" by Ernest Shackleton.
"Rear Admiral Byrd and the Polar Expeditions," by Coram Foster.
"Little America," by Rear Admiral Richard E. Byrd.

Le Bourget

PAUL E. LAMARCHE, JR.

> **Explanatory Note.** Flying fields are to aviators as seaports are to sailors. The principal fields of the world will some day be as well known to the reader of the daily newspaper as are the ports of entry to the leading countries. Le Bourget has military as well as civil hangars. The architects were farsighted enough to make space for larger planes than have ever been built. Some fields are already handicapped by having hangars inadequate in size. It was at this field that Lindbergh landed at the end of his world-famed flight of 1927.

LE BOURGET, the airport of Paris, is probably the best known of all European airports to Americans. As a goal for transatlantic flyers it has become associated with American achievements in the air more than once. A Ryan plane landed there on a direct flight from New York. A Bellanca has landed there after crossing the ocean, and last summer a Fairchild took off from this field, piloted by Collyer, who, with Mears, circled the globe in twenty-three days. Every year thousands of Americans use this airport when they come to Paris or leave by the route of the skies. To Europeans it is one of the three most important airports of the Old World, together with Croydon in London and Tempelhof in Berlin. To France it is her premier and most important airport, and to her people this field associates itself with some of her greatest efforts and most successful endeavors in the air. It was from this field that Nungesser and Coli in a Levasseur biplane took off one early morning in May of 1927, and it was from this field that Costes and Le Brix took off on a trip that carried them across the South Atlantic and over two hemispheres before they again brought their faithful Breguet *dix-neuf* down on the sod of this field amidst the acclaim of thousands.

374 *Romance of the Airman*

Le Bourget airport is one of the most important air centers of western Europe, and its location has largely brought this about. It is the principal air field of the second largest city in Europe, with a population in excess of three millions, and a location that is, as everyone knows, very central. Air lines radiate in every direction from this field in daily services, and it is visited by the planes of many nations in the maintenance of these services. The airport is situated twelve kilometers from the Opéra, which is the heart of Paris, and six kilometers from the Porte de la Villette, the northeastern extremity of the city limits through which passes the Route de Flandres, an important highway that continues past the air field in the direction of St. Denis. The field is actually just beyond the small town of Le Bourget-Dugny, from which it derives its name.

According to French history two massacres took place in Le Bourget during the Franco-Prussian War in October and December of 1870, so that, besides being famed for its airport, Le Bourget is thus recognized and known in Europe. Before the war the land which is now one of the finest airports of Europe was merely farm land outside of the town; and at that time much of the flying around Paris was from the old field of Issy-les-Moulineaux, which, though now abandoned, retains many historic associations with early French aviation. It was at this old field that Farman made the first flight in France in a plane built by Gabriel Voisin twenty-five years ago.

During the war the French government took over various tracts of land in the Paris region to use as airports for military operations, among them being the field at Le Bourget. Le Bourget was built as a military port and was known in French army parlance as a *réserve générale d'aviation*, which means that planes and forces were assembled there before going to the air stations at the front.

The Airman becomes a Pathfinder

Le Bourget, the Most Important Airport in France

It was also used for air squadrons whose duty it was to protect the city of Paris from air attacks. Though not at the front, this field saw much activity as a military field, and it was used alike by big Farman bombers, Caudrons, and other large planes as well as the little Spads, with their now old-fashioned rotary motors, that bore the brunt of the work among French combat planes.

The field itself is approximately 325 acres in area. The ground is usually in excellent condition except at times during the winter when the turf is soggy and two-ton commercial planes leave deep ruts behind them in taxiing over the field. It is very level, and, compared with many airports, the surface is smooth and free of stones or depressions in the turf. In shape the field cannot exactly be called square, but rather is suggestive of the shape of the state of Nevada as it appears on a map, though Le Bourget is perhaps not so angular. Although the field assumes more or less the shape of a rectangle, the southwestern corner makes the difference. The longest take-off

376 Romance of the Airman

runs north and south, and the greatest length in this direction is 1500 meters, or about 4500 feet. At the southern end there are some low military hangars behind which is a row of poplar trees, while to the north there is no immediate obstruction rising from the ground, although there is a small stream, known as the "Tranchée de la Morée," which winds its way along this boundary of the field and into which planes occasionally come to grief. The width of the field is at the widest point 1000 meters, or about 3300 feet; and hangars line both sides for the entire length of the field, so that planes taking off across the field must allow for these obstructions. In all, this air field is comparatively free of large obstructions, and the country beyond is quite level for a considerable distance. The altitude of the field is 44 meters above sea level.

Le Bourget is identified from the air by a large white circle across which is written the word LE BOURGET. A smaller white circle, near to the apron in front of the customs office, can also be seen from a distance. Signal posts and wind cones are placed at various points along the borders of the field and serve for both the military and the commercial aircraft. When a commercial plane arrives from a foreign country, it taxies to the apron in front of the customs office, where the passengers descend. Here passports are inspected, and the travelers enter the customs room, where the baggage is examined. They are then transported into Paris by a bus provided by the air line.

Le Bourget is completely equipped for night flying; and while none of the commercial lines using this port fly by night as yet, the field is equipped with the most modern lighting facilities. Several experimental night flights have been made between London and Paris, and Strasbourg and Paris, and at times the army planes practice night flying. Le Bourget is easily found at night, and in good weather

The Airman becomes a Pathfinder 377

can be identified at a distance. At the airport is a large steel pylon, or lighthouse, that stands about one hundred feet high and on top of which are installed a projector and eight tubes of neon lights.* In clear weather and when flying at a good altitude a pilot can see these lights from a considerable distance. These neon lights are the most effective type of lights used in European airports for penetrating through the fog and mists. The experience of Commander Byrd in the *America* when he vainly tried to reach this field during very bad weather conditions seems to show that even these lights are not good enough to conquer fog; but, on the other hand, there is much speculation as to whether he was actually near to Paris at any time before the end of the flight.

A large letter *N* illuminated at night identifies Le Bourget, and this letter designation is particularly useful in identifying the field from the lights of the city and railroad yards beyond. A large letter *T* on a mast which is illuminated at night shows the pilot the direction of the wind, while a system of colored lights on the roof of one of the buildings tells the night flyer whether the apron, or *piste*, as the French call it, is clear or not by showing green if free and red when occupied. Flood lights are placed at corners of the field as well as on the apron in front of the customs office. These lights are mounted on wheels so that they can be moved at will. At the extreme limit of the field is a powerful projector that is operated on a double circuit; that is, by the regular electric current on the field as well as by a gasoline set that can be used in an emergency if the current should fail. As on all air fields equipped for night flying, all obstructions, such as the roofs of the hangars, wireless masts, boundaries of the field, and other hazards, are clearly marked with red lights.

378 *Romance of the Airman*

The Le Bourget airport is owned and operated by the French government. Until recently the field was managed by a government organization known as the "Service de la Navigation Aérienne," which was under the control of Maurice Bokanowski, the Minister of Commerce. The *administrateur* of the Le Bourget airport is M. M. Renvoise, who was appointed by this organization. The organization under him is responsible for the maintenance of the airport in general and the operation of the weather bureau, radio department, and other departments. His is an organization that receives government support and supervision. The air lines themselves operate independently, as well as the army section of this field, and have their own forces of mechanics.

A tram line, from the heart of Paris, which ends in the town of Le Bourget is to be extended to the field, and one of the municipal bus lines will also be extended. Mail is usually picked up by the busses on the way out from one of the central post-office bureaus; but just at present plans are under way for an air chute from the Pantin post office, one of the more important branches in the north of Paris, directly to a branch which will be organized at the field for the handling of mail.

Words and Phrases

To aid in understanding this selection

neon lights: lights produced by a gas; similar to the northern lights.

Route de Flandres: road to Flanders.

To add to your vocabulary

premier	commercial aircraft
air squadrons	meter

The Airman becomes a Pathfinder 379

Informal Test (Multiple-Choice)[1]

1. The most important airport in France is **Le Bourget Croydon Tempelhof Trepassey**

2. The second largest city of Europe is **London Berlin Paris Madrid**

3. The Route de Flandres is an important **river highway railroad air line**

4. During the war the French government took over various tracts of land in the Paris region to use for **commercial operations military operations manufacturing centers**

5. The field of Le Bourget is usually kept in **excellent condition fair condition poor condition**

6. The shape of the Le Bourget field resembles that of the state of **Maine Kansas Kentucky Georgia Nevada**

7. The altitude of the Le Bourget field is **thirty-four forty-four fifty fifty-one** meters above sea level.

8. Le Bourget is **poorly fairly completely** equipped for night flying.

9. A large letter **N M L T** aids in identifying Le Bourget at night.

10. On all air fields used for night flying, such obstructions as roofs, hangars, etc. are clearly marked with **green red orange** lights.

Exercises and Topics related to your Other Subjects

1. What reasons can you find from your geography why Le Bourget should become an important flying field?

2. Compare the history of French aviation with that of American aviation.

3. Make a list of pioneers of aviation.

[1] For directions, see page 95.

380   *Romance of the Airman*

4. Make a sketch map of Europe locating the three noted flying fields named in the article read.

5. Make a map of the Le Bourget field.

6. What advantages has Kansas City as an important airport?

Other Readings

From other sources

The American Aviator, Airplanes and Airports.

Airports, a magazine devoted entirely to airports.

"Airports and Landing Fields" and "Airport Management," aëronautical bulletins published by the United States Department of Commerce.

The First Dirigible to circumnavigate*
the Globe

Explanatory Note. The first flight round the world was made by the American Army Air Service in 1924. The planes, which were heavier-than-air craft, left the United States from Seattle on April 6 and returned on September 28, covering a distance of 27,534 miles in one hundred and seventy-five days.

The first airship (lighter-than-air craft) to circumnavigate the globe was the *Graf Zeppelin*. This palace of the air is a German-built lighter-than-air ship which looks like a great silver cigar 776 feet long and 98 feet in diameter. A peek inside reveals interesting compartments. Most interesting is the control room, in which are seen the instruments of navigation and the highly skilled engineers who are experts in their particular fields. The radio room, containing receiving and sending apparatus and marine charts, is just behind the control room. Just across the aisle is the captain's room. Immediately behind these rooms are the kitchen and the dining-room. The dining-room is also used as a salon. It is furnished with light tables and chairs; and when dinner is over, it has the appearance of a drawing-room arranged for afternoon bridge. Behind the salon are the cabins. There are two berths in each of the little rooms. The lower one is used as a settee in the daytime, and the upper is swung to the ceiling very much as are the berths in a Pullman train. The first airship made by Ferdinand von Zeppelin was completed in 1900. The *Graf Zeppelin* represents the climax of more than a quarter of a century's devotion to airship construction.

WHEN the *Graf Zeppelin* set out from Lakehurst, New Jersey (the naval air station of the United States of America), on August 8, 1929, and returned 21 days, 7 hours, and 25 minutes later, it set many new records in the annals of aviation. All save one of these records will serve as challenges for others to surpass. The *one* record which will always be associated with this eventful flight is that it is the *first* time that a lighter-than-air ship ever made a flight round the world.

After the most careful preparation had been made under

382 *Romance of the Airman*

the direction of Dr. Hugo Eckener, the German dirigible with its twenty-two passengers aboard started away on its flight round the globe. The military band played the very appropriate song "There's a Long, Long Trail a-Winding" as the passengers set out on the greatest adventure since man learned to use his wings.

A ton of food, hundreds of letters, baggage for the twenty-two passengers, and a crew of forty-one persons were the necessary equipment of the *Graf Zeppelin*. When the "All aboard" signal was given, the land crew of four hundred and twelve American Marines, working under the direction of Lieutenant Scott Peck, U.S.N., weighed the ship, removed ballast here and placed it there in order that perfect equilibrium be established, moved the ship from the hangar to the center of the field, and finally released it to the skies. The wonderful silver airship floated away like King Solomon's magic carpet.

Truly, a magic carpet of the twentieth century the *Graf Zeppelin* proved to be; for in 55 hours and 24 minutes the great ship ended the first leg* of its flight. When it landed at Friedrichshafen, Germany, at 1.03 P.M. on August 10, the largest dirigible had covered approximately four thousand two hundred miles. The news of the arrival, several hours earlier than was expected, spread like wildfire through the city of Friedrichshafen, and great crowds hurried to the Zeppelin works to welcome the airship. Soldiers and police held back the cheering crowd, which went wild with enthusiasm and shouted "Hoch Eckener!" as the commodore made a spectacular landing. For days butchers and bakers had been working overtime preparing for the guests that would fill the hotels and private homes to welcome the arrival of the famous ship, as well as to celebrate Germany's Constitution Day on August 10. The celebration of Constitution Day in Germany is as

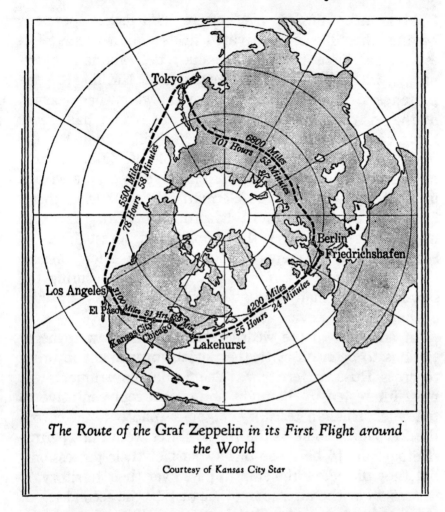

The Route of the Graf Zeppelin *in its First Flight around the World*

Courtesy of Kansas City Star

important an event as is our celebration of the Fourth of July. Another celebration was held on the day of the arrival of the *Graf Zeppelin*. It was the sixty-first anniversary of the birth of its famous commander, Dr. Hugo Eckener.

The second leg of the trip around the world was begun at five o'clock on August 15. The goal was Tokyo; the distance, sixty-six hundred miles. This leg of the journey was anticipated as one full of wonders. Truly it exceeded the most riotous imagination of any passenger aboard.

384 *Romance of the Airman*

Gold-domed churches everywhere in Russia; peasants herding their flocks; cultivated fields; fallow lands; forests; small lakes; silvery streams; the Siberian wilderness, — all these were spectacular and thrilling to the passengers. The inhabitants, some of whom had learned of the visit over the radio, others of whom had never heard of a dirigible, must have been thrilled too when the majestic ship passed over. The people of Yakutsk must have been excited when the ship lowered to drop a wreath upon the graves of some German soldiers buried there. This was by far the most hazardous part of the world flight. The route over the uninhabited forest lands of Siberia, across the steppes of Russia, within a few miles of the Arctic Circle, warranted Dr. Eckener in securing the services of Germany's most noted meteorologist as chief of the weather service aboard the ship.

In addition to the weather hazards, there were negotiations to be made with the Soviet government in order to cross Russian territory. The Soviet government was most interested in the flight and sent a representative to tell when Russian territory might be photographed from the *Zeppelin*. Some of the Baltic states would not permit photographs to be made of any part of their possessions, but they did allow the ship to pass over their territory.

At 6.40 of the afternoon of August 19 the second leg of the flight was ended — 101 hours and 50 minutes' flight from Friedrichshafen to Tokyo. The detour over Tokyo and Yokohama made the distance six thousand eight hundred and eighty miles according to the official reports. Europe now lies less than five days from the Far East. Tokyo greeted the *Zeppelin* and its passengers with strains of the German national anthem and with cheers and hand-clapping. After a brief customs examination of the passengers, a formal reception was held at the airport, and

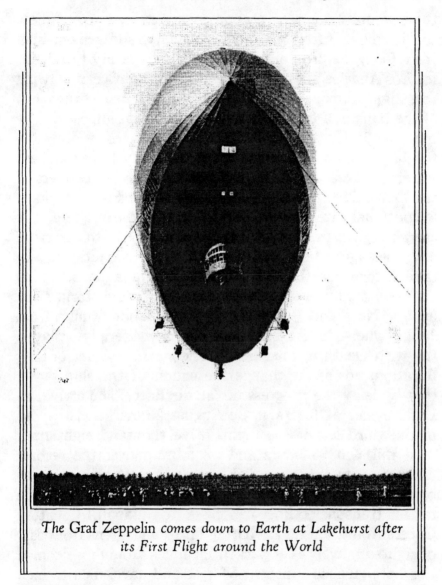

The Graf Zeppelin comes down to Earth at Lakehurst after its First Flight around the World

refreshments, consisting of dried chestnuts, dried cuttlefish, and sake,* were served with traditional Japanese ceremony. A dinner and entertainment followed, and for three days the passengers were fêted as an expression of hospitality when East meets West. If kindness could kill,

386 Romance of the Airman

there would have been no passengers or crew to complete
the journey. After refueling, regassing, and replenishing
their food, the crew and passengers were ready to set out
for Los Angeles and to conquer the Pacific Ocean. Owing
to a slight damage to the ship while it was being drawn out
of the hangar, a twenty-four-hour delay was imposed. The
naval authorities ordered destroyers to be in readiness at
the Japanese naval bases to assist the *Zeppelin* in Japanese
waters if there should be any mishap. Seven steamers of
the Dollar Line lay along its course in the Pacific to keep
in continual wireless communication with the dirigible. Six
carrier pigeons were taken on board at Tokyo to carry the
first messages. It is well that all these precautions were
taken; for when the *Graf Zeppelin* left Japan at 3.13 P.M.
on August 23, it encountered the most severe storm since
leaving New York. It was only three hundred miles from
Japan when Dr. Eckener and his crew literally "played
tag with Death in the skies." The storm was not of long
duration, nor did it change the course of the ship or seriously delay the progress of the air liner. The arrival at
Los Angeles at 5.11 A.M. on August 26 marked the close
of the third leg of the flight. Five thousand eight hundred miles in 78 hours and 58 minutes was the record.
This, the first nonstop flight across the Pacific, was accomplished in less than one third of the time that the
fastest transpacific liner can cross from Japan to Seattle.
Cheers from thousands, roaring horns and sirens from cars
of sightseers who were parked for miles around, welcomed
the distinguished visitors. Marine and naval men trained
for the occasion grasped the ropes dropped down to draw
the aërial monster to the ground, and safely anchored it
for a brief visit. The passengers were fêted in true American style. On August 27, at 12.14 A.M., the dirigible again
took off on the last leg of its epoch-making trip.

The Airman becomes a Pathfinder 387

Passing over Yuma, Gila Bend, El Paso, Kansas City, Chicago, Detroit, and Akron, the *Graf Zeppelin* reached its destination on August 29 at 8.13 A.M., having made the trip of three thousand one hundred miles from Los Angeles to Lakehurst in 51 hours and 59 minutes. Traveling nearly twenty thousand miles, going through almost every conceivable kind of weather and atmospheric conditions, the majestic ship landed serenely after having accomplished in a little more than 21 days what Magellan, four hundred years before, had required one thousand and eighty-three days to do.

The *Graf Zeppelin* set a new record for crossing the Atlantic (55 hours and 24 minutes), a new record for flying from Europe to Japan (101 hours and 50 minutes), a new record for crossing the Pacific Ocean (being the first), and a new record for a round-the-world flight (21 days, 7 hours, and 25 minutes). Who will accept the challenge of the *Graf Zeppelin*?

Words and Phrases

To aid in understanding this selection

circumnavigate: to sail around.
leg: a nautical term referring to one of the stages of a journey.
sake (sä′kĕ): a Japanese beverage made by the fermentation of rice.

Informal Test (Completion)[1]

1. The first flight round the world in a lighter-than-air ship was made by the _____ _____ in the year _____.

2. The time required to make the flight was _____ days, _____ hours, and _____ minutes.

3. The starting-point was _____ _____.

4. The voyage was divided into _____ parts called legs.

5. The crew numbered _____ men.

[1] For directions, see page 14.

388 *Romance of the Airman*

6. Calculate the total number of miles and the average number of miles per hour required to make the flight round the world. Use the data from the following tabulation:

Division of Flight	From	To	Distance in Miles	Time	
				Hours	Minutes
First leg	Lakehurst, New Jersey	Friedrichshafen	4200	55	24
Second leg	Friedrichshafen	Tokyo	6880	101	50
Third leg	Tokyo	Los Angeles	5800	78	58
Fourth leg	Los Angeles	Lakehurst	3100	51	59

Exercises and Topics related to your Other Subjects

1. Read the story of Magellan's voyage round the world. On a map locate the route taken by him.

2. What instruments of navigation did he use?

3. Others that circumnavigated the globe after Magellan and before the *Graf Zeppelin* were Nellie Bly (1889), 72 days, 6 hours, 11 minutes; George Francis Train (1890), 69 days, 12 hours, 3 minutes; Charles Fitzmorris (1901), 60 days, 13 hours, 29 minutes; Henry Frederick (1903), 54 days, 7 hours, 20 minutes; Colonel Burnley Campbell (1907), 40 days, 19 hours, 30 minutes; Andre Jaeger-Schmidt (1911), 39 days, 19 hours, 43 minutes; John Henry Mears (1913), 35 days, 21 hours, 35 minutes; Evans-Wells (1925), 28 days, 14 hours, 36 minutes; Mears-Collyer (1928), 23 days, 15 hours, 21 minutes. Learn from your reference books the motive of each and the route taken by each.

Other Readings

In this book

"The Story of Zeppelin's Early Projects," page 208.

From other sources

"The Outline of History," by H. G. Wells. (Page 745 gives a map of Magellan's voyage of exploration.)

"Around the World in Eighty Days," by Jules Verne.

"Skylarking," by Bruce Gould.

V. The Airman soars to Fame

His fame was great in all the land.
LONGFELLOW, "Tales of a Wayside Inn"

Columbus of the Air

AUGUSTUS POST

> *Explanatory Note.* In the months following his successful flight, newspapers, magazines, and books were filled with articles about Charles Lindbergh and his achievement. From the great mass of material this article has been chosen because it is a fine tribute to the young aviator and gives the significance of the flight.

ONE night in May, 1927, a tall, good-looking American boy stands in line unnoticed before a New York moving-picture house, like anyone else; a few hours later he drops from the sky in Paris, and the theater before which he stood is crowded to the roof to see the world's hero upon the screen. No man since men began to make history has risen so swiftly to world-wide fame as this young American, Colonel Charles Augustus Lindbergh. The man, the deed, and the hour combined to make this the event most quickly and widely known to the greatest multitude of rejoicing human beings. He had just come from San Diego, California, alone, in twenty-one hours, the fastest air time across the continent, and a record that would have put him on the front page of the newspapers in quieter times than these. But this was only tuning up for the flight that he was about to make; crossing the Atlantic on a sandwich and a half and a few swallows of water; landing at night, on unknown ground, in a machine with not a spot of oil on it nor a sign of having come from across the globe. It seems to be the peculiar attribute of Lindbergh to do the formidable, the fantastic, and the incredible in the simplest and most everyday fashion, and to keep this everyday simplicity through the fire of the most intense and exhausting publicity that has ever been turned upon a single individual.

392 *Romance of the Airman*

It was eight years ago, while Lindbergh was still a schoolboy, that Alcock and Brown made the first air crossing of the Atlantic, linking America with England. This fired Raymond Orteig of New York City, a passionately patriotic Frenchman, with the determination to do something not only to advance aviation but to bring France into these new world relations. I was at that time secretary of the Aëro Club of America, and it was to me that he telephoned to ask my assistance in formulating plans.

It was clear that the best way would be to link Paris with New York by air. This would require a machine to do double what had ever been done before — new instruments, and scientific navigation in addition to piloting. Naturally Mr. Orteig thought the French would be the first to do it, and so did I; he drew up a deed of gift for twenty-five thousand dollars, and I drew up the rules to win this prize that was a challenge to aviation. Five years passed, however, without a start from either side. The general public did not take it seriously; indeed, up to the very day of Lindbergh's starting, Mr. Orteig was berated in letters to the press for instigating men to go to their deaths for a deed not only impractical but impossible of accomplishment.

Mr. Orteig, however, extended the time, when an entry came from the foremost French flyer, René Fonck, and an attempt was made. In the following year, 1927, several entries were made from this side, and from France two of the most intrepid flyers of the world, Nungesser and Coli, flew out into the unknown and disappeared. Finally, on May 20, in the mist before morning, Lindbergh rose alone from Roosevelt Field, Mineola, Long Island; was sighted along our coast to the tip of Newfoundland; surprised a fisherman in Dingle Bay by asking from the clouds, "Is this the road to Ireland?" and before the day ended was in Paris.

The Airman soars to Fame

Lindbergh, Ready to take off on his Historic New York-to-Paris Flight, May, 1927

The keynote then struck was soon to swell into a world symphony of homage: as he passed from France, to Belgium, to England, kings and commoners joined the acclaim and expressed, each in his own way, the long-waiting joy of humanity at the coming of the first citizen of the world, the first human being truly entitled to give his address as "The Earth," the first Ambassador-at-large to Creation. Brought home in an American warship, he received the official welcome of his nation at the hands of the President at Washington, was greeted in New York with a demonstration to which that of Armistice Day alone might be compared, and set sail for home in the plane that he had always recognized as part of himself and partaker of his glory.

The reader of this survey of events, reviewing the great

394 *Romance of the Airman*

day of Le Bourget from the perspective of even a comparatively brief interval, may be permitted to ask, Why all the excitement? Just what is the significance of Charles Lindbergh's achievement that a world no longer looking on the aëroplane as a marvel — a world that had already acclaimed the crossing of the Atlantic, the circumnavigation of the globe by air, and the traversing of the North Pole by aëroplane and dirigible — should thrill to this exploit as if life were in some way beginning over again? The answer is that the world is right. Aviation is beginning over again. An epoch in air history was closed by the flight of Lindbergh, and with it an epoch begins.

Before the hero of the New York-to-Paris flight had regained New York on the *Memphis*, another American youth had crossed the Atlantic, this time with a passenger — Clarence Chamberlin with Charles Levine. Steering for Berlin, their gasoline supply had lasted to within a comparatively few miles of their destination, when they were forced down. Chamberlin is another type of American airman in time of peace; he was a "gypsy flyer," the picturesque phrase for a picaresque* way of life. The gypsy flyer owns his plane and picks up a living by it however and wherever he can, taking up passengers, buying and selling second-hand machines, taking photographs, and especially stunt-flying at fairs or other open-air assemblies. The gypsy flyer has been quite naturally looked down upon by the profession as a sort of aërial acrobat and camp follower, but he furnishes some of the most interesting and significant types of young Americans. The country is, if not full of them, at least well sprinkled with bronzed and competent youths who may drop from clouds almost anywhere over the countryside and earn a living by their skill, their courage, and their often brilliant resourcefulness.

The Airman soars to Fame 395

While all this was going on, a scientific expedition, headed by Commander Richard E. Byrd, was awaiting suitable weather conditions for an Atlantic flight in the giant monoplane *America*. The crew consisted of Bert Acosta, chief pilot; Lieutenant George O. Noville, radio operator; and Bernt Balchen, reserve pilot. They were not competing for the Orteig prize, but intended to chart the weather at various altitudes and generally to accumulate scientific data in regard to storms and air currents that would be of value to aircraft plying between America and Europe. Commander Byrd is yet another type of American airman: engineer, naval officer, scientist, and explorer, intrepid and devoted. His flights over the pole and Arctic regions were made in the interests of exploration, and he is at this writing arranging an expedition to the South Pole. He not only sustains the tradition of the American navy, but represents a family that has been prominent in the councils of the American nation since the time of Washington.

After waiting, like a good sportsman, for the return of Lindbergh to this country, the *America* took off from the very field from which the other two flights started, kept in touch with shore stations all the way by wireless, — which neither of the other planes did, — but was exceptionally unfortunate in running into dense fog which obscured the ocean for the greater part of the course. When the voyagers reached the coast of France the weather was so thick they were unable to determine their position, and their compass went out of commission for some unaccountable reason; but in spite of these disheartening difficulties they were able to return to the seacoast, and by the best of airmanship made a fortunate landing at Ver-sur-Mer, in the ocean, coming to shore in their collapsible life-raft.

Brief as the time has been since 1903, when the Wright

396 *Romance of the Airman*

brothers rose from the sand dunes of Kitty Hawk and opened the era of aviation, it is already divided into clearly defined periods, with each of which everything may be said to have started all over again. A man still in middle age might have lived through them all; it has been my good fortune to be so placed that I could watch all these developments at close hand. The first division was the period of the Inventors and Builders, such as the Wrights and Curtiss in America, the Voisin brothers and Bleriot in France. It would be hard to separate builders from inventors; for though the arch-inventors approached the subject by way of laboratory experiments in aërodynamics, and others of their type sought results by elaborate calculation, there were yet others who made valuable contributions to the changing machine by empirical methods, approaching the subject by trying one thing and then another, working "by guess and by gosh," as the farmer built his bridge, and acting as developers in the building process.

Immediately after this came the era of the Demonstrators, the age of "aërial jockeys." At first these were the inventors and builders themselves — Wilbur Wright at Le Mans, France; Orville Wright at Fort Meyer; and Glenn Curtiss elsewhere in the United States. But soon this duty of demonstration fell to a generation of pupils who did not add a nut or a bolt to the construction of the machine, who flew what was given them, but who, by their intrepid use of what they had, constantly set the constructors new tasks and constantly required of them new machines that would respond to their abilities and fulfill their demands.

It was this generation that by concentrating on flying proved possibilities undreamed-of by the public and only remotely hoped for by the builder. Pegaud's feat in loop-

The Airman soars to Fame 397

ing the loop was reviled by the unthinking as foolhardiness, serving no good purpose — a reproach that has never been withheld from any stage of development of air flight, and from which even Lindbergh himself has not been free. But by Pegaud the aëroplane builder was challenged to provide for all future flyers a machine that would withstand the strain of this new maneuver, to the general improvement of the plane and to the vast enlargement of the possibilities of flight, especially in warfare. During this period these expert demonstrators developed the plane by races and contests in reliability and speed, and carried it to undreamed-of altitudes. They were enlarging the pattern; already by the close of this era the Atlantic flight was on the horizon as the greatest possibility of all in the way of demonstration.

But this period was to come to a violent end. The World War intervened. Only to compare the little, light machine that went into the war with the deadly efficiency of the engines that emerged from it is to see for oneself that this period brought about developments in aviation comparable only to those in surgery and in chemistry. The vital necessity that made surgeons and chemists take chances that a century of peace would not justify sent men into the clouds to perform the impossible and make it the commonplace of a flyer's day. This period added armament to the plane and made the gun its *raison d'être*,* with flying only a means to this end instead of an occupation for all the powers and energies of hand and brain as heretofore. It not only developed a type of flyer who could run his machine almost automatically, reserving his darting intelligence for the exigencies of conflict, but it laid upon the builder the necessity of providing him with a plane whose mechanism would respond at once to the most sensitive control. When the war stopped, the Ace had been evolved,

398 *Romance of the Airman*

a creature whose personality extended to the tips of its wings and in whom mind and motor were one.

Opportunity for the Ace stopped with the war; and with the coming of the fourth period, Commercial Aviation, the machine began to take first place in the public mind — the machine and the organization that made its operation possible on a large scale. Air lines opened in every direction in Europe and became in a short time a valued method of transportation, not only in respect to speed, but for the even more important qualification of safety. The Channel as a barrier had crumbled under Bleriot and disappeared during the war; it was now to be crossed daily by steady air-going craft used by tourists no more freely than by staid business men desiring conservative and speedy methods of transportation for themselves and for fragile merchandise. From every airport of Europe lines crossed and recrossed the map. The globe was circled, Australia linked to the mother country, the Sahara opened, and Darkest Africa illuminated; the Atlantic, North and South, was crossed no less than fifteen times by airship and aëroplane; the islands of the Pacific, Hawaii and the Aleutian Islands, were joined to the mainland, the flights depending in each instance not only upon the skill of the pilots in flying and navigating but upon long preparation, organization, and teamwork of their supporters — in some instances, of supporting governments. But although our government took some part in this procession, the peak of our activity in this period was the air mail, a fine example of organized support of individual bravery and skill.

The actual achievement of Lindbergh is easily set down. In a monoplane named, for the city of his financial backers, the *Spirit of St. Louis*, built for him in sixty days, he flew on May 20–21, 1927, thirty-six hundred and ten flying

The Spirit of St. Louis *is now treasured by the Government of the United States in the Smithsonian Institution at Washington, D.C.*

miles, without stop or deviation from a determined course, in thirty-three hours and twenty-nine minutes. His only new instrument of importance was the earth inductor compass; this he constantly watched, and in order to fly, as he flew, on the arc of a great circle, it had to be adjusted about every hundred miles. He had continually to judge the side drift of his machine and allow for it, and also to use his judgment in maneuvering around fog and storm centers. The distance he covered constituted the world's record for nonstop flight at the time, but this was never emphasized in the popular mind, and I doubt if one man in a thousand who cheered Lindbergh could have told offhand the number of miles that he had flown in those memorable hours above the ocean.

There are some flights that make records and some that make history; this was a history-making flight. As with

400 *Romance of the Airman*

all the other periods of flying history, everything is beginning over again with it. Attention is again directed not only to the machine, but to the man, as in the first days, when aviation was a matter of great individuals. Old and young share in the thrill; for youth acclaims the young . hero, and to those who lived through the pioneer days, the days of pioneering begin anew. In 1926 Commander Byrd's magnificent feat in crossing the North Pole roused the admiration of the world; but once done, it was, so far as the public mind was concerned, done with, while Lindbergh's flight, almost immediately followed by Chamberlin's and then by Byrd's, seems even to the unimaginative the opening of a new era of transportation. As important as its being done was the fact that it was done on time, and, again, it was the aspect of ambassadorship that loomed large in the public imagination. America is a long way off from Europe, and, with the best will in the world, professional diplomacy does not always tend to diminish the distance. Radio —whose development has progressed step by step with aviation, as the telegraph accompanied the railroad, and the telephone the automobile — was doing much to bring the two hemispheres together in thought; but it needed the actual crossing, at a single step, of this level-headed boy, bringing a greeting no more official than his first words, "I'm Charles Lindbergh," but with a smile that carried with it those assurances of good will that words are more apt to obscure than to explain. There is no doubt that Europe took his coming in this spirit; and Lindbergh was fulfilling a sacred trust to humanity when in his brief speech to the multitudes at Washington and to the thirty millions of radio listeners he spoke only of the affection for America that he had seen and felt everywhere displayed in France, in Belgium, and in England, and of his sense of obligation to bring back

The Airman soars to Fame 401

with him the impression of this frame of mind, undimmed by time, and transmit it to his countrymen.

People appreciate what comes within their experience. Though the public thought the flight was great, it was even more impressed by the flawless tact with which Lindbergh met the kings of the Old World and the crowds of the New, and the unerring judgment that steered him past the two storm centers of sentimentality and commercialism. He conveyed far more by his actions than he did by his words, well chosen as they invariably were; he brought new power and vitality to diplomacy by the addition of the dramatic element.

His actions the public could see; but what it could only faintly envisage was, after all, the flight itself. This, strictly speaking, not more than a dozen men can really appreciate: these are the aviators who have had at least a similar experience; who have made, or partly made, a transoceanic flight. They know the fierceness of the forces that block the road through the unknown, the icy mist that may reduce the lifting power of the wings and in a moment change success to failure, life to death; the swift-springing storms or blinding fog that may, as they did for Byrd, blot out land and sea for nineteen hours together; and the immeasurable waste of waters whose very thought pulls down the mind — the waters that hold somewhere the secret of Nungesser and Coli. But aviators in general, given even a slight amount of imagination, can appreciate all this indirectly, and it is from them that the praise most valued by Lindbergh has come. It is they also who can value the exploit of Byrd as it should be valued. With the public at large the disposition had been to regard it as a flight that failed only in its avowed objective, though it was beset with incidents of dramatic grandeur. The superhuman skill and the highest science

402 *Romance of the Airman*

of aërial navigation on the part of Commander Byrd, and the cool bravery and heroic courage of each member of the crew, brought them through imminent dangers in safety to a well-earned ovation from the nations of the world as well as from all their fellow citizens of America. Chamberlin, heading for Berlin, found himself in a cucumber patch in Kottbus; the fact that this was some miles farther than Lindbergh had flown did not count with the crowd in comparison with the fact that it was some miles short of the spot he had expected to reach, though he had carefully refrained from making official announcement of this expectation. Byrd, in the *America*, carried three times the weight, chanced three times the motor difficulties, and, with four times the human risk, completed a tremendous scientific experiment, revealed the possibilities of radio communication almost as remarkable as those of the aëroplane, and demonstrated, against almost inconceivable dangers and difficulties, that it was by no mere lucky fluke that the others had made the flight, and that the crossing could be made in almost any weather.

The transpacific flight of Maitland and Hegenberger,* which took place with brilliant precision at almost the same time as Byrd's, was but another proof to the public of the marvelous state of accuracy to which the navigation of aircraft had reached; such small objects as the Hawaiian Islands, after a flight of twenty-five hours and fifty minutes, could be hit "plumb on the nose," although they were a distance of twenty-four hundred miles away over water. But long-distance flights are becoming of everyday occurrence, and the public no longer complains that human life is being risked for only a brief moment of glory. The mortality rate has always been lower for aviation than people generally believed, for the emphasis has been not upon the man that flies but the man that falls; now the

The Airman soars to Fame 403

expectation is that the pilot will win through, just as the traveler on the railroad train believes that he will reach Chicago on time. If there is a train wreck the papers do not at once complain that the steam engine is an affront to Providence.

Lindbergh's perfect flight revealed the highest and noblest characteristics of man: daring, skill, calculation, and genius. It brought into the limelight of public knowledge the vast height of attainment and the tremendous possibilities even now at our command in the aëroplane of today; and as a flash of lightning illumines the landscape for a moment so that we see the mountain peaks upon the horizon, so this brilliant deed revealed to the imagination of man a clear vision of the future. He had faith not only in his motor but, what is still more important, in himself, and he was upheld by the wishes, the hopes, and the prayers of the whole nation.

Today not only the airmen but the earthmen are planning and prophesying. In 1914 I wrote an article called "Columbus of the Air," and I said:

A man is now living who will be the first human being to cross the Atlantic Ocean through the air. He will cross while he is still a young man. All at once Europe will move two days nearer; instead of five days away, it will be distant only thirty hours. . . . It would seem out of keeping with the general economy of weight, when even the parts are not duplicated, that the pilot should be carried in duplicate. . . . As for keeping awake and alert for the whole time of the flight, every aëronaut knows that this is possible. I myself have kept alert for longer periods than this several times in international balloon races. Whoever crosses the ocean through the air for the first time will be too busy to be lonesome. . . . Imagine then, the welcome that awaits the "Columbus of the Air"! The cable warns of his departure; before him flies the wireless announcing his progress. Ship after ship, waiting the

404 *Romance of the Airman*

great moment, catches glimpses of the black dot in the sky; ocean steamers bearing each a cityful of human beings train thousands of glasses on the tiny winged thing, advance herald of the aërial age. The ocean comes to life with gazing humanity; above all he rides, solitary, intent. There will have been no time to decorate for his coming; flags will run up hurriedly, roofs in an instant turn black with people, wharves and streets white with upturned faces, while over the heads of the multitude he rides in, to such a shout as the ear of man has never heard. No explorer ever knew such a welcome, no conqueror, as awaits the "Columbus of the Air."

To say that within less than a decade America will be covered with commercial air lines is only to remind the public that America is now far behind Europe, where time-tables for air routes are at this time as much a part of a business man's equipment as those for land and sea. Landing devices must be improved; this is most evident in the case of airships. Indeed, the main reason for the lagging behind of the dirigible is that it must be pulled down to earth by a swarm of men. Imagine the *Leviathan* being warped into her dock by an army of men each pulling on a rope, and you have something like the present anachronism in the working of the dirigible. That this will be overcome there can be no doubt, nor that the landing devices of aëroplanes will be made safer than they are at present. The parachute as an emergency measure with the aëroplane is of comparatively recent date, and in its present improved form provides something like that "sky-hook" the old-timers used to declare every aviator needed. Platforms over city blocks and piers will make every city a port of the air and bring to pass the famous predictions of Kipling's "With the Night Mail." There will be "floating islands" in the ocean, and moored ships for weather reports, with *ballons sondes* * and kites for high-altitude data; mail

The Airman soars to Fame 405

and passengers will be flown to shore from Atlantic liners, cutting two days off the passage. New and better instruments will come — a capacity indicator to show how high you are above the surface of the ground will make crossing mountains less perilous, an instrument will measure distance traveled over the earth's surface, and an automatic pilot keep a predetermined course as set by an earth inductor compass, as is done now on ocean liners by what is known to seamen as "Metal Mike." We shall have devices to dissipate and to guide through fog, the greatest enemy of all craft, especially to assist pilots to land; neon lights and wireless beacons and powerful radio direction stations to transmit meteorological information and give bearings must be generally established, with observation stations in the polar regions, on the ice cap of Greenland, and in the Antarctic. In the course of these investigations and discoveries great flights must soon be made. No spot on the earth will be unseen by man. The Pacific will be crossed in a single flight, the world circumnavigated in fifteen days. Heights of fifty thousand feet will be reached, and it may be possible to utilize the vast possibilities of speed at very great altitudes. We may see "superterranean" machines with apparatus for supplying passengers with air under pressure mixed with oxygen — Bréguet built such a machine in France; and, on account of the reduced resistance of the air, speeds of five hundred miles an hour might be attained, according to some authorities. Experiments are now in progress in the use of the reactionary principle in propulsion, doing away with the propeller and motor as used in the present plane and substituting the exhaust of liquid air through nozzles. Wireless transmission of power is still distant, but not below the horizon. Machines have been refueled in the air, enabling them to make continuous journeys of indefinite duration.

406 *Romance of the Airman*

By the time the earthbound reader has reached this point in this conservative forecast, his mind may be preparing to let go, and it is time to round off this survey of reasonable possibilities of the future of air transport.

Words and Phrases

To aid in understanding this selection

picaresque: roguish or adventurous.

raison d'être: reason for being.

Maitland and Hegenberger: flyers who crossed the Pacific from California to Hawaii on June 28, 1927.

ballons sondes: small balloons sent up to make automatic records of atmospheric conditions.

To add to your vocabulary

formidable

Technical term

earth inductor compass

Informal Test (Completion)[1]

1. Lindbergh flew from San Diego to New York in _____ hours.

2. Raymond Orteig was a citizen of _____.

3. Chamberlin had been a _____.

4. Byrd's trip across the Atlantic was for the purpose of _____.

5. The greatest achievement of the period of commercial aviation was _____.

6. Emphasis in the past has been not on the man that flies but on the man that _____.

7. In "Columbus of the Air," Mr. Post said that the first human being to cross the Atlantic will be _____.

8. He prophesied that men will reach heights of _____.

[1] For directions, see page 14.

The Airman soars to Fame 407

Exercises and Topics related to your Other Subjects

Read Kipling's "With the Night Mail" and bring, for reading to the class, selections that forecast what might actually happen today.

Lindbergh flew alone, which proves that he was an expert pilot, a mechanic, and an aëronautical engineer. Other positions in the field of aviation are those of airport designer and constructor, radio operator, advertising and publicity man, salesman, airport ground man, factory man. The Department of Commerce, which licenses all trained men, says, "A recognized method of securing experience as an aëronautical engineer is to attend a college or university with a complete course in aëronautical engineering." What subjects in high school form the foundation for a course in aëronautical engineering? Ask your high-school principal to assist you in making out a program of courses for you to follow in senior high school as a preparation for aviation as a career.

Subjects for oral themes

Lindbergh's most Admirable Qualities.
The Truth of Mr. Post's Prophecy of 1914.
Floating Islands.
The Explanation of Neon Lights.

Other Readings

In this book

"American Youth honors Lindbergh," page 414.

From other sources

"With the Night Mail," by Rudyard Kipling.

Wings of Lead[1]

NATHALIA CRANE

Explanatory Note. The entire world was thrilled when Charles A. Lindbergh made his nonstop flight from New York to Paris on May 20. 1927. The plane in which he flew, the *Spirit of St. Louis*, is now preserved at the Smithsonian Institution, to be honored by the generations to come.

After Lindbergh's flight the name "Lone Eagle," as he was called, was on the lips of everyone, but no one had been inspired to the point of interpreting his feat through the medium of poetry. Eventually a publisher offered $500 as a prize for the best poem on the theme of Lindbergh's flight. The prize was awarded to Nathalia Crane, a little girl of fourteen years, in competition with four thousand entrants. Her explanation of the title is as follows: "Why, 'wings of lead' signifies the impossible. You see, Lindbergh just came in unknown and said he would do it; and everyone said, 'Ridiculous, impossible.' Then he did it — the impossible."

Nathalia's poem is in the Kipling manner, a narrative of the flight: a picture, first, of the gods looking down on a dull world, and deciding to stimulate it to extraordinary achievement. Their challenge to Lindbergh was accepted. The middle section represents the world's excitement over the challenge, and the last part is the triumph that places Lindbergh's flight among the greatest in history.

THE gods released a vision on a world forespent and dull;
They sent it as a challenge by the sea hawk and the gull.

It roused the Norman eagerness, the Albion cliffs* turned
    red:
"You fly the wings of logic — can you fly the wings of
    lead?

It's been done in faded ages, changing titles for each writ —
The wheel, the keel, the pinioned heel, the longbow and the
    bit;

[1] From "Venus Invisible," by Nathalia Crane. Copyright, 1928, Coward-McCann, Inc.

The Airman soars to Fame 409

The tiller and the javelin, the harp with leaden string,
The pewter lens that Homer used, the ore in David's sling.*

Locations in all latitudes where heroes left the ground
Still show the clots of cinnabar* that marked the last re-
bound.

We set no rules on engines or the drive of whirling gear —
Our course is but a thousand leagues of doubtful atmosphere.

Designers may parade a moth or rack the condor's* spread,
One simple stipulation — that the pinions be of lead."

* * *

The hawks were dropping challenges from Tokyo to Rome;
The gulls delivered cartels* from Cape Town to tousled
Nome.

The Nagasaki* coal girls stopped to wipe their smutty
eyes;
The damsels of Ferghana* saw new rug tints in the skies.

A thousand ardent oilers swung the long spout 'twixt their
nods,
And tried to glimpse a meaning in the challenge of the gods.

And then one night there landed on a Mineola swale*
A plane that looked like pewter, with a carrier of mail.

Its wings were tinged like tea-box skins, each truss* of
shadow gray,
Its cabin but an alcove slung beneath a metal ray.

The Spirit of St. Louis was inscribed upon the lee;
It came from out a province that had never seen the sea.

Romance of the Airman

The pilot entered for the course, the quarter-quadrant
glide —
To fly the full Atlantic and the tag ends of the tide.

He listed in as "Lindbergh" — just one pace beyond the
ranks;
He had a moon-stained paddle and some star gas in his
tanks.

Invisible, he passed the word, the barograph was sealed —
A plane with leaden wings went down the Mineola field.

It rose and fell and rose again and then attained to breath —
The raiment of the bubble when the bubble goes to death.

And somewhere near the noontime as the fishes turned to
scan,
They saw a pearl-gray monoplane slide east of Grand
Manan.*

A single-motored miracle, a lead mine on each flank;
Below a shadow swept and awed the hundred-fathom bank.

Upon a billow rocked and cheered a lanterned spindle
buoy,*
The offshore bells were chanting for the *Spirit of St. Louis*;

For o'er the darkened deep there flew a carrier of mail,
His engine drunk with star gas and a berserk* in the flail.

He made the course the gods had set, the quarter-quadrant
glide;
He flew the full Atlantic and the tag ends of the tide.

* * *

The Airman soars to Fame   411

'Tis a feat that sends Old Richard* groping down a ghostly
   van,
Starts a Joan* doing high steps on an ancient barbican.*

And the eyes of all look upward seeing sign-word drawing
   nigh,
The stony wings of Egypt coming back across the sky;

We hear the clinking tambourine of Miriam* anew;
We believe in every miracle since Lindbergh flew the blue —

The wonder of the long draw when the bowstring is a
   thread —
The beauty of a courage that can raise the wings of lead.

Words and Phrases

To aid in understanding this selection

Albion: England; the name is used especially with reference
   to the white chalk cliffs that face the sea on the southeast
   coast.
ore in David's sling: David, born at Bethlehem about 1050 B. C.,
   killed Goliath, a gigantic Philistine, with a sling.
cinnabar: red mercuric sulphide; used as a pigment.
condor: the largest and most powerful of flying birds.
cartels: notes of defiance or opposition.
Nagasaki: a seaport in the northwestern part of Kyushu Island,
   Japan.
Ferghana: a province in Russian Turkestan.
swale: a low plain or valley.
truss: an iron fitting to support a structure.
Grand Manan: an island in the Bay of Fundy; part of Char-
   lotte County, New Brunswick, Canada.
buoy: a floating device to indicate the position of a rock or
   other object below the surface of the water.

412 *Romance of the Airman*

berserk: in Norse legend a warrior who fought with frenzied fury (known as "berserker rage"), who could assume the appearance and ferocity of a wild beast, and whom fire and iron could not harm.

Richard: probably refers to Richard Cœur de Lion.

Joan: probably refers to Joan of Arc, "Maid of Orleans," who led the French army against the English with success in 1429.

barbican: outwork of a castle or fortified place.

Miriam: sister of Moses (see Exodus xv, 20).

To add to your vocabulary

        buoy   barbican

Technical terms

    quarter-quadrant   barograph   monoplane

Informal Test (Multiple-Choice)[1]

1. The plane looked like   **iron**   **skin**   **pewter**   **wood**

2. The challenge was given by   **gulls**   **hawks**   **the seas**   **the gods**

3. The *Spirit of St. Louis* came from a region that is accustomed to   **sea**   **land**   **long air flights**   **water**

4. Nathalia Crane is   **a pilot**   **a girl**   **a teacher**   **an aviatrix**

5. The plane was a   **biplane**   **monoplane**   **triplane**   **dirigible**

Informal Test (Matching)[2]

1. **Lindbergh has taught us**   that the gods had set.

2. **The fishers saw a**   to believe in miracles.

3. **O'er the darkened deep**   pearl-gray monoplane slide east of Grand Manan.

4. **He made the course**   flew a carrier of mail.

5. **The offshore bells chanted**   for the *Spirit of St. Louis.*

[1] For directions, see page 95.   [2] For directions, see page 9.

The Airman soars to Fame 413

Exercises and Topics related to your Other Subjects

1. Mark on a map all the places mentioned in this poem.

2. List the words that speak of color.

3. List all the terms that are applied to Lindbergh's plane.

4. What lines do you think tell of very tense moments? Write them.

5. List all the words that you think describe the challenge the gods gave.

6. What lines bring out Lindbergh's extraordinary courage? Write them.

7. Write three things about the poem that interest you.

8. List as many titles for this poem as you can think of.

9. Nathalia Crane was the age of many junior-high-school pupils when she wrote this poem. What topics in history, literature, and science had she read? With what Bible stories was she familiar?

Other Readings

From other sources

"We," by Charles A. Lindbergh.

Mitchell Kennerley in *Saturday Review of Literature* (July 16, 1927), Volume III, pages 977 ff.

Poems about Lindbergh in the *Literary Digest* (November 13, 1927), Volume XCV, page 34.

"The Lone Scout of the Sky," by James E. West.

American Youth honors Lindbergh

JOHN H. FINLEY

Explanatory Note. After Colonel Charles A. Lindbergh made his memorable flight from New York to Paris in May, 1927, the entire world was eager to pay him homage. The official reception in New York City was attended by many distinguished Americans. The most brilliant speech of the occasion was made by Dr. J. H. Finley, who, in behalf of the youth of America, presented a gold medal to Lindbergh. Dr. Finley, a member of the Executive Board of the Boy Scouts of America, was a most pleasing representative of American youth upon this occasion. His speech is especially valuable because of the literary and historical allusions it contains.

I HAVE never been prouder in my life than at this moment, in being called upon to represent the youth of America. But I should like to have Colonel Lindbergh know that I also have a flying record. That ambassadorial land pilot, Mr. Herrick, beloved of all of us, once introduced me in this fashion. He said, "Mr. Finley has beaten Moses all to pieces, for it took Moses and the children of Israel* forty years to go from the Land of Goshen to the Land of Canaan; whereas Mr. Finley covered the distance in two hours and thirty-five minutes." And then he added that Moses had only a "look-in" when he got there. Mine is not much of a record by the side of yours, but I recall it as a brother aviator.

In speaking of Ambassador Herrick, that capable land pilot, I should like also to mention that other wise ambassadorial pilot who sent you safely back to us, Colonel Lindbergh — Ambassador Houghton.

In Sir Walter Scott's description of the castle in his "Quentin Durward," there were three moats* that had to be crossed, three drawbridges that had to be let down, three speeches of welcome that had to be received, before the

The Airman soars to Fame 415

approaching knight was actually admitted into the heart
of the castle. You, my young knight, who departed so
unceremoniously from us, have had a more difficult time
in getting back into your own land. You crossed the first
moat, which is as wide as the Atlantic, and the national
drawbridge was let down. You crossed the second moat —
I do not know just how you came in; I have been away
today — and have been welcomed by our hospitable Mayor
at City Hall. And now that the Governor has pinned on
you the badge of the state's welcome, it may be said that
you have crossed the Harlem River moat and are actually
back in America at last.

One has never really entered America who has not come
to New York; but one who has never been in the valley
where we were born (the *we* meaning in this instance
"you and I") cannot really know America. And speaking
of this pronoun *we*, as former Commissioner of Education I am sorry that I must call attention to the Mayor's
error in grammar. He used *we*, in the sentence "We go
with *We*," in the objective case. I am not criticizing him;
we shall just simply have to revise our grammars hereafter,
so that *we* may be used either in the nominative, possessive,
or objective case.

I have a special pride in the privilege that is accorded
me tonight because I was born in the same valley with you,
some little distance down the river below Little Falls, on
the flat prairie, as flat as the ocean, though my particular
village — and you will excuse me if I mention this fact,
for I shall never have such an opportunity to call attention
to my native place — my particular village was called,
with utter disregard of the topography, "Grand Ridge."
It becomes a real eminence tonight, a real "ridge," in the
fact that I, as one of its sons, salute you, the son of the river
that runs through the heart of America, and whose falls

416 *Romance of the Airman*

will sing your praises so long as water runs downhill and linden trees grow and mountains stand; for, as I suspect, your Anglicized* name is Linden Mountain.

In my own schooldays out there on the prairies where you were born (and I) we used to sing this school song:

> Once a man from Androscoggin
> Or from some outlandish place,
> With a view to see this country,
> To the westward set his face.
>
> He was weary at Chicago,
> So he sat him down to rest,
> But 'twas only there the center
> Of the famous land out West.
>
> 'Tis away out in the West,
> 'Tis away out in the West,
> Oh, I fear we ne'er shall find it,
> 'Tis *so* far out in the West.

But in these years since those days a new age has dawned — an age which twenty years ago I began to call the "televictorian age," the age of the conquest of the far. The most widely known symbol of the earlier ages is the image of the "Winged Victory."* Mr. H. G. Wells, seeing one of these little statues in every Boston parlor, spoke of it as the "symbol of the terrifying unanimity of æsthetic discrimination" in that cultured city. But the feet of that "Winged Victory" were attached to the prow of a ship. We have, however, in this tall, slim stripling the living symbol of the new age — a youth who has

> pushed the sea and land
> Farther away on either hand,

and who in his flight has even

> split the sky in two
> And seen the face of God shine through.

The Airman soars to Fame 417

He typifies the being for whom the other ages have been longing and waiting — the creature with wings. The prophet Ezekiel, in captivity by the River Chebar, twenty-five hundred years ago had a vision which suggests your landing at Le Bourget. He saw a great cloud come out of the sky, and out of the midst of it the likeness of a man — "with the hands of a man under its wings." Ancient kings had likenesses of themselves graven with wings. It was beings with wings who knelt over the Shekinah of the children of Israel and who carried the mail for the gods of Olympus.* It was with wings fastened on with wax that Dædalus is imagined to have made the first nonstop flight from Crete to Sicily and that his son Icarus flew till, nearing the sun, which melted the wax, he fell "headlong through the affrighted air" and sank in the sea. It was of such a flying man as you that Leonardo da Vinci prophesied when he said, "There shall be wings" (*Spunteranno le ali*).

It was of you that Samuel P. Langley said to a group of us about the table, only a few months before his death, that we should see man fly, though, alas, he should not. It was of you that the Wright brothers, with whom I sat at dinner here but a little later, gave augury* from the flight at Kitty Hawk, as the ancient augurs divined the will of the gods from the flight of birds. The whole world has welcomed you not only because of your intrepid* spirit, your daring to go alone into the "last wilderness," your incarnation of what it most loves in youth and manhood, but because you came out of the skies in the guise in which man has dreamed of a higher destiny — as an angel. And how the angels must have applauded this young man when they saw him flying. Oliver Wendell Holmes would have said of you, "The angels laughed, too, at the good you have done." We need no longer say of man that he is "a little lower than the angels."

418 Romance of the Airman

There has been a poetic fitness, if you will allow me to say so, in your selection for this pioneer exploit. I think the Lord had a great deal to do with it. An old professor whom I knew at Princeton would have said that "it was almost providential," leaving some credit to you as a free moral agent.

In the first place, being of Norse descent you most appropriately returned the call which a Norseman, one Leif Ericson* (believed to be the first European to visit our shores), made when, nearly a thousand years ago, he

> came rowing up the Charles
> In the sea-battered dragon-ships,
> Stroked by the strong, blond carles.

They called him "Leif the Lucky," and as Leif the Lucky he has been sung in sagas across the centuries. He welcomes you, "Lindy the Lucky," as his companion through thousands of years to come.

In the next place, the river on whose banks you were born (as I was), was discovered by the French explorers and priests who evoked that greatest valley — the valley of the new democracy — from the unknown: Father Marquette, Joliet, La Salle, Tonty. Except for the French the *Spirit of St. Louis*, which has flown back across the seas, would never have found its nest in that valley.

Then there was something of Irish blood in your veins that must have told your instinct the way back to Ireland. You needed not to ask that frightened fisherman whether you were on the way to Ireland. But fortunately you did not land there, for had you, you would never have come back to us. You would have done what one of James Stephens's angels in "The Demigods" did: instead of going back to heaven with the other and older angels, he lost his heart to Ireland (or more particularly to Mary McCann), stripped himself of his wings, and stayed.

The Airman soars to Fame 419

And if Pope Gregory the Great* could have seen you as you flew over the coasts of England, he would surely have said (as, according to tradition, he did say), "Not Angles, but Angels"; and they too, the descendants of the Angles, are proud to claim you as one of their descendants. You have stretched "hands under wings across the sea."

But, above all, you are an American composite youth, of the best that has been and a promise of the best that is to be.

Shakespeare speaks of his young Prince Hal as "witching* the world with noble horsemanship." But it is something more than your noble horsemanship among the clouds that has witched our greater world: it is the modest nobility with which you have borne yourself in all this acclaim in many tongues, an acclaim which but tells the desire that the world has in its heart for its youth. We are prouder than ever of America in being proud of you. And we think the better of ourselves because we care so much for you. May our youth live up to this winged ideal, and may you be ever true to the boy that is in you.

An American poet, recounting Leif Ericson's voyage into the "land as lonesome as a star," — our land that "God had set aside for mortals not to mar," — said:

> Not till Leif's sons set foot upon the moon
> Will such a deed as his be done again.

But you, one of the sons of Leif, have done a more daring deed than he did; and if you should ever set foot upon the moon, even there it would not be necessary for you to say, "I am Charles Lindbergh," for the moon had sight of you on that immortal flight.

I ask the privilege, however, and I do this on behalf of the youth of America, since I have been appointed to represent them, of giving you this small gold medal with the

420 *Romance of the Airman*

figure of a youth upon it. It is not for your breast, as are these other medals and decorations, but for your pocket — a medal originally for those who walk, but who may some day fly, *à la sainte terre**; so that in years to come, when age has so changed your countenance, — which is now known in every home in America and in other parts of the world, — so changed your countenance that you may need to be identified here on the earth, you will have upon you this time-defying certificate with this inscription:

> This is Charles Lindbergh.
>
> Though Time may change his youthful face
> It never can his deed erase;
> He was the first, and first will be
> When Time becomes Eternity.

• Words and Phrases

To aid in understanding this selection

Moses and the children of Israel: read from the book of Exodus the story of the national migration led by Moses.

moat: a ditch, usually filled with water, surrounding a fortification.

Anglicized: here, translated into English.

"Winged Victory": a famous statue representing the winged goddess on the prow of a ship. Figuratively, it typifies success.

Olympus: a mountain of Greece anciently fabled to be the abode of the greater Grecian gods.

augury: the art of foretelling by signs or omens.

intrepid: fearless.

Leif Ericson: "Leif the Lucky," a Norwegian explorer who is credited with being the first white man to come to America.

Pope Gregory the Great: in 597, missionaries from Rome were sent to England by Pope Gregory. The story goes that years before this date some fair-haired, good-looking English boys

The Airman soars to Fame 421

were put up for sale in a Roman slave market. In answer to his inquiry he was told that they were Angles. "Not Angles, but Angels," he said, "had they but the Gospel."

witch: to charm by magical influence.

à la sainté terre: to the Holy Land.

Informal Test (Completion)[1]

1. The word *Lindbergh* means _____ _____.

2. Lindbergh is of _____ descent.

3. Lindbergh was born in _____, on the _____ River.

4. "Valley of the new democracy" refers to the _____ Valley.

5. Da Vinci prophesied, "_____ _____ _____ _____."

Exercises and Topics related to your Other Subjects

1. Look up in your reference books the nationality of each person mentioned in this selection.

2. Analyze the word *televictorian*.

3. Locate on a map all the places mentioned in this selection.

4. Explain how *we* can ever be in the objective or the possessive case. Think of other words that have undergone similar changes.

5. Make a list of all the quotations used in this selection and find the source of each.

Other Readings

In this book

"Dædalus and Icarus," page 11.

"Da Vinci Did it First," page 114.

"Lindbergh, America's Ambassador of Good Will," page 459.

"Early Scientific Experimenters," page 101.

From other sources

"The Story of the Bible," by Hendrik Van Loon.

"We," by Charles A. Lindbergh.

"Heroes of the Air," by Chelsea Fraser.

[1] For directions, see page 14.

Floyd Bennett, Martyr of the Air

NOT so many years ago two quite obscure members of the American navy who were then connected with MacMillan's Greenland expedition were flying northward over the great Greenland ice cap. The clear-blue ice pack shimmered like glass beneath their speeding plane, and looming up before them was a range of towering, jagged mountains, their snow-clad crests hidden and enveloped by billowy clouds — the familiar " woollies " of the Arctic regions. The least-known of the two men was at the controls. Suddenly the motor began to miss, cough, and spit. The pressure in the oil gauge jumped up hastily. The temperature outside the closed cockpit was around 60 below zero, and the plane was miles from its base.

"Here, take the controls," the pilot said to his commander.

"Why?" the commander asked.

"I'm going out on the wing and fix that engine before it stops completely," the pilot answered.

The commander took over the controls, and the pilot climbed out of the closed cockpit into the open air stream that was pouring past at a hundred miles an hour. And while the plane was sinking toward the ice pack, and the bitter wind gnawed into his bones, the man on the wing fixed the engine and crawled back into the cockpit, all but frozen stiff.

That man was Floyd Bennett, who was at that time an enlisted man with the rank of Aviation Machinist's Mate. His commander was Richard Evelyn Byrd, then a more or less obscure lieutenant commander in the navy. Bennett had been picked blindly, along with other enlisted men of the navy, to accompany Byrd on that expedition. But no choice could have been better. Bennett was an instinctive,

The Airman soars to Fame 423

natural flyer, and knew motors from cotter pin to crankshaft. He was "one man in a million," as his commander, Byrd, has often said since.

Out of Byrd's experience in Greenland came his dream of the conquest of the North Pole by airplane, and with him on the *Chantier* when it started out from America for Spitsbergen was Floyd Bennett. Bennett was second in command and billed to pilot the plane to the pole and back.

How well Bennett did his job of piloting need not be told here. All the world knows that he and Byrd made a memorable flight and came safely back. What many do not know is that during all that flight, soon after the plane left the northern coast of Spitsbergen, one motor threatened to go dead. Bennett knew it.

"Shall we turn back?" his commander asked.

"When we have reached the pole," Bennett replied.

He nursed that defective motor along the Arctic sky trail and got to the pole and back again in record time. Few others but Bennett could have done it. Many might have had the courage to try as he did, but in only a very few is there the combination of courage, of innate flying ability, and of technical knowledge of motors which Bennett possessed.

When Byrd planned his Atlantic hop Bennett was scheduled to be his chief pilot; but in a preliminary test of the plane to be used, with Anthony Fokker, its designer, at the controls, the plane became unmanageable (by Fokker) and crashed, injuring Byrd and Bennett seriously — Bennett so much so that his life was despaired of for some time. But, fighting desperately with that courage which was his, he pulled through, though still on crutches when Byrd's plane, the *America*, winged its way across the Atlantic.

Byrd's Antarctic expedition was already planned, and Bennett was to be chief pilot and second in command. He

424 *Romance of the Airman*

looked forward anxiously to that event as the crowning achievement of his life; so he took good care of his slight strength and tried to build himself up for the Antarctic ordeal, that he might not fail in his part.

In the meantime the German-Irish crew of the *Bremen** had succeeded in winging their way across the Atlantic in a westward flight, but they never made the mainland. Their plane crashed on a small island off the coast of Belle Isle Straits. Bennett volunteered to fly a relief plane to their rescue with food and spare parts so that they could continue their flight. He was in no condition to try it, but he rose from a sick bed to do so. He was taken sick in the air, and when he landed near Montreal was taken to the hospital stricken with pneumonia. He had not fully recovered from his previous injury and lacked sufficient reserve strength to throw off the ravages of the disease.

Bennett died with his old commander at his bedside. Today his body rests in the Arlington National Cemetery, among the other heroes of the army and navy who have won undying fame.

Words and Phrases

To aid in understanding this selection

> *Bremen:* an airplane that in April, 1928, made the first westward nonstop flight across the north Atlantic from Dublin, Ireland, to Greenely Island, Canada, covering a distance of 2124 miles in 36 hours and 30 minutes.

Informal Test (Completion)[1]

1. Floyd Bennett was enlisted in the _ _ _ _ _ _ with the rank of _ _ _ _ _ _ _ _ _ _ _ _ _ _ _ _ _ _.

2. He accompanied _ _ _ _ _ _ _ _ _ _ _ _ on his polar flight.

3. _ _ _ _ _ _ said of him that he was "one man in a million."

[1] For directions, see page 14.

The Airman soars to Fame 425

4. The first expedition in which Bennett took part was _ _ _ _ _ _
_ _ _ _ _ _ _ _ _ _ _.

5. The conquest of the North Pole by airplane was from _ _ _ _ _ _
to _ _ _ _ _ _, thence to _ _ _ _ _ _.

6. Because of illness Bennett was not able to make the trip across the _ _ _ _ _ _ with _ _ _ _ _ _.

7. The last service rendered by Bennett was to fly a relief plane to _ _ _ _ _ _ to aid the _ _ _ _ _ _ crew whose ship, the _ _ _ _ _ _, had been forced to the earth.

8. The exposure attending this courageous attempt resulted in his _ _ _ _ _ _ at _ _ _ _ _ _.

Exercises and Topics related to your Other Subjects

Prepare a report on MacMillan's Greenland expedition.
Locate on a map Greenland, Belle Isle Straits, and Spitsbergen.

Other Readings

In this book

"Floyd Bennett laid to Rest as the Elements Rage," page 426.
"Byrd's Flight to the North Pole," page 275.

From other sources

"Skyward," by Richard E. Byrd.
"Heroes of the Air," by Chelsea Fraser.

Floyd Bennett laid to Rest as the Elements Rage

W. A. S. DOUGLAS

> *Explanatory Note.* Read "Floyd Bennett, Martyr of the Air" to learn of the career of this hero. This selection is the report written by Mr. W. A. S. Douglas of the Washington Bureau of the Baltimore *Sun* in the April 28, 1928, issue of the *Sun*. It was so artistically written and of such literary value that it won the *Bookman* prize for the month of April, 1928.

UP ON TOP of the highest hill in Arlington Cemetery — as close as they could rest him in death to the skies he had loved to roam in life — Machinist Floyd Bennett, United States Navy, was buried this afternoon in a driving wind and rainstorm, a fitting dirge from the elements the hero had dared and met and conquered.

"Greater love hath no man than this, that a man lay down his life for his friend," said Chaplain Curtis H. Beckins as Bennett was being consigned to the grave.

As this was spoken the ropes which held the flag-draped coffin were loosened in the hands of Bennett's eight comrades — like himself, enlisted men in the navy. Then a rattle of bullets, repeated three times, and followed by the long, mournful notes of a bugle blowing "taps." Another prayer from the chaplain, and the services ended.

Floyd Bennett, modest, unassuming, self-effacing hero and companion of heroes, was asleep among other heroes. All around him, up and down the slopes of his own Virginia hills, were strewn the white-stone tents of other soldiers and sailors — little white slabs by the thousands marking the graves of those who had gone forth to war. A marker atop the highest hill, Floyd Bennett's hill, told his story and their story:

The Airman soars to Fame 427

On Fame's eternal camping ground
Their silent tents are spread.
And glory guards with solemn round
The bivouac of the dead.

To the east of his own hill are spread the hundreds of slabs beneath which sleep, as Bennett sleeps, the dead of the Great War.

Now has come Bennett, the polar flyer, to join these men who laid down their lives in France in honorable combat. The difference was that Bennett had laid down his life for the nation that these new comrades had fought against.

Blinding rain fell as they brought the body from the Union Station. Things were hurried along, perhaps in a rather unseemly manner, to anybody who did not know Bennett. Other heroes have been carried in slow, dignified procession all along the way. But Bennett, the polar flyer, moved fast in life, and his wish would have been to go along speedily in death.

The crowds waited beside the grave for hours. The rain poured and the wind moaned, but the throng increased. Herbert Hoover, arriving at 2.30, stood for more than two hours to pay homage.

There was no shelter other than a skimpy tent over the grave, and another, even smaller, which covered the hundred or more wreaths that had been sent by the high and by the low, one from the President of the United States and one from a sailor who had enlisted with Bennett eleven years ago.

Between these two tributes were separate piles of flowers from representatives of the great nations of the world, from cabinet officers, from admirals, from generals, from governors and from states.

Truly the world was paying homage to Machinist Bennett.

428 *Romance of the Airman*

Planes hovered over the hillside for a while, coming from escort duty to the funeral cortège. They droned high up in the heavens, one great bomber circling about with engine shut off as it passed over Bennett's own hillside. Then came a group of five navy airships, which circled twice and flew away as the sounds of the navy band were heard from the hollow, below the cemetery, where lies Fort Myer.

Two companies of sailors followed the musicians, which procedure is not at all according to proper navy rank and precedence. Such a gathering means that a commissioned officer is being buried, and Bennett held only a machinist's rating. But the navy broke its precedent and, in passing, would not have had to break it but for Bennett himself. He refused commissioned rank when it was offered him after his return from the North Pole flight with Commander Richard E. Byrd.

The six-horse gun caisson* halted on the brow of the hill. Bennett's enlisted comrades bore the coffin to the edge of the grave. The crowd forced the ropes and thronged over the inclosure until they stood close-packed around the coffin. Passageway had to be forced for the widow and the dead man's two brothers. Commander Byrd, unable to get closer, had to stand on the edge of the crowded mourners, almost an outsider at the burial of the man who had crossed over one pole with him and had been designated to accompany him on his approaching attempt to conquer the other.

The Reverend L. E. Smith, pastor of the Christian Church of Norfolk, Virginia, Bennett's pastor, followed the coffin and began the funeral services. Behind him came Chaplain Beckins in the cap, the gown, and surplice of the Episcopal Church.

"The Lord is my shepherd, I shall not want," the Rev-

The Airman soars to Fame 429

erend Mr. Smith read in loud, clear tones. "He maketh me to lie down in green pastures" —

And so he read through the Twenty-third Psalm. All around in the valley of the dead stretched green "pastures," bright with the rain and losing none of their spring sheen through the grayness of the skies. Over the "pastures" were thousands and thousands of white slabs above the graves of the flyer's new companionship of men.

The words Chaplain Beckins used epitomized Bennett's deed as no other words could have done.

"Greater love hath no man than this, that a man lay down his life for his friend."

Tears ran down the cheeks of the slim, blond-haired German ambassador. Surely the man who had died as a result of bringing succor to his countrymen must have forever healed the wound between the two nations.

Earth pattered on the coffin, and the throngs moved away. The flyer was at rest on his hillside. Beside him on his right lies Admiral Robert E. Peary, discoverer of the earth's rim over which his neighbor flew. At his head rest Lieutenant General John Coulter Bates and Brigadier General Morgan Lewis Smith. On his left is Lieutenant General Samuel B. M. Young. Machinist Bennett sleeps his last sleep in a goodly company.

Words and Phrases

To aid in understanding this selection

caisson: a chest for ammunition, mounted on two wheels.

To add to your vocabulary

homage	epitomized
cortège	bivouac
liturgy	

430 *Romance of the Airman*

Informal Test (Completion)[1]

1. Floyd Bennett was a resident of the state of _ _ _ _ _ _.

2. He was a member of the _ _ _ _ _ _ Church.

3. His body lies in _ _ _ _ _ _ Cemetery.

4. Bennett is referred to as the _ _ _ _ _ _ flyer.

5. At his burial his pastor read the _ _ _ _ _ _ Psalm.

6. _ _ _ _ _ _ _ _ _ _ _ _ body lies to the right of Bennett in Arlington Cemetery.

7. Bennett had enlisted in the service of the United States _ _ _ _ _ _ years before.

8. Words that best describe Bennett's personality are _ _ _ _ _ _, _ _ _ _ _ _, _ _ _ _ _ _.

Exercises and Topics related to your Other Subjects

1. Find in the World Almanac some facts concerning the National Cemetery at Arlington, Virginia.

2. Look up in your history the career of each of the following: John Coulter Bates, Morgan Lewis Smith, Samuel B. M. Young.

3. Find the name of the blond-haired German ambassador who wept because of Bennett's death.

4. Use as a topic for a theme "Arlington Cemetery on a Rainy Afternoon in April." Use the phrases found in this selection.

5. Find from a map of Washington, D.C., and vicinity the distance between the city of Washington and Arlington Cemetery.

Other Readings

In this book

"Floyd Bennett, Martyr of the Air," page 422.
"Byrd's Flight to the North Pole," page 275.

From other sources

"Heroes of the Air," by Chelsea Fraser.

[1] For directions, see page 14.

Gjoa — To Amundsen

JOHN J. JURY

Explanatory Note. Roald Amundsen, a Norwegian explorer, began his seagoing life at the age of twenty-one. He spent a number of years exploring the district about the North Magnetic Pole. In 1903 he undertook an expedition in a small vessel, the *Gjoa*, with the hope of relocating the North Pole, and was the first to thread the Northwest Passage from the Atlantic to the Pacific. After Peary's discovery of the pole, Amundsen sought the unconquered lands of the Antarctic. He was one of the first explorers to consider seriously a flight to the polar regions. In 1914 he had plans to fly to the North Pole, but because of the World War the attempt was not made until 1925. An account of the disastrous ending of this first flight is given on page 262. His dream was realized in 1926 when he flew over the North Pole in the semi-rigid airship the *Norge*. The career of Amundsen ended in his attempt to rescue General Umberto Nobile and the crew of the *Italia*, who were stranded in the ice fields of the North (see page 297). Only the icy seas of the North can reveal the fate of the renowned explorer. The poem "*Gjoa* — To Amundsen" is the lament of the small craft (now in Golden Gate Park, California) for its lost master.

O WINGED WINDS of the North —
Winds from the world's white rim —
Out where the lamps of the stars
Hang low and their lights are dim,
Tell me — what of my Captain —
Fearless Viking of Storms —
What has become of him?

Once I was free as you
Upon the nights that stun,
And felt the sharp white teeth of ice,
And spears of sleet and hail,
And the splashing swords of rain.
But against the dauntless will of One,
How could these prevail?

432 *Romance of the Airman*

Now from my deck the sparrows fly,
My masts are bars as a stringless harp.
Except for you, O Winds,
Only the ghosts of the sea come nigh.

Again, I call to you!
Winds from the world's white rim,
Where is Amundsen —
Viking of Storms —
What has become of him?

The *Dixmude*, Mystery of the Air

IRVING CRUMP

Explanatory Note. It is an occasion for regret whenever life and property are lost for any reason. It is more regrettable when such losses are sustained in the name of progress. This crew, bent upon a mission of unselfish service to mankind, should be thought of as heroes who lost their lives in the name of progress.

SICILIAN fishermen, about six miles off the coast, in December, 1924, saw a dead body floating in the waves. They lifted the corpse out with Latin formality and turned it over to duly constituted authorities. Several days later, other Sicilian fishermen found, floating about in the sea, a head, with the skull cracked, and some badly twisted pieces of wreckage. With due formality these fishermen too turned their find over to the officials.

And there, in a few words, is the sequel of the flight of the *Dixmude*, French government rigid dirigible, which left Toulon December 18, 1924, to establish a new nonstop endurance record for the world. What happened to the giant airship and her crew of fifty is destined to remain one of the unsolved mysteries of the air; for the rigid dirigible, after having remained aloft for at least three days, never was seen again.

Because the Sicilian fishermen found the body, which turned out to be that of Lieutentant Du Plessis de Grenedan, commander of the craft on its ill-fated voyage, the French government came to the official conclusion that the *Dixmude* was lost in the Mediterranean; and due to the discovery of the pieces of wreckage the government was enabled to inscribe "Lost by fire" at the end of her record — but that is all.

When the airship with her brave crew left Toulon, the

434 *Romance of the Airman*

eyes of the entire world were upon her; the press of every nation on earth carried the story of her auspicious start and was prepared to give hourly reports of her progress, so great was the general interest in her flight. This was because the naval experts of the world differed as to the efficiency of the rigid type of dirigible, and France was determined to discover, once and for all, whether or not it should continue to develop this type. The flight, then, was a French experiment with a ship that had been built in Germany during the latter days of the World War for the express purpose of crossing the Atlantic Ocean to bomb America.

According to Major William Hensley, at that time commander of the United States Army Air Station in Mitchel Field, the ship was nearly ready for service when the Armistice was signed, in November, 1918, and had a cruising radius of ninety-five hundred miles and a fuel capacity of eleven thousand gallons of gasoline. Thus it can be seen that the *Dixmude* was virtually the queen of the air. When in the hands of the Germans, she was known as the *L-72*. She had been turned over to France as part of the war indemnity.

When the *Dixmude* took off from Toulon she was fully equipped and, so far as anyone knew, was in the best of condition for the trip. The weather was considered ideal. She pointed her nose due south, and thirty-five hours later was over a point in the Desert of Sahara known as Insulah. The following day she registered by wireless from Biskra, also in the desert, and on December 21 she sent a message from over Tunis, on the northeast African coast of the Mediterranean Sea, that all was well.

That wireless was the last definite word heard from her, except that five months later a bottle was found on the Corsican coast containing a message scrawled in French,

The Airman soars to Fame   435

which, translated, read [as follows]: "Gasoline given out. We are adrift. Wind like a tempest. Crew of the *Dixmude*. Adieu and *vive la France*."* Perhaps the message was written the day the *Dixmude* was over Tunis, but no one can tell that.

Apparently the machinery in the ship had gone wrong and had rendered the wireless apparatus useless as well as left the giant craft a toy of the winds. The *Dixmude* was seen many times during the five or six days succeeding her final message. At one time she was seen far back in the desert over oases she had crossed on her way south from Toulon. Again she was seen over the Gulf of Gabes, port of Tunis. Truly, if ever an earthly, man-made object was a toy of the winds, the *Dixmude* was. Her fate undoubtedly was the worst in the history of aëronautics, for it is known that her crew of fifty must have been without food for many days. It is known, too, that the crew must have suffered horribly from the cold; for even over the Desert of Sahara, after the sun has set, the air is bitter cold, often many degrees below Fahrenheit zero.

When the body of Lieutenant de Grenedan was found, officials in the Italian government concluded that the ship had been burned, the conflagration caused by the explosion of some of the hydrogen cells. It was pointed out by naval aëronauts that these bags could easily be expanded to the bursting point in the rarefied air high above either the desert or the sea. The mystery as to the fate of the ship was deepened at the same time, however, when other airmen, quite as experienced as the Italians, advanced the theory that the gondola which served as the commander's cabin had broken away from the craft and dropped into the sea, leaving the dirigible to fly her uncertain way over the desert.

Those in Sicily who believed the *Dixmude* to have been

436 *Romance of the Airman*

the victim of an explosion declared that observers on the coast near Sciacca noticed at 2.30 o'clock in the morning a momentary illumination of the skies out at sea. Coincidental with this, the watch of the dead French officer was found to have stopped at that moment.

In order not to have left anything undone toward the rescue of the crew of the *Dixmude*, or toward discovering what her fate had been, the French government sent all of its available craft into the Mediterranean with orders to scan every square rod of its surface for relics or clues. This search proved fruitless. At the same time scores of airplanes were sent out over the Sahara Desert with the same orders, but no trace of the missing craft or of its crew could be found.

Many airmen believe that the crew of the *Dixmude*, or part of them, at least, could have been saved had anyone on the craft given the necessary orders. After the ship had disappeared, there were those who remembered that when the ship was over Tunis she had, in addition to reporting "All well," communicated the fact that some of her motors were not functioning properly, and that only one was going at all times for the purpose of maintaining radio communication with the land. Some of the men believe that the ship should have been brought down at that time. The consensus, after it was certain that the ship was lost, was that the commander should have attempted to effect a landing even at the peril of some of the lives of his crew and of rendering the craft a wreck. If this had been done, it is almost sure that not all of the fifty lives would have been sacrificed.

Following the first shock of the loss of the *Dixmude*, a great storm of criticism arose, and it was declared on all sides that someone in official circles had not acted to the fullest extent on information that was in his possession

The Airman soars to Fame 437

at the time the craft was known to be in distress. The controversy became acrimonious; and one charge after another was hurled at the authorities, who combated it with statements that everything possible had been done to effect a rescue when it was feared the *Dixmude* was adrift.

It was said on many sides that aviators in airplanes could have made trips to the craft while she was flying as a free balloon, and could have carried supplies, medicines, and parachutes with which the crew might make their escape. Some went so far as to say that the ship should have had an airplane escort at every second after she was known to be drifting, but others controverted this by showing that airplanes at that time were not equipped with facilities for staying in the air so long a time. It was later shown to the satisfaction of the French public that to send a plane so far from its base as the interior of Sahara with no opportunity to refuel would only have added another casualty to the list.

In early February, to satisfy public clamor, the French government conducted an exhaustive and impartial investigation into the destruction of the *Dixmude*, and concluded that the craft had been struck by lightning. The commission of inquiry was headed by Marshal Fayolle. In its report it said that the ship was intact until it was struck by lightning, and that it was reasonable to suppose that, barring the accident, the ship eventually would have landed safely.

The commission found that, with regard to the loss of the ship, it could not raise the question of responsibility, and added:

The time chosen for the voyage, the winter solstice,* was the most favorable time of the winter in the western basin of the Mediterranean. The period offered the least risk of meeting storms

438 *Romance of the Airman*

that are more dangerous than tempests for metal-surfaced dirigibles. Consequently there can be no reproach against those fixing the date of departure.

The condition of the *Dixmude* and its ability to make the voyage give rise to no criticisms. The tests preceding its departure eliminate all responsibility on this point also.

The next point touched upon by the commission in the report almost without doubt gives the key to the main cause of the fate of this ship, for it shows that there had not been sufficient thought given to the possibility of refueling the craft. As written by Marshal Fayolle's commission, it stands on the records of France as follows:

The provisions for temporary mooring and supplying fresh gasoline were insufficient. If there had existed an encampment at Tugurt or Wargla, which the dirigible left in fine weather, it would have returned and obtained fresh supplies and resumed the voyage to Baraki in better condition to meet emergencies.

The report ends by saying that such eventualities, while regrettable, are to be looked for in any field of exploration, and that progress in unexplored domains must be accomplished even at the cost of painful experiences and catastrophes.

The report also says, "The commission unanimously considers that the collective responsibilities herewith noted should not be followed by any prosecution, and that no individual can be held responsible."

There are those who believe that some day, in the wilds of the Sahara, someone will come upon the bleached bones of forty-nine men twisted in the wreckage of a rigid dirigible. Who knows?

The Airman soars to Fame 439

Words and Phrases

To aid in understanding this selection
  vive la France: long live France.
  winter solstice: December 22, the time of year when the sun is
    at its greatest distance from the equator.

To add to your vocabulary
  consensus   facilities

Technical term
  airplane escort

Informal Tests (Completion and Multiple-Choice) [1]

1. The power for sending radio messages was obtained from
_____.

2. The temperature over the Sahara at night is _____.

3. Communication was sent from the *Dixmude* by _____.

4. The *Dixmude* was on a voyage to **England   America
Africa   Italy   the Azores**

5. The Sahara Desert is in **Europe   Asia   Africa**

6. The crew consisted of **five   three   twenty   fifty   ten**
men.

7. The trip was **for pleasure   for exploration   for the
purpose of taking supplies to the sick   for experimentation**

8. Aëronautics is the study of **medicine   aviation   bird life
the stars   the weather**

9. The dirigible *Dixmude* left **France   Egypt   Italy   Spain
Sicily**

10. The *Dixmude* was the name of **a boat   a hotel   an airplane   a dirigible**

[1] For directions, see pages 14 and 95.

440 *Romance of the Airman*

Exercises and Topics related to your Other Subjects

1. Trace on a map the route taken by the *Dixmude* from the start to as far as is known.

2. Study the important working parts of a dirigible and make a drawing showing their location.

3. Find out the fuel capacity of a dirigible of the type of the *Dixmude*.

4. The *Dixmude* carried fifty people on its fateful voyage. Explain how they were accommodated during the voyage as to food, sleeping quarters, points for observation, and the like.

5. On the map you have made, show the place where the bottle containing the message was found, and the distance from the last-known location of the *Dixmude*.

Other Readings

In this book

"Crossing the Atlantic," page 299.
"Andrée's Polar Expedition," page 250.

From other sources

"What became of Andrée?" by Walter Wellman, in *McClure's Magazine* for March, 1898.

The Lost Fliers, Nungesser and Coli

ISABELLE ELLING

Explanatory Note. The tragic disappearance of the French aviators Charles Nungesser and François Coli a few days before Lindbergh made his transatlantic flight wrung the hearts of all Americans and inspired this poet to write "The Lost Fliers."

I HEARD the motors roar, I saw the take-off and the rise;
I felt the rush of wind beneath the wings,
And upward raised my eyes —
You cleft the clouds — you rode the trackless air —
A strange and shining star.
A meteor shot from the fields of France
To span a distant shore.

... I drooped my head to cup my hands
Against my eyes.
'Tis a moment all my life
I shall be sorry for!!
For in that moment you had left the world and me.
And though I heard a faint hum
Drifting from those hills of mist —
And though I strained my eyes through tears
To film a glimpse of you
I could not see —
I knew that you were gone.

... All my days I shall be listening now,
Heart-startled with every plane I hear,
With every little sound like engines from afar.
But always, it is just a gust of wind —
Or the throbbing of the Sphinx-like sea
Beneath a lonely and impervious sky.

Some Historic Aircraft

ALONG with the *Pinta*, the *Santa Maria*, the *Constitution*, the *Maine*, and other ships of the sea, with their thrilling historical associations, history will soon place the *Los Angeles*, the *Shenandoah*, the *Spirit of St. Louis*, the *Graf Zeppelin*, the *Question Mark*, and other aircraft of equal importance.

Just what have these eliminators of distance done that they are now historic? Let us see. Everything or every person that comes into existence and does something that spells progress becomes a part of the annals of mankind. To be *first* to do a thing that gives man a better method, a better tool, an inspiration, or a challenge is to merit recognition. Someone has said, "If you can make a mousetrap better than anyone else, the world will beat a path to your door." Mousetraps aren't particularly beautiful nor absolutely necessary, but fine workmanship is, and is usually rewarded. These ships of the air are the embodiment of the spirit of progress and the personification of some person or group of persons that have through these as instruments done a bit in the world's work. The aircraft mentioned in this selection are representative of others mentioned in other selections in this book and of those that may be added in the future.

It was not until after the close of the World War that the manufacture by American chemists of an alloy composed of copper, magnesium, and manganese, called duralumin, made it possible for America to build successful lighter-than-air craft. Before this, Germany alone had held the secret of the successful dirigible. After three years of experimentation had produced and tested duralumin to the satisfaction of the United States government,

The Shenandoah, *the First Airship built by the United States Government*

Courtesy of the Smithsonian Institution

the navy built, from materials produced exclusively in America, its first airship, the *Shenandoah*. This "Daughter of the Stars" was 680 feet long and 78.74 feet in diameter. Imagine a structure as long as three city blocks and as high as a five-story building. This beautiful airship cost more than two million dollars to build, and one filling of helium cost a quarter of a million dollars. She was originally equipped with six 300–350-horse-power engines and had a cruising radius of about four thousand miles. One engine was later removed. Her dead weight was about thirty-eight tons. On January 17, 1924, while undergoing a mooring test at Lakehurst, New Jersey, the ship was torn away from the mooring mast by a seventy-mile gale.

444 *Romance of the Airman*

The nose was badly torn and the rudders were damaged. The ship was carried northward before the gale until she reached the vicinity of New York City. The presence of mind of Captain Heinen, civilian expert aboard, and the reliability of her engines saved the ship and made it possible to return her in safety to the hangar at Lakehurst. Repairs were needed because the storm had shattered her nose, and the *Shenandoah* was not heard from again until the fall of 1924, when, with her crew of forty men, she started on a record-breaking nine-thousand-mile cruise over the United States. Taking the Southern route over West Virginia, the Carolinas, Georgia, Alabama, Mississippi, and Louisiana, she arrived at Fort Worth, Texas, early in the evening of the second day, and paused for a night's rest. The trip over the mountains, which was considered the most difficult part of the journey to the coast, lay ahead, and everything was put in shipshape order before continuing the flight to San Diego, the goal. After a coastwise cruise as far north as Seattle, Washington, and return, the *Shenandoah* set out toward the Atlantic coast, and within four days was safely at home beside her adopted sister, *ZR–3*, now called the *Los Angeles*. This trip was the first test of an American-built dirigible made of material produced in America and manned by an American crew. It proved two things that had been doubted by experts: that mountains are not insurmountable, and that it is more practical to use helium than hydrogen gas in lighter-than-air craft. When this, "America's Queen of the Air," was nearing the second anniversary date of her first cruise, she set out again on what promised to be an equally glorious trip. Instead it proved to be her last flight: the *Shenandoah* was lost in a storm on the morning of September 3, 1925, while flying over Ohio. Fourteen members of her crew were killed. The official report states that the

The Airman soars to Fame 445

ship became uncontrollable and broke into several pieces. Various reasons were advanced for the disaster. Captain Heinen, probably the foremost authority in America, attributed it to the removal of valves. Experts failed to agree. The Naval Court of Inquiry, after an exhaustive investigation, failed to state definitely the cause of the accident.

The *ZR–3* was built by the most expert craftsmen, under the direction of the highest-trained engineers of the Zeppelin works in Germany. According to an agreement of the Council of Allied Ambassadors, Germany was to build for the United States, on the reparation count, a dirigible to be used exclusively for experimental work and peace-time pursuits.

The *ZR–3*, subsequently renamed the *Los Angeles*, arrived in America on October 15, 1924. It is a rigid airship slightly larger than the *Shenandoah*. It is 656 feet long and 90 feet in greatest diameter, with a displacement of 2,472,000 cubic feet. The ship has a cruising radius of about five thousand miles and a dead weight of about forty-five tons. It has accommodations for from fifteen to twenty passengers. It has compartments like the berths in a railway car or a steamer. Two sofas, opposite each other, are made up as berths at night, and provide for four occupants. There is a kitchen, a pantry, a storage room, and toilets and lavatories for men and women. It is not a military craft. The Navy Department has ordered that the *Los Angeles* be set apart for commercial purposes and peace-time development.

Ever since Columbus, a native of Genoa, Italy, set out to explore a new route to India, Italians have been thrilled at the thought of the possibility of other worlds to explore. Very naturally, when Premier Mussolini's coöperation was sought by Roald Amundsen, the Norwegian, and Lincoln

446 *Romance of the Airman*

Ellsworth, the American, he fostered the undertaking of these explorers. He made it possible for them to secure the Italian-built airship *Norge* at a nominal price and commissioned Colonel Umberto Nobile, who had built the *Norge* and was therefore familiar with every part of it, to pilot it on its flight to the North Pole. The purpose of the expedition was to learn something of the unexplored regions of the North. The *Norge* was the best type of craft in which to make such a flight. It was about half the size of the *Los Angeles* and was of the semi-rigid type. Three engines, each of 250 horse power, gave it a speed of seventy-five or a hundred miles per hour. The ship was so built that one engine could drive it about forty miles per hour, and, if necessary, the craft could remain in the air a whole month at a time, navigating as a free balloon, or it could land on water or the ground without the aid of a ground crew.

The *Graf Zeppelin*, which was named for Count (German, *Graf*) Zeppelin, the inventor of dirigibles, was not built merely for an experiment. It is the intention of Dr. Eckener, director of the Zeppelin works, that it shall some day cross the Atlantic as frequently as any of the ocean-going liners. This, the largest rigid dirigible airship which was built in almost a quarter of a century after the invention of the flying machine, has luxurious accommodations for passengers.

A gondola a hundred feet long, directly attached to the bottom of the fore part of the airship, contains the passenger accommodations. Entry to the gondola is made by a ladder on the right side, which leads to a small corridor. The corridor opens into a beautiful and comfortably furnished salon. The salon covers about two hundred and seventy-two square feet of space and will accommodate thirty persons on day trips and twenty during ordinary day-and-night trips. Two large double windows on each

Mealtime in the Graf Zeppelin
Courtesy of the Smithsonian Institution

side assure adequate light and ventilation. Owing to the effective streamlining of the ship two panes of each window can be opened without creating a draft. The walls of the room are of inlaid mahogany up to one third of their height, and the upper parts are covered with silk brocade which harmonizes with draperies and upholstery.

At mealtimes the salon becomes a dining room, where food, skillfully prepared by an expert chef in the kitchen, is served to the passengers.

The kitchen is a marvelous place of shining pots and pans. It is equipped with an electric stove of aluminum which has three heating plates and two ovens for the preparation of hot meals. A closet holds the china and glassware.

Aft of the salon are ten staterooms, five on each side of a wide passageway. Each stateroom has a window and is equipped with a table, two closets, a chair, and a com-

448 *Romance of the Airman*

fortable sofa. At night an arrangement similar to that in use on Pullman cars converts the room into comfortable sleeping quarters containing an upper and a lower berth. The washrooms, with warm and cold running water, and the toilets are located aft of the passenger staterooms.

The accommodations for the crew, which averages about thirty men, are within the airship proper. Here also are the stowage rooms for mail and freight.

The *Graf Zeppelin*, carrying a crew of forty, a passenger list of twenty, sixty-five thousand letters, and considerable freight and express, was hailed as a messenger of good will on October 15, 1928, when she reached Lakehurst, New Jersey, from Friedrichshafen, Germany.

The route taken by this ship is interesting to study. From Friedrichshafen over Lyon (in France), to Spain, through the Strait of Gibraltar to the Madeira Islands, then to the Azores, the Bermudas, and Cape Hatteras, over Washington, D.C., and New York City, to Lakehurst, New Jersey. When President Coolidge saw the *Graf Zeppelin* soar above the city of Washington, he sent this message to President von Hindenburg of Germany:

I wish to congratulate you upon the splendid achievement of your compatriots in accomplishing the voyage from Germany to the United States on the *Graf Zeppelin*. This flight has filled the American people with admiration and has marked another step in the progress of the development of air communication.

The historic flight around the world is described in the selection "The First Dirigible to circumnavigate the Globe."

On January 1, 1929, the *Question Mark* added a chapter to the history of aviation. The purpose of this flight was to test the method of refueling in the air. This was done by means of a two-and-one-half-inch hose thirty feet long, weighted by a twenty-pound weight, which was thrown

Refueling the Question Mark in the Air
Official Photograph, United States Army Air Corps

450   *Romance of the Airman*

from a transport plane that soared above the *Question Mark* carrying a hundred gallons of gasoline to be transferred from this "aërial filling station" to the tanks of the larger plane. About three thousand gallons were transferred in the entire flight. Oil, food, radio messages, and even the daily newspapers were delivered to the airplane, which not only tested the possibility of refueling in the air but made the world's record for endurance, having cruised in one hundred and fifty hours, forty minutes, and sixteen seconds a distance equal to almost halfway round the world.

The flight was conducted under the direct supervision of the War Department, for the announced purpose of keeping the plane in the air as long as its engines would function. Rear Admiral William A. Moffett, chief of the navy's bureau of aëronautics, declared that the flight demonstrates the possibility of a nonstop flight round the world.

The purely physical aspects of the flight may be stated simply: The *Question Mark* took off from Metropolitan Airport, Los Angeles, at 7.26.46 A. M. on the first day of 1929 and landed at 2.07.01 P. M on the seventh day. During that time 36 contacts were made, and 5200 gallons of gasoline were burned by the three Wright Whirlwind engines. The *Question Mark* took on 21 tons of supplies during the long test and flew a total of 11,500 miles.

The airplane which Captain Charles Lindbergh used when he made his memorable flight from New York to Paris on May 20 and 21, 1927, was appropriately called the *Spirit of St. Louis* for the city which was his home. Captain Lindbergh received his built-to-order plane just sixty days after he had given the order for it.

The *Spirit of St. Louis* is now at the Smithsonian Institution at Washington, where the thousands who visit the nation's capital annually may see the silent partner of the company called "We." It weighs 2150 pounds when

The Airman soars to Fame 451

empty, but when ready to make its flight it weighed 5130 pounds. Lindbergh is credited by the Geological Survey with having covered 3610 miles on his nonstop flight across the Atlantic. The time for the flight was $33\frac{1}{2}$ hours, and his average speed was 108 miles per hour.

The *Spirit of St. Louis* was a stock monoplane with a few alterations. These were the addition of 10 feet to the wing span, increasing it to 46 feet; the fairing up of the ship in every possible way, placing the huge gasoline tank of 425 gallons capacity in lieu of the passenger compartment, and totally inclosing the pilot's cockpit. The inclosing of the cockpit was intended to improve the speed and to economize fuel. That it achieved these ends is shown by the maximum speed of the craft, estimated at 135 miles an hour, and by the fact that at the end of the flight fuel for 400 miles remained.

The plane, fully loaded for the trip, weighed 5130 pounds. This meant a loading of 26 pounds per horse power and, with a wing area of about 320 square feet, a loading per square foot of wing of 16.2 pounds. The plane had difficulty in getting off, touching the ground twice before the final get-away and showing the slowest possible rate of climb at the start.

The actual cost of the monoplane was $6000. It was built and ready to fly in sixty days. The instruments and the engine cost $6900, bringing the total cost to approximately $13,000. This can hardly be considered expensive for the result achieved.

Words and Phrases

To add to your vocabulary

      coastwise   premier

Technical terms

    dirigible   semi-rigid   duralumin   helium

452 *Romance of the Airman*

Informal Test (Completion) [1]

1. American chemists developed an alloy called _____ that is used in making dirigible airships.

2. The *Shenandoah* was _____ feet long and _____ feet in diameter.

3. The historic cruise of _____ miles was begun in the fall of _____.

4. The *ZR–3* was rechristened the _____ when it became American property.

5. The *Los Angeles* was built by _____ and can be used for _____ or _____ purposes.

6. The *Los Angeles* is of the _____ type and is slightly larger than the _____.

7. The *Norge* was built by _____, a native of _____.

8. _____ fostered the expedition made by the *Norge*.

9. The *Norge* was so constructed that it could remain in the air for a _____ as a free balloon.

10. The *Graf Zeppelin* was built in _____. It made its first visit to America in the year _____.

11. The *Question Mark* began its test flight on the _____ of _____ in the year _____.

12. The purpose of the flight was to test the method of _____ in the air.

13. The plane in which Lindbergh made his transatlantic flight was a _____ in type.

14. The distance from New York to Paris as flown by Lindbergh was _____ miles, which he covered in _____ hours.

15. The *Spirit of St. Louis* is now in the _____ _____.

[1] For directions, see page 14.

The Airman soars to Fame 453

Exercises and Topics related to your Other Subjects

1. Contrast the time the *Shenandoah* would take to go from Lakehurst, New Jersey, to Tacoma, Washington, with the time required for making the same trip in a covered wagon.

2. Contrast the development of the country at the period when the covered wagon was the mode of travel with its condition at the time of the *Shenandoah* as to methods of communication, growth of cities, methods of farming, and density of population.

3. Contrast Lewis and Clark's experiences with those of the crew that manned the *Shenandoah*.

4. Trace the route of the *Shenandoah* and locate the principal cities visited.

5. What properties does duralumin possess that are not possessed by other metals?

6. Indicate the points where the crew would have to turn their watches back when making the east-to-west flight, and forward when going from west to east.

7. Tell why the trip was made by way of Fort Worth, Texas, instead of directly west from Lakehurst.

8. Compare helium and hydrogen as to weight and usefulness.

9. Distinguish between static control and dynamic control.

Other Readings

In this book

"Byrd's Flight to the North Pole," page 275.
"Crossing the Atlantic," page 299.
"The *Southern Cross* visits the Fiji Islands," page 338.

From other sources

"Conquering the Air," by Archibald Williams.
"Skyward," by Richard E. Byrd.
"Modern Aircraft," by Victor W. Pagé.
"Historic Airships," by R. S. Holland.

Homage to the Lilienthal Brothers by a Frenchman

[*Explanatory Note.* The following is an editorial that appeared in the *Des Moines Register*, August 17, 1929.]

IN BERLIN the other day a French glider expert named Irlagasse placed a wreath on the monument to Otto Lilienthal, German pioneer with gliders, and with the wreath was placed a French flag and the inscription "Homage to the Lilienthal brothers by a Frenchman." Gustave Lilienthal, one of the brothers, and his family were present at the little ceremony.

No doubt German feelings have been touched by the incident because of the period of wartime hatred. In other fields, notably sports, Germans and Frenchmen have been on the finest of terms for two or three years now. But the "tribute" part of this ceremony and the simplicity of it were bound to appeal. And, besides, there is involved a recognition of the vital rôle of the German Lilienthals in preparing for the whole modern development of aviation. While the other great pioneers — the Wrights in America, for instance — have all along given the Lilienthals full credit, the credit thus given has never "registered" with the world public. For a Frenchman to take the lead in public testimonials, which ultimately should fix the Lilienthals' place where it belongs, has special value.

The Lilienthals did not have a power plant of the kind that came with the internal-combustion engine and that made power flight possible. But the principles of airplane design that they worked out experimentally and scientifically with their early gliders were sound principles. They were adopted by the Wrights and all other successful later

The Airman soars to Fame 455

experimenters, improved upon in some important respects, and proved. The curved instead of the flat wing surface can probably be regarded as a Lilienthal contribution. It was a vital one.

Exercises and Topics related to your Other Subjects

Subject for oral theme

The Airman as a Peacemaker.

Subjects for written themes

Public Tributes paid to Pioneers in Aviation.

What Different Nations have contributed to Aviation (consult your notebook as suggested on page 123).

Other Readings

In this book

"Otto Lilienthal, Inspirer of the Wright Brothers," page 124.

From other sources

"Conquering the Air," by Archibald Williams.

VI. The Airman Serves

The Winged Pony Express

Does the tempest cry halt? What are tempests to him?
   The service admits not a "but" or an "if."
While the breath's in his mouth, he must bear without fail,
   In the name of the Empress, the Overland Mail.

Kipling, "The Overland Mail

Lindbergh, America's Ambassador of Good Will

ARCHIBALD WILLIAMS

Explanatory Note. This selection tells of the reception accorded Colonel Charles Lindbergh when he reached Mexico City. No other visitor received such a welcome as was given "America's most attractive citizen."

ON DECEMBER 13, 1927, Colonel Lindbergh had left Bolling Field, the army's air station, just across the Potomac from Washington. The starting time was 11.29 A.M. He was on a new and hazardous venture to a foreign land. Drama was in the scene; but Colonel Lindbergh, by his business-like attention to the last details, made it appear commonplace.

Overhead there was a fringe of storm clouds, thick and low, forecasting rain; underfoot the field was a soggy, mud-bespattered morass. The conditions required just that supreme moral and physical courage and consummate skill which we have learned to associate with the clear-eyed and clear-headed hero.

The great plane had been wheeled by a score of enlisted men from the hangar to the north end of the field. Sergeant Hooe climbed on top of the machine and began pouring gasoline into the tanks, using, altogether, 368 gallons. The plane's total weight was 4750 pounds, a tremendous weight to lift on such a soft field.

The colonel appeared. He made a final inspection or two. Then he disappeared behind an automobile, reappearing dressed in his baggy, loose-fitting, one-piece flying suit. It was the Lindbergh adored of his country. He stepped into the machine. The sergeant gave the propeller

460 *Romance of the Airman*

its start, and Colonel Lindbergh turned on the engine. A hand-wave from the cockpit was the signal to free the chocks.

The propeller began to purr; then, to roar. The soldiers walked along with the plane, pushing strenuously. As the plane gathered speed the helping hands were withdrawn. Down the runway it went.

One minute and nineteen seconds after the start, a bit of daylight showed between plane and earth. The distance was about four thousand feet. This left only a thousand feet before the field ended at the river's bank.

As the beautiful silver-gray plane left the muddy field the spectators were dismayed. It seemed that he must strike the hangars on the right or the trees on the left. It did not seem possible, with the poor take-off, that he could avoid both obstacles. But the undaunted spirit of Lindbergh, coupled with his great skill, brought the other Spirit higher and higher, little by little, until "We" had risen to a height of two hundred feet before these hazards were reached. The great plane had again been imbued with the intrepid spirit of its master and again had stood the test.

Colonel Lindbergh was off for Mexico City!

Circling with an upward tilt he reached the open air and pointed the nose of his plane south-southwestward. In a few minutes he was gone, merging into the cloud-banked skies.

On December 17 more than thirty thousand spectators gathered in the Mexico City stadium for a public fête arranged by the Department of Education. More than ten thousand school children performed before their hero in a series of songs, drills, and dances. The next day about a hundred thousand workmen marched the streets as an expression of admiration and affection. Honor after honor was paid the distinguished visitor until even Mexico could think of nothing further to do.

Mexico City welcomes Lindbergh

Concrete, material results—political, social, economic—of the visit were quickly seen in Mexico. Aviation, with Lindbergh as its personification, had captured the imagination of the Mexicans, as, indeed, it has of all peoples, more than anything else in recent years; for love of the heroic is a fundamental emotion common to all men.

Hardly had Lindbergh landed in Mexico before the Central American republics, keenly alive to the interests of their peoples in the great American, telegraphed invitations to him to visit their countries before returning home. These invitations were accepted, to the great satisfaction of President Coolidge, who was intensely interested in extending the good-will mission at least as far as Panama. It afforded a splendid opportunity to sweep off by

462 *Romance of the Airman*

one dramatic gesture much ill feeling against the United States which had been reported for some time past.

At the time of going to press, his route was to take him to Guatemala, Honduras, San Salvador, Nicaragua, Costa Rica, and Panama, in the order named. Brief stays were to be made in each capital. From there it was his intention to fly back to Yucatan, whence he could take off for the comparatively short flight over water for Havana. It was hoped that he would attend the Pan-American Conference in Havana* in January, 1928.

Speaker Longworth has called Lindbergh "America's most attractive citizen." This he certainly is. It is truly amazing that he is unspoiled by acclaim from presidents, ambassadors, and kings such as no other private citizen has ever received. There is something about this young aviator, a magnificent simplicity, which baffles any attempt at explanation. Frank, simple, courageous, he represents the chivalric spirit of America. He makes visible every ideal the American pictures for himself. Colonel Lindbergh seems destined to make men forget their differences in a common admiration of his splendid manhood. The Frenchman, the Englishman, the Belgian, the Mexican, alike so came under his spell that they could not tell whether they had higher regard for Lindbergh the airman or Lindbergh the private American. His experiences in Europe were repeated in Mexico and Central America.

So the thousands of Mexicans who thrilled over the memorable flight, who later saw Lindbergh on the streets of Mexico, the children who sang for him, the one hundred thousand workmen who marched in review before him in a monster parade, took him into their hearts. They decided that after all there must be something to these Americans. A wave of sentiment broke down the invisible barriers of distrust which they had felt for us. They felt

The Airman Serves 463

that a country which could produce a man so heroic and so modest could not be a secret enemy. Our unofficial ambassador crystallized this emotion into a feeling of accord between the two nations which could not have been effected by diplomacy.

We can make treaties with other countries; we can reach agreements with governments. But a feeling of friendship between the people of two nations is more important than anything a statesman may accomplish. After all, Lindbergh to foreign peoples means America and all it connotes. He visited the countries to the south of us in the guise of a friend, but he went consciously as a representative of the prevailing American hope to be able to live on good terms with our neighbors. We are trying to understand them better and we are trying to help them understand us better. For that object nothing could be more useful than the quickening of sympathies across frontiers of land and sea which always follows the flights of Lindbergh, American Ambassador of Good Will.

Words and Phrases

To aid in understanding this selection

the **Pan-American Conference in Havana:** a meeting of unusual interest and importance to which all the republics of Latin America sent delegates.. Among the important proposals acted upon at the conference held in 1928 was an aviation treaty which was regarded as an admirable means for the encouragement of postal, commercial, and passenger flying in the Western Hemisphere.

To add to your vocabulary

fête   intrepid   consummate   morass

Technical terms

chocks   hangar

464 *Romance of the Airman*

Informal Test (Completion)[1]

1. Lindbergh was called _____ _____ _____ _____.

2. The date of his first visit to Mexico is _____ _____ _____.

3. _____ spectators gathered to honor him.

4. _____ school children engaged in the fête.

5. Among the Central American countries that Lindbergh visited were _____, _____, _____, and _____.

6. The plane carried _____ gallons of gasoline.

7. Speaker Longworth has called Lindbergh _____ _____ _____ _____.

8. The purpose of Lindbergh's visit to Mexico at this time was _____ _____ _____.

9. Lindbergh was _____ by the workmen of Mexico.

Exercises and Topics related to your Other Subjects

1. Write a theme telling what you imagine Lindbergh saw as he passed from Washington, D.C., over the United States south-southwest en route to Mexico.

2. Give a two-minute talk on the political, social, and economic results of Lindbergh's visit to Mexico.

3. List adjectives that describe Lindbergh's personality.

4. Locate on an outline map the cities that Lindbergh visited.

5. Look up some historic reasons for Mexico's distrust of the United States.

6. Calculate the years since Lindbergh started to Mexico City (December 13, 1927).

Other Readings

In this book

Read "Ave, Lindbergh!" page 465. This poem was written by a Mexican poet upon the announcement of Lindbergh's approach.

[1] For directions, see page 14.

Ave, Lindbergh!*

GEORGE GODOY

Explanatory Note. This poem, from the pen of a Mexican poet, is a beautiful tribute to Lindbergh and the motive of his visit to Mexico. It appeared in *El Universal*, "The Mexican Independent Daily," on the day that "America's Ambassador of Good Will" arrived.

At 2.39 P.M. on December 14, 1927, Lindbergh, with an escort of Mexican airplanes, circled the field and brought the *Spirit of St. Louis* to a graceful landing. The crowd of one hundred thousand people, many of whom had been waiting since five o'clock in the morning, went wild. He was greeted officially by President Calles and his cabinet and by Ambassador Morrow, our official ambassador to Mexico. President Calles issued a proclamation making December 14 a national holiday in honor of the event. This was the first time in history that such an honor had been paid to a citizen of another country.

Now doth the air-cleaving eaglet of powerful wing
And dauntless heart,
The bird imperial,* beloved of the air and sun,
Strain eagerly on his high mountain perch
To scan with piercing eye the vast expanse below,
And spreading his golden pinions
Catch with the sure instinct of his breed,
The winds that bear him onward in his course
To the distant, tempting valley that he seeks.

Cometh he like the eagle of ancient lore
Who led a migrant nation to its home,
Lured by the diamond waters of our lake,
To plunge his ravening talons in her bosom
And leave it crimson?
Or doth he obey some falconer*
And dart unhooded, like a feathered shaft,
At his helpless quarry*?

466 *Romance of the Airman*

Perchance the President of the Stars and Stripes,*
Or the gold lords of Wall Street,*
Are his master?
What fancies, fleeter e'en than his swift flight,
Flit through his mind as he sweeps across
Mountains filled with silver
Or broad plains fat with oil?
What brings this bird of war and prey?

But no!
Dismiss distrust of violence and guile.
Oh, land of Cuauhtemoc,
Bedeck thyself for welcome,
And take him to thy bosom.
For it is Lindbergh, the poet of the air,
The prince of aviation,
Who, as the spirits Dante* places in the realm divine,
Comes flashing through the ether like a ray of light,
To set our hearts on fire
And with radiant visions fill our souls.

Words and Phrases

To aid in understanding this selection

Ave, Lindbergh! hail, Lindbergh! *Ave* is the Latin word for "hail."

imperial: of supreme authority; Lindbergh is here likened to an eagle.

falconer: a person who hunts with falcons. A falcon is a bird of prey which is capable of being trained to capture other birds.

President of the Stars and Stripes: president of the United States.

lords of Wall Street: men of wealth who control the money market.

The Airman Serves 467

Dante: the foremost Italian poet. The reference is to the good spirits in Paradise, described in Dante's greatest poem, the "Divine Comedy."
quarry: a beast or bird hunted or chased.

To add to your vocabulary

dauntless   prey   scan

Exercises and Topics related to your Other Subjects

1. Make a list of words that mean the same as *hail!*

2. Learn why the citizens of Mexico should fear the "lords of Wall Street."

3. Has Mexico ever had any reason to fear the "President of the Stars and Stripes"? Read of the war between Mexico and the United States in 1845.

The Perils of Flying the Night Air Mail

The Story of the Heroic School that trained Lindbergh

HOWARD MINGOS

> *Explanatory Note.* This selection recites many incidents of daring achievement, of heroic self-sacrifice, of courageous facing of death for a cause. Such incidents make up the history of the early air-mail service of this country. Blazing the trails of the sky has been as hazardous an undertaking as was that of the explorers who made their way through the trackless forest. The same indomitable spirit that characterized the early period of American history is found in the pilots who have proved the practicability of air-mail service from coast to coast. This selection was written in 1927.

VETERANS assert that a trained aviator requires at least two full years in the mail service before he can be depended upon to do the right thing in an emergency. In that period, they say, he will have many accidents, and on the average will wreck two or three planes, with excellent chances of being killed. In the last nine years, since the first air-mail route was established, about forty pilots have been killed, though not more than that number have been employed at any one time. The majority of them had been flying the mails less than two years.

Mail planes are now flying between New York and Chicago both day and night, and between Chicago and Salt Lake City, between Salt Lake and Los Angeles, and between Salt Lake and San Francisco. Other branch routes extend to distant cities, linking up San Francisco, Portland, Seattle, and Vancouver, British Columbia; Chicago with Kansas City and Dallas, Texas; New York with Boston and Cleveland; and Chicago with Detroit. Other routes are being opened this summer. In winter even the daylight routes demand much flying after dark.

The Airman Serves 469

Fog is the worst handicap. It hides everything. In the air, fog is as thick as soup. One morning a veteran hovered over the mail field at Bellefonte, Pennsylvania, for an hour and a half. It was a dismal situation. The gauges registered only a few gallons of gasoline, and he could only guess that he was somewhere near the field. He could see nothing below. Now and then a tree-fringed hilltop would appear, sticking above the sea of mist like an island and indicating the limits of the valley which he thought must hold his airport. By mere luck he managed to find a hole in the fog, got a fleeting glimpse of the field, and glided into it with his fuel tanks utterly drained.

The mountain route at night is the most dangerous of all. Pilots flying the Alleghenies between New York and Cleveland rarely see the gigantic aërial beacons and intermediate lights between Youngstown, Ohio, and Easton, Pennsylvania. They are hidden by the mist. The pilots learn to fly by dead reckoning, high up and over the top, wherever possible.

Wesley L. Smith is one of the old-timers in the service. He has been flying the mails ever since the first route was established in 1918. He admits that he has been exceptionally lucky. The majority of pilots who entered the service the year that he started have "gone west," cracked up in their planes, though in the early days they did not wear parachutes and were unable to jump and save themselves if anything went wrong.

Smith had flown the Cleveland–New York division so often that he knew every landmark. Twice a week, and often three or four times in a similar period, he had made round-trip flights. Then one day he came eastward and headed into black fog. He could not see the earth, but continued on, flying a compass course, quite sure that the air would clear before he reached New York. After an hour and a half of blind flying he concluded that he must

470 *Romance of the Airman*

be somewhere near the seaboard. He zoomed low in an effort to get his bearings. His altimeter recorded that he was almost on the surface, but still he could see nothing.

The minutes passed, and he came down much lower. This time he got a glimpse of it through a break in the fog. Instead of land, it was water he saw, and, judging by the waves, he was far off the coast. Lacking a horizon or any other landmark, he had no means of checking up on the direction, so he cruised about in circles. He had about decided that his gas would become exhausted before he got anywhere, when he found another hole in the fog, and through it there loomed up a lightship. He recognized it, and knew just how to steer in reaching a flying field on Long Island. There he landed without further trouble. Had he not seen the lightship his disappearance might have remained a mystery.

Some of the pilots lost their lives by fire. In the early days experimental mail planes or inadequate and ancient war equipment were responsible. The machines would either catch fire in the air or burn up as soon as they struck the ground. Conditions are much better today; but one must always be prepared for freak accidents.

Crossing Great Salt Lake one afternoon a pilot noticed his engine thermometer registering above the danger point. As he watched, the mercury rose to the limit and the radiator cap blew off. He throttled down for a glide across the lake, saw that he could not make it that way, and, not wanting to land in the water with his load of mail, again throttled wide open. The engine burst into flame. He continued to glide, sticking to his post, and managed to reach shore, jump out of the machine, and fight the fire with his chemical pump until he thought it was extinguished. After pulling some fifteen pouches out of the compartment, he fainted from overexertion.

The Airman Serves 471

Regaining consciousness, he saw the flames spreading back under the plane and endangering the pouches, which lay near by. Again he carried them several feet away. Then he made a futile attempt to put out the fire. As he was turning away from it he saw that the wind was blowing the flames through the dry greasewood directly toward the mail. Running back and forth through the fire he carried the pouches to the other side and sat down to rest. At that moment the gasoline tank burst, and the blazing fluid jetted out in a graceful curve to fall directly on the pile of pouches. That time he could not save them. It was the only mail destroyed in a twelve-months period, and resulted in having all radiators on the mail planes replaced by those of another type.

The pouches contained considerable banking paper from San Francisco institutions. In order to insure clearance and proper credit after the loss, the banks were put to much bother and expense. In one instance the cashier entered the office of the president and remarked that he did not believe they should trust the air mail further.

"Why not?" asked the president. He had been a banker in the stagecoach period. He had lost money in hold-ups and later in train wrecks.

"We have been sending mail by air for some time," he said. "This is the only loss. Let us forget it." He then ordered all items of more than $400 shipped by air mail.

The pilots know that upon the regularity with which their service is maintained depends the patronage of the public. They know that there is danger in bucking storms; in flying the mountain ranges at night when bad weather prevents seeing the emergency fields,* which lie at regular intervals, lighted by caretakers and ready to receive a plane in distress. Only those pilots who have operated machines over the routes in daylight become night-mail carriers.

472 *Romance of the Airman*

Some of them fly for months, even years, without accident; many of them average fifty thousand miles of flying every twelve months. And then, after a long period of perfect success, one of them will disappear.

Charles H. Ames flew out of the New York terminal at New Brunswick, New Jersey, in the evening, taking the usual load westward over the mountains of Pennsylvania, his first stop Bellefonte, Pennsylvania. Below him he had an emergency landing field every sixteen miles, with lighted markers so located that he always had three of them in sight, when he could see anything at all. He also had a great aërial beacon at Bellefonte capable of sending its rays for a hundred miles pitched one degree above the horizon. On clear nights a pilot could see it fifty miles away.

Ames never reached Bellefonte. The land crew awaited his arrival throughout the night. Telephone calls to the emergency fields developed information that he had been heard passing over some of them in very thick weather, with dense fog hanging closely to the surface, especially in the valleys. Search parties scoured the wood; and ten days later a boy hunting about four miles east of Bellefonte found Ames. The torn and splintered wreck of the mail plane lay in the undergrowth, with the body of the pilot still strapped in his seat. Parts of the machine were caught in the trees, and broken branches showed just how it had crashed through them, probably before Ames realized that he was so near the earth. He evidently had no time to jump.

Pilots dislike the idea of jumping when over the mountains; they believe that they might be dropped into the top of a tree, or the parachute so caught that they would be rendered helpless, and there, unable to get down, await a lingering death. The majority prefer to stick to their planes over rough country.

The Airman Serves 473

Paul Scott was flying westward out of Salt Lake City. He met with both fog and snow, and his path became dark as night. He finally turned aside southward to circle a mountain range, and there saw a small hole between the fog bank and the clouds, directly over Saddle Pass, on the main route. At a mile and a half above the surface he dove through it, but not quite through. The hole closed up in front like a blind alley. He banked his plane and turned about.

He could not see twenty feet in any direction. The plane pitched up and down like a bucking broncho. He started to climb; but at that instant felt a slight jolting, then another. His wheels were swishing through the tops of cedar trees. When he came to his senses he was buried in snow. His right hand fumbled for the switches, mechanically trying to turn off the current and prevent an explosion. His left shoulder was dislocated. His arm hung numb and useless. Struggling down the mountain side to keep from freezing, he slipped on the shale rock and rolled for yards. The fall snapped his shoulder back into place again. He got up and struggled on. Hours later he reached a railroad and managed to flag a train. Mechanics who climbed up to the wreck found it had cut a path forty feet wide along the ridge, at one place clipping off a tree sixteen inches thick. But the mail was saved. In spite of the difficulties, the mail goes through about 97 per cent of the time on all of the nine thousand miles or more of cross-country air routes.

Landing a machine in trouble is always difficult. In the mountains it is especially dangerous. On the Nevada side of the Sierras it is a tight squeeze if one is to avoid hitting the crags. Storm clouds closed in on a pilot crossing them late one afternoon. Night came upon him before he knew it. He set his machine down in Truckee Cañon, barely

474 *Romance of the Airman*

scratching the wings; but when the salvage crew came up they had to take it apart to remove it from the gulch. On another occasion a pilot flopped into the Rockies, and they had to take his machine apart and pack it out of the mountains with mules.

Snow is almost as bad as fog. It is not unusual for sleet to weight a plane down and change the shape of the wings so that it cannot remain in the air. The pilot comes down, kicks off the ice, and goes up again. Very often his flight becomes a series of hops across country. Lindbergh had excellent training for his transocean flight, for he had encountered all kinds of weather on his air-mail route.

Weather is tricky, particularly in the Rockies. Jim Murray was heading toward Cheyenne one October afternoon. He found the Medicine Bow Range enveloped in clouds. Toward Elk Mountain on the south he saw a gap where the storm apparently had split apart. He reached it as it closed again. All he could see was a blanket of tree tops underneath and a thick, white wall ahead. He commenced climbing until he felt the controls sag. The plane was stalling. The trees rose up to meet him.

Those who have flown in all kinds of weather are probably the most skilled and the least fearful when they are forced down. They say that landing in the mountains is not so bad, but that it requires skill and presence of mind. Their method is to cut the ignition, drain the gas tank, remain up as long as possible to cool the engine and thus prevent fire, then land uphill. Murray put his machine down in that fashion, uninjured. He climbed out and walked through the night in three feet of snow; and when he became exhausted, sat down under a tree and went to sleep. His fur-lined flying suit prevented freezing. Next morning he discovered a cabin standing within a hundred feet of the spot where he had camped out. He did not

The Airman Serves 475

linger, however, but kept on going — for twenty-four hours. He staggered into Arlington, Wyoming; and though his clothes and shoes were worn to tatters, the first thing he did was to telegraph the Post Office Department requesting a pair of snowshoes. He got them, too; and after that carried them strapped to his machine.

Flying out of San Francisco on a winter afternoon, Claire Vance nosed up until his altimeter recorded 11,500 feet above sea level. He was crossing the Sierras. Inside of thirty minutes he had plunged into a snowstorm without much warning. He continued on; and twilight was fading into night when Vance realized that he had become lost in the air, unable to see where he was going, and knowing that lack of fuel would soon force him to earth. He had to come down, and he managed to land in a light timber patch. He built a fire between two huge logs, lay down, and slept fairly comfortably all night.

The next day he walked for hours down the mountain slopes until he stumbled upon the little town of Last Chance, famous in the gold-rush days. There he procured a pack-mule team and went back to the wreck, got the mail, and pushed on to the railroad. As there was no telephone in Last Chance, days elapsed before he reported to the outside world, though brother pilots had searched the mountains and given him up for lost. Vance heard the planes buzzing through the valleys and along the ridges, but had no means of signaling them.

Civilian operators have been trying to procure trained pilots for a wage of $3600 a year, which indicates that attempts will be made to cut the pay of pilots generally. The mail pilots say, however, that it will be unwise to employ untrained aviators on the regular routes, and that they are worth every cent of what the pilots received from the Post Office Department when it operated the

476 *Romance of the Airman*

transcontinental route between New York and San Francisco. They then averaged between $5000 and $8500 a year. They explain that they do more cross-country flying than any other group, and that half of their flying is done at night, much of it in bad weather. Over the mountains and occasionally during a storm in the Middle West, particularly along the Great Lakes, the winds are so strong that they sometimes hold a plane aloft, swaying first over one spot, then over another, while the pilot works to the point of exhaustion in a brave effort to prevent being turned upside down.

Bob Ellis left Rock Springs on the usual four hours' hop into Salt Lake City. As he approached a mountain wall rising nine thousand feet, he nosed up to hurdle it, as he always had done, and was shocked to find a mighty stream of cold air flowing over it like a Niagara Falls. It caught the plane and pushed it earthward. Ellis cut his switches an instant before he struck the face of the mountain. Badly damaged, its nose shattered and wings broken, the plane began sliding backward until it halted on the very edge of a precipice. Gingerly Ellis eased himself out of the machine, climbed up, and up. He worked his way through the snow to the top of the ridge, then down a slope, waded knee-deep for hours, and finally procured help. He led all hands back to the upper edge of the snow line. They formed a human chain for a hundred feet down to the wreck. One by one the mail pouches were passed up over the ledge.

Another pilot lost in those mountains found the snow so deep that he could not get through it. He had no snowshoes, but he had an overcoat and a traveling bag, used when he had to put up overnight at the end of his run. With the coat in one hand and the bag in the other he was able to stay on top of the thin crust. But he could only

The Airman Serves 477

crawl. He crawled for two days and nights through ravines and over treacherous barriers. On the second evening he lay down, wondering how long he would require to fall asleep permanently. One last glance about him. What was that? A light? Absurd! There couldn't possibly be a light so near. But it was a light, glimmering through the window of a forest ranger's cabin. There he was put to bed, remaining for days, until he was able to sit on a horse and ride into town.

In his statements Lindbergh has constantly reiterated his belief that the people have not given the air-mail pilots enough credit. He has pointed out that each individual is a hero, and those familiar with that brotherhood agree whole-heartedly.

Forced down on the Nevada desert near Secret Pass, a pilot set out walking toward the nearest settlement. After several miles he found a horse grazing. It permitted him to mount, and then promptly threw him off, breaking his ankle. He hobbled for hours until he reached a ranch house, where he telephoned for help. A reserve plane was flown to the ranch. He got in it and flew back to his own ship, left the others there to make repairs, got in the plane, after transferring to it all the mail, and flew on into Elko, Nevada. There his ankle was set in a plaster cast. Next day he again went out on his regular run.

The man who got his letter by way of that flight probably cursed broadly because of the ten or twelve hours' delay, but it is more than likely that he received it more quickly than if it had traveled by train. Once in a while the delays are longer.

Johnny Eaton had engine trouble on the Nevada desert, about seventy miles from the nearest habitation. He remained with his plane, knowing that he would probably die of thirst if he left it; and there he drank sparingly of

478   *Romance of the Airman*

the water in the radiator. He knew his comrades would be out looking for him, and they were. But when, three days later, they dropped down alongside, they found him doubled up in agony. He had contracted metal poisoning from the radiator water. After that, army canteens were issued — just another development from the school of harsh experience.

A sand storm is about the most deadly thing that a pilot can run against in the air. There have been times when machines flying in opposite directions have missed one another by inches simply because the pilots were blinded, not being able to see past the noses of their planes, and with every turn of the propeller sweeping clouds of sand back into their faces, the sticky, humid air smearing their goggles and rendering them useless. The wind often whips into a terrific blast on the plains.

One night the Cheyenne mail plane flying eastward ran squarely into a windstorm which the pilot had hoped to escape. But when some of the beacon lights failed to appear, he decided to land at Chappell, Nebraska, where he saw the field lights shining brightly and all clear. He throttled his engine and glided down to within five hundred feet of the surface, when a blast struck the machine, turned it over and over, and knocked the pilot senseless against the instrument board. The plane then politely landed on the air-mail field, crashed, tipped up on its nose, threw the unconscious aviator out and clear, then continued on its erratic course, blown like a leaf by the wind hundreds of yards away. A few minutes later the pilot and the caretaker of that field removed the mail. After the storm another ship came in and sped it on its way into Omaha. Later it was learned that a Union Pacific passenger train had been slowed down to five miles an hour because the engineer feared the wind would blow the train off the tracks.

The Airman Serves 479

If there is one kind of weather worse than another, it is a thunderstorm. The pilots are afraid of lightning, though they have to fly through it often. J. D. Hill had the most terrifying experience. Flying eastward from Bellefonte, Pennsylvania, toward New York, Hill had put his machine up over the mountain ridges, which stand like hurdles, four or five of them along that night route. He felt a blast of chill air as it struck sidewise against his plane. His propeller blades commenced biting into masses of wet black clouds, and a streak of lightning leaped at him without warning. He tried to climb above it, for it would have been foolhardy to risk a landing on such a night — better to keep on.

Before he had climbed more than a few hundred feet he was in the heart of the storm, such was the speed at which he had entered it. He had all he could do to keep his plane from being rocked into a bad stall or sent nose-first out of control. Still he climbed, with lightning splashing about the machine on all sides, until it seemed to be part of the storm, a roaring thunder god crashing through space, with a long tail of sparks from its open exhaust and crowned with a halo of lightning. But Hill kept on. There came another and particularly vicious crash, and then another, close at hand this time, followed almost instantly by a burst that seemed to stop his ship in mid-air, rendering him blind for the moment because of its brilliant flash. Hill felt himself tumbling, knocked out of the sky. It was only for an instant. He realized what had occurred. The engine had been struck by a lightning bolt, but it had picked up again. The propeller twirled merrily; so Hill continued on.

When he landed at Hadley Field, New Brunswick, he told of his experience, but the mechanics could find no evidence that lightning had struck ship or engine. They took Hill's word for it, however. They were also inclined to

480 *Romance of the Airman*

believe that he had flown through the worst electrical storm of the season when next day they learned that a passenger train had been derailed by a washout almost underneath that part of his air route where Hill had been struck. And all others familiar with aviation admit readily that for sheer heroic flying these pilots of the night mail, and the day mail too, as a matter of fact, are entitled to the first prize. Their daily work is producing our Lindberghs; and when flying becomes safe for the average person we shall look back and credit these pioneers with having forced the improvement of commercial planes, gradually, through their experiences with indifferent equipment.

Words and Phrases

To aid in understanding this selection

emergency fields: every twenty-five or thirty miles one of these fields furnishes a safe landing in case of necessity. It is not equipped with facilities for shelter, supply, or repair of aircraft. The boundaries of both emergency and landing fields are outlined with small white lights placed one hundred and fifty or three hundred feet apart, and all obstacles are marked with red lights. Between the fields smaller beacons are located, approximately every three miles. Most of this lighting is so controlled that the lights go off when the sun comes out, and come on when the sun ceases to shine. The lighted airway and the radio service are under the Department of Commerce.

To add to your vocabulary

greasewood   jetted   gulch   gingerly

Technical terms

dead reckoning   stalling
blind flying   altimeter
zoomed

The Airman Serves 481

Informal Test (Completion)[1]

1. A reliable mail pilot requires _____ years of service.

2. The weather handicaps mentioned in this selection are _____.

3. The president of a bank in San Francisco ordered all accounts of over $_____ to be sent by air.

4. Pilots dislike a parachute jump in the mountains, because they are afraid of _____.

5. After the pilot was made ill from metal poisoning, the Post Office Department provided pilots with _____.

Exercises and Topics related to your Other Subjects

List the things mentioned here that the Post Office Department learned in "the school of harsh experience."

Subject for oral theme

Explain a chemical fire-extinguisher.

Suggestions for written themes

The life and work of the forest ranger.

Use this as an opening sentence: "I remember once in stagecoach days, _____." Finish the bank president's story of how money was sent. Consult reference books and make your story accurate as to the time required for travel, the description of the stagecoach and the driver, and the dangers encountered. Make your own title.

Other Readings

In this book

"Lindbergh makes a Parachute Jump," page 492.
"Flying the Mail," page 482.

From other sources

"Winning the West," by Theodore Roosevelt.
"The Oregon Trail," by Francis Parkman.

[1] For directions, see page 14.

Flying the Mail

DONALD WILHELM

> *Explanatory Note.* This article is based upon the experiences of Randolph Gilham Page, one of the oldest pilots in the mail service, who is now in charge of the tests given to the candidates for the service. He was an instructor in aviation in both America and France during the World War and was also assigned to service on and over the German lines. The discussions of the science of aviation and the use of wireless and other instruments are the result of reports and interviews with members of the Air Mail Service and the Army Air Mail Service, and with army and air-mail pilots themselves. The article has been checked and approved by these authorities.

Now the conference that night late in February, there on the Omaha field, was critical. Strictly, it wasn't up to Knight to fly those four hundred and twenty-four miles on to Chicago, over a course he had never flown. He was hungry and he was sleepy, he said, after he circled the field, "jazzing" his motor by way of greeting, as his habit is, and set down. "Bill" Votaw, field manager, let him drift over, across from the field, to get a bite to eat. Good "Mother" Andrew Bahm had coffee and sandwiches ready for him, at 1.15 in the morning.

Then "Bill" broached the big question very gently.

He didn't order, or even urge, Knight to go — night flying was voluntary!

But if he didn't go — if he failed to fly that gap in the run from sea to sea — if the service failed to get the mail across the continent in twenty-five hours or so of flying time, at the rate of nearly two miles a minute — the next day Congress might renounce even the small appropriation it had been giving us to carry on the largest and most significant of all experiments in commercial aviation anywhere in the world.

The Airman Serves 483

We had, before that twenty-third of February, when our appropriation was to come up before the House, flown the mail more than a million miles — more than forty times round the equator, with a loss of life of eleven pilots, a loss of life smaller, you'll find, than has ever occurred in all the long history of transportation in any attempt to cover a distance so great. Yet all through the progress of our experiment, which we have carried on with no more than absolutely necessary equipment, some Congressmen and Senators have always been ready to damn us for our enthusiasm.

So you can see; when the next day was appropriation day, why Knight's trip and those others were so vital to a service whose loyalty and devotion some poet ought to sing.

But there was just one plane available, and that *D–H4* had flown nearly five hundred miles. And there was just one pilot, who had traveled half as far!

Knight had brought the mail — some sixteen thousand letters or so — from North Platte to Omaha, 248 miles in the air. But the two pilots who got to Chicago from Cleveland, bound west to Omaha and scheduled to return therefrom, could not leave Chicago — one went aloft to try! And Harry Smith, in an epic flight between 7 and 11.30 at night, had flown his lap all the way from Cheyenne to Omaha, an air-line distance of 458 miles — enough for one night! So there was just one plane fit. There was just one fit pilot — Knight — and he had already flown from North Platte, a distance greater by a third or so than the air-line trip from Boston to New York.

Then that conference, with his wife awaiting word that he had got that far through the night with not much more than the instincts of a bird to guide him.

Outside, it was dark and cold. Up aloft the cloud

484 *Romance of the Airman*

packs were moving. The moon glowed through a moment, and then disappeared.

Knight divined the situation after "Bill" had let him get a bite to eat. He considered that impending flight — 424 miles at night, over a course he had never traveled even on a railroad train. He considered — about one minute! "Sure, I'll go," he volunteered.

And he knew the danger well.

Less than two weeks before, he had crashed in broad daylight. Read his routine explanation to the department and you know the kind of man he is:

On February 14 I was scheduled to make the Cheyenne–Salt Lake trip. I was sitting in my ship warming it up at 6.30 in the morning. The motor was running smoothly on the ground and turning up exceptionally well (about 1520 R.P.M.* on the ground). Oil pressure 35, temperature of 170, and air pressure of $3\frac{1}{2}$.

It was a clear morning, with a fifteen-mile southwest wind blowing. I took off about twelve minutes before sun-up and headed west. Time of take-off, 6.35.

Climbing to 9800 feet above sea level (about 3500 feet above Cheyenne), I throttled to 1480 R.P.M. and headed west. Fifteen minutes out of Cheyenne, at 6.50, my instruments read R.P.M. 1480, oil 25, gas $3\frac{1}{2}$, temperature 185, altitude 9600.

A down current of air always hits us about Horse Creek and drops us 600 to 800 feet. This is on the eastern edge of the Laramie Mountains. Then, when we get within a few miles of Telephone Cañon, we invariably hit a current of air that boosts us 1200 to 1600 feet. This is a singular condition that is experienced and vouched for by every pilot on this division.

At the eastern edge of the Laramie Mountains I was flying at approximately 8800 feet. For safety's sake I started to follow a telephone line that leads from Horse Creek to Laramie. When I got within fifteen miles of Laramie my oil pressure dropped to 9 or 10, motor temperature ran 195, and suddenly my motor dropped to 1200 R.P.M. My only salvation was to attempt to land up the side of a steep mountain slope in a big snowdrift.

The Airman Serves 485

The shock of the impact knocked further details from my system, but when I came to and looked around I found myself lying several feet from the cockpit in a lot of blood. The motor, with the propeller attached, was sticking in the snowdrift seventy-five to eighty feet up the slope, and the fuselage had rolled down the slope, lodging up against a few trees and rocks.

I must have crashed about seven o'clock, but when I woke it was 8.35. Outside of bad cuts on my face, a broken nose, . . . and numerous aches and pains all over my anatomy, I was O.K.

Had a tough time, though, climbing mountains and trying to find civilization; but, with the aid of the sun and good luck, finally came to a ranch house about seven miles from the wreck, at 10.30. The rancher drove me five miles to Laramie, where I called up headquarters at Cheyenne, made arrangements for disposal of the mail with the postmaster, and then went to a doctor for medical treatment.

Now, less than two weeks later, Pilot Knight locked himself in a bare little room in the shack we use as office. What he thought of, of course I don't know. What he did we know. He studied a map,— a map quite like any other.

At Chicago, 424 miles away, lay victory and the safety of the cause. If he could get those sixteen thousand letters there early next morning, the other pilots— Webster, a newcomer in the service who had never flown the route to Cleveland, and Hopson and Allison—would get the pouches to New York.

He studied that map for exactly twenty minutes. Quite deliberately, then, by permission of "Bill," he tore out a part of it. "I'm on my way," said he.

He started out. "Wire my wife," he called back, "that I'm going to see this through."

He crawled into his ship and buckled himself in. He called "Off!" With the switches cut, the faithful mechanics turned the propeller over.

486   *Romance of the Airman*

Then, "Clear!"

The blades spun.

He taxied out, swerved into the wind, waved a hand, was gone.

They saw him hover a moment overhead against the moon and clouds; then he was off like a homing pigeon, at 1.59 in the morning, for Iowa City and Chicago.

And here, now, is the rest of his story . . . :

Well, I steered a compass course out of Omaha, crabbing into a twenty-five-mile north wind. The visibility was fair until about Des Moines, where I encountered fog and snow flurries lasting to Iowa City.

This first leg of the trip is not well landmarked with towns or railroads. Towns show at night; the business sections are lighted even when the people have gone to bed. I figured, though, that I could hit Des Moines, which is one hundred and forty air miles east of Omaha, by steering by compass, and I did — I hit it right on the nose!

Altogether, the first half of the trip was all right. But I got pretty lonesome. At times the moon was totally obscured by a heavy black layer of clouds. It looked as if the whole blooming world was sleeping hard, and oh, man, I envied most of 'em. It was dark as hob up there. There's a sense of isolation that's hard to describe. But my faithful old Liberty roared out, fighting the wind and dragging my ship along at about a hundred miles per hour.

I sighted Des Moines in an hour and five minutes. I could see the lighted dome of the Capitol plainly. And Fort Des Moines showed plainly under my right wing a bit later. I spotted it as a good place to land if my motor missed. The parade ground was illuminated by a light on each corner. But the engine was hitting on all twelve, and I passed over the southern edge of the city fifteen minutes later.

Beyond Des Moines about ten miles a layer of white clouds began to drift in under me. I didn't dare lose sight of the ground. So I dropped down from half a mile to fly at a hundred feet. Flying was pretty bad at this altitude. The air was rough, and the valleys were packed with fog. Next I began to get snow flurries,

The Airman Serves 487

and by checking my compass course I knew, with the wind shifting, I was slowing to eighty-five miles an hour. Then I lost my horizon and got to wondering if I'd reach Iowa City.

But I watched the landmarks carefully, stuck to the railroad all I could, and wagged along, hoping soon to hit Iowa City. Well, I did hit it — right on the nose! But where in the world the landing field was I had no idea. I had to get down for gas and oil. I'd never seen the town before, and there were no traffic cops handy. I flew all around, in and out the town, dodging steeples and looking for that field. For a good twelve minutes I ran around; then several red flares were lighted on the field. I judged as well as I could the general characteristics of the field and then, more by luck than skill, made a perfect landing at 4.45.

No. 172 was reserviced while Knight phoned Chicago, and got a bite to eat, and had a smoke or two. Then, with a weather report justifying his idea that he could make Chicago, he took off again into the darkness and winged away, on the last two hundred miles of his trip.

Now, as all pilots know, it's these last laps that tell the story. He had traveled a good five hundred miles in the air — add a fourth or so more miles for land distance and you have the equivalent of a journey from London to Paris with a couple of hundred miles to boot, from Berlin to Bern, New York to Cleveland, or half the distance from New Orleans to Buffalo.

He was tired, of course. And he was sleepy. Later on he had to pinch and slap his cheeks to keep his eyes open.

But luck and the weather were with him; fog and bad weather couldn't jinx him now! He flew for an hour, he says.

Then [he goes on] a faint streak showed up off to the east. Down below, lights began to flash around farmhouses — the farmers were out with lanterns to feed their cattle. And in towns, too, people were stirring. The old world was waking and getting on the job again, and I guessed after all I'd have breakfast with my wife in Chicago.

488 Romance of the Airman

But at Clinton, Iowa, I hit into a fog that had been boosted up, I suppose, from down below. But daylight was breaking, and I hopped it. I climbed up to five thousand feet and ran on, trusting to drop down beyond the Mississippi. I ran for some time up there, then dropped down and began picking up landmarks in the suburbs of Chicago.

I spotted the landing field in Maywood from a long way off. Then the motor missed.

But as I was within gliding distance of the field, I said, "Just spit, old boy; we're here!"

My mail was transferred to another ship. In less than fifteen minutes Webster was piloting it on to Cleveland, flying low, under fog, doing one stretch of one hundred and four miles in an hour, with Allison romping home at better than two miles a minute.

They got it through, ahead of schedule, in a little over thirty-three hours out of San Francisco, in less than twenty-six of actual flying time.

And I went to bed.

P.S. It might be well to add that it was simply my good luck that gave me the chance at this trip, and that any other pilot in the Air Mail Service would have gladly tried the flight and probably gotten away with it as good or better.

Words and Phrases

To aid in understanding this selection

R.P.M.: revolutions per minute.

Technical terms

cockpit   propeller   fuselage   visibility   ceiling

Informal Test (True-False)[1]

1. Pilots are ordered to do night flying.

2. It is very important to get the mail across the continent on schedule time.

3. The loss of life in the air-mail service has been greater than in any other kind of transportation.

[1] For directions, see page 54.

The Airman Serves 489

4. Knight argued against making the night trip.

5. Knight was well aware of the dangers in the night trip to Chicago.

6. The landing at Iowa City was a perfect one.

7. Knight realized that he was the only pilot who had the skill to make the trip.

Exercises and Topics related to your Other Subjects

1. Make a list of the things in Knight you would want a poet to praise.

2. Compare the spirit of the mail pilots with that of the messengers in Browning's poem "How they brought the Good News from Ghent to Aix."

Other Readings

In this book

"Peace on Earth," page 490.

From other sources

"How they brought the Good News from Ghent to Aix," by Robert Browning.

Loading a Mail Plane at Hadley Field, Chicago

Peace on Earth

DR. ABBUH RANDLAW

DAWN from the mountain tops greets his eyes,
  On the valleys it sheds its glow,
Red'ning the clouds, as eastward he flies
  O'er the peaks of perpetual snow.

The Air Mail is en route: the post's on the wing
  High in the heavens so blue.
Yesterday's vision; today's glory sing;
  Tells victory triumphant and new.

Homeward-bound traveler, bearing the mail,
  Only the God of us all
Marking the sparrow's flight, ne'er does He fail.
  Protecting His own who might fall.

The Airman Serves 491

Safely he's landed; the journey is o'er;
　Of service and duty — 'tis done.
Night shadows behind him and mankind before
　With tasks that come with each sun.

Homes brought together; friendships are bound
　In ties closer now than before;
Till the world ends its tumult, and peace may be found
　Echoing down from the skies as of yore.

Exercises and Topics related to your Other Subjects

Explain what is meant by "yesterday's vision." Read Tennyson's "Argosies of the Air," page 97.

Subject for oral theme

How the Mail Pilot brings Homes Together.

Subject for written theme

The Post from Horseback to Wing. (Consult reference books
and find out how mail has been carried from earliest times
in America to the present.)

Lindbergh makes a Parachute Jump

CHARLES A. LINDBERGH

Explanatory Note. Lindbergh enlisted in the 110th Observation Squadron of the 35th Division, Missouri National Guard, in November, 1925, and soon was commissioned a first lieutenant. The next spring he began his mail-flying, as told in this selection from the United States Official Postal Guide, Monthly Supplement, June, 1923. On one of his night trips in the fall of 1926 he conceived the idea of making the New York – Paris flight. The jump told of here was his fourth jump. The plane was wrecked about five hundred feet from where he landed, but it could not be located that night. Lindbergh went into Chicago for another plane, returning the next day to find the wrecked plane and to rescue the mail, which had received only slight damage.

I TOOK off from Lambert–St. Louis Field at 4.20 P.M., November 3, arrived at Springfield, Illinois, at 5.15, and after a five-minute stop for mail took the air again and headed for Peoria. . . .

I encountered darkness about twenty-five miles north of Springfield. The ceiling had lowered to around 400 feet, and a light snow was falling. At South Pekin the forward visibility of ground lights from a 150-foot altitude was less than one-half mile, and over Pekin the town lights were indistinct from 200 feet above. After passing Pekin I flew at an altimeter reading of 600 feet for about five minutes, when the lightness of the haze below indicated that I was over Peoria. Twice I could see lights on the ground, and descended to less than 200 feet before they disappeared. I tried to bank around one group of lights, but was unable to turn quickly enough to keep them in sight.

After circling in the vicinity of Peoria for thirty minutes I decided to try to find better weather conditions by flying northeast toward Chicago. I had ferried a ship

The Airman Serves 493

from Chicago to St. Louis in the early afternoon, and at that time the ceiling and visibility were much better near Chicago than elsewhere along the route.

Enough gasoline for about an hour and ten minutes' flying remained in the main tank, and twenty minutes' in the reserve. This was hardly enough to return to St. Louis, even had I been able to navigate directly to the field by dead reckoning and flying blind the greater portion of the way. The only lights along our route at present are on the field at Peoria; consequently, unless I could pick up a beacon on the transcontinental route my only alternative would be to drop the parachute flare and land by its light, together with what little assistance the wing lights would be in the snow and rain. The territory toward Chicago was much more favorable for a night landing than around St. Louis.

I flew northeast at about 2000 feet for thirty minutes, then dropped down to 600 feet. There were numerous breaks in the clouds this time, and occasionally ground lights could be seen from over 500 feet. I passed over the lights of a small town, and a few minutes later came to a fairly clear place in the clouds. I pulled up to about 600 feet, released the parachute flare, whipped the ship around to get into the wind and under the flare, which lit at once, but, instead of floating down slowly, dropped like a rock. For an instant I saw the ground; then total darkness. My ship was in a steep bank, and for a few seconds after being blinded by the intense light I had trouble righting it. I then tried to find the ground with the wing lights, but their glare was worse than useless in the haze.

When about ten minutes' gas remained in the pressure tank and still I could not see the faintest outline of any object on the ground, I decided to leave the ship rather than attempt to land blindly. I turned back southwest

494 *Romance of the Airman*

toward less populated country and started climbing in an attempt to get over the clouds before jumping.

The main tank went dry at 7.51 and the reserve at 8.10. The altimeter then registered approximately 14,000 feet, yet the top of the clouds was apparently several thousand feet higher. I rolled the stabilizer back, cut the switches, pulled the ship up into a stall, and was about to go out over the right side of the cockpit when the right wing began to drop. In this position the plane would gather speed and spiral to the right, possibly striking my parachute after its first turn. I returned to the controls and after righting the plane dove over the left side of the cockpit while the air speed registered about 70 miles per hour and the altimeter 13,000 feet.

I pulled the rip cord immediately after clearing the stabilizer. The Irving chute* functioned perfectly. I had left the ship headfirst and was falling in this position when the risers whipped me around into an upright position and the chute opened.

The last I saw or heard of the *D. H.* (airplane) was as it disappeared into the clouds just after my chute opened. I placed the rip cord in my pocket and took out my flashlight. It was snowing and very cold. For the first minute or so the parachute descended smoothly, then commenced an excessive oscillation, which continued for about five minutes and which I was unable to check.

The first indication that I was near the ground was a gradual darkening of the space below. The snow had turned to rain; and although my chute was thoroughly soaked, its oscillation had greatly decreased. I directed the beam from the 500-foot spotlight downward, but the ground appeared so suddenly that I landed directly on top of a barbed-wire fence without seeing it.

The fence helped to break my fall, and the barbs did

The Airman Serves 495

not penetrate the heavy flying suit. The chute was blown over the fence and was held open for some time by the gusts of wind before collapsing. I rolled it up into its pack and started toward the nearest light.

... I delivered the mail to Maywood* by plane, to be dispatched on the next ship out.

Words and Phrases

To aid in understanding this selection

chute: parachute. Leonardo da Vinci is credited with the invention of the parachute. In one of his manuscripts he gives a drawing of a pyramidal structure, beneath which a man is suspended. He describes it thus: "If a man have a tent roof of calked linen [*calked* means "made waterproof"] 12 braccia broad [roughly a braccio equals a yard] and 12 braccia high, he will be able to let himself fall from any great height without danger to himself." Aviators say of the parachute, "If you need it and haven't got it, you'll never need it again."

Maywood: a suburb of Chicago.

To add to your vocabulary

oscillation

Technical terms

ceiling	dead reckoning	altimeter	air speed
visibility	flying blind	stabilizer	rip cord
ferried	parachute flare	stall	risers

Informal Test (True-False)[1]

1. Lindbergh took off to St. Louis.

2. It became dark soon after he left Springfield.

3. He landed at Peoria.

4. He had gasoline enough for less than two hours' flying.

[1] For directions, see page 54.

Romance of the Airman

5. The air route between St. Louis and Chicago was well lighted at that time.

6. He was unable to find the ground with the wing lights.

7. He considered a parachute jump safer than a blind landing.

8. At the time the tank went dry he was only two thousand feet from the ground.

9. He was forced to make the jump without any preparation.

10. He landed in a blinding snowstorm.

11. The barbed-wire fence helped to break his fall.

Exercises and Topics related to your Other Subjects

Subjects for oral themes

A Parachute and How it Works.

Flying the Mail as a Preparation for the Paris Hop.

"The Caterpillar Club."

Other Readings

In this book

"The Perils of Flying the Night Air Mail," page 468.

"American Youth honors Lindbergh," page 414.

From other sources

"We," by Charles A. Lindbergh.

"The Lone Scout of the Sky," by James E. West.

"Modern Aircraft," by Victor W. Pagé (pages 679–685, on parachutes).

"Down to the Earth in 'Chutes," from "The Big Aviation Book for Boys," by J. L. French.

The Westbound Mail

PHIL BRANIFF

A DRIZZLING rain was falling.
 A near-by clock tolled eight.
They watched the sky with an eager eye,
 For the Westbound mail was late.

The rain beat down on the old tin roof.
 The hangar-chief stood by.
Then the drumming tone of a motor's drone
 Came from the misty sky.

The beacon sent its welcome beam
 To the rider of the night,
'N he brought her down the soggy ground
 Up to the landing light.

They swap the mail 'n shout "Okay!"
 Then she roars 'n lifts her tail,
She's up again in the snow 'n rain
 On with the Westbound mail.

The dim, blurred lights of a city
 Loom in the space below.
Their work is done, but the mail flies on
 And on through the blinding snow.

The rain is freezing on her wings.
 She seems to feel the weight.
It'll soon be dawn, but she staggers on
 Hopin' she won't be late.

498 *Romance of the Airman*

The crystals stick on the windshield,
  Formin' a silvery veil.
Icy struts 'n a man with guts
  'N a sack o' Westbound mail.

Over the peak of a mountain now,
  Clear o' the treacherous rim,
Away up there in the cold night air,
  Just God 'n the mail 'n him.

His thoughts turn back to a summer night
  'N a girl, not so long ago,
Who shook her head 'n firmly said,
  "As long as you're flying, No!"

He tried to quit the bloomin' job
  'N stick to the concrete trail,
But the wish came back for the canvas sack
  'N the feel o' the Westbound mail.

The wind kept whisperin' secrets
  It had heard the stars confide,
So back he went to the big blue tent,
  Back to the long black ride.

The sleet 'n snow were far behind
  Before the night was gone,
Out of the rain the gray dawn came
  'N found him flyin' on.

He tilted her stick 'n banked her in.
  She seemed to feel the gun
'N voiced her wrath at the cinder path
  At the end of a perfect run.

The Airman Serves — 499

Three points touched 'n she taxied in
 Up to the hangar rail.
He stretched a grin as they checked him in
 "On time" with the Westbound mail!

Exercises

Prepare this poem to read aloud to the class.
Which lines do you think give the most vivid picture?

Plant Protection by Airplane

S. R. WINTERS

Explanatory Note. Barnstorming, sky-writing, and other spectacular stunts usually have about the same connection with the airplane that joy-riding has with the automobile. More and more we find the airplane being accepted as a necessity of man. This selection tells of some projects that the different departments of the United States government have coöperated in advancing.

IT WAS in August, 1921, that the airplane was first introduced to the then spectacular undertaking of spraying insect-killing dust on destructive pests. The Air Service of the United States army, in coöperation with the State Experiment Station of Ohio, launched a sweeping air attack against a swarm of insects that was stripping a grove of catalpa trees of their foliage. By the very daring nature of this innovation, the announcement of the attempt was received with skepticism — classified as a "publicity stunt" or a feat for exploitation by motion-picture producers. It fell into the same category, at least in the mind's eye of the public, with the subsequent undertaking of breaking up ice formations in rivers by dropping bombs from airplanes, or the more recent spectacular demonstration of the transfer of postal matter from a flying machine to a train. But the novel experiment of arresting tree-insect depredations was successful on its face value, and, what was of far greater significance, it at once suggested the possibility of employing the airplane for the control of insect pests. From this feeble beginning emerged the definite project which has since consistently enlisted aircraft as the ally of plant protection against the attacks of insects.

One year later — in the cotton-growing season of 1922 — the airplane was drafted as an instrument of warfare against

Spraying Catalpa Trees
Official photograph, United States Army Air Corps

the rapid and damaging encroachments of the cotton-boll weevil, then, as now, under indictment for inflicting a $200,000,000 loss annually to cotton-growers of the South. Two borrowed airplanes, as well as pilots and other personnel and equipment from the Air Service of the United States army, furnished the basis for undertaking the tests. The poisonous dust, in the preliminary flights, was carried in bags and in limited quantities. The insecticide,* consisting of calcium arsenate, was dropped on the cotton fields over the side of the airplane by hand or poured through an opening in the bottom of the fuselage. Later, through the varying stages of evolution, came the hand-crank hopper and finally the air-suction hopper, which distributes the clouds of poisonous dust with an absence of

502 *Romance of the Airman*

human equation. Curiously enough, the first application of the airplane as an agency of insect control in cotton fields was evidently fraught with such misgivings that the attacks were not directed against the boll weevil at all. Instead, the cotton-leaf worm, which, as the term implies, feeds on the plant leaf and is clearly exposed, was the object of the preliminary airplane flights.

It is a far cry from the initial test flights in Louisiana in 1922 to the well-defined, officially approved project of cotton-dusting from the air in 1928. The field laboratory at Tallulah, Louisiana, owned and operated by the Bureau of Entomology* of the United States Department of Agriculture, is composed of five buildings, and, including the flying field, the laboratory grounds cover about seven acres.

The tests are largely confined to Louisiana, although the airplane — in its sweeping reach — may fringe the borders of Arkansas and Mississippi in cotton-dusting operations. The government experiments have answered in the affirmative the three question marks that were so conspicuous during the preliminary tests of six years ago, namely: Can the planes be operated over a cotton field in such a manner that the field will be thoroughly subjected to the cloud of dust? Can the dust be forced down from the plane into the cotton plants and be made to adhere to them in a quantity sufficient to control insects? Can dusting be done economically from the air?

The latter question is answered by the Department of Agriculture with a proviso, namely: "The operation could be only considered as a community affair or for planters whose acreage would be large enough to justify purchasing more than one plane. Many districts in the South have now reached the point in public sentiment where the desirability of community weevil control can be seen, and it is only by some such method as the use of the airplane that

The Airman Serves 503

such community poisoning can be attempted in the near future." This serves to introduce the commercial airplane cotton-duster, just as commercial flying concerns are now carrying the mails, fighting forest fires, and making airplane surveys and maps of cities. The commercial cotton-duster may be hired by cotton farmers whose crops are infested with ravaging insects. This and similar organizations furnish the airplanes, the pilots, the insecticides, and other equipment necessary to adequate dusting operations. The cotton-grower pays a stipulated figure for each acre dusted, and the dusting corporation offers its services to any community guaranteeing at least five thousand acres of cotton to be sprayed with insecticides from airplanes. The cost to each farmer does not exceed that of ground methods of applying the poisonous dust — the one-mule dusting machine, for example.

B. R. Coad, in charge of the Bureau of Entomology field station at Tallulah, Louisiana, outlines some of the advantages as well as disadvantages of dusting cotton from airplanes: The flying machine, unlike the one-mule dusting machine and similar ground methods, does not have to postpone operations because of a soggy soil; stumps do not offer the slightest obstacle to the airplane; and the planes can be manipulated so that all portions of a field may be treated without delay. On the other hand, timber lines offer some obstruction to airplanes for low-flying dusting, and in the hilly sections of the cotton belt it is dangerous to use planes as a regular operation. Withal, to quote J. L. Webb, associate entomologist of the United States Department of Agriculture, who has followed the progress of airplane dusting from the beginning:

It is by far the most expeditious means of putting insecticide on cotton. An airplane can accomplish in one day what a hun-

504 *Romance of the Airman*

dred of the best and most efficient ground machines could accomplish in the same time. Airplane dusting is a permanent agricultural project — it is here to stay!

The Office of the Cereal Investigations, United States Department of Agriculture, in its investigations to determine the distribution of spores, which cause rust of wheat, sought the airplane as the only suitable vehicle for exploring the upper air. The airplane was employed in preference to balloon, kite, or similar device, because the traps to ensnare these minute organisms, when attached to an airplane, could be exposed at varying altitudes, and the direction of the flight could be changed at will. An ordinary microscope slide (3 inches by 1 inch), smeared with vaseline on one side, was exposed in three different ways. Of these methods that of the mechanical spore trap was satisfactory. This trap had six compartments, each containing a slide. The trap was attached to the wing struts of an airplane, and it was provided with a wire control operated by the observer in the cockpit. One pull on the wire opened the first compartment and exposed slide No. 1; a second pull closed this compartment and terminated the exposure of the slide. This procedure was repeated with respect to the other compartments. This method enabled the scientist to expose one slide at a time for the desired period, at varying altitudes and at widely separated points.

On one of the slides, exposed five minutes at an altitude of about two miles near Fort Crook, Nebraska, 244 spores were trapped. On another slide, exposed for the same length of time at an altitude of eight thousand feet, 827 spores of known identity were trapped and about 200 spores unidentified — a total of approximately 1000. The highest altitude, attained between Waco and San Antonio, Texas, was more than three miles, at which height only two spores

The Airman Serves 505

were identified. "The results of these experiments," concludes the Bureau of Plant Industry of the Department of Agriculture, "indicate that large numbers of spores and pollen grains are carried several thousand feet above the surface of the earth during the growing-season. Probably they are carried long distances by the upper air currents, the direction and velocity of which are quite different from those near the surface. If the spores retain their viability,* as some of them quite probably do, it is conceivable that a local epidemic might occur in one locality as a result of the blowing in of spores from an infection center in another distant locality."

And here again the Department of Agriculture places its stamp of approval on the airplane as a utility device in detecting these minute organisms and thus possibly preventing a disease epidemic among plant life. "The airplane," emphasizes this government bureau, "is a great aid in studying the distribution of spores of pathogenic fungi.* It is likely to be very useful in epidemiology studies, and it may also be useful in determining the value of establishing quarantine lines. . . . Airplanes probably will be useful in studying the dissemination of many pathogenic fungi, and probably will aid in the solution of problems connected with the development of epidemics of plant diseases."

The dusting of Paris green from airplanes to control the breeding of mosquitoes was an innovation introduced five years ago by the Bureau of Entomology, United States Department of Agriculture, in the swamp and marsh areas of Louisiana. A light metal hopper, holding three hundred pounds of insecticide, was built in the rear cockpit of the plane, and the poisonous dust was released through an opening in the bottom of the fuselage on the mosquito-infested areas. Similar experiments are now in progress

506 *Romance of the Airman*

near Quantico, Virginia, the Bureau of Aëronautics of the United States Navy Department using seaplanes for distributing one part of Paris green to one hundred parts of an inert carrier — road dust, for instance. Thus, the airplane is not only offering protection to our potential bread supply and source of cotton cloth, but, in destroying mosquitoes by the wholesale, this modern dissipator of distance* makes it possible to enjoy our food and clothing supplies with the minimum amount of annoyance from pests.

Words and Phrases

To aid in understanding this selection

insecticide: a preparation for killing insects.

Bureau of Entomology: the division of the United States Department of Agriculture which collects and disseminates information about insects that damage plant life.

viability: ability to live, vigor.

pathogenic fungi: disease-producing fungi. Fungi are plants that grow on dead or living organic matter; for example, mildew, mold.

dissipator of distance: here means the airplane.

To add to your vocabulary

inert   insecticide   ally

Technical term

fuselage

Informal Test (Completion)[1]

1: There are two insects that are enemies of the cotton-planter. They are _ _ _ _ _ _ _ _ _ _ _ _ and _ _ _ _ _ _ _ _ _ _ _ _.

2. The experimental use of the airplane in the destruction of injurious insects has been made in the states of _ _ _ _ _ _, _ _ _ _ _ _, _ _ _ _ _ _, and _ _ _ _ _ _.

[1] For directions, see page 14.

The Airman Serves 507

3. An airplane can accomplish more in one day when scattering insecticides than _____ ground workers can do in the same time.

4. The United States Department of Agriculture owns and operates a Bureau of Entomology in the state of _____.

5. A well-known insecticide is _____ _____.

6. It is _____ expensive to spray cotton fields by airplane than by the ground method.

7. Experiments have been made that lead scientists to conclude that insects (**are, are not**) found far above the surface of the earth.

8. Thus far three distinct things have been accomplished by the use of the airplane in protecting plants; namely, _____, _____, _____.

Topics related to your Other Subjects

1. Read from government bulletins about the attempt to destroy the boll weevil.

2. From your geography learn the cotton-producing states, and make a list of them in the order of the number of bales produced.

3. Contrast the methods of raising cotton today with the methods used before the Civil War.

4. Make a list of the contributions which the United States Department of Agriculture has made to more adequate tilling of the soil, better care and protection of crops during the growing-season, and better methods of harvesting and marketing crops.

Other Readings

From this book

"Aviation's Varied Uses in Business," page 532.
"Life-saving Airplanes," page 516.
"Hunting Whales by Airship," page 508.

Hunting Whales by Airship

ROMAN J. MILLER

HUNTING whales via the aërial route is a most fascinating adventure. This pleasure was afforded the writer a few years ago while on duty as an airship pilot at the Naval Air Station, San Diego, California. The adventure was only an experiment, but it savored of future possibilities. It came about in this way:

An old whaling captain of the Pacific coast had invented a rather ingenious harpoon. It was designed to be dropped from an airship into the body of a poor, unsuspecting whale. Whales were appearing off the coast of southern California at that time.

Authority to conduct the experiment was readily granted by the Bureau of Aëronautics.* The airship designated for this work was a single-motored ship of nonrigid type — one hundred and sixty-five feet in length and of ninety thousand cubic feet capacity. It carried the pilot-mechanic, the whaling captain, and a photographer. The harpoon in question was a combination bomb and harpoon embodied in one unit. In general appearance it was not unlike a gigantic steel tubular arrow seven feet in length and weighing about one hundred pounds. A sort of line-carrying rocket, so to speak. It contained a high explosive, a detonator, a delayed-action fuse, and a highly compressed lighter-than-air gas. The arrangement was such that when the harpoon would enter the body of the whale, a trigger arm would fire the explosive charge into the body of the victim, inflicting a mortal wound. The delayed-action fuse would then operate within a period of about a minute and release the highly compressed inflating gas. This gas, filtering into the body of the whale under high pressure,

The Airman Serves 509

would inflate it so as to make the carcass float. Attached to the ring end of the harpoon was a coil of durable water-laid rope, several hundred yards in length, wound on a cask-like buoy. Attached to the buoy was also a flag, vivid red in color and about four feet square.

This outfit was arranged on the outside of the airship at the whaling captain's station. It was further arranged in such a manner that the harpoon, line, and buoy could be released simultaneously by the mere pulling of a lever. The harpoon itself also acted as a sighting bar along which the captain would sight in making the shot. The method of attack was for the airship to attain a position at an altitude of about five hundred feet directly above the whale, found basking or feeding on the surface of the sea. The airship would then spiral slowly down to an altitude of about one hundred feet above the whale, hover over it, release the harpoon line and buoy, then climb to the higher altitude again, and watch the show.

If the shot was successful, the explosive charge in the harpoon would mortally wound the whale. The inflating gas would keep the carcass afloat, and the line buoy and flag mark the kill. Then the whaling tug would be notified by radio from the airship, and could come to the location and secure the catch.

The time selected for the experiment was a most delightful day, as most days are in southern California. The ship took off from the landing field, circled over the city of Coronado, and then headed out over the calm blue waters of the Pacific toward Los Coronados Islands. These islands, by the way, are a singular group of mountain peaks, three in number, rising from an azure sea some seventeen miles from Coronado Beach. They are really off the coast of Mexico, just across a line with the border.

To those who have never experienced a ride in an air-

510 *Romance of the Airman*

ship it may be of interest to know that it is a most delightful kind of a ride. One is not subjected to a headaching, teeth-chattering vibration. But rather one soars along through a sky of adventure in a peaceful, soothing calm. Unlike an aëroplane, the airship has the advantage of static control, not depending entirely upon the motor to keep it aloft. Consequently the motor may be idled, and the ship, balloon-like, may hover over a certain spot in observation.

As we soared aloft on this delightful morning, an alluring picture of Mother Earth unfolded in a brilliant kaleidoscopic panorama, a gorgeous nature painting of mountain, land, and sea wrought by the Divine Artist, which no mortal man can successfully imitate. Far to the eastward the dark, purple-blue mountains of two countries rose through the morning mist in serrated, somber beauty. The foothills adjoining merged into shiny green slopes adorned with orange and lemon groves, and further dotted with villages, towns, and cities of ivory mosaic, with white lines of surf rolling upon their silvery shores. Beneath us sparkled the sea, rivaling in blue the arching dome of heaven above, with the horizon line but dimly traced. Directly ahead, the Los Coronados Islands appeared like dream castles floating upon the bosom of the sea. As we soared above we looked down into the azure depths of the sea and observed a scene of fascinating marine beauty.

The islands are of rugged, barren nature, uninhabited by human beings. But on the rocks were seals and sea lions in great numbers, and what appeared to be a sea elephant, basking by his lonesome in a detailed shallow. Sea birds in thousands, including pelicans, gulls, and petrels, soared about.

A marine forest of kelp surrounds the islands and offers refuge for myriads of rock bass, sheepshead, white fish, and

The Airman Serves 511

the great, lumbering black bass which afford famous sport for deep-sea anglers. To the west of Los Coronados, we passed over Tanner Bank. It was so named after Captain Tanner, U.S.N. Legend refers to it as the Lost Island, where old bells toll on stormy nights and weird craft are seen sailing as phantoms across the shallows. Many a romance has been written with this bank as an inspiration. There it is supposed once stood a Pacific Atlantis,* and now in its mystic depths mermaids of entrancing beauty hold court. Richly colored sea plants wave invitingly in the currents which sweep about the bank in rhythmic cadence. It is the home and abiding place of countless denizens of the deep.

Near at hand is the leaping tuna, the long-finned tuna, the yellow fin, the white sea bass, the leaping swordfish that jumps and outfights the tarpon, the yellowtail, and a host of others which would make any place famous. To these fascinating waters we came by airship in quest of whales. But we were so fascinated by the submarine scenery about us that we were given to daydreams and saw no whales.

But turning about we laid a course over the sea that would carry us to La Jolla, California, and kept a sharp lookout for signs of our quarry. Personally, I know little about whales, except that they are huge fishlike mammals of the sea, with a tail that lies on the water as flat as a pancake. Any fishlike mammal of the sea, large or small, with that kind of a tail is a whale. The tails of fish are in a vertical plane.

At a point about fifteen miles off La Jolla, the whaling captain espied the spouting of a school of three of the big mammals. In the vernacular of his profession he called out above the even purr of the motor: "Thar she blows! Thar she blows!" The ship, with increased speed, soared

512 *Romance of the Airman*

over in the direction of the nearest one, and was soon in a position some five hundred feet above it. The captain said it was a large male. Observed from the airship the whale appeared not unlike a gigantic distorted cigar, silver gray in color. He seemed to be lying on the surface of the sea, basking in the sun, with the waves running freely over him. Spiraling down to an altitude of scarcely a hundred feet above the whale, the motor was idled, and the airship hovered over the spot. The captain sighted the harpoon, let go, and it dropped downward with the speed of a bomb. The harpoon struck the whale amidships, wavered for an instant, and then slid off sideways. Evidently it did not have energy enough to penetrate the skin and blubber of the whale. Harpoon, line, buoy, and flag disappeared from view. The whale did not seem unduly alarmed for the moment, and another shot could easily have been made. But the captain had only the one harpoon on this trip, and owned but one other, which was to be used on other tests.

As the harpoon struck the whale he slowly assumed a perpendicular position and revolved slowly about, as if to scan the sea all around. The water oozed from his jaws and spilled down into the sea like miniature sparkling waterfalls. He seemed to be about fifty feet in length, but of enormous bulk. Finally, he swung from side to side, sweeping a radius of some thirty feet with awful violence. The concussion of the tail churned the spot into a mass of foam, and the air was filled with spray. Then suddenly, with an angry hissing surge, he dived vertically down to the depths below. We could easily see the course of the monster beneath the surface of the sea, speeding along like a big white cigar. Occasionally he came to the surface to blow and spout. During these blowings, which lasted about ten minutes, he could easily have been shot or harpooned.

The Airman Serves 513

In the course of the day two other whales were sighted, and the ship brought down in photographic view of each without alarming them. On the bulging bulk' of one we dropped a bag of sand weighing thirty pounds. This landed with a resounding whack, and the whale scurried for parts unknown. Needless to say, we returned to the landing without a whale, but rich in pleasant adventure.

I afterwards learned from the captain an interesting theory why it was so easy to approach a whale via the aërial route. It appears that the eyes of all whales are located far aft and well down near the angle of the jaw. The whale, therefore, has an extremely limited field of vision. It is said that each eye covers no more than thirty degrees of vision in advance of the straight side line of sight, and about thirty degrees behind it. Therefore the whale's eyes do not portray a single view upon the brain, as does the human eye. It is reasonable to infer, then, that the whale thus sees and comprehends two distinct fields of vision, one ahead and one astern, but none directly above. When he raises his head perpendicularly and revolves slowly around to gaze in all directions, he is simply confirming previous impressions as well as exploring new fields. Consequently it is an easy matter for an airship to hover above a whale at a low altitude and, with an improved device, to fire an explosive bomb or harpoon into it.

An aëroplane, on account of its excessive speed and its inability to hover over a spot, would encounter more difficulty. However, an aëroplane fitted with a helicopter element might be successful.

It is the writer's candid opinion that aircraft will eventually be used with phenomenal success in the whaling and fishing industries.

514 *Romance of the Airman*

Words and Phrases

To aid in understanding this selection

Bureau of Aëronautics: a division of the United States Department of Commerce. A private citizen must secure permission in order to use government property for private or experimental purposes.

Pacific Atlantis: *Atlantis* is the name given to a mythical island in the Atlantic Ocean in which ideal conditions prevailed. *Pacific Atlantis* refers to a similar island in the Pacific Ocean.

To add to your vocabulary

myriads phantoms aft

Technical terms

helicopter static control detonator

Informal Test (Completion)[1]

1. Hunting whales by _____ has proved to be successful.

2. The airship descends to a distance of about _____ feet before the harpoon is thrown.

3. The body of the wounded whale is kept afloat by means of _____, which is injected into the body.

4. A whaling tug notified by _____ would locate the carcass by means of a _____.

5. Los Coronados Islands are _____ by human beings.

6. An airplane is less successful than an airship in hunting whales because of its _____ _____ and inability to _____.

7. A whale differs from a fish in that the tail of the former is in a _____ plane, whereas the tail of the latter is in a _____ plane.

For directions, see page 14.

The Airman Serves 515

Exercises and Topics related to your Other Subjects

1. Ask your English teacher to assist you in making a list of romantic stories that have the scene of this selection as a setting.

2. Locate on a map the places mentioned in this story.

3. Read from your reference books about whale-hunting and the uses of whale carcasses.

Other Readings

From this book

Selections pertaining to the uses made of the airplane.

Life-saving Airplanes

S. R. WINTERS

Explanatory Note. The Life-saving Service is a branch of the Treasury Department of the United States government. The Massachusetts Humane Society established the first stations of a life-saving service which operated along the eastern coast of the country. In 1837 the president of the United States was authorized to employ ships to cruise along the shores of the country and render assistance to ships in distress. William A. Newell introduced a bill in Congress in 1848 to provide for the establishment of life-saving stations along the eastern coast. From this beginning the life-saving service has grown to the proportions told of in this selection.

OVERTHROWING a precedent of nearly one hundred years' duration, something new — the airplane — enters the service of life-saving. The present-day interest in aviation, stimulated to the point of accepting the miraculous, finds added impetus in an invention of Lieutenant Commander C. C. Van Paulsen. About five years ago Commander Van Paulsen quietly began experiments at the recently abandoned aviation station at Morehead City, North Carolina, and has perfected a revolutionary method of throwing out rescue lines by aircraft. This method has been adopted at two aviation stations of the United States Coast Guard, located at Gloucester, Massachusetts, and Cape May, New Jersey.

The old tar* who related his narrow escapes and gave full credit for his deliverance to the "breeches buoy"* would indeed have something to tell for the rest of his days should he be saved by aircraft. Various methods have been practiced for rescuing ships in distress, but those of the old school most frequently refer to the "cannon." Briefly, this system made use of a miniature cannon, from which was shot a projectile, with life line attached, to the ship in

The Airman Serves

An Airplane carrying a Life Line to a Ship in Distress
Photograph by United States Coast Guard

distress. The stricken crew seized this line and made fast a cable carrying a large life preserver to which was attached a pair of canvas trousers, with lines for hauling the breeches buoy to and from the disabled vessel. One by one the stranded crew stepped into the "breeches," which formed a sort of cushion for the life preserver, and were towed safely to shore.

And now, the airplane has been accepted by the Coast Guard of the United States Treasury Department as the vehicle for carrying out the life line to ships in distress. In this radical safety measure the line on shore is coiled around a number of upright sticks attached to a wooden frame. The rope is so wound around these sticks as to play out freely when an airplane is taking the line to a disabled vessel. The end of the life line is led through clips to the tops of two slender masts, which are planted on the shore, spaced about two hundred feet apart and landmarked by fluttering pennants.

518 *Romance of the Airman*

Immediately upon intercepting distress signals by means of the radio equipment aboard, the airplane takes off, picking up the rope, which is held taut by the masts. The method of this pick-up is unique, although by no means difficult in procedure. A rope of the usual close-line variety is suspended from the craft, and a weight attached to the floating end keeps it in a more or less stationary position. By flying low, the rope from the airplane intersects the rope between the poles, and the weight intervenes to prevent it from slipping. The rescue rope, released from the poles, is then carried seaward to a point within reach of the distressed vessel.

The pick-up line, once caught in the rigging of the disabled ship, or otherwise secured on board, performs the function of trailing aboard a larger line to which is attached the end of the hawser. To the latter is attached a breeches buoy, — the life preserver and canvas trousers employed in the time-honored method of rescue. This buoy, with simple tackle, is detailed on its life-saving errand, bringing the crew and passengers safely ashore.

That the airplane is quicker and more certain than the old method is attested by the fact that in a recent demonstration twenty-seven life lines were shot from a miniature cannon mounted on a Coast Guard cutter before contact was established with a ship on the rocks. Then, too, the record distance covered by a line ejected from such a contraption is 695 yards, while the new method of delivery is said to be capable of carrying a rescue line a mile or more.

Certain limitations, however, attend this new means of extending succor to disabled vessels. For instance, a seaplane cannot take off from rough waters; and should it take off from still waters, the chances are that it would be too far removed from the wrecked ship to offer the needed assistance. While a land plane in this case might be able

The Airman Serves 519

to take off from a near-by shore, a forced landing would render it helpless. In recognition of these handicaps the Coast Guard is using amphibian aircraft at the aviation stations where this method of life-saving has been introduced. This, of course, means that the planes used in carrying rescue lines to disabled ships can take off from either land or water — preferably from the former, owing to the usually high winds encountered near a storm-swept vessel.

Another possible application of airplane activities as an aid in lessening the hazards of seafaring is suggested as a result of the success of conveying life lines. Menacing icebergs that threaten life and property in the traffic lanes of the North Atlantic Ocean have proved stalwart foes to attempted placements of TNT. The reason for such a slight degree of success in the proposed explosions is the difficulty encountered in making a true placement of the dynamite. Now, by means of amphibian planes, it should be relatively easy to get a line over the top of an iceberg for the attachment of a high explosive bomb.

Maintaining more than two hundred and fifty stations, stretching along the ten thousand miles of treacherous coasts, the Coast Guard was authorized, under the provisions of the First Deficiency Act of 1926, to maintain and operate five seaplanes for use in performing the duties with which this branch of the service is charged. The five new planes are developments of army and navy aircraft features and are designed to give maximum cruising distance. Arrangements for the construction and operation of these planes were made under the general direction of Lieutenant Commanders S. S. Yeandle and E. F. Stone, and the army and navy officials extended every possible coöperation. Two types were decided upon — the *OL–5* amphibian and the *UO–4* seaplane. Three of the former and two of the latter have been constructed.

520 *Romance of the Airman*

The *OL–5* amphibian planes, which have proved peculiarly adaptable to life-saving work, are equipped with inverted Liberty engines; have a gas capacity of 140 gallons, an estimated cruising radius of 500 miles at a cruising speed of 75 knots, and a speed range of 55 to 103 knots; are equipped with a Lewis machine gun; and have weight and space allowance for radio installation. These planes are capable of landing on and taking off from the water and good flying fields. They are of the three-seater type and have a 45-foot wing span. Two amphibians and one seaplane are stationed at Gloucester, Massachusetts, while the other amphibian and seaplane are assigned to Cape May, New Jersey.

Paramount among the duties of the Coast Guard is life-saving and rescuing seafarers from peril. More than two hundred life-saving stations are maintained on the coasts of the Atlantic Ocean and the Gulf of Mexico alone — each manned by a crew of seven to ten men. They are subjected to a rigid course of drills and well-defined duties, which necessitates their keeping long day and night vigils for disasters on gulf or sea. The life-saving apparatus of every Coast Guard station includes a surf boat, with air chambers to make it unsinkable; a self-righting and self-bailing boat equipped with gasoline engine, sail, and oars; a breeches buoy; an iron-covered life car capable of carrying five or six persons at a time, and operated like a breeches buoy; a bronze cannon capable of shooting lines up to six hundred yards; a rocket, with a coil of rope at its head, which is sometimes used instead of the cannon, and which can travel one thousand yards; a beach cart; a pulmotor; and now an amphibian plane for rescue work.

That the added duty of apprehending rum-smugglers has not decreased the life-and-property-saving efficiency of the Coast Guard service is attested by the following statement,

The Airman Serves 521

made by Lieutenant Commander Stephen S. Yeandle, aide to Commander F. C. Billard.

The record for the year 1926 in the primary function of the Coast Guard — the preservation of life and property from the perils of the sea — continues to show, most gratifyingly, that the law-enforcement work in connection with the prevention of the smuggling of liquor into the United States from the sea, also calling heavily and increasingly on the service forces, has in nowise been permitted to intrench upon, break down, impede, nor diminish what is undoubtedly the highest form of service it is the duty of the Coast Guard to perform.

Commander Yeandle's statement is backed up by the annual report of the United States Coast Guard, which shows that last year alone 3037 persons were rescued from peril — a higher number than any year since the organization of the present service in 1915.

There were some 4831 instances of assistance rendered during the year; 2240 of these cases involved saving of life or property or both — termed major assistance. The remainder of this stupendous figure represented such services as warning vessels standing into danger; furnishing food, fuel, and water to vessels in distress; succoring the shipwrecked; rendering medical and surgical aid to the sick and injured; assisting at neighborhood fires, and fires occurring at buildings, wharves, and other structures on the shore line; fighting forest fires; assisting at floods and other calamitous visitations; dragging the waters for bodies; burial of bodies cast up by the sea; sheltering wayfarers overtaken by storm or other misfortune; preventing theft and invasion by those maliciously inclined; protecting wrecked property; acting as pilots in cases of emergency; coöperating in the enforcement of the Federal laws; etc.

After bringing in the unfortunate who has floundered in the waters, the duties of the Coast Guard are by no means

522 *Romance of the Airman*

at an end. Frequently the life-saving crews are called upon to undertake the restoration of persons taken from the water in a helpless or an unconscious condition. Out of fifty-six cases of resuscitation attempted by the service crews during the year, twenty-five were successful, the persons being restored to consciousness; and of these twenty-five, at least five were apparently dead when they were taken in charge by the crews from the life-saving stations.

The station crew of the Coast Guard is divided into regular watches of two men each, who, during the hours from sunset to sunrise, patrol the beach, keeping a sharp lookout seaward at all times. The schedule of watch is: first watch, sunset to 8 P.M.; second watch, 8 P.M. to midnight; third watch, midnight to 4 A.M.; fourth watch, 4 A.M. to sunrise. While the patrolman is out, his watch-mate takes the station watch, which is kept in the tower or on the beach abreast of the station, as conditions may require. If the station is connected with the service telephone line, the station watchman makes it his business to be within hearing distance of the bell at regular intervals. In addition to keeping watch seaward, he is on the lookout for signals and telephone calls from the patrolman.

Each patrolman carries a number of red Coston signals with which to warn a vessel standing too close inshore or to notify a vessel in distress that he has gone to summon assistance.

A quite complete system of communication has aided greatly in the work of the Coast Guard. With radio at their service, it is now possible for ships in distress to inform shore stations of their plight; and by means of radio and wire telegraph systems on land, the nearest life-saving station to the scene of the disaster can be reached. These fast means of communication have robbed the hungry ocean of many of its terrors.

The Airman Serves   523

And the time has now arrived when the master of a disabled ship may look forward to assistance and rescue by means of a life line thrown from that messenger of progress and annihilator of distance — the airplane.

Words and Phrases

To understand this selection

old tar: a slang term for *sailor*.
breeches buoy: a life-saving device consisting of a rubber belt, filled with air, to which is attached a support resembling a pair of trousers (breeches).

To add to your vocabulary

projectile   knots   taut

Technical term

amphibian

Informal Test (Completion) [1]

1. There are more than _____ life-saving stations maintained on the coasts of the Atlantic Ocean and the Gulf of Mexico.

2. Detection of rum-smugglers is a duty assigned to the _____ _____ of the United States.

3. The First Deficiency Act of 1926 authorized the Coast Guard _____.

4. On the basis of the annual report of the United States Coast Guard for 1926, approximately _____ lives are saved annually.

5. Four types of minor assistance rendered by the Coast Guard are
   a. _____
   b. _____
   c. _____
   d. _____

6. The station crew of the Coast Guard is divided into _____ regular watches of _____ men each.

[1] For directions, see page 14.

524 · *Romance of the Airman*

Exercises and Topics related to your Other Subjects

1. Consult an encyclopedia for a complete description and picture of the breeches buoy.

2. Read from your books on civics about the work of the Treasury Department.

3. According to this selection, life-saving stations have been maintained for about a hundred years. Look up in your historical readings the exact time that this work was first sponsored by the United States government.

4. Read the story of Grace Darling and the rescue of passengers on the *Forfarshire*. Compare the methods used at that time (1838) with the methods used today.

Other Readings

From other sources

"Two Years before the Mast," by Richard H. Dana.
"When Lighthouses are Dark," by Ethel C. Brill.

Alaska's Flying Gold Hunters

JAMES M. NELSON

> *Explanatory Note.* The Alaskan Geological Survey Expedition of the United States government returned in December, 1927. More than two thousand square miles of Alaskan and adjacent territory had been mapped. A new river, with a drainage basin of eleven hundred square miles and a current of fifteen miles an hour, was discovered and named Chatkachatna; a large lake, the source of the river, was discovered and named Chakachamna.
>
> Heretofore the chief industries of Alaska have been mining and fishing, but recently the wood-pulp industry has shown very promising developments. The engineers of the Department of Agriculture have estimated that the forests of Alaska may supply 1,300,000 tons of newsprint annually, and that there is an ample water supply available for the development of power projects. Already huge plants representing investments of millions of dollars are being built in the vicinity of Juneau and Ketchikan.

FOR more than two months the ancient quiet of mighty forests in southeastern Alaska has been disturbed by the roar of four amphibian planes systematically criss-crossing thousands of square miles in that district. High above precipitous crags, expert aërial photographers have been recording the secrets of a coastal region so rugged as to make mapping by ground methods almost impossible.

With the airplane tender * *Gannet* and a 140-foot barge as a base, the planes have spent weeks taking pictures of little patches of land which, when pieced together by the Geological Survey at Washington, will result in the first really accurate maps of the region.

The expedition, known as the Alaskan Aërial Survey Detachment, is continuing work begun in the summer of 1926, when three navy planes took some 17,000 photographs of 10,000 square miles of territory. Patching those photographs together like a gigantic cut-out puzzle, government

Navy Mapping Planes over Twin Glacier Lakes, near Juneau, Alaska

Official photograph, United States navy

draftsmen constructed a map that has contributed greatly to our knowledge of the "Panhandle," as the region is known. Information obtained at the time also proved of great value to the Forest Service in pointing out distribution and extent of forests and available water power. It is said that the survey of 1926 advanced the wood-pulp industry in southeastern Alaska by several years.

For nearly thirty years the Geological Survey has carried on topographic mapping* in Alaska; yet in that time less than half its vast area has been covered. The two aërial

The Airman Serves 527

expeditions have accomplished in half a dozen months what otherwise would have taken many years of laborious effort.

Surveying an extensive area from the air requires a systematic plan for taking the photographs and matching them together into a complete, unbroken photographic map. Elaborate flight charts are prepared in advance, showing the parallel lanes to be traversed by the planes. An altitude of 10,000 feet was adopted in the Alaskan surveys, giving the photographs a scale of one inch to 1666 feet on the ground. In recording each small division of territory three photographs are taken simultaneously: one straight down, one at an angle to the left, and one at an angle to the right. Each set of three represents an area of about eleven square miles. Proper·timing between exposures allows for an overlapping of the photographs — 60 per cent in the direction of flight and 25 per cent to the sides, giving plenty of landmarks to aid the mapmakers in combining the many photographs.

Each plane's crew consists of a navigator, pilot, and photographer. The pilot's job is to keep his plane on the designated flight lane, at the proper altitude, and on an even keel. The navigator keeps a constant check on the pilot, signaling directions to him by means of electric lights set in a panel. The camera alone occupies the photographer's attention.

The present expedition has been photographing the islands of Kuiu, Chichagof, and Baranof, as well as several thousands of square miles on the mainland.

Map-making is only one of a dozen services the airplane is performing in Alaska, all developed since 1920. In the summer of that year Captain St. Clair Street led a band of United States army flyers on an epoch-making flight from New York to Nome, Alaska, blazing an air

528 *Romance of the Airman*

trail over trackless wildernesses. Soon afterwards business men of Alaska purchased a plane to see if commercial flying would prove practical there. They selected as pilot Carl Ben Eielson, a young high-school science teacher at Fairbanks, Alaska, and former war flyer. It was this same Eielson who piloted Sir George Hubert Wilkins on the first flight across the Arctic ice from Point Barrow, Alaska, to Spitsbergen.

Eielson's pioneer commercial flying was so successful, and interest in aviation grew so rapidly, that today a network of airways spreads across the country. Fifty-seven airports are maintained in summer, and with skis on planes in winter any smooth stretch of snow or ice becomes a landing field.

Nine planes in Fairbanks maintain regular service to remote points of the territory. One aviation company there is headed by Noel Wien, who not long ago completed a hazardous 2300-mile flight to Cape North, Siberia, and return, the first round-trip flight between the Western Hemisphere and Asia. Carrying half a ton of food supplies for a fur-trading ship caught in the ice off the coast of Siberia, Wien returned to Fairbanks four days later with $150,000 worth of white-fox furs which otherwise would have remained on shipboard until the ice broke up.

So successful was this flight that fur-trading companies are considering further flights to Siberia to bring back sable and squirrel pelts. The Soviet government also is negotiating with Wien to carry provisions to Wrangell Island,* where a group of colonists have been isolated for three years. Thirty men and two women were last reported on the island.

Throughout Alaska and Canada prospectors and mining companies have been quick to take to the air. Maintaining base camps in cities or towns, they fly to their diggings,

The Airman Serves 529

completing in a few hours journeys that would take dog teams several days. The Canadian Department of Civil Aviation estimates that planes flew 630,000 miles over the Northland in mining transportation and exploration last year without a casualty. In that same period at least forty-two prospectors, using old-time methods of transportation, lost their lives.

One large Canadian company engaged in aërial explorations for minerals maintains three big camps in the North, each stocked with food for two years, and twenty-six bases where gasoline and oil are cached. Some individual prospectors fly their own planes. Many free-lance flyers carry passengers and freight to all parts of the Northland. Some of the sealing ships carry along planes to do their scouting. Until recently a lookout from the masthead was the only means of sighting seals, and whole herds often were overlooked.

One of the greatest services the airplane is performing is that of bringing the outside world to communities hitherto isolated from civilization. Regular arrivals of fresh food and news of the day have given the prospector a new life. The drone of the airplane motor means something far more important, too, because in all interior Alaska there are no physicians except at Fairbanks. From this center planes carry serums and medicine to far-off communities, or return with prospectors requiring hospital attention.

The airport at Fairbanks is the finest in the territory. It has two runways, each more than two thousand feet long and four hundred feet wide. It is the only illuminated airport in Alaska. The government recently established a weather bureau in that city, adding greatly to flying safety. Previously pilots had been forced to rely on private advices of Army Signal Corps observers scattered about the territory.

530 *Romance of the Airman*

Words and Phrases

To aid in understanding this selection

airplane tender: an ocean vessel used as a base of operation by airplanes.

topographic mapping: mapping the natural features of a region.

Wrangell Island: Stefansson raised the British flag on this island and claimed it for Great Britain in 1921. In 1924 the Russian Soviet government ousted Stefansson's party and took possession of the island.

To add to your vocabulary

precipitous	casualty
aërial photographer	cached
pelts	

Technical term

amphibian plane

Informal Test (Completion)[1]

1. There were _ _ _ _ _ _ amphibian planes.

2. The mapping told of here is of the region known as _ _ _ _ _ _.

3. The Geological Survey has been making topographical maps of Alaska for _ _ _ _ _ _ years.

4. The two aërial expeditions have worked _ _ _ _ _ _ months.

5. The photographs are made from an altitude of _ _ _ _ _ _ feet.

6. For each division of territory _ _ _ _ _ _ simultaneous photographs are taken.

7. Each plane's crew consists of _ _ _ _ _ _.

8. The number of airports maintained during the summer is _ _ _ _ _ _.

9. Fairbanks has _ _ _ _ _ _ planes in regular service to remote sections of Alaska.

[1] For directions, see page 14.

The Airman Serves 531

10. By old-time methods of transportation _____ prospectors lost their lives last year.

11. The finest airport of Alaska is at _____.

12. The government weather bureau for Alaska is located at _____.

Exercises and Topics related to your Other Subjects

On a recent map of Alaska locate the "Panhandle"; the islands of Kuiu, Chichagof, Baranof, and Wrangell; Chatkachatna River and Chakachamna Lake; the cities of Fairbanks, Juneau, and Ketchikan.

Subjects for oral themes

The Industrial Future of Alaska.

Alaska as a Playground.

Explain the use of a scale of miles in map-making.

Other Readings

From other sources

"Wilderness," by Rockwell Kent.

"The Call of the Wild," by Jack London.

"The Young Alaskans," by Emerson Hough.

Aviation's Varied Uses in Business

P. G. JOHNSON

> **Explanatory Note.** Twenty years ago Rudyard Kipling made the following prophecy: "The time is near when men will receive their normal impressions of a new country suddenly and in plan, not slowly and in perspective; when the most extreme distances will be brought within the compass of one week's — one hundred and sixty-eight hours' — travel, when the word *inaccessible*, as applied to any given spot on the surface of the globe, will cease to have any meaning."
>
> This selection shows the extent to which this prophecy has been fulfilled.

THE airplane is no longer an experimental, once-in-a-while, spectacular vehicle. Its career lies ahead of it, while other forms of transportation have approached their maximum speed and lowest operating costs. Experiences of our own company in selling planes to corporations and individuals for business use, and of our transportation system in interesting business men to travel on and use the regularly scheduled ships, are typical of the story of factories and air-transport companies over the country.

Some specific cases should prove interesting, and at the same time indicate a definite trend. From them other businesses and other business men may get an idea as to how this new business tool can be adapted to their needs — and as to how it may influence their regular, everyday operations.

Oil companies were among the early purchasers of planes to transport executives between headquarters, branch offices, and oil fields, and their planes range from single-engined cabin jobs to multi-motored transports. One executive has a plane with sleeping accommodations, buffet, dictaphone, and all the conveniences of his office.

Colonel E. A. Deeds, a director in a New York City bank,

The Airman Serves 533

maintains a flying field at his home in Dayton and flies in his tri-motored plane wherever his business takes him.

A candy company has a fleet of planes used for transporting salesmen and, incidentally, to entertain customers.

Newspapers are purchasing planes to obtain wider distribution and to cover important news events. The *Des Moines Register* and *Tribune-Capital* call their plane *Good News*, a name selected out of six thousand suggestions received. In six months it was flown thirty thousand miles and is now considered indispensable. Newspapers find the airplane a splendid aid in showing prospective national advertisers or their agents the extent of a trading area. One ship is equipped with maps and charts to facilitate this function.

M. C. Meigs, publisher of the *Chicago Herald-Examiner*, is not only a frequent traveler on established air lines, but flies his own "ship." He was active in forming one of the first local transport companies in Chicago, which has served scores of businesses and scores of business needs. The *Los Angeles Times* flies its papers to the San Francisco Bay district after midnight. The *Wall Street Journal* gets papers to financial houses in Chicago's "Loop" at the same hour New York bankers are reading the morning edition in Wall Street.

One motor-car company has been operating a multi-motored cargo plane between Buffalo and Detroit on a schedule as regular as a train, and has found that it has saved its cost of operation by rushing replenishments of parts, the lack of which would have tied up certain production, entailing large loss of pay roll and interfering with production schedules.

If you want aërial advertising — another business ramification of this new industry — you can take your choice between sky-writing at so much a letter; aërial broadcasting, where your message booms out from a plane with

534   *Romance of the Airman*

charges fixed on the basis of population within hearing distance of the aërial broadcaster; or a plane with illuminated letters on the wings, which advertise your favorite cigar or gasoline — or what you have.

Versatility of air-transport craft is shown by the log of a tri-motored plane which recently completed half a million miles in the air. Its varied cargo had included two baby grand pianos and six passengers. It was used as a studio for the first successful radio broadcasting from the air, and later as the original flying cigar store. It also acted the part of a German bomber in the movies.

Nothing has been said of the part played by aviation in the campaigns of both national parties. The radio gets the laurels. However, the ability of an air-mail company to move a broadcasting device from Chicago to Oklahoma saved the day for the Republican National Committee, which had paid $20,000 for a broadcast by Senator Borah.

Even the farmer finds air transport a valuable ally. When California honey-producers found themselves with a surplus, they used the air mail for a sales campaign and sold the excess in three weeks. Like carrying coals to Newcastle,* they disposed of a considerable amount in Ohio and certain other Eastern honey-producing states.

In Nebraska five hundred farmers assisted by an airplane and three aviators, who directed the affair, had a successful wolf hunt to rid the countryside of animals that had been raiding farms.

California citrus-growers use air mail to send manifests East instead of wiring them, as in the past. Apple-shippers in the Rogue River Valley boost the Medford, Oregon, post-office air-mail receipts substantially in the summer months, when selling orders, bills of lading,* car-tracers, orders for supplies, and other seasonal requirements demand speedy handling.

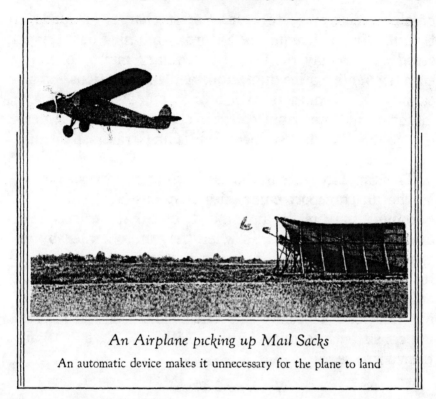

An Airplane picking up Mail Sacks
An automatic device makes it unnecessary for the plane to land

An outbreak of anthrax in the Klamath Country was halted by air express. Cattlemen were losing fifteen head a day, and prices were averaging $150 a head. This loss was stopped as soon as vaccine was rushed from California by Pacific Air Transport.

A thousand-acre field in Coos County, Oregon, was successfully seeded from the air at a third of the expense of hand-seeding, and an excellent stand of grass obtained. The experiment was so successful that large areas on the Pacific coast will be similarly planted this year.

Air-mail companies report various firms using air mail for handling of all correspondence between offices where a saving in time can be made over train mail; announcements of new products; soliciting new accounts; in place

536 *Romance of the Airman*

of night telegrams; to save interest charges on funds in transit; for mail requiring Saturday-morning delivery instead of Monday delivery by ordinary mail; collecting slow accounts; price quotations and specifications; maintaining closer contacts with branch offices and salesmen; all forms and important communications to agencies, dealers, jobbers, and customers, and filing tracers by traffic departments.

This rapid increase in the use of air transport has proved to the air-transport companies that business is not only becoming universally air-minded, but that business men are ready to use airplanes when they are operated by responsible companies with equipment of the type and quality required, and when proper educational methods are employed to acquaint the public with the advantages of air transport. Not only this, but business men themselves are consistently coming forward with new ideas as to air-transport use.

Words and Phrases

To aid in understanding this selection

"**carrying coals to Newcastle**": making offerings to those who have an abundance of the thing offered. The proverbial expression alludes to the city of Newcastle upon Tyne, England, which has a great quantity of coal supplied to it from the mines along the banks of the Tyne.

bills of lading: written receipts given by a carrier for goods delivered to him for transportation.

To add to your vocabulary

facilitate	citrus	tri-motored

Technical term

log

The Airman Serves 537

Informal Test (True-False)[1]

1. The airplane as a practical means of transportation is still in the experimental stage.

2. The *Good News* is a plane owned by a Mid-Western newspaper.

3. Farmers cannot make use of the airplane.

4. Freight is never carried by airplane.

5. Business men are becoming air-minded.

Exercises and Topics related to your Other Subjects

1. Clip from the daily paper accounts of the uses of airplanes. Classify these according to the type of enterprise; as, news-distributing, use on the farm, salesmanship, air mail, etc.

2. Find, from magazine material, statements concerning the motives for such flights as the trip of the *Graf Zeppelin* round the world.

3. Write a prophecy of conditions twenty years hence similar to that made by Rudyard Kipling twenty years ago.

4. Lindbergh says that it is entirely possible and will probably be true that business men will live one hundred or two hundred miles away from their work and, by use of the airplane, will go to their offices as easily as they now cover twenty miles in an automobile. State what possible changes will accompany such conditions.

Other Readings

In this book

"Argosies of the Air," page 97.

[1] For directions, see page 54.

Chronology of Aviation

YEAR   EVENT

1783 The first balloon flight. Made by the Montgolfier brothers, of France, with animals as passengers. See "The Montgolfier Brothers, Inventors of the Balloon," page 170, and "The First Flyers," page 181.

1891–1896 The first successful gliders. Otto Lilienthal made over one thousand flights in gliders. Read "Otto Lilienthal, Inspirer of the Wright Brothers," page 124.

1903 The Wright brothers' first flight at Kitty Hawk, North Carolina. This was the first heavier-than-air machine to stay aloft. Read "The Wright Brothers, the First Successful Flyers," page 185, and "The Experiments of a Flying Man," page 197.

1909 Bleriot flew the English Channel, covering 25 miles in 40 minutes. Read "Bleriot crosses the English Channel," page 257.

1919 The first nonstop transatlantic flight. Captain Sir John Alcock and Lieutenant Sir Arthur Brown of England flew from Newfoundland to Ireland, a distance of 1960 miles, in $16\frac{1}{2}$ hours. Read "Crossing the Atlantic," page 299.

1924 The first round-the-world flight. Made by three United States army planes, which completed 27,500 miles in 375 flying hours.

1926 The flight to the North Pole. Made by Commander Richard Evelyn Byrd and Floyd Bennett, who started from King's Bay, Spitsbergen, and covered 1300 miles in 15 hours. Read "Byrd's Flight to the North Pole," page 275, and "Floyd Bennett, Martyr of the Air," page 422.

1927 The first New York-to-Paris flight. Made by Charles A. Lindbergh, who flew alone, covering 3610 miles in $33\frac{1}{2}$ hours. Read "Columbus of the Air," page 391.

540 *Romance of the Airman*

YEAR   EVENT

1928 The first east-to-west flight across the Pacific. Made by
Captain Charles Kingsford-Smith and three others, with
stops at Honolulu and the Fiji Islands. The distance
covered was 7400 miles, in 83 hours and 15 minutes.
Read "The *Southern Cross* visits the Fiji Islands,"
page 338.

1929 The first refueling in mid-air. Made by the *Question Mark*.
Read "Some Historic Aircraft," page 442.

1929 The first round-the-world flight in a dirigible. Made in
the *Graf Zeppelin*, which traveled eastward from Lakehurst, New Jersey, and again arrived at Lakehurst in
21 days, 7 hours, and 25 minutes. Read "The First
Dirigible to circumnavigate the Globe," page 381.

1930 Richard E. Byrd's Antarctic expedition returned from the
most extensive expedition of discovery and surveying
of new territory ever recorded. Read "Preparation for
the Antarctic Expedition," page 352.

Glossary

This glossary is made up of technical and semi-technical terms that are found in the selections of this book. The definitions of the technical terms have been taken largely from Report No. 240 of the National Advisory Committee for Aëronautics, United States Department of Commerce, entitled "Nomenclature for Aëronautics," and simplified for the junior-high-school pupil. The report of the National Advisory Committee for Aëronautics, published in 1928 by the United States Government Printing Office, Washington, D.C., should be used as the authentic source of correct terminology. The definitions of the semi-technical terms are taken from the New Century Dictionary, copyrighted 1927.

aërial: of or in the air.
aërodrome: a hangar.

> NOTE. Alexander Graham Bell applied this term to the flying machine.

aërodynamics: that branch of dynamics which treats of the motion of air.
aërologist: one who knows the science of the air.
aëronaut: one who travels in the air.
aëronautical: pertaining to aëronautics.
aëronautics: the science and art of the flight of aircraft.
aërostat: a balloon or flying machine capable of floating in the air.
aërostatics: as an aëronautic term it relates to those properties of lighter-than-air craft which are due to the buoyancy of the air.
aërostation: the art of operating balloons or other lighter-than-air craft; distinguished from *aviation.*
aircraft: any weight-carrying device or structure designed to be supported by the air, either by buoyancy or by dynamic action.
airplane: a mechanically driven aircraft, heavier than air, fitted with wings and supported by the dynamic action of the air.
> **amphibian:** an airplane designed to rise from and alight on either land or water.
> **biplane:** an airplane with two main supporting surfaces, placed one above the other.

542   *Romance of the Airman*

flying boat: a form of seaplane which, when resting on the surface of the water, is supported by a hull or hulls providing flotation in addition to serving as fuselages. The term *boat seaplane* is now obsolete.

landplane: an airplane designed to rise from and alight on the land.

monoplane: an airplane which has but one main supporting surface, sometimes divided into two parts by the fuselage.

multiplane: an airplane with two or more main supporting surfaces, placed one above another.

pusher airplane: an airplane with the propeller or propellers in the rear of the main supporting surfaces.

quadruplane: an airplane with four main supporting surfaces, placed one above another.

seaplane: any airplane designed to rise from and alight on the water. This general term applies to both the boat and the float type, though the boat type is usually designated as a "flying boat."

ship-plane: a landplane designed to rise from and alight on the deck of a ship.

tandem airplane: an airplane with two or more sets of wings of substantially the same area (not including the tail unit), placed one in front of the other and on about the same level.

tractor airplane: an airplane with the propeller or propellers forward of the main supporting surfaces.

triplane: an airplane with three main supporting surfaces, placed one above another.

airport: a locality, either of water or land, which is adapted for the landing and taking off of aircraft and which provides facilities for the shelter, supply, and repair of aircraft; or a place used regularly for receiving or discharging passengers or cargo by air.

airship: a flying machine provided with a propelling system and with means of controlling the direction of motion. When its power plant is not operating, it acts like a free balloon. The term *airship* is sometimes incorrectly applied to heavier-than-air craft, either in full or as *ship*, which is a slang use of the word and should be avoided.

Glossary 543

non-rigid airship: an airship whose form is maintained by the internal pressure in the gas bags and ballonets.

rigid airship: an airship whose form is maintained by a rigid structure.

semi-rigid airship: an airship whose form is maintained by means of a rigid or jointed keel in conjunction with internal pressure in the gas containers and ballonets.

air-speed indicator: an instrument for indicating the speed of an aircraft relative to the air. It is actuated by the pressure developed in a suitable pressure nozzle or against a suitable obstruction and is graduated to give true air speed at a standard air density. The speed indicated by the instrument is termed the "indicated air speed." (The indicated speed is a direct measure of the lift or drag exerted on the airplane at any altitude. Stalling at all altitudes occurs for the same value of the indicated speed.)

altigraph: an altimeter equipped with a recording mechanism; a barograph whose scale is designed to read heights.

altimeter: an instrument for measuring or indicating the elevation of an aircraft.

amphibian: an airplane designed to rise from and alight on either land or water.

angle, wing–dihedral or **dihedral:** the acute angle between the transverse reference line in the wing surface and the lateral axis of the airplane projected on a plane perpendicular to the longitudinal axis.

aperture: an opening in a telescope; the diameter of the exposed part of the object-glass.

ballast: heavy material carried by a ship to give it steadiness.

ballonet: a compartment, constructed of fabric, within the interior of a balloon or airship.

balloon: an aërostat without a propelling system.

barrage balloon: a small captive balloon used to support wires or nets which are intended as a protection against attacks by aircraft.

captive balloon: a balloon restrained from free flight by means of a cable attaching it to the earth.

544 *Romance of the Airman*

constant-pressure balloon: a supply balloon arranged to maintain a constant pressure of gas in a moored or docked aërostat.

free balloon: a balloon, usually spherical, whose ascent and descent may be controlled by use of ballast or with a loss of the contained gas, and whose direction of flight is determined by the wind.

kite balloon: an elongated form of captive balloon, fitted with lobes to keep it headed into the wind and usually deriving increased lift owing to its axis being inclined to the wind.

observation balloon: a captive balloon used to provide an elevated observation post.

barograph: an instrument for recording the barometric, or static, pressure of the atmosphere.

basket: the structure suspended beneath a balloon, for carrying passengers, ballast, etc.

biplane: an airplane with two main supporting surfaces, placed one above the other.

blimp: a small non-rigid airship. *Airship* is to be preferred.

blind-flying: flying without accurate knowledge of position or direction, owing to atmospheric conditions.

bump: a rapidly rising current of air which, when encountered by an airplane, gives it a jolt or upward thrust.

buoyancy: the upward air force on an aërostat, derived from aërostatic conditions. It is equal to the weight of the air displaced.

Bygrave slide rule: a device used in engineering for rapid calculation.

camber: the convexity of a plane.

car: that portion of an airship which is intended to carry the power unit or units, the personnel, cargo, or equipment.

ceiling, absolute: the maximum height above sea level at which a given airplane would be able to maintain horizontal flight, assuming standard air conditions.

chock: a metal casting through which a cable passes.

chronometer: any instrument for measuring time.

cockpit: an open space in which the pilot and passengers are seated. When the cockpit is completely housed in, it is called a cabin.

Glossary 545

compass, induction: a compass the indications of which depend on the current generated in a coil revolving in the earth's magnetic field.

compass, magnetic: an instrument for determining directions, consisting essentially of a freely moving magnetized needle which points to the magnetic North or South.

control stick: the vertical lever by means of which the longitudinal and lateral controls of an airplane are operated. Pitching is controlled by a fore-and-aft movement of the stick; rolling, by a side-to-side movement.

controls: a general term applied to the means provided to enable the pilot to control the speed, direction of flight, altitude, and power of an aircraft.

    air controls: the means employed to operate the control surfaces of the aircraft.

    engine controls: the means employed to control the power output of the engines.

cord: see **rip cord.**

dead reckoning: the calculation of the position of a craft without the use of instruments, as in flying in a storm or heavy fog.

detonator: something that explodes, or causes another substance to explode.

dirigible: that which can be directed; as, a dirigible balloon.

drift: the lateral velocity of an aircraft due to air currents.

drift-indicator: an instrument for measuring the deviation of an aircraft from a set course.

duralumin: an alloy of aluminum and other metals which is much used in aëronautics, especially for the structure of airships and airplanes.

dynamic factor: the ratio between the load carried by any part of an aircraft when accelerating and the corresponding basic load (that is, the load carried in normal flight).

endurance: the maximum length of time an aircraft can remain in the air at a given speed and altitude.

float: a completely inclosed water-tight structure attached to an aircraft in order to give it buoyancy and stability when in contact with the surface of the water.

546 *Romance of the Airman*

fuselage: the structure, of approximately streamline form, to which are attached the wings and tail unit of an airplane. In general it contains the power plant, passengers, cargo, etc.

glide: a descent with reference to the air at a normal angle of attack and without engine power sufficient for level flight in still air, the propeller thrust being replaced by a component of gravity along the line of flight. Used also as a verb.

gondola: the car of an airship. This use of the word is borrowed from the Italian, through the German. *Car* is to be preferred.

hangar: a shelter for housing aircraft. More properly applied to heavier-than-air craft.

helicopter: a form of aircraft whose sole support in the air is derived directly from the vertical component of the thrust produced by rotating airfoils.

inclinometer: an instrument for indicating the attitude of an aircraft. Inclinometers are termed fore-and-aft, lateral, or universal, according as they indicate inclination in the vertical plane through the fore-and-aft axis or in the vertical plane through the lateral axis, or in both planes, respectively.

keel: the assembly of members at the bottom of the hull of a semi-rigid or rigid airship which provides special strength to resist sagging and also serves to distribute the effect of concentrated loads along the hull.

kilo: short form for *kilogram*. A kilogram equals 2.2 pounds.

kilometer: a measure of length equal to 3280.8 feet.

kite: an aircraft heavier than air, restrained by a towline and sustained by the relative wind.

landing crew: a detail of men necessary for the landing and handling of an airship on the ground; a "ground crew."

landing gear: the understructure which supports the weight of an aircraft when in contact with the surface of the land or water.

leeward: toward the region in whose direction the wind is blowing.

leg: one of the distinct portions, or stages, of any course.

lift: that component of the total air force on an aircraft or airfoil which is perpendicular to the relative wind and in the plane of symmetry. It must be specified whether this applies to a

Glossary   547

complete aircraft or to parts thereof. In the case of an airship this is often called *dynamic lift*. Its symbol is *L*.

lodestone: a variety of magnetite possessing magnetic polarity.

log: a record of the events of a journey.

magnetic compass: see compass.

monoplane: an airplane which has but one main supporting surface, sometimes divided into two parts by the fuselage.

neon lights: lights using a gaseous element occurring in the earth's atmosphere.

permeability: the measure of the rate of diffusion of gas through intact balloon fabric; ordinarily expressed in liters of hydrogen per square meter of fabric per twenty-four hours, under standard conditions of pressure and temperature.

pontoon: a float.

propeller, adjustable-pitch: a propeller whose blades are so attached to the hub that they may be set to any desired pitch when the propeller is stationary.

propeller, controllable-pitch or variable-pitch: a propeller whose blades are so mounted that they may be turned about their axis to any desired pitch while the propeller is in rotation.

quadrant: the operating lever, made on the arc of a circle, of a control surface of an airship; for example, rudder quadrant, elevator quadrant.

rate of climb: the vertical component of the air speed of an aircraft; that is, its vertical velocity with reference to the air.

rip cord: the rope running from the rip panel to the car or basket. The pulling of this rope tears off or rips the rip panel and causes immediate deflation.

rudder: a device for steering an airplane.

runway: a track along which a plane or ship moves into its hangar.

semaphoring: sending messages by means of signals.

sextant: an astronomical instrument used in measuring the sun's altitude in determining latitude and longitude.

skid: a runner used as a member of the landing gear and designed to aid the aircraft in landing or taxiing.

548 *Romance of the Airman*

soupape: probably refers to nitroglycerin soup and is the slang term for this explosive.

spiral: a maneuver in which an airplane descends in a helix of small pitch and large radius, the angle of attack being within the normal range of flight angles.

stabilizer: a normally fixed airfoil whose function is to lessen the pitching motion. It is usually located at the rear of an aircraft and is approximately parallel to the plane of the longitudinal and lateral axes. Also called *tail plane.*

stall: the condition of an airplane when, from any cause, it has lost the air speed necessary for support or control.

station, airship: the complete assembly of sheds, masts, gas plants, shops, landing fields, and related equipment required to operate airships and supply their needs. (A station may include all or a part of the items enumerated.) The base from which airships are operated.

strut: a compression member of a truss frame. For instance, the vertical members of the wing truss of a biplane (interplane struts) and the short vertical and horizontal members separating the longérons in the fuselage.

tail-skid: see **skid.**

taxi: to run an airplane over the ground, or a seaplane on the surface of water, under its own power.

triangulation: a small captive balloon used as a mark in making a survey. Refers also to the determination of height trigonometrically.

triplane: an airplane with three main supporting surfaces, placed one above another.

visibility: capability of being seen.

winch: the rigging by means of which the lift and drag of a kite balloon are transmitted from the envelope to the towing, or traction, cable.

wing-dihedral angle: see **angle, wing-dihedral** or **dihedral.**

wing span: the distance from wing tip to wing tip.

zoom: a term used to denote any sudden increase in the upward slope of the flight path.

Classified List of Related Topics

The exercises given at the close of the selections are here re-arranged by subjects for ready reference; they are for use by teachers in various departments in unifying the work.

Literature

PAGE

Compare Irving's description of the Dutch in "Knicker-bocker's History of New York" with Poe's description of the Dutch in Rotterdam — 70

Compare Clayton's description of "absolute silence" in the balloon with Irving's description of "one of the quietest places in the world" in the "Legend of Sleepy Hollow" — 249

Compare Percy Bysshe Shelley's description of daybreak as found in his poem "The Boat on the Serchio" with the description of dawn by Clayton — 249

Read examples from Kipling's "With the Night Mail" that show the influence of Poe — 70

Compare Jules Verne's imaginary story of the natives' conception of the balloon with Kingsford-Smith's true story of the natives' conception of the *Southern Cross* — 344

Compare Mark Twain's and Jules Verne's imaginary flights across Africa with Lady Heath's flight — 351

Tell how Irving happened to write "The Alhambra" — 55

Compare the spirit of the mail pilots with that of the messengers in Browning's "How they brought the Good News from Ghent to Aix" — 489

Read to the class Tom Sawyer's explanation of the meaning of the word *welkin* (See "Tom Sawyer Abroad," Chapter V) — 184

Bring to the class selections from Kipling's "With the Night Mail" that present incidents which might actually happen today — 407

Subjects for oral themes

Short biographies of

Washington Irving — 55

Edgar Allan Poe — 70

550 *Romance of the Airman*

	PAGE
Jules Verne	82
Robert Louis Stevenson	344
Alfred, Lord Tennyson	98
Charles Algernon Swinburne	274
Report on the Newbery Prize Medal for Juvenile Literature	169
Report on President Eliot's "Five-Foot Shelf"	372

Geography

Africa

Trace Lady Heath's voyage across Africa	350
Name the British East African territories and locate the other British possessions in Africa	350
To what governments did Lady Heath refer in her suggestion for their coöperation in providing radio instructions for flyers in Central Africa?	350
Read about Stanley's and Livingstone's explorations and write a theme on "Exploring Africa by Foot and by Plane"	351
Make a short report on the geography of the region around Lake Victoria Nyanza	82

North Polar Region

Make a map showing the polar expedition of Byrd	288

Locate

Dane's Island and Virgo Bay	256
Peary Land, the Magnetic Pole, Gray Hook	288
Cape Prince of Wales	298

Location by latitude and longitude

Andrée's location (82°. 2' north latitude; 15° 5' east longitude)	256
Amundsen and Ellsworth's landing (87° 44' north latitude; 10° 20' west longitude)	274
Nobile's location in Alaska (71° north latitude; between 157° and 158° west longitude)	298

Classified List of Related Topics 551

South Polar Region

	PAGE
Locate Dunedin, New Zealand; Bay of Whales; Mt. Erebus and Mt. Terror; Marie Byrd Land	371
On a map of Antarctica locate the discoveries and explorations made by Byrd's party	372

United States

| Write a theme giving an account of the country Lindbergh viewed on his flight from Washington, D.C., to Mexico | 464 |

Subjects for oral themes

| The National Cemetery at Arlington | 430 |
| What advantages has Kansas City for being an important airport in the United States? | 380 |

Europe

What reasons do you find in your geography why Le Bourget should become an important flying field?	379
Locate on a map of Europe the three flying fields named	380
On a map of Europe locate Bleriot's starting place and his landing place	261

Subject for theme

| The Zeppelin Works at Friedrichshafen, Germany | 306 |

South America, Mexico, and Central America

| Locate the cities visited by Lindbergh on his "good-will flight" | 464 |
| Locate Lima, Callao, Valparaiso, and the Falkland Islands | 146 |

Alaska

| Locate the "Panhandle" of Alaska; the islands of the "Panhandle" region; a recently discovered river and lake | 531 |

Subjects for themes

| The Industrial Future of Alaska | 531 |
| Alaska as a Playground | 531 |

552 *Romance of the Airman*

Miscellaneous

	PAGE
Mark on an outline map the location of places of departure and of landing, on both sides of the Atlantic, for all the transatlantic flights given in "Crossing the Atlantic"	306

Subjects for themes

The Fiji Islands	344
Brisbane, a Modern City	344
Why there were Indian Police in Suva	343
The Use of a Scale of Miles in Map-making	531

Social Sciences

Historical Characters and their Work

Subjects for brief oral themes

Alexander the Great	10
Charles V, Emperor of Germany	10
The Many-sided Franklin	153
Franklin, Editor and Author	153
Places in Philadelphia made Memorable by Franklin	154
Treaties between the United States and France negotiated by Franklin	154
Franklin's Thrift Maxims	154
The Story of the Invention of the Telephone	161
The Life of Alexander Graham Bell	161
The Important Work of John Coulter Bates, Morgan Lewis Smith, and Samuel B. M. Young	430

Pioneer Period in America

Subjects for themes

Carrying the Mail in Stagecoach Days	481
The Post from Horseback to Plane	491

Exploration

Subjects for themes

Comparison of what "Land!" meant to Columbus with what it meant to Nobile	298
The Voyages of the *Mayflower* and the *NC–4* Contrasted	306

Classified List of Related Topics   553

	PAGE
The Seven Years' War and the French and Indian Wars	146
Magellan's Voyage	388
Colonial Possessions of Portugal in 1700	134
Stanley discovers Livingstone	85
Stanley as an Explorer	85
Peary's Expedition to the North Pole	288
MacMillan's Polar Expeditions	288
Shackleton's Antarctic Expeditions	372
The Race between Amundsen and Scott for the South Pole	372

The Old World, Ancient and New

Consult a map of ancient Greece and locate the places mentioned in the selection from Ovid	14
Look up pictures of buildings of ancient Persia	49
Read about the invasion of Britain by Cæsar	261

Subjects for oral themes

Life in Rural Germany Today	325
Political and Economic Conditions in England in 1842	98
An Interesting Event which happened to Granada the Year that Columbus discovered America	55

Present-Day Topics

Subjects for oral themes

How Treaties between Nations are Made	154
The Reasons why Mexico distrusts the United States	464
The Political, Social, and Economic Results of Lindbergh's Visit to Mexico	464
The Briand-Kellogg Peace Pact	98
The Life-saving Work of the United States Government	524
The Work of the Treasury Department	524
The Smithsonian Institution	161
The Guggenheim Foundation	372
The Daniel Guggenheim Fund for the Promotion of Aëronautics	372
"Floating Islands" as Refueling Stations	407
How a Patent is secured from the Government	179

554   *Romance of the Airman*

General Science

	PAGE
Explain why the sun compass was for Byrd what the magnetic compass was for Columbus	288
When the reading of the thermometer is 11.5° centigrade, what would it be on the Fahrenheit scale?	274
In the account of "A Record-breaking Balloon Voyage," why was the thermometer whirled outside the balloon?	249
Make a report on the work of the Department of Agriculture for better tilling of the soil, better care and protection of crops during the growing-season, and better methods of harvesting and marketing crops	507
Report on the efforts to destroy the boll weevil	507
List the cotton-producing states in the order of the number of bales produced	507

In a sentence for each, give the important work of the following men:

Newton	123
James Watt	123
Harvey	123
Copernicus	123
Galileo	123

Why would throwing sandbags out make a balloon go higher?	249

Subjects for oral themes

The Uses of Paper	179
How the Blowpipe controlled the Balloon	82
The Uses of Monel Metal	372
The Advantages and Disadvantages of Duralumin	453

Mathematics

Problems in Longitude and Time

Byrd reached the pole at 9.04 A.M. on May 10, Greenwich time. What time was it by his mother's clock in Richmond, Virginia? What time was it at San Francisco?	288

Classified List of Related Topics 555

PAGE

Alcock and Brown landed at Clifden, Ireland, at 8.04 A.M., Greenwich time. What time was it by the clocks in Chicago? by the clocks in your town? 306

Metric System

Andrée's balloon was 600 meters high. How many feet was this? 256

Amundsen's plane flew at an altitude of 1000 meters. How many feet was this? 274

The diameter of the ice cake was 200 meters. How many feet was this? 274

Miscellaneous

Consult the market report and your grocer for prices of the different kinds of foods that Byrd took with him on his Antarctic expedition. Calculate the cost of the list of provisions given 372

An experiment: Blow up a football or a basket ball as full as possible. Weigh it carefully. Allow all the air to escape; then weigh it again. Calculate the weight of the air the ball held 180

Calculate the weight of a balloon, filled with air, the cubical content of which is the same as that of your schoolroom 180

How many miles would the machine go at the rate of 200 leagues a day? 134

Art

Bring to the class pictures of works of art representing Mercury, Perseus, Andromeda, Dædalus, Phaëthon, Pegasus, Neptune, Medusa 10

Subjects for themes

Leonardo da Vinci, the Artist 123

The Controversy over "La Belle Ferronnière" 123

556 *Romance of the Airman*

Guidance (Educational)

Latin

PAGE

The story of the wooden pigeon is told in a work entitled " Attic Nights," by Aulus Gellius.   **10**

Subject for theme

The Necessity for some Latin Students in Each Generation   **10**

The explanatory note on the translation of "Dædalus and Icarus," from Ovid's "Metamorphoses," points out that this great Latin work is often read by classes in Latin in high school and college   **11**

Modern Languages

Subject for theme

The Value of the Study of Foreign Languages   **325**

Guidance (Vocational)

Lindbergh flew alone, which proves that he was an expert pilot, a mechanic, and an aëronautical engineer. Other positions in the field of aviation are those of airport designer and constructor, radio operator, advertising and publicity man, salesman, airport ground man, factory man. The Department of Commerce, which licenses all trained men, says, "A recognized method of securing experience as an aëronautical engineer is to attend a college or university with a complete course in aëronautical engineering." What subjects in high school form the foundation for a course in aëronautical engineering? Ask your high-school principal to help you in making out a program of courses for you to follow in senior high school as a preparation for aviation as a career   **407**

Books listed in "Other Readings"

A B C of Aviation. *Victor W. Pagé.* Norman W. Henley Publishing Company.

Alexander Graham Bell. *Catherine MacKenzie.* Houghton Mifflin Company.

Alhambra, The. *Washington Irving.* Ginn and Company.

American Explorers, Stories of. *W. F. Gordy.* Charles Scribner's Sons.

Andrée's Balloon Expedition in Search of the North Pole. *Henri Lachambre* and *Alexis Machuron.* Frederick A. Stokes Company.

Arabian Nights' Entertainments, The. *M. A. L. Lane.* Ginn and Company.

Around the World in Eighty Days. *Jules Verne.* A. L. Burt Company.

Artificial and Natural Flight. *H. S. Maxim.* The Macmillan Company.

Autobiography. *Benjamin Franklin.* Ginn and Company.

Aviation. *A. E. Berriman.* Doubleday, Doran and Company, Inc.

Balloon Hoax, The. *Edgar Allan Poe.* Thomas Y. Crowell Company.

Benjamin Franklin. *S. G. Fischer.* J. B. Lippincott Company.

Benjamin Franklin. *Edward L. Dudley.* The Macmillan Company.

Big Aviation Book for Boys, The. *J. L. French.* McLoughlin Brothers.

Boys' Own Book of Great Inventions. *F. L. Darrow.* The Macmillan Company.

Boys' Trader Horn. *Kenneth P. Hempton.* Simon and Schuster, Inc.

Call of the Wild, The. *Jack London.* The Macmillan Company.

Classic Myths. *Charles M. Gayley.* Ginn and Company.

Conquering the Air. *Archibald Williams.* Thomas Nelson & Sons.

Conquest of the Air. *A. L. Rotch.* Moffatt, Yard & Company.

Famous Leaders of Industry. *E. Wildman.* The Page Publishing Company.

Five Weeks in a Balloon. *Jules Verne.* E. P. Dutton & Company.

Flight of the *Southern Cross,* The. *C. E. Kingsford-Smith* and *C. T. P. Ulm.* Robert M. McBride & Co.

Four Years in the White North. *D. B. MacMillan.* Medici Society of America, Inc.

From the Earth to the Moon. *Jules Verne.* Everyman's Library.

Girls who became Famous. *Sarah K. Bolton.* Thomas Y. Crowell Company.

Gulliver's Travels. *Jonathan Swift.* Ginn and Company.

Hans Pfaall. *Edgar Allan Poe.* Thomas Y. Crowell Company.

Heroes of the Air. *Chelsea C. Fraser.* Thomas Y. Crowell Company.

Heroes of the Farthest North and Farthest South. *J. Kennedy MacLean.* Thomas Y. Crowell Company.

Historic Airships. *R. S. Holland.* Macrea-Smith Company.

558 · *Romance of the Airman*

How I Found Livingstone. *Henry M. Stanley.* Charles Scribner's Sons.

Hunters of the Great North. *Vilhjalmur Stefansson.* Harcourt, Brace and Company.

Labrador: the Country and People. *Wilfred T. Grenfell.* The Macmillan Company.

Last Voyage of the *Karluk*, The. *R. A. Bartlett* and *R. T. Hale.* Small, Maynard & Company.

Log of the H. M. A. *R–34*, The. *E. M. Maitland.* Hodder and Stoughton.

Lone Scout of the Sky, The. *James E. West.* The John C. Winston Company.

Lost in the Jungle. *Paul B. Du Chaillu.* Harper & Brothers.

Man, the Miracle Maker. *Hendrik Van Loon.* Horace Liveright, Inc.

Marvels of Aviation. *C. C. Turner.* J. B. Lippincott Company.

Masters of Science and Invention. *F. L. Darrow.* Harcourt, Brace and Company.

Mechanical Investigations of Leonardo da Vinci. *Ivor B. Hart.* Chapman and Hall.

My Airships, a Story of my Life. *Alberto Santos-Dumont.* The Century Co.

My Kalulu. *Henry M. Stanley.* Charles Scribner's Sons.

My Life as an Explorer. *Roald Amundsen.* Doubleday, Doran and Company, Inc.

Oregon Trail, The. *Francis Parkman.* Ginn and Company.

Our Polar Flight. *Roald Amundsen* and *Lincoln Ellsworth.* Dodd, Mead & Company, Inc.

Record Flights. *Clarence Chamberlin.* Dorrance & Company, Inc.

Romance of Aëronautics, The. *C. C. Turner.* J. B. Lippincott Company.

Scott's Last Expedition. *R. F. Scott.* Dodd, Mead & Company, Inc.

Sky High. *E. Hodgins* and *F. A. Magoun.* Little, Brown & Company.

Skylarking. *Bruce Gould.* Horace Liveright, Inc.

Skyward. *Richard E. Byrd.* G. P. Putnam's Sons.

Story of the Bible. *Hendrik Van Loon.* Boni and Liveright.

Story of Henry M. Stanley. *V. Golding.* E. P. Dutton & Company.

Story of Mankind, The. *Hendrik Van Loon.* Boni and Liveright.

South. *Ernest Shackleton.* The Macmillan Company.

Tenderfoot with Peary, A. *George Borup.* Frederick A. Stokes Company.

Tom Sawyer Abroad. *Mark Twain.* Harper & Brothers.

Tragedy of the *Italia*, The. *Davide Giudici.* D. Appleton and Company.

20 Hrs. 40 Min. *Amelia Earhart.* G. P. Putnam's Sons.

Two Years before the Mast. *Richard Henry Dana.* E. P. Dutton & Company.

Uncle Sam, Wonder Worker. *W. A. DuPuy.* Frederick A. Stokes Company.

Voyage of the *Discovery*, The. *R. F. Scott.* Dodd, Mead & Company, Inc.

Books listed in "Other Readings"   559

We. *Charles A. Lindbergh.* G. P. Putnam's Sons.

When Lighthouses are Dark. *Ethel C. Brill.* Henry Holt and Company.

Wild Life under the Equator. *Paul B. Du Chaillu.* Harper & Brothers.

Wilderness. *Rockwell Kent.* G. P. Putnam's Sons.

Winning of the West. *Theodore Roosevelt.* G. P. Putnam's Sons.

With the Night Mail. *Rudyard Kipling.* Doubleday, Doran and Company, Inc.

Wonder Book, A. *Nathaniel Hawthorne.* Houghton Mifflin Company.

Wonderful Balloon Ascents. *F. Marion.* Charles Scribner's Sons.

Young Alaskans, The. *Emerson Hough.* Harper & Brothers.

Zeppelins and Super-Zeppelins. *R. P. Hearne.* John Lane, The Bodley Head Limited.

A List of Books, Periodicals, and Bulletins on Aviation

This list is made up of publications of interest to junior-high-school pupils and to teachers who wish to assist pupils in locating materials for classroom work and for leisure reading. The following specifications were set up as a guide in selecting these publications:

1. They should be up to date.
2. They should be complete and well balanced.
3. They should be technically correct, yet nontechnical in treatment.
4. They should avoid propaganda and sentimentality.
5. They should be well illustrated.

Aëroplane Photography. *Herbert E. Ives.* J. B. Lippincott Company.

Around the World in Twenty-eight Days. *Linton Wells.* Houghton Mifflin Company.

Aviation Chart. *Victor W. Pagé.* Norman W. Henley Publishing Company.

Book of the Sky, The. *M. Luckiesh.* E. P. Dutton & Company.

Boys' Book of Airmen, The. *Irving Crump.* Dodd, Mead & Company, Inc.

Boys' Book of Model Airplanes, The. *F. A. Collins.* The Century Co.

Building and Flying Model Aircraft. *Paul E. Garber.* Ronald Press Company.

European Skyways. *Lowell Thomas.* Houghton Mifflin Company.

Explorer in the Air Service, An. *Hiram Bingham.* Yale University Press.

First Crossing of the Polar Sea. *Roald Amundsen* and *Lincoln Ellsworth.* Doubleday, Doran and Company, Inc.

First World Flight, The. *Lowell Thomas.* Houghton Mifflin Company.

Flying the Arctic. *Sir G. H. Wilkins.* G. P. Putnam's Sons.

14,000 Miles through the Air. *Sir Ross Smith.* The Macmillan Company.

Gods of Yesterday. *James W. Bellah.* D. Appleton and Company.

How to Make and Fly a Model Aëroplane. *F. O. Armstrong.* Practical Arts Publishing Company, Elizabeth, New Jersey.

If you Want to Fly. *Alexander Klemin.* Coward-McCann Company, Inc.

Our Atlantic Flight. *Harry C. Hawker* and *K. MacKenzie Grieve.* Methuen and Company, Ltd.

Physics of the Air. *W. J. Humphreys.* Franklin Institute, Philadelphia.

Piloting the United States Mail. *Lewis E. Theiss.* W. A. Wilde Company.

562 *Romance of the Airman*

Strategy and Tactics of Air Fighting. *Oliver Stewart.* Longmans, Green & Co.

Things Worth Making. *Archibald Williams.* Thomas Nelson & Sons.

Aëro Digest. 220 West Forty-second Street, New York City.

Aëronautics. 608 South Dearborn Street, Chicago, Illinois.

Air Travel News. 1500 Buhl Building, Detroit, Michigan.

American Aviator: Airplanes and Airports, The.

Aviation, Merit Badge Series. Boy Scouts of America, 2 Park Avenue, New York.

Bibliography of Aëronautics. Smithsonian Institution.

Blue Book of American Airmen, 1925. Gardner Publishing Company.

The following bulletins on aëronautics will be sent free, on request, by the United States Department of Commerce, Washington, D.C.

Civil Aëronautics in the United States
Construction of Airports
Aëronautics Trade Directory
Air Markings for Cities
Airports and Landing Fields
Aëronautical Publications
Air Commerce Regulations
Airway Map of the United States
Air Transport Routes in Operation
Airway Strip Maps
Airway Distance Map of the United States
Airway Operation Costs
Civil Air Accidents and Casualties
Air Traffic Rules
Airport Rating Regulations
Airport Management
Abstract of State Laws on Aëronautics

Index

Aërodrome, Dr. Bell's, 158
Aëronautical Society of Great Britain, 107; *Journal of the Royal Aëronautical Society*, 114
Aëronautics, Bureau of, 514
Africa, 71–81, 83–84, 345–349
Ahmed Al Kamel, Prince, 50–53
Air mail, perils of flying, 468–480, 482–488; in "Peace on Earth," 490–491; Lindbergh as pilot of, 492–495; the westbound, 497–499; uses of, 535–536
Alaska, *Norge* sails over, 292–296; uses of airplane in, 525–529
Alcock, Captain John, 181, 301–303
Alexander the Great, 7
"Alhambra, The," 50
Allen, "Scotty," 329, 358
Amundsen, Roald, and Ellsworth expedition, 262–273; and expedition of the *Norge*, 276, 289–296; greets Byrd, 285; lost in searching expedition, 297; lament for, 431
Andrée, Salomon August, polar expedition of, 250–254, 262–263
Andromeda, 4–5
Antarctic continent, 120, 352, 368–369
Antarctic expedition, Byrd's, 352–370; Scott's, 365
"Arabian Nights' Entertainment, The," 43
Archytas, 8
"Argosies of the Air," 97
Aviation, the first official recognition of, 131–134; Dr. Bueno on, 139–142; Benjamin Franklin as a patron of, 147–152; progress of, in England in 1784, 150; Alexander Bell's contribution to, 155–159; actual beginnings of, 194; periods in development of, 395–398; uses of, in business, 532–536

Balchen, Bernt, 365, 395
Balloon, Hans Pfaall's, 61–62; Dr. Ferguson's, 71–81; principle of, 116; hot-air, 133; Franklin's interest in, 147–152; invention of,

170–178; first named, 172, 173; Charles's ascent in, 172–176; carries first passengers, 181–183; Count Ferdinand von Zeppelin's, 208–212; Santos-Dumont's, 217–222; meteorological investigations with, 225–226, 269; record-breaking voyage of, 225–248; sounding, 231, 248; Andrée's voyage in, 250–254
"Balloon Hoax, The," by Poe, 56, 299–300
Bacon, Roger, 101
Bell, Alexander, 155–159
Bellerophon, 8, 16–41
Bennett, Floyd, expedition of, to North Pole, 278–286; Byrd's tribute to, 365; martyr of the air, 422–424; burial of, 426–429
Biplane, Lilienthal's, 126; Redwing, 158; Voisin's, 193
Birds, flight of, as basis of aviation, Lilienthal's writings on, 109, 124, 127–129; Da Vinci's manuscript on, 114, 166; study of, by Santiago de Cárdenas, 137–139; Borelli's work on, 141; Wilbur Wright on, 197
Bladud, 6
Blanchard, Jean Pierre, 257–258
Bleriot, Louis, crosses the English Channel, 167, 194, 257–260
Blue Hill Meteorological Observatory, 225–226
Breeches buoy, 516, 518, 523
Bremen, the, 424
Brown, Lieutenant Arthur, 181, 301–303
Byrd, Rear Admiral Richard E., flight of, to North Pole, 275–286, 400, 422–423; with MacMillan's expedition, 278, 422; sells the *Friendship*, 326; Amelia Earhart's acquaintance with, 329; Amelia Earhart carries book by, 330–331; preparations of, for the Antarctic expedition, 352–370; fails to find Le Bourget, 377; crosses the Atlantic, 395, 402

563

564 *Romance of the Airman*

Cayley, Sir George, 105–106
Central America, 461–462
Chamberlin, Clarence D., 319–324, 394, 402
Chanute, Octave, 155
Charles, Professor, 172–176
Chimera, 23–41
Circumnavigation of the globe, first, by air, 381; first, by a dirigible, 381–388; by Magellan and others, 388
City of New York, the, 352
Clothing for the Antarctic expedition, 360–364
Columbia, the, 319–324
Costes and Le Brix, 373
Curtiss, Glenn H.. 158

Dædalus and Icarus, 4–5, 11–14, 87, 88, 102, 140
"Darius Green and his Flying Machine," 86–94
Da Vinci, Leonardo, 114–121, 124, 166
Dirigibles, 208–212, 381–388
Dixmude, the, 433, 438
Dog teams, 358–360
Dove, wooden, of Archytas, 8

Eagle, mechanical, 8
Earhart, Amelia, 326–336
Eckener, Dr. Hugo, 304, 382–387
Eielson, Carl B., 370, 528
Eleanor Bolling, the, 352
Ellsworth, Lincoln, and Amundsen expedition, 262–273; with the *Norge*, 276, 284–286, 289
"Enchanted Horse, The," 43
Entomology, Bureau of, 502–503, 505–506
Experimenters, early scientific, 101–110
Experiments of the Wright brothers, 197–205

Fairbanks, airport of, 529
Farman, Henry, 193, 375
Finley, Dr. John H., 414
Flyers, the first, 181; the first successful, 185
Flying chariot, 7, 102
Flying horse, 8

Flying machine of Darius Green, 86–94
"Flying Warrior of Uganda, The," 83
Franklin, Benjamin, 147–152
Friedrichshafen, landing of the *Graf Zeppelin* at, 382–383
Friendship, the, 326–336

Germany, landing of Chamberlin in, 319–324
Gjoa, 431
Gliders, Montgomery's, 107–108; Lilienthal's, 109, 124–129; built by Wright brothers, 187–189, 199–204; Bleriot's, 257; Ferber's, 192–193
Globe, hollow, 101, 103–104
Gordon, Lou, 326–336
Gordon Bennett balloon race, 225–248
Graf Zeppelin, the, circumnavigation of the globe by, 181, 381–387; building of, 208; description of, 446–448
Guggenheim, Daniel, 316
"Guide-roping," 220–221
Gusman, Bartholomew Laurence de, 104–105. *See also* Guzmao
Guzmao, Bartholomeo de, 131–134. *See also* Gusman

Hanson, Malcolm P., 367
Hans Pfaall, 56–69
Hawker and Grieve, 301
Hawthorne, Nathaniel, 16
Haynes, William C. ("Cyclone"), 367
Heath, Lady Mary, sells plane to Amelia Earhart, 334; flies across Africa, 345–349
Helicopter, 105
Henson, William Samuel, 106
Herring, Augustus, 155

Icarus and Dædalus, 4–6, 11–14, 87, 88, 136, 140
Iobates, King, 24–25

James Gordon Bennett Cup, 83, 225
Jeffries, Dr., 257–258
Josephine Ford, the, 278–286
June, Harold I., 365

Index

565

June Bug, the, 158
Jupiter, 6, 14

Kill Devil Hill, 185, 199, 200–201
Kingsford-Smith, Captain C. E., 338–342
Kipling, Rudyard, 56, 404, 532
Kite, Dr. Bell's, 155–159; tetrahedral, 156; Hargrave box, 159
Kite-flying, Santiago de Cárdenas's interest in, 137; Alexander Bell's interest in, 155–159; principles of, 156; Chinese, 165
Kitty Hawk, 110, 185, 188, 199

Lana, Francesco, 103–104
Langley, Samuel P., 109–110, 155, 194
Lansdowne, Lieutenant Commander Zachary, 303
Larsen, Riiser, 295
Latham, 258
Le Bourget, 373–378
Legends, Greek, 3, 4, 6, 8; Swedish, 4; Chinese, 4, 6, 7; Persian, 7, 8, 43–48; Indian, 7, 43; Mohammedan, 7, 50–53
Leif Ericson, 418–419
Lilienthal, Otto, as inspirer of the Wright brothers, 109, 124–129, 186, 188, 194, 197–198; Selfridge as student of, 158; homage to, 454–555
Lindbergh, 373; flight of, across the Atlantic, 391–406, 408–411; American youth honors, 414–420; America's "ambassador of good will," 459–463, 465–466; as a mail pilot, 474, 477, 492–495
Loadstone, 104, 131, 135
Los Angeles, the, 208, 304–305. *See also ZR–3*

Machine, internal-combustion, 105; heavier-than-air, 105, 155; flapping-wing, 107, 116; bat-wing, 116; Lilienthal's, 125; inventors of heavier-than-air, 159, 185
MacMillan's polar expedition, 278, 286
Magic carpet, 7–8, 50–53
Magic carriages, 6

Magic horse, 43–48, 50
Magic shoes and boots, 4
Maitland and Hegenberger, transpacific flight of, 402, 406
Mark Twain, 300
Maxim, Sir Hiram S., 108–109, 155, 210
Mechanical devices for flying: dove, 8; eagle, 8; magpie, 8; horse, 8, 43–45, 47–48
Medusa, 3–4, 8, 16
Mercury, 3
Mexico, Lindbergh as America's "ambassador" to, 459–463, 465–466
Monoplane, first, 106
Montgolfier brothers, 116; Franklin's interest in, 147–148; inventors of the balloon, 170–178; patent granted to, 170, 176–177; and balloon bearing first passengers, 181–183
Montgomery, John J., 107–108
Moon, Hans Pfaall's trip to, 56–69; the *Victoria* taken for, 71–81; eclipse of, and arrival of the *Southern Cross*, 341–342
Myths, 3–8, 11–13. *See also* Legends

NC–4, 300–301
Newbery Medal, 165
Nobile, 276, 284–286, 289–296
Norge, the, 284, 289–296
Nungesser and Coli, 305, 307–317, 373, 392, 441

"Opus Majus," 101
Orteig prize, 305, 307, 311, 319, 392

Parachute, 102, 116, 495; Lindbergh makes a jump with, 492–495
Patent, entered for Henson's machine, 106; first issued for a flying machine, 131–134; granted for the Montgolfiers' balloon, 176
Peary, 263, 275
Pegasus, 8, 16–41
Perseus, 3–4, 8, 16
Peru, 136
"Peruvian Aviator of the Eighteenth Century, A," 136–144
Phaëton, 6

566 *Romance of the Airman*

Pirene, Fountain of, 16–28, 40
Pizarro, Francisco, 136
Poe, Edgar Allan, 56, 300
Portugal, 131–134
Prehistoric tales, 3

Question Mark, the, 448–450

R–34, 303, 304
Raynham and Morgan, 301
Rönne, Martin, 353, 363
Rosier, M. Pilatre, 150
Rotch, Lawrence A., 225–226

Samson, the, 352, 353. *See also City of New York*
Santiago de Cárdenas, 136–144
Santos-Dumont, 193, 212; first balloon ascent of, 217–222
Seaplane, 519–520
Shenandoah, the, 443–445
Southern Cross, the, 338–342
Spirit of St. Louis, 398–399, 450–451
Spitsbergen, 263–264
Stringfellow, John, 106–107
Stultz, Wilmer, 326–336
Suva, 338–343

Tennyson, Alfred, Lord, 97, 248
Tokyo, landing of the *Graf Zeppelin* at, 384–385
Transatlantic flights, 299–305; Nungesser and Coli's attempt, 307–317; Chamberlin, 319–324; Amelia Earhart, 326–336
Transpacific flights, 338–342, 402, 406
Triplane, 107
Trowbridge, J. T., 86

Uses of airplane for plant protection, 500–506; to control mosquitoes, 505–506; for hunting whales, 508–513; for life-saving work, 516–523; for mapping areas, 525–527; for fur-trading, 528; by newspapers, 533; for advertising, 533–534; for transportation of vaccine, 535; for seeding ground, 535

Van Loon, Hendrik, 165
Verne, Jules, 56, 71

Walden, Arthur, 358–360
Wellman, Walter, 262–263
White Bird, the, 307–317
Wieland the Smith, 6
Wilkins, Sir George Hubert, 367, 370, 528
Wilkins, John, 102–103
Wing, curved, 105, 107
"Winged hat," 3
Winged horse, 16–41
Winged man, 100
"Winged Victory," 416
Wisting, Captain, 294, 296
Wright brothers, awarded the Langley Medal, 159; first flight of, 167; inventors of heavier-than-air machine, 170; as first successful flyers, 185–195, 197–205; as inventors, builders, and demonstrators, 197–205, 395–396

Zanzibar, 72, 73
Zeppelin, Count Ferdinand von, in American Civil War, 208; work of, 208–212; first airship of, 381
Zeppelins, 167–168, 208–212
ZR–3, crosses the Atlantic, 304–305; description of, 445–446. *See also Los Angeles*

𝕿𝖍𝖊 𝕬𝖙𝖍𝖊𝖓𝖆𝖚𝖒 𝕻𝖗𝖊𝖘𝖘

GINN AND COMPANY · PRO-
PRIETORS · BOSTON · U.S.A.

LaVergne, TN USA
09 December 2010

208053LV00005B/6/A